Born in 1969 outside Göteborg on the Swedish west coast, Fredrik T. Olsson spent most of his childhood writing, acting and producing plays. Refusing to grow up, this is pretty much what he has kept doing since. A full-time screenwriter for film and television since 1995, Fredrik has written scripts in genres ranging from comedy to thrillers, as well as developing, show-running and head-writing original material for various Swedish networks. He is also a standup comedian and makes occasional contributions as a director.

Also by Fredrik T. Olsson

Chain of Events

ACTS OF VANISHING

FREDRIK T. OLSSON

TRANSLATION BY
MICHAEL GALLAGHER

sphere

SPHERE

First published in Great Britain in 2017 by Sphere
This paperback edition published in 2018 by Sphere

1 3 5 7 9 10 8 6 4 2

A CIP catalogue record for this book
is available from the British Library.

ISBN 978-0-7515-5336-9

Typeset in Bembo by M Rules
Printed and bound in Great Britain by
Clays Ltd, St Ives plc

Papers used by Sphere are from well-managed forests
and other responsible sources.

MIX
Paper from
responsible sources
FSC
www.fsc.org   FSC® C104740

Sphere
An imprint of
Little, Brown Book Group
Carmelite House
50 Victoria Embankment
London EC4Y 0DZ

An Hachette UK Company
www.hachette.co.uk

www.littlebrown.co.uk

ACTS OF
VANISHING

Prologue

No one could possibly have known that he was going to be right here, simply because he hadn't known himself.

He hadn't made his final decision until two days before. He had booked trips to various destinations, rebooked, and then collected tickets he had no intention of using. Quite deliberately, he had left everything open until the very last minute, and yet he couldn't shake the feeling that someone must have known exactly what he was thinking. Of course no one could – that was impossible, he of all people should know – but even so, the thought sent a chilling anxiety through him.

He'd got rid of the greying, tufty beard. He'd trimmed his hairline to make it look like he was receding, even though he wasn't. His eyebrows, which over the years had converged into a single, long and bushy skein, had been plucked and tweaked into two thin lines. For the first time in his life he had spent hours standing in front of a mirror, concentrating on his own face. By the time he was finished he wasn't sure if he'd be able to pick himself out in a crowd.

He'd rented a year-old BMW in a garage that could, at best, be described as dubious. He had paid in cash without proving his identity, and no one could have seen him, no one could know where he had gone. He was safe.

And yet, here he was. Sitting in the dry silence of the car, hearing nothing but the thud of his own heart, and the rhythm of rain against the roof.

Maybe he should've known something was up.

Perhaps not as soon as the level-crossing barriers blocked the road in front of him, not then, even if he'd felt a twinge of fear in his belly as he rounded the long bend. As the red-and-yellow pole reached across the road in front of him, right there in the darkness, the bell hammering peevishly alongside.

He had stopped with the blinking red eye of the crossing gate just in front of him, one lone car in the darkness. Waited a minute, maybe two. No trains passed, yet the bell stopped.

That brought another wave of anxiety. The silence as the clanking died out, the mechanical movement as the barriers rose, leaving just him and the level crossing, strangers in the silent winter night, deep in rural Skåne. All he could see was the darkness and the wide expanse of field on the far side of the tracks. Empty slabs of rock-hard clay seemed to go on for ever until they disappeared into the grey-white mist, red dots glared at him from high in the air where lonely turbine blades rotated out of sight.

He had forced himself to snap out of it. There was nothing to be afraid of. The train must have passed before he arrived, or maybe it had broken down or got stuck at the points somewhere – it didn't matter. What mattered was he needed to get going. He was in a foreign country, with a long trip ahead of him, and no time to lose.

He'd started the engine and gently rolled up and over the tracks. And that's when everything had happened.

The world around him had gone black. The whole car switched off at a stroke: the headlights that should have illuminated the road ahead, the rear lights that should have cast a faint red glow behind the sloping rear windscreen, and above all – the engine.

He turned the key in the ignition to restart it. Nothing. Once more, and then again, and he heard himself bark *Start for fuck's sake*, slamming his hands against the wheel.

The moment he grabbed the door handle was the moment he realised what in fact he knew already: that no matter how much he heaved and strained, the doors would stay closed and locked, and nothing was going to change that. It was the same with the windows: however hard he pushed, however much he stabbed at the buttons in the door panel, no matter how he struggled, the car was going to stay just as locked and dark and dead.

It was then that the barriers started coming down again. It was then that he heard the hissing, and it was then that he knew.

He was lying stretched across both front seats when he caught the first glimpse of the lights. He stamped his soles against the window, his pulse raging inside his eardrums, the taste of terror and iron and blood even in the few seconds left until it would happen.

He could see the glass shudder under his soles but not give way, the approaching headlights flooding the dirty surface, and he closed his eyes and all he could hear were the sounds. The wailing thrill from the rails beneath him. The heartbeats thick in his mouth.

And then the horn as the train driver spotted the blacked-out car, a relentless honking that would be the last thing he ever heard, the grating scrape of iron biting into iron, trying to brake when it was already too late.

Day 1. Monday 3 December

AMBERLANGS

I have no first memory.

No matter how hard I try to look back, I can't.
   I remember no birth.
   I remember no places.
   All I know is that I am alive now, that behind me is an infinite then, and somewhere within that is all that is my past.
   And I cannot stop wondering what it was.

I have no first memory.
   I just think to myself that if I had had one, everything would have been better.

1

The days that change your life for ever start off like all the others.

No one wakes you saying today might be a bit tough, so have another piece of toast, take your time and enjoy your coffee, because it will be a while before you learn to enjoy life again. There's no one putting an arm around you, preparing you for what's about to happen. Everything is as normal, right up until the point where it no longer is.

As the afternoon gloom descended over Stockholm on Monday the third of December, no one knew that the threat level in the country had just been raised to 'elevated'. No one knew that inside the Swedish Armed Forces' great brick-built headquarters on Lidingövägen, men and women with uniforms and name badges were sitting waiting for the worst to happen.

And no one knew that the massive power cut that was about to hit at six minutes past four was just the start of something much bigger.

The men sitting inside the white van up on Klarabergsviadukten, the road bridge over Stockholm's Central Station, had no idea what they were waiting for. Or rather, *who*. They didn't know what he was going to do, who he was going to meet, how it was all going to look. Nor did they know *why*, which was of course what worried them most.

Inside the van's cramped loadspace, the silence was absolute. From the outside, it looked like any other anonymous delivery vehicle. Presumably, it had seemed spacious and generously proportioned when they bought it. After that, they seemed to have got carried away. Someone had given free rein to a team of technicians with an extravagant budget, and now the van was so full of screens and electronics that it felt less like a workplace and more like a boy's bedroom full of expensive kit.

A cubic metre's worth of space nearest the driver's cab had been consigned to computers and other electronic gizmos that probably carried out important tasks, but appeared not to do much more than flash red and green. Along one side hung two banks of flat screens, and behind a long thin desk below the screens sat four grown men, which was at least two too many.

The two who sat at the keyboards were of markedly different ages but unfortunately shared a similar BMI. Immediately behind them were the two men in charge: the one who the others called Lassie when he was out of earshot, and the one called Velander, an IT expert in civilian clothes, of completely indeterminable age, with glasses that seemed to get constantly steamed up in the heat inside. They stood hunched against the roof, shoulder to shoulder, eyes glued to the screens and the fuzzy grey CCTV images being relayed from within the station.

It was the older man who spotted him first, two minutes ahead of schedule.

'What the fuck are you doing here?'

His voice was no louder than a whisper, but everyone heard, and once they'd spotted the subject they saw it too.

It might have been something about his movements – the jerky gait, perhaps – or maybe something else. Whatever it was, a burst of concentration filled the tiny space, the same sudden alertness that comes when you catch sight of an ex in the corner of your eye during the interval at the theatre, someone you haven't seen for years but who stands out from the crowd and holds your gaze.

He'd changed.

He was trotting, rather than running, his hair untidy in the breeze, as though he'd just got up – although it was late afternoon. This from a man who'd always been so well dressed, so well coordinated. Who'd been sharp, in good shape, who no one quite believed when he told them he'd turned fifty – *several times*, as had been the standing joke these last three birthdays. *Last time was so much fun I thought I'd turn fifty again this year.*

It was as though, in the space of just three months, age had suddenly caught up with him. He looked tired, broken, with his overcoat hanging as if it had just been thrown over him and his jeans soaked with slush up to the knees. As he jostled through the crowds and across the blue-grey marble floor, a blue-grey mac in a sea of blue-grey passengers, he did so with movements that were forced and spasmodic, full of a buzzing intensity.

He kept appearing and disappearing as he moved between cameras, rushing onto the vaulted concourse, past the great frescoes and over towards the new escalators at the far end.

Surely it wasn't him they were waiting for? But if it wasn't, what was he doing there, now?

'What do we do?' asked the one with the steamed-up glasses.

'We wait,' said the one whose name wasn't Lassie.

And then, for two long minutes, not a word from anyone inside the van.

It had been only seven minutes to four when the bright yellow taxi stopped on Vasagatan outside Stockholm's main station to drop William Sandberg off into the slushy afternoon gloom that was Monday the third of December.

Thick layers of dark grey cloud hung where the sky should have been, the air so thick with mist that the noise of the traffic and all the roadworks seemed to meld into a single indistinct clamour. Construction lights and Christmas illuminations struggled gamely to overcome the murk, and the scaffolding and tarpaulins that clung to the surrounding buildings gave the impression that someone had clad the whole city in an orthodontic brace to reset it.

He was tired today, just like yesterday, and the day before that. If he'd given it any thought he would probably have noticed that he was hungry too, but if there was one thing he'd managed to cut out it was thinking of stuff like that. He'd stopped when he realised that his feelings were consuming him, literally eating him up: they were gnawing him from the inside with big, brutish bites, and now what was left of what was once William Sandberg was at least ten kilos lighter.

It's the method the tabloids forget, he used to say. *Find yourself something really worth worrying about.*

—

He picked his way through the heavy, wet snow outside the main entrance, following it into the departure hall, where it turned to a cinnamon-brown mush, and where the fusty smell of dirt and damp clothes mixed with the aroma of takeaway lattes and people on their way home.

William Sandberg, though, noticed none of it. Not the smell, not the flush of his face as the wind gave way to the still warmth indoors, or the irritated elbows that jerked out in frustration as he pushed his way through the crowd towards the northern exit.

It had been less than two weeks since that first email, and in precisely seven minutes' time he'd be in position, on the Arlanda Airport Express platform.

Precisely, because that's what it had said.

All he felt was hope – and fear – they came in tandem.

He'd been waiting by the bright yellow ticket machine for at least five minutes before he realised that he'd been looking for the wrong thing.

The platforms had been full of businessmen with briefcases, people with blank looks who seemed to be hibernating inside their own heads, waiting for a train to take them to somewhere they didn't want to go. But William had been looking for something else: faces that didn't want to be seen, people in dirty coats, with heavy plastic bags and loop after loop of damp scarves muffling their restless, freezing eyes. The kind who hid themselves behind bulky clothes, layers protecting them from both the biting cold and any unwanted contact with the rest of the world.

Maybe, he'd allowed himself to think – maybe one of them had finally got in touch. Someone, at last, with something to tell him, who'd made contact to reveal an address or even point the way, anything at all that would help him along.

Sandberg had hoped. And if only he hadn't, he probably would have seen the man on the other platform much sooner.

He was well over thirty. He had a headset in one ear, a studied vacant look despite being perfectly alert, and clothes so painfully ordinary that once you'd noticed him he stuck out like a child trying to hide behind a curtain.

His suit was silver grey. On top of it he wore a short overcoat that was so tightly buttoned at the waist that the bottom of his suit jacket poked out like a short pleated skirt, and below his trousers sat a pair of clumpy, anonymous trainers. All in all, it was a look that screamed *discreet!* as loud as it possibly could.

What caught William's eye, though, was the phone call. It seemed to contain more silence than talk. There were long periods when the thin wire just hung from his ear with nothing to do, and when the man eventually did open his mouth it was for single short interjections. That was it. In between he stood waiting impatiently, head darting distractedly from side to side looking at nothing in particular.

Slowly, William felt himself moving to a state of readiness.

It was already five past four by the time the Arlanda train rolled in to the platform. The driver's cab stopped by the buffers just in front of him, the train's hundreds of yellow tons puffing and dripping as the passengers wove their way past each other to board or alight. Gradually the swathes of people formed streams in various directions – to the main hall, the taxi ranks, other platforms – and gradually too it emerged that there were some who weren't going anywhere at all.

The discreet man with the headset, for one – and then someone else. He stood on the same side of the tracks as William, further down the platform, and he too was wearing a headset, sporting the same bland clothing, and having the same kind of conversation, short, sharp responses into the mic: they were talking to each other.

Something was wrong. William had been instructed to be in situ at precisely four p.m., and the word 'precisely' bothered him, because five minutes had passed and no one had shown up – no one, but for the two with the headsets. Were they waiting for the same person as he was? Or worse still – waiting for him?

He looked around. The crowds along the platform had slowly thinned out, and everyone not boarding was heading somewhere else. William had noticed the men with the headsets because they weren't doing either, and now he was making the same mistake.

He hesitated for two seconds before making up his mind. The

13

meeting, as far as he was concerned, was cancelled. He looked for a gap in the stream of passengers, sidled in and turned to follow the crowd towards the station hall.

He managed a single step.

'*Amberlangs?*'

The man blocking William's path had a chest so broad that it might have looked funny in another situation. Now, though, it was too close for comfort. He was wearing the day's third improbably discreet outfit – maybe they'd bargained for a discount – and now he stood massively still, with his legs apart and arms ready at his sides. But ready for what?

'And you are?'

In his mind, he bit his tongue as he was saying it. Shouldn't he be playing dumb?

'Nice and calm,' the man replied. Northern accent, a cold, curt order. 'You come with us and nothing will happen to you.'

Us? Who were they?

'When you say "happen",' William said, to buy some time. 'Would you care to elaborate on that?'

When the Northerner slid his jacket to the side, the weapon across his chest was all the elaboration William needed.

The days that change your life for ever start off like all the others. Everything normal, right up until the point when it isn't.

When the power went, at six minutes past four, leaving vast tracts of Sweden in total darkness, it was just like any other day. A damp, cold afternoon in the no-man's-land between seasons, neither autumn nor winter. At Stockholm Central Station the lights went off, the waiting locomotives lost power and lapsed into silence, screens and signs went dark. At hospitals and airports, emergency generators swung into action, on the roads and rails the lights and the signals disappeared, causing jams and confusion. It was irritating, for sure, and a bloody scandal too – with people getting stuck in lifts or on trains with no signal and what kind of society do we live in anyway. But for most people, that was all it was.

For William Sandberg, on the other hand, it was the start of an evening that would see his life lose its meaning.

For the men in the white van up on Klarabergsviadukten, it was confirmation that things were getting worse.

2

It hit the city centre first.

In the metro tunnels, the lights and the motors died at once. Darkness enveloped carriage after carriage, and passengers toppled en masse as the automatic brakes slammed on, forcing the trains to a halt in a few dozen metres. Above ground the street lights and the advertising hoardings fell dark. Escalators stopped, espresso machines died in the middle of filling cups, swearing and frustration everywhere. In a matter of moments the darkness marched out in a widening circle, from one neighbourhood to the next, out from the city, through the peripheral concrete estates and further on across the country. At the centre lay Stockholm, like a pitch-black maze in the pitch-black afternoon.

Everything stood still. And in the middle of the junction between Sveavägen and Rådmansgatan sat Christina Sandberg in the back seat of a taxi.

Her driver had spent the first part of their journey from Sollentuna endangering both of their lives, sitting with his eyes fixed on his yellow monochrome display, frenetically tapping away at various codes in the hope of landing his next fare, whilst simultaneously displaying an impressive range of expletives every time a fellow motorist happened to distract him from it.

They had just turned off Birger Jarlsgatan when Christina thought to herself that maybe she had better put her belt on. The next minute, though, it was too late.

At first she didn't grasp what was going on. It was as if they'd just entered a tunnel, but there were no tunnels on Rådmansgatan, and she looked up, out at what seemed to be a blacked-out version of her home town. No illuminated window displays, no Christmas decorations, no traffic lights, no visible lighting anywhere. That was the last thing she managed to discern before everything, suddenly and without warning, was replaced by blurred perpendicular lines.

It wasn't the HGV that hit them, the one that came roaring from their left, whose driver must have interpreted the disappearing red light as the signals turned green. Say what you like about the world-class swearer in the front, but there was nothing wrong with his reflexes. He slammed on the brakes and spun the wheel in a single manoeuvre, flinging Christina across the back seat as she felt the car jolt and shudder across the slush beneath them, and maybe it was professionalism, maybe just good fortune, but whatever it was it gave the lorry room to sneak past them with just millimetres to spare.

But when the bus came at them from the opposite direction, they didn't have a chance. It appeared behind the vanishing lorry, speeding flat out and straight ahead, and now there was no time to react. The collision with the taxi's offside wing was like two pool balls smashing into each other, and Christina felt herself sailing along the leather seat, weightless and in slow motion, helplessly floating like a crash-test dummy in a blazer and immaculate make-up.

So there she was, sitting in the middle of the Sveavägen–Rådmansgatan junction, alive but dazed, squashed into one corner of the back seat and with a view of a bonnet with a heavy bus wedged across it like a huge red vice.

The silence was almost overwhelming. All she could hear was the sound of her own breath, blending with the breathing from the front seat, and the quiet static hum seeping out of the car stereo.

'Are you okay?' she asked.

She saw a nod, two shocked eyes in the rear-view mirror.

'Are you?'

When she confirmed that she was, he mumbled something about terminating here and all change please and that she didn't need to worry about the fare.

The first thing she noticed as she clambered out was the way the darkness seemed to stretch in all directions. The sky was black, below it the street lamps loomed invisible and dark, and then below them the leaden fronts of buildings spreading in all directions, disappearing into nothing.

One direction led towards the high-rises around Hötorget's marketplace. The opposite direction was towards the tower of the Wenner-Gren Center. But none of it could be seen. The sole relief came from the cold, dimmed lights of the cars that had stopped around them, the fine drizzle drifting through the headlight beams and the odd driver still behind their wheel, face glowing faintly in the light from the dashboard.

Out of nowhere, she could feel the darkness closing in around her, her pulse racing for no reason. An almost paralysing terror, a wordless, exhilarating sensation that reality had ceased to operate: someone had flicked a switch on all the world, and from now on, this was how things were going to be.

She knew that feeling far too well, and shook it off. It was just a power cut, she told herself, someone had drilled through a cable somewhere or forgotten to calibrate a fuse. There was no reason at all to release a load of pent-up thoughts that weren't going to lead anywhere.

Instead, she looked around her and tried to turn her thoughts somewhere else. A quick assessment of the news value: Central Stockholm Plunged into Darkness. Wasn't that your headline right there?

Of course it was, and she pulled out her phone to ring the news desk, then stopped as the display lit up.

No signal.

She braced herself as the fears came back at her, focused even harder on the job. This, she thought to herself, was more than a headline. This was a massive story. If the inhabitants of Sweden's capital were stuck without electricity, with no means of calling for help, and if it was also going to stay this way for a while ... This was a security issue. This was about society as a whole. That made it worth whole tanks of ink.

Christina Sandberg looked around her. She raised her phone above her head, fired off a few shots with the camera pointing straight at the darkness, the junction with all the stationary cars, crumpled bodywork strewn around, the odd motorist using the light from their phones to inspect the damage.

She'd already composed the first few lines by the time she passed Tegnérlunden's open space on her way to her office on the island of Kungsholmen.

Across the platforms and trackbeds at Stockholm Central Station, darkness fell like a cupped hand. Pupils that had accustomed themselves to the artificial light struggled to see again, and at once all points of reference disappeared – contours, colours, everything.

Hearing, though, was a different matter, and what William could hear was the cocking of a gun.

Just a few inches in front of him, the Northerner had raised his weapon, and William closed his eyes in a pointless reflex, utterly sure that he was about to die.

But in that case, what did he have to lose? The darkness was his saviour, he told himself, and flung himself headlong into the crowd, not knowing who he fled from, or why, but determined to try.

He raced towards the station building, his arms like snowploughs, dislodging anyone in his path, determined that if he could just get into the big hall he'd be able to melt into the crowd and get away. He could hear footsteps coming after him, voices calling him to stop, as if they thought maybe he would change his mind and turn around if only they suggested it loudly enough.

Ahead of him, the main building was getting closer. He could see the weak light sources in there, the green phosphorescent EXIT signs telling him he was on the right track, and he picked up the pace—

The glass doors into the hall could not be seen in the darkness, but they could be felt. The pain was so intense that he was convinced at first that he'd been shot. He'd been sprinting for what seemed like safety, and in the darkness the plate-glass doors had been completely invisible, with the motors that should've slid them from his path as dead as everything else.

He felt his whole body scream in pain, heard his neck crick, and his face and his ribs and a metallic taste in his mouth; maybe this was what dying felt like ... It took him only a second to realise that he must be still alive. Otherwise he wouldn't have felt the pain redouble as they grabbed him from behind. First as the stranger's hand grabbed his, then as he pushed William's forearm up between his shoulder blades, and then again as his face and chest slammed up against the glass for a second time and were held there.

Ahead lay the dark main hall of the station, on the far side of the door. Behind him were three invisible men in discreet clothing, and in between he could feel his face squashed ever flatter against the glass as if to yield a vacuum-packed version of himself. And whatever he might've been expecting by the airport express at precisely four o'clock, it sure as hell wasn't this.

Sandberg had allowed himself to hope. Now the hope was gone. Slowly, he stopped resisting.

Christina Sandberg had got as far as the bridge over to Kungs-holmen before she stopped for the first time.

From there, the whole of Stockholm should have been visible, in all directions. The city centre with Södermalm as the back-drop. The TV masts in Nacka that should've been pulsing with sharp, white flashes behind the silhouettes of hotels and office blocks. They weren't though. Wherever she looked she could see nothing but darkness. Kungsholmen, Karlberg, Solna, Vasastan, invisible, lost in a dense, impenetrable night.

For a second, she felt her mind wander. From out of nowhere came the thoughts of *her*, the guilt and the sorrow that always waited just around the corner. She would be out there some-where, too, she who had turned her back on them, betrayed them, and, to be honest, who had helped force her and William apart. That kind of thinking was forbidden, yet she couldn't help it. It was impossible not to lay some of the blame onto her, and the mere thought of doing so spread a new layer of guilt on top of all the others, set the anxiety spinning like a child pushing a roundabout in the playground and not stopping until it's going way too fast.

She was out there somewhere. In all likelihood so was he, always on the move, running from whatever it was that kept him moving, himself or his conscience, or maybe from Christina, and – fuck it. She was the news editor at one of Sweden's largest tabloid newspapers, and to stand here feeling sorry for yourself gets nothing done.

All around, the city lay in darkness. She set off again, over the bridge, then on between the buildings. This, she reminded herself, was big news.

3

The girl who was about to die but didn't know it yet was struggling against two different things at once.

First was the struggle against her own body, this body that couldn't quite manage to hold her upright, or move as fast as she wanted. The one that had aged so grossly – though it was only twenty years old – that it made people recoil, as much as she wished they wouldn't. This body that right now was elbowing its way through the vast and impenetrable darkness of the metro station under Hötorget's marketplace.

Then there was the struggle against the tide of pumping panic. *What the fuck had she done?*

Everything was in darkness. Everywhere, invisible puffer jackets seemed to be heading at random in all directions, the only things visible being the EXIT signs, glowing in feeble pale green along the walls. How could all this have been her fault?

She shouldn't even have been here. She should have stayed home – whatever *home* meant – home where she could keep out of people's way and live her own so-called life. The amusement park had closed for the winter in September, so if you managed to avoid the security guards and the builders, if you knew the hideouts no one bothered to check, you could sort yourself a place to live for six months – nicely enclosed, and under a roof and with heating. What more could you want?

Home, she could have replied, if anyone had asked, was on the exclusive island of Djurgården. Quite the hotspot.

No one asked though.

Home was where she'd loved to be as a kid, where lamps had flashed their gaudy colours, where cars rattled along the roller coasters and voices screamed with happiness – and from time to time one of the voices had been her own.

Now the lamps were off. Tarpaulins were stretched over the rails and over the metal and fibreglass cars. It was like the aftermath of a party when everyone's gone home. And in the middle of all that, behind thin wooden walls and corrugated iron, was her home. Cold, damp, insecure – and yet it still made her proud in a way she couldn't quite explain. She had her own life – a shitty life, okay, but it was *her* shitty life and not theirs, and that was all that mattered.

At least that's how she'd used to feel. But things change. Now she was here, struggling through the pitch-black metro station, up the motionless escalator, out into the cold damp evening air. The darkness went on up here too. It was daytime, but also night: rows of vegetables and cut flowers lined up under unlit awnings, and on the far side of the square the giant cinema's glass frontage looked like an empty black cube.

How could she have caused all this?

Maybe, she told herself, she hadn't. Maybe this was her distorted perception of reality, and she was pushing it all too far. She hadn't taken anything for days, so maybe all this anxiety was a kind of symptom, a new version of that grating, sweaty restlessness that was always overtaking her, and that sooner or later always pushed her off the wagon.

But not this time. That was a promise she planned to keep.

She walked on past the stalls, away from the square, on the alert for voices or shouts or footsteps catching up with her. It was just a matter of time till they came looking, she was certain of that, and as long as she roamed around the town like this, dirty and shaking from cold turkey, and with the thin nylon rucksack ready to fall apart under the weight of the twenty-thousand-krona computer inside it, it wasn't going to take an expert criminologist to work out that she was the one they were looking for.

What choice had she had, though? She had cut the power off. She didn't know how, or why, but it had to be her. And still, that wasn't what bothered her most. Nor was it the darkness, or even the fear of being caught and arrested for what she stole. None of that.

The worst thing was knowing what she should have done.

It was ten past four on the afternoon of the third of December.

Everything was darkness and ink and wet, heavy snow. There she ran, Sara Sandberg, the girl who was about to die, and somewhere in the cold leaden hell that was Stockholm was a man who called himself her father.

In her rucksack she carried a warning for him.

Now whether he would receive it or not was all down to her.

4

William Sandberg's eyes stared back at him from the mirror, two white circles, glistening in the light of the battery-driven emergency light on one of the walls.

He leaned forward into the mirror, let his eyes scan from left to right. A sharp, accusing stare straight into the room that he knew was on the other side.

'If this is a stag-do prank you can come out now,' he said, his voice hard and impatient, strained through gritted teeth as though every word was forcing its way out from his chest against his will. And then, quieter, and with an aftertaste more bitter than he'd intended:

'Because in that case you've got the wrong end of the marriage.'

No reply. Just the mirror, the silence, the darkness.

He'd been on the other side of the glass often enough to know that you never feel quite safe. Every time a suspect's stare meets yours, a shiver runs through you, no matter how well you know that they can't see through the mirror, and if William transmitted a little share of that, then all the better. *This one's on me.*

How long had he been here now? An hour at least, maybe two. In an interview room at his own workplace – or rather, he corrected himself, his former workplace.

During that time, his thoughts had swung from rage to fear and back again. He'd repeated the same question time and time again, and now it seemed as though they grew bigger and more uncomfortable with each passing minute. What the fuck was he doing here? Why had they been waiting for him?

Presumably they were SÄPO – the security police. Either that or military police, but who gives a shit, either way they had dreadful taste in clothes. When they had finally tired of pressing him up against the glass door at the Central Station, they had led him through the darkness towards Vasagatan and a waiting black Volvo. They'd fixed him inside using the seatbelt, carefully and precisely so that he wouldn't get hurt if they happened to crash, which he had to admit was considerate given that they'd seemed all set to knee his spleen out of his body just moments earlier. After that they had driven him through Stockholm in stony silence.

Darkness had yawned from everywhere. Every building they passed, every street, tunnel, junction – all of it completely pitch-black. Shop windows stood like empty mirrors, Christmas decorations hung lifeless above the streets, neon signs writhed like dark serpents over the entrances to cinemas and theatres.

'What's happened?' he had asked, but none of the men in the front seat had shown any inclination to reply.

Eventually they had turned off Lidingövägen and rolled past all the security gates, down into the car park under the hideous redbrick rectangular building that was the headquarters of the Combined Armed Forces. That's when they'd taken his phone, watch and coat and put him in here. Then, time had been permitted to pass.

The power still wasn't back on, which bothered him more than he cared to think about. Not because there was an awful lot to see in there – the room he sat in was a box with grey walls and a grey floor. Apart from the mirror, the furniture comprised a table and four cheap chairs.

It wasn't the darkness itself that troubled him, it was the coincidence. The emails, the meeting, the arrest, the power cut – they were connected in some way, but how? There was no pattern, no logical link. All he could do was wait for his old comrades to haul themselves out of their chairs in there, behind the mirror, drag their arses the three metres along the corridor outside and come in and tell him the score.

He heard himself snort at that thought. *Comrades*. Yeah right. With friends like these, and so forth. 'I've read that manual too,' he barked at the mirror. 'Just so you know, I'm also waiting you for you to blink first.'

They were waiting for him to fall apart, to reveal himself insecure and afraid. He had no intention of allowing them that much fun.

'Here's how we're going to do this. I'm going to go and sit down, so you can write down all my tics and little movements, and then, when you've seen enough, you're all welcome to come in. Does that sound okay to you?'

He sauntered over to the table. Sat down, staring straight at the mirror, choosing his body language with care. One arm on the back of the chair, the other on the table, spread out, relaxed. Open, confident.

As he did, his thoughts caught up with him. How come they had been waiting for him just there? How could they have known that he was going to show up just *there*, and *then?* Had they been bugging him? Reading his emails? Or, worse still, had they been following his mobile phone, tracking all his movements? If so, for how long?

In an instant, it was as if everything fell into place, as though suddenly he could see himself through their eyes, and he was overcome by a helpless desire to defend himself even though he still hadn't been accused of anything. He'd been convicted in advance. Of what he didn't know, but convicted he was, and he started to go through everything that had happened over the last few weeks, months, the whole fucking autumn, inside his head.

Everything from that Thursday, three months ago, when he'd trudged out through Reception for the last time, dropped his key card and ID onto the floor instead of handing them in through the hatch, as though taking it out on some innocent lad on the front desk might somehow make things better. From that, to all his trekking around night after night, in the chilly autumn rain and this bloody damp that was supposed to be winter. Things that the people behind the glass couldn't possibly know about. Or could they?

He closed his eyes.

And then there were the emails. Obviously they were going to ask him about them. Obviously they were going to ask him about all of it, but how the hell was he going to answer?

At the moment he opened his eyes again he realised that he'd just let them win. He'd forgotten himself. Dropped his guard. He was sitting with his legs tight together, feet tucked in under his chair, with his back twisted and hunched – a perfect reflection of how he was feeling. Or, to be honest, how he had been feeling for months.

He looked over at the mirror.

'Insecure,' he said. He gestured up and down with his hand to draw their attention to the way he was sitting. 'Uneasy, perhaps even nervous. Write that down, and let's get this over with.'

He felt the fatigue closing over him, and this time he couldn't hold out. He couldn't face sitting here, couldn't deal with the brooding or the wondering. He'd already spent far too much time on that.

'Come on. I think both you and I have better things to do with our time than sit here and stare at this mirror.'

A pause. Then, more honestly than he'd intended: 'Especially since neither of us is probably all that fond of what we're looking at.'

There were fewer eyes watching from the other side of the glass than William thought.

Half of them belonged to a Major named Cathryn Forester, and she was closing them with a silent sigh, not of fatigue but a frustrating mix of other emotions. Stress. Restlessness. Anxiety. There was no time for fatigue.

'Please,' she said.

She said it in English, and though the word entailed a single syllable, her understated British intonation made it seem as though the man beside her was twelve years old and had just claimed not to have smashed the coffee table despite standing there blushing with cricket bat in hand.

'There is no *type*,' she went on when the silence continued. 'No one is the type, until suddenly it turns out that they are. When their neighbours are standing on the news saying who would have thought, he was such a friendly bloke.'

The man next to her stood straight and determined, staring into the interview room.

'I know him.' That was all he said.

He was tall, at least six feet, with neatly cut grey hair. He was probably twenty years older than her, dressed in the Headquarters' grey-blue uniform, which made him look like an officer from any country in the world, only washed in really cheap laundry powder.

The others called him Lassie behind his back. She didn't know why, just that he hated it, which somehow made him even more pitiful.

'What does "know" mean?' she asked.

'We worked together for almost thirty years . . . '

'I *know* that. I mean philosophically speaking.'

His eye-rolling wasn't even half as elegant as her *please*.

'I don't know how you run things over at your place, but Swedish intelligence doesn't do philosophy.'

'Really?' she said. 'Well, maybe you should.'

She noticed the sharpness in her voice, and regretted it at once. She wanted to avoid any conflict. After all, she was the one in charge, not him, and if either of them should be feeling squeezed and powerless it wasn't going to be her.

But there was something about the Swede that always put her back up. Part of it was the fact that he had chosen to speak English with her, although she was a qualified interpreter and spoke Swedish almost as well as he did. In some odd way it gave him the upper hand, signalled that she was the temporary visitor and that he was, in effect, the one in charge, and that it was only through his good manners that she was admitted.

The fact was, it wasn't like that at all. And the last thing she wanted was to waste time on asserting herself, not here, not now, not *still*.

Cathryn Forester had grown up in a family with four brothers, and if anyone ever got what was coming to them, it was men who tried to put her in her place. Men who patronised her, cocked their heads to one side, and showed how charming they thought she was, charming and inoffensive and perhaps on the dim side. They had been there at home, at school and at university, and over the years she'd learnt how to take them, how to pretend that it didn't bother her at all, even if that was hardly true. When, at the age of thirty, she'd started to work in intelligence, she had developed armour that could deflect whole armies of cocked heads. Literally.

The problem with the Swede was that he didn't do any of that. He was arguing on behalf of a friend. He was objective and restrained, and he was certain that he was right, but now it happened that so was she.

In a way, they were both right. And she had no armour for that.

'I'm not stupid, I know what it looks like,' he said eventually. 'But none of us were expecting this.'

'Really?' That British understatement again. 'None of us? This?'

Major Forester flung her arms out in the darkness, pointing to the *this* that was going on around them. The darkness, the power cut – what she had warned them about, the very things they'd always known would happen again, just not when, not where, and not how big they would be.

It's like having your arteries on the outside of your body.

Those were the words she'd used three weeks before, standing in the so-called briefing room. She'd stood there in front of the entire Swedish staff, the walls behind them covered in maps.

That's how vulnerable we are.

No one had challenged her then, because they'd all known she was right, and if the Swedish officer next to her was now claiming that this had all come as a surprise, then this was a discussion she simply couldn't be bothered to engage in.

'He *is* AMBERLANGS,' she said.

'I know,' he said.

And for a moment they just stood there, their faces lit only by the faint emergency lighting on the other side of the mirror: one tall British officer in civilian dress, with high-heeled boots, ice-clear eyes, and boyish, strawberry-blonde hair, and the man the others called Lassie, whose real name was Lars Erik Palmgren and who was probably close to retirement. But who had suddenly found himself working with her, without any say in the matter.

On the other hand, she had never asked to work with him either.

'So what comes next?' he asked her at last.

Forester picked up the file from the table in front of them.

'Five more minutes,' she said. 'Then we go in.'

5

It smelled like Christmas, but no one was in a Christmassy mood. The sweet scent of blown-out candles hung thick over the conference room. On the table in the middle, a warm yellow light shone from the tea lights and candle stubs that someone had dug out of the drawers in the kitchenette – the sort that were left over from celebrating Saint Lucia or departmental parties, just because they might come in handy some time in the future.

Outside the twentieth-storey window of the great newspaper building, Stockholm spread out like a pitch-black miniature landscape, an abandoned model railway where only brilliant queues of vehicle headlights etched the darkness with creeping luminescent ribbons.

'How far out does it reach?' asked Christina. Try as she might, she could see no sign of an end to the darkness.

'We took photos from up on the roof,' someone at the table behind her chipped in. The silence that followed summed up the situation: nothing visible from higher up either.

Christina nodded but did not speak. There was no point in struggling against it now: that feeling had returned, the one that had overcome her in the darkness downtown, that she'd managed to almost forget over the years. *You're so easily scared when you're young, aren't you?*

Thirty years ago, it had had her waking up in the middle of the night, stricken with fear that this might be the day when someone pushed the button that would set the superpowers annihilating the world. The sense that each new second balanced on a thin film of ice, and beneath the film lay the end of everything.

She turned back towards the room. All her colleagues were sitting around the table, and now they were waiting for her.

Pull yourself together.

'Right,' she said, and heard her voice cut slightly too sharply through the silence. 'So none of us can make any calls?'

Shaking heads all round.

'I've got a mate who can do smoke signals but he's not answering.'

The voice came from the far end of the table, a slicked-back hairstyle that spoke without looking up. His name was Christopher, but he had a surname so impossible to pronounce that his name had long since been shortened to CW, for the sake of efficiency. He was a journalist of the old school, something he was keen to remind them of at regular intervals, even if it didn't, as far as Christina could tell, mean much more than that he smelt unusually strongly of tobacco.

'How's it going?' asked a colleague sitting next to him.

A big ghetto-blaster lay facedown in front of him in the candlelight. They'd found it in the window by someone's desk, and it had of course been as dead as everything else. The only batteries available had been far too small, plundered from keyboards and peripherals from across the whole floor, but there he was, working like a nicotine-scented surgeon attempting to insert the batteries into too big a compartment, with sticky tape and paper clips to hold them in place.

'It's fucking fiddly,' CW said, concentrating on the table in front of him. 'But if anyone's got a better idea let's have it.'

Christina observed him from her seat at the table. She looked at the dark office landscape beyond the glass walls behind him, the quiet restlessness that was gripping her staff.

Everyone had a job to do, but no one knew how to do it. The constant ringing and bleeping of phones was eerily absent, the fax machines, the internet – all of it was down. The only way to find out what was happening was via good, honest, old-fashioned radio, but it seemed Sweden's most modern tabloid wasn't quite ready for that technology yet.

And the whole time, those nameless terrors were waiting at the back of Christina Sandberg's mind, waiting to roam freely, the way they used to on those sleepless nights back in the seventies. What happens if the power doesn't come back on? How long can we keep going? How long will the warmth last, how long will there be food in the shops—

'Wait!'

CW's voice. Moments later she heard the crackling. He looked up at them all, full of pride.

There was a weak, quiet hum from the speakers – the empty gap between two stations, but radio nonetheless – and an intake of breath went all around the table in anticipation of finding a channel where someone would tell them what was happening.

The crackling lasted two seconds. That was the time it took for the paper clips to come loose and break the contact with the batteries. All the same, it had shown that the method could work; Christina nodded approvingly and told him to give it another go.

Onwards, she said to herself, and then, turning to the others: 'Angles?'

No one answered, but then it had been a rhetorical question.

Around the table, ballpoint pens were clicked in readiness; lined A5 notepads were brought into the weak light. Here and there, the odd face was lit by the screen of a laptop or a tablet that still had some battery power, and Christina couldn't help but turn towards them.

'Great idea. Unless the power cut lasts and you're left sitting

30

there with the world's best copy trapped on your hard disc and not a cat in hell's chance to retrieve it until it's old news.'

No protests. Just screen after screen going dark around the table.

'First off,' she continued, 'the practical. What has happened, how many are affected, are there any prognoses? Who do we approach?'

Someone suggested the power company, another the city council, someone else said the government's press office. Christina nodded, delegated the tasks by pointing, and watched her staff make notes in the gloom. There were cars in the basement, others had bikes, the ones who had neither would just have to walk. The only way they were going to get any answers was by moving around.

'Second,' she said, 'society. How vulnerable are we? Who's in charge? What's happening with the emergency services number, what's the score with essential services?'

More scribbling, new suggestions.

'Third.' She paused. A tone of gravity. 'The consequences.'

She was about to conclude her dramatic pause when she saw hands going up around the table again. *Hang on*, said the hands, and then came shushing from all directions, and finally the click as CW snapped the battery compartment closed for the second time. He carefully placed the radio upright so that he could get at the controls.

The room fell silent. On the far side of the table she saw CW clicking his way up through the frequencies, and the digits on the display increased in half-megahertz increments up through the FM band.

Static. Static. Static.

Interminable waiting.

Static.

Eventually he stopped. Opened his mouth to say something but couldn't remember what. He had been through the whole dial, without passing anything that even resembled a transmission.

'Anyone know where P1 is?' he said. 'Or Radio Stockholm?'

Embarrassed smiles showed through the gloom. Who memorised that sort of thing nowadays? Technology took care of all the necessary information – codes, addresses, even phone numbers of our nearest and dearest – and now, when there was suddenly no search engine to find them, no one had any answers.

But then again, it didn't make any difference. Once CW had finished the third cycle through the whole of the FM band, step by step and with a little pause after each click of the button, the facts of the matter were obvious to everyone.

No one was broadcasting. The radio was dead.

Christina felt the dam break inside her. If all the signals were down, if there really was nothing at all out there in the ether, what did that mean? How far did an FM signal reach? How big was the area affected by the power cut? What had happened?

Her catastrophic thoughts took on a momentum of their own, and she could feel them spinning out of control. What if Stockholm had actually got off lightly, and was in fact at the periphery of a much bigger catastrophe . . . ?

'Wait!'

CW again. Proud eyes once more.

'The AM-band,' he said. 'I searched the AM-band. I think this is Dutch.'

The relief was like everyone in the room breathing out. The voice from the speaker was incomprehensible and intermittent, but at least it was a voice. An over-energetic presenter talking to a caller who was even less audible, with both of them laughing for no reason, the way people do on the radio. Judging by their tone it was probably a quiz, but honestly, who gave a shit what it was: it meant the world was still there. Somewhere not all that far away there were people untroubled enough to spend time competing on a phone-in, which meant that whatever else had happened, life was not surrendering today.

Christina gulped hard, cursed herself for allowing those teen-age feelings to get to her.

'Third,' she resumed. The final point. 'The consequences.'

The questions spilled out of her. How long will society survive? What happens to Sweden? First hour, second hour, after a *day*?

'As of now, we don't know how long the power is going to be out, and let's hope for the best, but suppose this continues, how long *can* we survive? What sort of reserves do we have? Water? Food? Healthcare?'

One by one her colleagues got up from their places, some in teams of two, others on their own, before trickling out through the open-plan office, pulling on their coats as they went.

They weren't, of course, about to get any answers. Everyone would be blaming someone else, but that would be news too, and every step would lead to new people to question. Handled right, this was a press opportunity, and they couldn't ignore it just because they didn't have electricity.

No one knew how long that would last.

But, when it was all over, you wanted to have a story to tell.

Christina stood at the window long after the last of her colleagues had gone, staring out into cold and darkness.

'Are you thinking about her?' the voice behind her asked.

'Amongst other things,' she answered. 'A whole lot of other things.'

The woman standing in the doorway was a photographer, even though the paper officially didn't have any.

She was older than Christina, older and heavier and still panting from climbing the stairs, probably for the first time in years. She was wearing a big print dress with loose, multicoloured fabrics over the shoulders, thin material that fluttered at the slightest movement giving her the appearance of an old-fashioned screen-saver. All of which did nothing to make her look smaller, which was probably the idea.

Above all, though, she was a friend. A prized colleague. Following a couple of vivid arguments when someone else had booked her before Christina, she had become Christina's unofficial companion, and that was the way it had stayed.

Beatrice Lind. Saviour in her hour of need. Literally.

'How are you finding the flat?' she asked, as though tuning in to Christina's thoughts.

Christina turned to face her before answering.

'It's perfect,' she said. 'If you like vintage, that is.' A pause, then she couldn't help adding: 'And if by vintage you mean old stuff that just tends to smell a bit off.'

Beatrice nodded. 'In that case my boss at my old job was vintage.'

They exchanged invisible smiles through the darkness, an island of normal in the middle of all the terrifying weirdness. Eventually Beatrice took a deep breath and asked the question on everyone's lips.

'What's going on out there?'

Christina took an age before she spoke, then she nodded to Beatrice to follow her down to the car park.

'Work,' she said.

6

As the woman with the long dark hair opened the door to the apartment on Ulica Brzeska, she knew that she was never going to see him again. She let the creaking of the door and floor subside, and stood there waiting with a pounding heart until she could be sure that no one had heard her, that no one else was lurking in the damp stairwell or had seen her take the short cut across the back yard and possibly followed her in. All she could hear was the odd sound from the trams down on Targowa or Kijowska, the singing rails as a train passed through Warsaw Wschodnia, the slamming of a door in a nearby building.

Apart from that though, nothing. No music greeted her, the way it always did when he was home before her. No jazz trumpet floating over the top of elegant standards, no whirring from the giant industrial fan, the one that would usually be humming away above the stove, trying in vain to remove the scent of garlic and oils and vegetable stock from the air. Aromas that would normally hit her here.

But it was his voice she missed most of all, his articulate, gentle, intelligent . . . she bit her lip. Memories are memories. This was now. Michal Piotrowski was gone, and he wasn't coming back.

—

She found tufts of his hair in the bathtub, great tufts as though he'd grabbed fistfuls of his shaggy hairstyle and shorn himself like a sheep. He had altered his appearance, just as he'd said he would, over the wine and the candles and the rough, worn dining table, right through clasped hands and a love that grew stronger and tougher for each day they were forced to keep it secret. If it happens, he had said, if he had to disappear, then it would go just like this.

She had laughed at him, a little too loud and too shrill, because he'd made her feel afraid and uneasy and the only way to shed all that was to pretend that he was joking. But he wasn't.

When she'd rinsed him out of the bath and watched the final hairs disappear down the plughole, when no traces remained of his transformation, she went out into the big living room. Running along one of the interior walls was a long plank of coarse dark timber, fitted like an outsize desk from one corner to the other, and above that hung rows of shelving, and that's where she eventually found them.

The photo albums. The memories. The days they had got to spend together, the trips they took – always far away, always in secret, waiting for a permission that was never going to come.

One by one, she took photos out of the albums, looked herself in the eyes as she eased the corners from their mounts: smiling, happy eyes that gazed back at her from glossy paper. She put them in a pile on the table, each new memory slightly fresher than the one before.

She'd got past halfway when she opened a brown envelope and saw the photos change character. These were photos that she didn't recognise. They were taken from a distance, clearly in secret and with a telephoto lens, of a man and a woman and a teenage girl in a city she didn't recognise. Sometimes they were together, sometimes on their own, here getting out of a car and into an apartment, there just doing their own thing. The young girl on a café terrace. Coffee and cigarettes. The man climbing into a taxi, outside a boxy redbrick complex. She stared at them for ages without understanding.

Who were these people? What were they doing in his shelves?

But there was no one to ask, and the next pictures were of her, and they brought back the memories of the travel and of missing him so much it hurt all over again, and she carried on purging album after album until nothing remained on the shelf.

The realisation hit her like a slap. Suddenly, there were no more pictures. Their relationship had deepened and lasted so long that the world had changed around them – analogue had become digital, and the last photo of them was seven years old. After that there were no physical prints.

How many years was that, lying on the table? Five?

Altogether it had been twelve years. Twelve years of her life. One technology had replaced another, borders had been redrawn, entire countries established and abolished. Their relationship had stayed in the same place.

Until now.

She carried the photos into the kitchen. Placed them at the bottom of the big sink. Next to the gas stove were the same piles of matchboxes as always, and she placed them all on top of the pictures, took a clutch of unused matches and struck them in a single sweep.

Saw her own face crumple in the heat. Saw the pieces of photographic paper curl up as if to repel the flames for a few more seconds, before they went black and hovered up over the worktop like thin weightless veils of soot.

It was for her own sake, so he had said. But the worst part remained, and even if she didn't know why, she had promised. One more task, and after that, memories would be all she had.

Because memories don't burn.

7

William Sandberg leaned over the table in the darkness. Just a movement, a change of position, yet it expressed an underplayed sarcasm; a tired protest, mute and invisible, but that no watcher would have missed.

'I,' he said. Then: 'Don't. Know.'

They had let him wait in silent solitude for another twenty minutes before at last they opened the door. Then they had almost hovered into the room, their features blue in the emergency lighting, and in the darkness the smallest sounds had become near-tangible events: clothes rustling as they moved, chair legs scraping against the floor as they sat down, papers being laid on the table.

The one on the left had introduced herself as Cathryn Forester, as though that was something very special and worth boasting about. And as Major, as if that was too. And then, in perfect Swedish, only with a slight English accent, she had introduced the face next to her.

William had long since recognised him. The height, the heavy gait, the presence. *The bastard.* Not that he'd had any reason to make assumptions, he knew that too, but as his former colleague had floated into his seat across the table, William had realised that deep down, he'd been assuming that Palmgren wasn't part of this. Lassie, he'd thought, would be on his side. Regardless of why William had been brought in, whatever all this was about, Palmgren would intervene like the older cousin in the playground, protesting and rushing to help as soon as he heard he was there.

Instead he'd sat down and set out his papers, every bit as formal and reserved as the English Major to his right. Clicked nervously with an invisible pen, hidden in the darkness without saying a word.

She, on the other hand, had managed more. She had asked methodically and at length about things they already knew, name, age and kiss my arse, he'd thought to himself but made sure not to say out loud.

Then there was that question that kept coming up, again and again, the one William would have been only too glad to answer if he could. Except that he did. Not. Know.

'So you keep saying,' she said.

'Oh, you did hear then,' he answered. 'I thought that, since you had to ask so many times, maybe your hearing went with the lighting.'

He found himself playing for time without even knowing why, resorting to sarcasm to slow the conversation down, no matter how unviable a strategy. What was she doing here, a foreign officer, in an interrogation room inside the Swedish Armed Forces HQ? It was all deeply alarming. In more ways than one.

'Is it a person?' she said. 'An organisation? Is it an acronym?'

This time he didn't answer at all, and when he didn't she steeled herself before repeating the original question, for the umpteenth time. Word for word, the same deliberate, over-articulated delivery.

'*Who. Is. Rosetta?*'

'It is a *sender*,' he told her. 'What more do you want me to say?'

'We know that. But who?'

William shook his head. His energy was draining. The darkness sapped him, as did the lack of time perception, and there were moments when he thought he saw a movement in the blackness, as if one of them had raised a hand, or there was some fourth person in here that he hadn't seen until now. Each time, though, he realised that it was just his brain filling in the gaps of its own accord.

'I realise that you have to ask me that,' he said, straining to maintain his focus. 'But I've run out of synonyms now. I don't know.'

'Which brings us on to question number two,' she said. 'Isn't it rather odd that you ended up going there?'

Here we go again.

'Isn't it odd that you show up at just the right spot, at just the right time, with no idea who asked you to?'

He could feel his pulse rate rising. They'd just begun to scratch the surface, yet already they had questions he couldn't answer. Waiting in line were others, ones that he didn't *want* to answer.

Please, he said to himself. *Please don't go there.*

'Tell me,' he said instead, a last attempt to seize the initiative. 'Tell me why I'm here.'

From the other side of the table, silence.

'I understand that this has to do with the power cut. I just don't see how.'

'What makes you think that?'

He saw Forester's teeth twinkle opposite. Was she smiling? Her voice certainly wasn't.

'Because I struggle to believe it's pure coincidence. You jump me at Central Station. At that very moment, this happens.'

He made an invisible gesture out into the darkness, towards the walls, the ceiling, all the things that should be bathed in the sterile, bright white light of fluorescent tubes, but were not. 'So instead of asking me questions I can't answer, please: tell me what has happened.'

For a second, Forester breathed in as though she was negotiating with herself. As though, for an instant, she might consider answering. Instead, she reached for the stack of papers on the table in front of her.

On top of the stack was some sort of plastic document wallet, possibly white or yellow, but under the emergency lighting it was as ice blue as anything else. She laid both hands on top of it. Two rubber bands signalled that the folder was closed and would remain so for the time being.

'Can you tell me what happened three months ago?' she asked. *Not there. Not there.*

'I can,' he said. 'But you already know.'

'You were sacked.'

'I was encouraged to resign.'

'How did that feel?'

Feel?

'Is that why you're here? You're a shrink?'

'Did you feel hurt? Hard done by? Did you feel you'd been treated unfairly?'

William felt the sweat just starting to find its way down his back. *Here we go.* Whatever she suspected him of doing, it was utterly clear *why* she suspected it, which meant that the interrogation room was a corner he'd painted himself into, all on his own. Chances were she'd already heard colleagues telling her how he'd changed.

'Did you feel you wanted to demonstrate your skills? Show what you can do? Show your employers what they're missing?'

William shook his head. Across the table sat a woman making

accusations without saying what they were, and the one person who should be speaking on his behalf was sitting right beside her not speaking at all.

'Say something,' he said eventually. 'For fuck's sake, Lassie.'

The words found their way out of him, tired, almost silent, and he looked Palmgren straight in the eyes that he could not see. Come on. Show us which side you're on, now.

For the first time, he heard Palmgren breathe in.

'Why did you go to ground, William?'

Of all the things to say.

'Did I? Did I really?'

'We tried to get hold of you.'

'That's one of the drawbacks of sacking someone. They don't tend to be on call so much after that.'

Palmgren didn't respond. 'We needed your help,' he said instead.

William could hear the sarcastic retorts lining up inside his head, knew what he ought to say: 'I don't think I'm the right person to help you with anything, unless what you're looking for is someone to come in here and be obstructive. Unless you're suffering an acute shortage of people wallowing in self-pity and creating conflicts and – what else was it you said? – becoming a risk for the whole operation.'

That's what he should have said. And on another day, in another life, that's just what he would have done, and afterwards he'd have smiled with dark eyes and added, '*If* I'm wrong, *if* that is what you're looking for, then I think the team investigating the Olof Palme case still have a couple to spare.'

His weapon of choice was sarcasm, and after thirty years in the Forces it was the only one he had full command of. Now he was sitting there, and it was loaded and ready for use, but the anger had gone and all he felt was regret. Regret and resignation and please, let me go.

'For the last time,' was all he said, 'why am I here?'

The question hung, unanswered, in the thick, dry silence until Forester spoke again.

'Because we feel the same as you. We find it hard to believe that this was a coincidence.'

Every time Christina got into one of the paper's cars, she wondered what kind of people her colleagues really were. The light blue Volvo was only a year or so old. It had been driven only by adults travelling to interviews and reports, from A to B and back again. Yet somehow it still had the appearance of belonging to a sugar-addicted family on a road trip. There were crumbs and wrappers and remains that couldn't be identified, and Christina swept it all onto the floor, forming a pile of rubbish along with the stuff that other colleagues had swept down before her.

'Right,' Beatrice said as she got into the passenger seat beside her. 'What have you saved for us?'

'I'm shooting from the hip,' said Christina, 'but I know someone who ought to have a bit more information about this than we do.'

'And you think he's going to want to talk to you?'

'I *know* he doesn't want to talk to me,' she replied. 'But he hasn't been there in three months.'

Beatrice's response was a questioning silence, and instead of answering her, Christina leaned forward and turned the key in the ignition.

Christina lived a different life now. She had started again. And she had done so in a freezing cold flat in Sollentuna. It was described as 'furnished' in the ad, and had it not been Beatrice who'd found it for her, she'd probably have turned on her heel as soon as she set foot inside. Editor or not, every night Christina Sandberg left work she went home to a faded lino floor, a cathode-ray TV perched on a stool, and a single bed whose previous occupants she'd rather not speculate about. She hung her clothes on a hanger outside the wardrobe, since the inside stank of damp and neglect. Her nightly ablutions were performed in front of a wonky bathroom cabinet made of wafer-thin steel and above a washbasin scarred with permanent reddish-brown trails left by the constantly dripping tap.

It had already been a month. She hadn't realised until she saw the rent invoice lying on the hall floor, *a month of my life in this*

41

place, she'd thought to herself, but the truth was she'd been lucky to find anywhere to live at all.

A month since she cleared out her old wardrobe at Skeppargatan, jotted a concise explanation on a notepad she left on the kitchen table and then pushed her keys through the letterbox as she left. He still hadn't so much as called her. Maybe he hadn't even noticed that she'd left.

So no, he wouldn't want to talk.

'That's about the only thing we have in common right now,' she mumbled in response to her own thoughts, and put the headlights on full beam to light their way out of the car park.

It was Beatrice's yell that got her to slam on the brakes. She saw it first, the feeble yellow light that suddenly appeared as they pulled out of the garage and accelerated over the pavement and the bike lane. Her first thought was *what the fuck is that?* Her second was that it had to be a moped.

They felt the wheels lock and glide across the ice, the judder from the brakes as the car slid forward, then that instant of uncertainty before the bang came.

The noise of the moped's engine cut through all other sound. It cut through the crunch of metal on metal, the squeal of the parka gliding across the windscreen, the clatter as the whole thing finished its scraping course across the bonnet and fell off the other side, where a worrying silence followed.

Across the road they could see the darkness of the park, bare trees lined up in their headlights, and just in front of the bumper a steady moped headlight shone right up into the mist, signalling 'Here I am'.

Christina Sandberg had run someone over. And if they did need help, there was going to be no one to call.

She flung herself out of the car and undid her seatbelt, roughly in that order, which wasn't the right one, until she finally managed to extricate herself and cleared her own car door.

The man who lay in front of her car was staring straight at her. Two eyes sandwiched between a woolly hat and a full white beard. As far as she could see there was no blood, and at least that was something.

'Are you okay?' she asked. 'I didn't see you.'

His answer wasn't what she expected.

'Christina Sandberg?' A voice she didn't recognise, fevered and full of urgency.

'And you are?' she said.

'I've been calling you. You never call back.'

She leant over. Did she recognise him? But before she had time to speak he reached out, grabbed hard at her lapel, and then pulled himself up using her body as support until his face hung just inches from hers – harried eyes and damp, flushed cheeks bathed in the light of the car headlamps.

'They've known about this all along,' he puffed. Then with a penetrating stare: 'They knew that this was going to happen.'

'Thirty years you worked here, isn't that right?'

William let his silence concur.

'You're one of the Military's best cryptologists. You're a trusted, well-regarded colleague – that's what everyone's told me. Then suddenly, six months ago, out of nowhere – you're not any more. You start accessing systems you're not authorised to see. You conduct searches of sensitive directories with no supporting explanations. You refuse to answer questions, you engage in various forms of misconduct, you become unpredictable.'

He wobbled his head. It was a 'yes', a 'no' and a 'who gives a shit' all rolled into one.

'Am I mistaken?'

'If that's what it says in your notes then that must be the case.'

He said it with a glance at the file on the table, trying to provoke her into revealing its contents. She either missed his gesture in the darkness, or simply ignored it.

'Can you tell me why?' was all she said.

'I'm not a big fan of convention,' William said loudly, trying to sound authoritative, failing utterly. 'But wasn't there a good European one?'

It all came out a lot less cocky than he'd aimed for, and he was grateful to the darkness for hiding his regret. Hopefully they

43

would at least have grasped what he meant. Somewhere amongst all the articles and paragraphs of the European Convention on Human Rights there was a very applicable passage, and if they planned to breach it, he didn't mean to let it pass unnoticed.

All prisoner have a right to know what they are accused of.

'*Why?*' he asked again. 'Why am I here?'

He could feel glances being exchanged in the darkness. Was he imagining it, or was there something they weren't agreeing about?

William waited for them. Then, eventually, it seemed that their glances had produced a decision. Palmgren leant forward.

'William?' he said. His tone was direct and serious. Headmaster to pupil. Traffic warden to someone who's just parked his Porsche in a disabled bay and then cartwheeled off. 'We know that you respond to the codename AMBERLANGS.'

The word caused the ground underneath him to sway. It was the first thing they'd said to him on the platform, yet he'd managed not to make the connection until now: *that* was the evidence, right there. They *had* read his emails. What more did they know?

'We know that you showed up for a meeting at Central Station with a person or group of persons who might go under the alias ROSETTA. Not only that, we have reason to believe that they – and by extension you – are involved in one or more terror plots against Swedish and/or international targets.'

For a second, William looked for a smile in the darkness, but none came.

Was he being serious? Lars-Erik 'Lassie' Palmgren? *Dram of Lagavulin with a drop of water* Lassie? *Tennis twice a week until his Achilles packed in* Lassie, the man he'd known for almost thirty years – how could he be sitting there, suddenly transformed into *accusing me of terrorism* Lassie?

William clenched his jaw.

'There were a whole lot of assumptions in that sentence,' he said.

No answer.

'Would you like to tell me just why you've arrived at that conclusion?'

Palmgren gave Forester another quick glance. She had no objection. Palmgren got to his feet.

'Right now, a great swathe of Sweden is in complete darkness. The whole of the east coast, from Sundsvall down. We don't yet know exactly how many are affected – authorities can't communicate with one another, no information is getting to the public, masts and transmitters are all down. Telecoms, radio, TV, everything.'

William swallowed. He'd guessed it was significant, but on that scale? He felt the moisture of sweat creeping down over his back again.

'How?'

'Sixteen zero six today, this afternoon.' Palmgren was still doing the talking. 'A short circuit in a substation near Årsta caused a minor fire. The automatic fuses tripped and the security precautions worked as intended: the electricity supply was automatically diverted via other substations to avoid any overload. That caused another blowout somewhere else, and with each incident there were fewer and fewer alternative routings available to deal with an accumulating load. Eventually the system couldn't take any more and the whole system was knocked out.'

William said nothing.

'That,' Palmgren continued, 'is the official version.'

Oh shit.

'So there's an unofficial one?'

'The automatic fuses blew. That much is true. However.' Palmgren took a deep breath. 'There was no fire.'

'What do you mean by that?'

Forester made an invisible signal to Palmgren to take his seat again. That'll do, she said without saying a word.

'I am sure you'll understand if we don't share our information until you have shared yours.'

She picked up the file, the one that had been left lying on the table like a flat, unuttered threat, pulled the rubber bands away, one snap, two snaps, slowly and carefully like she enjoyed dragging it out. Inside was a single sheet of paper, which she illuminated with her phone as she slid it across towards William.

A laser printout. Almost completely devoid of content, except a single line of straight letters, striped and of varying clarity due to low ink levels. A toner cartridge somewhere was still being kept at work long after its due date. *Still having budget problems*, William thought. But said nothing. *We're expected to defend a nation but we can't afford stationery.* Didn't say that either.

Instead, he said: 'Yes,' then: 'I recognise that. That's one of the emails I got.'

'*One of?*' Forester's voice betrayed more surprise than she had probably intended.

'Yes. One of them.'

'Can you explain what it means?'

'It means what it says. What else could it mean?'

She was still waiting him out. And he could feel himself getting more frustrated.

'I don't know! What else can I say? If it means anything more than what it says, I don't know what that is.'

There was a hint of desperation in his voice now, and he could hear it himself. He didn't want to fall apart, but then again, why not? Maybe that was the only option left, a collapse and a breakdown that would force them to see that he knew nothing, that he was feeling tired and sad and fuck off, just let me go home and do that alone.

'Seriously,' he said, slowly, with a tone that contained all that, 'what is going on?'

Perhaps she saw him give up. Maybe she saw fatigue take him over. Whichever it was, she leaned back in her chair and turned off the light on her phone.

'You first,' she said.

8

When the blast hit, Rebecca Kowalczyk was sitting in her car. Tears found their way down her face, painting black stripes of mascara, but she left them there. No one could see them anyway. And even if they did, they wouldn't recognise her.

Her long dark hair was gone. The process had been more painful than she'd anticipated, first in her mind as the scissors sheared off years of growth and careful attention, then physically as the razor tugged its way across her scalp to finish the job. All because he'd made her promise. Because he'd told her that if one day he disappeared, she too would be in danger.

Sitting there now, at one end of Ulica Brzeska, with the car facing away just as Michal had taught her, she looked at the door she had shut behind her moments before. Saw the window panes in the storey above shatter, the flames erupting, grabbing at the oxygen, saw how what had once been their apartment now ended its life in a black, billowing inferno that everyone would simply put down to a gas leak.

Left rear-view mirror. Right. Centre. Switching between the three as though deep down she was hoping that the other mirrors might show something else, a reality where the windows were intact and everything as usual and she was the same Rebecca as ever.

But the house was on fire. And whoever she was, it was some-one she had never seen before.

She would get used to it. Her hair would grow back eventu-ally, everything that Michal had told her would turn out to be paranoid fantasy and life would go back to normal. That's what she told herself. But she knew she was lying. Still, as long as it made her feel better, a little white lie was hardly the worst thing she'd done today.

People came rushing out of the shops and nearby buildings, trying to approach the burning block. But none of them noticed the hire car starting and then pulling off at the far end of the street.

In her rear-view mirror, Rebecca Kowalczyk could see smoke and fire and people transformed into tiny dots, vibrating as the car shuddered along the uneven road surface. She swung out towards Targowa, continued past Praskiparken, let herself melt into the traffic and followed the flow, without knowing where she was heading. Or why she had done what she'd done.

The only thing she knew was that the one person she could have asked no longer existed.

9

Standing in the empty lunch room on the third floor, Christina was struck by how rarely you experience something that's never happened to you before. Even big, unexpected events tend to be familiar in some way, as if they'd already been built into your life, and somehow belong when they eventually turn up.

Hitting a moped rider, though, was a first. Especially in the middle of a massive power cut, and especially a man who knew her name and who demanded to be let into the building because he had something vitally important to show them.

Now he stood over by the sloping windows, his face floating in the darkness, lit up by the open laptop in front of him. On a chair beside him lay the dark grey plastic crate that he'd had tied to the old moped's rusty pannier rack. With a steady stream of 'Oh dear, oh dears', he proceeded to pull out all the electronic devices that he'd had to rescue out of the sludge down there, checked them one by one, connected them up with twisted cables and attached them to the filthy car battery at the bottom of the crate.

Normally, the cafeteria would be buzzing with activity at this time of day, but now it was deserted and empty. It had taken only minutes for the rolls and salads to disappear from the chilled cabinets, hungry colleagues stockpiling in case the power cut lasted, and on the now cool hotplates spherical pots offered only the very last, ice-cold dregs of coffee. A handwritten note was all that remained of the kitchen staff, and every now and then she would hear colleagues approach from the stairs, read that the power cut had closed the canteen, then shuffle off again in disappointment.

But Christina's focus remained on the man who stood by the windows: the weird homemade device taking shape, the seriousness in his face as he cobbled it all together. An uneasy sensation that this was indeed something she'd never experienced before.

'Maybe you should've hit him a bit harder.' That was Beatrice. She was standing next to Christina, leaning against one of the darkened fridges, her murmur barely audible. 'I've always wondered what he looked like. I have to say I'm disappointed.'

Christina smiled an invisible smile in the darkness.

His name was Alexander Strandell. And if they'd known that earlier, he wouldn't have been standing there at all.

His beard looked like it had climbed off the front of a packet of throat lozenges. He had zinc-white hair that it would be impossible to pull a comb through, that seamlessly wound its way into his equally white beard, framing a circular face that was pitted and swollen, marks left by an adolescence that had refused to pass unrecorded.

Tetrapak. That's what they called him. And even if neither of them had met him he had been a standing joke long before Christina had joined the paper. He was a medically retired amateur radio enthusiast, living in a small house in Alvik, and every time someone recounted a story about him there were more aerials in his garden, thicker layers of tinfoil on his windows, and still less credibility to his tip-offs.

No one knew who had been present at that meeting when his nickname was coined. It may be that it never even took place. The story went that it was the early nineties – even the Eighties, according to some – and even back then, Strandell had been notorious in the trade. There wasn't a single tips line at a single Swedish paper that hadn't at some point received a call from him, claiming to have intercepted some secret radio transmission, each time equally convinced that he had uncovered a global conspiracy that absolutely could not be discussed on the telephone.

Despite being constantly fobbed off with varying shades of polite professionalism, he continued to make contact – and then one day, towards the end of the last century, someone had finally agreed to meet him for lunch.

The first thing the man had done was to clear everything from the restaurant table. Saltshaker. Pepper mill. The little wilted pot plant. Everything had been shifted onto neighbouring tables because *they're always listening*, and according to the legend he'd then lowered his voice to explain how *anything could be a microphone*, his eyes darting around as he told them *you're not safe anywhere*.

What this earth-shattering tip had been about had long since been streamlined out of the tale, but when they got to the coffee, and the bowl containing the sugar and the small pyramid-shaped packets of milk were placed in front of them, the radio amateur had reacted as though something had just bitten him on the leg. He'd thrust the chair away from the table, imploring the waitress to remove the goods at once – *now, straight away, have we even ordered that?* – and there he sat, keeping his distance till she finally did as he'd asked.

In the end, the journalist couldn't resist. When lunch was over and they both stood up to leave, he took a detour past a nearby table and let one hand pluck a handful of the miniature milk tetras from the sugar bowl. Next minute, as they squeezed out through the revolving door, he'd dropped a couple into his visitor's overcoat pocket.

Not that he ever got to see the result, but the mere thought of the man's reaction when he got home and realised that his pocket held two of the terrifying packets, presumably having eavesdropped on him all afternoon – that alone had won the tale legendary status. Over the years, it had been told at Christmas dos and work parties so many times that it had in the end become true. Whether or not it had happened was neither here nor there.

After that lunch, Strandell's tip-offs had grown increasingly rare. Despite that, he would still make occasional contact, always to warn of some extreme event in store. And always, without exception, when there really was no time to listen to him.

It took him almost seven minutes to plug in all the devices on the table, and when he was done he got to his feet and beckoned the two women over.

'Background,' he said when they were in place. 'My name is Alexander Strandell. I've been in contact with you before.'

The pause that followed confirmed that this did not come as

a surprise to either of them. So he carried on talking, gesticulating as he did so to underline the importance of what he had to say.

'I'm not stupid,' he said. 'I know you don't take me seriously. But just give me these ten minutes. I think you're going to agree with me about this.'

'Seven of them have already gone,' Christina said. 'Tell us why we're in here with you and not out there doing our job.'

Instead of answering he bent over his little set-up on the table.

The computer was black, the size of an encyclopaedia volume, and might once have been considered both cutting-edge and ultra-portable. Seen with today's eyes, it was heavy and awkward, and the blue-green desktop screen revealed that the operating system was at least three generations too old. His dirty fingers hammered in commands via a keyboard whose letters and symbols had been worn away by years of use, and the result was a whirring from the hard drive along with a riot of windows and data tables. Some of them displayed barely discernible columns and values, while others displayed curves and wave movements that could stand for just about anything.

'The first time I heard it was back in summer,' he said as he carried on working. 'Early August, to be precise. This is my first note.' He pointed at a row of numbers as though it might help them to understand. It failed to do so.

'Heard what?'

'Their transmissions.'

Something about those words caused Christina to sit up straight.

'Who are they? What transmissions?'

He didn't answer. Instead, he used the arrow keys to steer the cursor up to the top number in one of the windows. A date, as far as Christina could make out, and next to it a time, and something resembling a graph showing peaks and troughs. A sound file?

He looked up at them. Pressed return.

For a second, Christina could feel her stomach protesting inside her. What the hell was this about?

Two. Four. Six. Nine. Three. One.

A voice. A woman's. It was so devoid of feeling, so monotonal, that it seemed to balance on the cusp of death. Crackling digits, read aloud in English in a slow, meaningless series, rang chillingly through the empty lunch room.

Seven. Nine. Nine. Two. Four. Four. Seven.

They stood there, listening without breathing, and when the dirge ended it was followed by a tone that played for a few seconds before the count resumed again. Exactly the same numbers, the very same monotone.

Two. Four. Six. Nine. Three . . .

When the bearded man finally turned it off, Christina was standing with her arms wrapped tightly around herself, her hands gripping firmly at her upper arms as though she was freezing with cold.

'What is it?' she said eventually, her unease sneaking through.

'It's a number station,' he said.

'And what is that?'

'That's the thing. No one knows.' He looked at them with deadly serious eyes, lowering his voice. 'Long story short,' he said. 'The shortwave band. It spans two to thirty megahertz. It is divided into countless transmission frequencies, all of which are arranged into area of use and type of traffic. In favourable conditions, you can hear transmissions from any part of the globe.'

He paused. Now he had their attention, and his enjoyment of that fact was plain to see.

'The first reports of this kind of number station came in the early nineteen hundreds. No one knows who the sender is, no one knows who the receivers are, just that they're there, on different frequencies. Spouting their sequences, incessantly, day in and day out.'

'Why?' Beatrice's voice sounded just as unsettled as Christina's.

'No one knows for sure. Coded messages? Signals to spies out in the field? Maybe. What we do know, on the other hand, is that most of them disappeared along with the Cold War.'

At that point he paused for several beats, as though having come to the heart of the matter he was about to share with them.

'And that's just it,' he said. 'This particular frequency has been dormant since the nineties. Until now.'

The room fell silent, and the bearded man known as Tetrapak looked at them with an ominous intensity, waiting for them to say something.

'Who is transmitting?' It was Christina who spoke first. 'What does it mean?'

'I believe it to be instructions.'

'Instructions for what?'

For a moment, he said nothing. Instead, he flung his arms wide, towards the windows. Towards the power cut and the silence and all that empty darkness out there.

'For today.'

There was something about the way he said it. In his voice, the devices strewn on the table, the meaningless numbers, in the implication that it had something to do with a Cold War that no longer existed and – *for Christ's sake*, she asked herself, had she really got snarled in the ramblings of a person afraid of coffee creamer?

'I don't understand what you mean,' she said, for want of anything better.

'After a while, the transmissions were altered,' was his reply. 'Significantly.'

'In what way?'

He bent down over the screen, clicked down to another date in the list, finger poised above the keyboard.

'This is the nineteenth of September.' A pause. And then he tapped the space bar.

As he did so, both women backed instinctively away. What came pouring out of the computer now was not words, but a prolonged blast of amalgamated, atonal noise, scraping and hissing and familiar yet not, a grating sound that lasted for almost a second before it disappeared again, just as sharply and abruptly as it had come.

What the hell was that?

Christina and Beatrice stood frozen as the echo disappeared into the empty lunch room, followed by a couple of interminable seconds of discomfort while their memories caught up.

It sounded like a modem. That was it. Like a computer connecting to the internet, that sound that could be heard at every desk in the mid-nineties until technology moved on and eventually disappeared like a species with no place in the food chain – but this sound was faster, deeper, richer.

'Suddenly it's as if the entire ether is awash with transmissions,' Tetrapak said before anyone had managed to distil their thoughts into words. 'They are all on frequencies surrounding the number station, unusually clear and pronounced, short blasts of sound that last for a few seconds. Day after day. At around the same time too.'

He returned to the lists on his screen, played a few new transmissions consisting of scraping noises, grizzling cacophonies that alternated as he made his way down through the list. They were becoming more and more frequent, he explained through the din, and above all they were coming at various levels of intensity and from different sources. Sometimes they were echoed at once by another transmitter, sometimes close by and sometimes from a completely different part of the globe. He had never heard anything like it before, and it had scared him, and then he had grasped what it was.

Receipts. The repeats were confirmations of delivery, from someone who had received the message confirming that it had arrived.

'It was as though they were fine-tuning a system,' he said, his face expressing pride and seriousness and foreboding in a single expression. 'As though they were constructing a whole new channel of communication. What we're listening to is computers talking to one another, on frequencies that haven't been used since the end of the Cold War.'

Christina looked at him. What he was saying was fascinating and terrifying at the same time. But isn't that also the mark of a good conspiracy theory? That it seems to have some basis in fact, that it's plausible, and if you get yourself sucked in from the likely angle then you don't see all the gaping holes elsewhere?

Even if what he said might actually be true – even if this was an entirely new and secret mode of communication – there was no evidence whatsoever pointing to any connection with the power cut. Even less to suggest that there was in fact anything strange about it.

'I still don't understand,' she eventually said. 'I don't understand what you think this has to do with today.'

At that point he turned to the computer again. He switched off the sound, letting the silence settle as the swirl of computer bleeps echoed out in the darkness.

'Shortwave,' he said. And then he expanded. 'Who uses short-wave when we've got the internet?'

'I don't know,' said Christina. 'You tell me.'

'Whoever knows that the internet's about to go down.'

10

The first email had arrived in the middle of the night. Outside, it was still November. A definite wintry chill had arrived from somewhere, taking Sweden by surprise the way it did every year, as predictable as the self-assessment tax return but equally impossible to remember. William Sandberg had made his way past abandoned cars, hazard lights blinking, their summer tyres unable to find grip in the thin layer of polished snow. He'd spent a whole night walking in the snowfall, silence settling around him as echoes disappeared between flakes, swarms of sparkling dots moving like insects in the wind. He was wet and freezing cold, and throughout he had forced himself not to feel any of it. Just as he always did it, night after night after night.

It had been staring out at him when he got home in the small hours of the morning, demanding his attention. Just an email, nothing more. A single message in an otherwise completely empty inbox, marked as a thick blue band across half his screen. Visible from across the room even as he came through the door.

Before long, his lungs were screaming inside his chest,

reminding him that he had just stopped breathing. It was as though he was experiencing a sense of elation and a falling all at once, and at first he didn't recognise the feeling. Was it a heart attack? Was it hunger?

It was hope.

This, he'd allowed himself to think, was the moment he'd been waiting for. What else could it be? And he had ended up standing in the doorway of his study, with the parquet flooring creaking beneath his feet as though quietly protesting against the law of gravity, with snow swirling past the window like a badly tuned television. Not daring to go inside, wanting to keep the hope alive for as long as he could.

The email address was one he hadn't used for years. He'd kept it because it was associated with memories, and it had remained untouched for years, because those memories were painful. At least that was partly why. Partly, it was also because grown-ups have grown-up email addresses: combinations of first and surnames, something that fosters trust, that's serious, anything but this. Not AMBERLANGS.

He'd simply hadn't had any use for it. If Sandberg communicated via email at all, he did so at work. And even if he knew that the computers in his home office were invisible to the outside world, hidden behind Virtual Private Networks and basically impossible to access from elsewhere, his trustworthiness would not be improved by asking people to contact him via a non-existent word on a free mailhost.

It wasn't until his life started falling apart that he'd logged on again. Much to his surprise, the account was still there, and that somehow gave him a sense of security, as though it was *meant to be*, even though looking for meaning was something he couldn't resent more. But his hope and his longing outweighed his good sense, and so that became the address he had chosen to give out to the ones he met on his nightly rambles. Morning after morning he had come home hoping to find something in the inbox, hoping that one among all those lonely, frozen people he'd met might have had something to tell him.

That was the simple truth. They were the only ones who knew about that address. No one else should have been able to email him there. But then again, nothing in William's life was as it should be any longer.

Eventually he had dared to approach the computer.

In an instant, he felt the hope replaced by something else.

He was tired, off-kilter and unbearably alone, and maybe it was that, or the darkness and the silence that made everything grow out of proportion. For Christ's sake, it was just an email. Yet still he could feel an icy chill spreading inside him, as though someone had opened a trapdoor in his groin.

What the hell was this?

He reread the text on his screen. On the left, where the sender should have been, was nothing. Underneath that was the subject field, also blank. Still, what ramped up his unease was the text in the message window on the right-hand side.

Contact me. I need your help.

Nothing more. No name, no subject, barely any content. Just an order, or maybe a plea, hard to know which. And he stood there for several minutes, paralysed, his heart pounding hard. It was as if the email itself was a sign, an omen of something bad, something unstoppable that was just about to take place.

In a way, he was right. But how was he to know?

In the end he'd forced himself to shrug it off. He'd taken a shower, donned clean clothes and made some coffee. Things he'd made habits of, because you must have habits. He'd sat at the kitchen table, with the newspaper open in front of him but without reading, and had gradually convinced himself that the email was just a mistake and had been meant for someone else. It was strange, sure, but it was trivial and meant nothing, and in the end he'd gone back to the computer and deleted it from his inbox.

Two days later, another email had arrived. *Contact me.* The same instruction, waiting in the morning gloom. But this time with an extra concise line beneath the first.

Please.

He spent hours trying to trace the sender. The 'from' box was empty, but technically it comprised a blank space. It was hiding a Hotmail address, and the name attached to the account was

57

ROSETTA1998, but that was as far as it was possible to get. That combination of letters and numbers didn't exist anywhere. He found no references, not as an email address, not as a term in any other context.

He split the email into its component parts. He searched the email's headers and concealed information, switched the letters around, ran it through various encryption software for analysis, tried to locate some other meaning. Not necessarily because he thought it would help, but he'd been doing it professionally for so long that he did it automatically, almost without thinking.

And just as he'd thought, it led nowhere. The message contained neither more nor less than what was visible – whoever had sent it didn't want to be traced. The question was why? Who asks for help without saying who they are?

Eventually he had sat down at the computer and written a reply. Just as brief, just as monotonal, just as cold. *Who's this?*

Silence followed: no new emails – not that day, nor the next, or the day after. And the unease had waned and turned to exasperation, and then the exasperation to apathy, the same apathy of eternal darkness and meaninglessness as life itself. He had allowed himself to forget about it.

Three days later, Sandberg had arrived home in the half-light of morning, as he did every day. He was exhausted, he had talked to people in tunnels and shacks, had asked and pleaded but with no reply.

And there, in his inbox, was a new message, same sender.

Stockholm Central Station, Arlanda Airport Express, third of December, 4pm precisely.

This time he didn't refrain. His fingers hammered the keyboard, as though the rage and fear and exasperation would come across the harder he typed. He asked who the fuck it was contacting him, how they'd got hold of his address, and above all why on earth William would go anywhere to meet anyone who he had never met and didn't know what they wanted.

But no more emails arrived. No one got back to him. For the second time, the unease left him – but what refused to go was the hope. The hope that someone would have something to tell him after all.

Three weeks later he arrived at Stockholm's Central in a yellow taxi, walked through the great hall to the northern platforms, and was knocked down by three discreet men.

'I don't understand,' the woman opposite said once William had gone quiet. 'Who did you think you were going to meet?'

He avoided their eyes as he answered.

'Someone,' he said. 'Anyone.'

When Forester's gaze made it clear that wasn't answer enough, he closed his eyes, took a deep breath, and let the words pour out in a long, toneless stream. Quiet and objective, as though this was actually about someone else.

'I haven't slept a whole night since I don't know when.' Wrong. He corrected himself. '*I don't know when* was in August. The third. A Friday.'

He looked between his two interrogators, felt their eyes, took care to avoid them.

'That was the last time I spoke to my daughter. That was the day I found her gear, and that she swore never to speak to us again, and ever since then I've been stuffing myself with sleeping pills and tablets and hoping it will work – every fucking night for four months. But sleep never comes. In the end I go out looking, not because I think I'll find her, but because it's the only way I can keep myself from falling apart.'

He told them about his nightly rambles, about the people he talked to, people he had always known existed but who he had always avoided, pretended not to see. People who slept in ditches and alleyways, in the damp and the cold, or who didn't sleep at all, just like him. The ones who sit on the streets, outside shops and in the entrances to the metro, the ones who would look at him, pleading for help.

Now he was the one pleading with them.

'I tell myself that one day, in the end, there must be someone who knows. Who has met her, seen her, heard something. *Someone* who has *something* to tell me.'

He sat there in stillness.

'And then,' he said, 'the email arrived. My mistake was that I allowed myself to hope.'

11

Alexander Strandell talked on for over twenty minutes, and those twenty minutes afforded him more respect than ever before. He showed them the lists where he had fastidiously recorded the time, strength and duration of the signals, and Christina took photographs of them with her phone, its charge diminishing with each shot, but it had to be done. And lastly he explained the Doppler effect and meteorology, and the way radio waves bounce off the ionosphere. How that makes it all but impossible to determine exactly where a signal originated.

'But radio amateurs are a helpful breed,' he said, and went on to describe how he had been assisted by other amateurs' antennae. How they had done calculations on delays and strength, and how, with the help of colleagues all over the world, he had arrived at estimates that were both detailed and reliable, and that almost certainly showed where the transmissions were likely to be coming from.

'First the UK. They're the ones calling. Then come the replies. Sometimes from America, sometimes from Brazil. France, Japan, the UK, Sweden.' He lowered his voice again. 'The whole world is in on this.'

Those words stopped Christina in her tracks.

His information had been relevant and fascinating, that wasn't the problem. And tinfoil hat or no, the man who spoke had gone from being Tetrapak to the real-life Alexander Strandell, and his enthusiasm had been difficult to resist.

But there was something about that sentence that reminded her who she was talking to. *The whole world.* All at once, the spell was broken, as if they were right in the middle of a would-be seduction and he had just happened to say *I don't mind you being a bit chubby.* She just had to say something.

'In *what exactly*?' she asked. 'Involved in *what*?'

'I don't know,' he said. 'What I do know is that *they knew*.'

She gave him a wary look, but he didn't notice. As far as he was concerned, the seduction was still in full swing, and the whole room rang with the dissonance between a man ready to crack open the champagne and put on the Barry White on the one hand, and two women who'd already started glancing at the exit on the other.

'Who are they?' asked Christina.

'The Authorities. The Military. Everyone.' He drew himself up. It was time for the finale, the point he'd been striving towards throughout the meeting, perhaps throughout his life, a life full of meetings that didn't happen and the media refusing to listen. He took a deep breath, his pockmarked face draped in strange shadows from the glow of the computer screen.

'I'm afraid that what we've seen is just the beginning.'

Alexander Strandell raised his arms, an impassioned plea and a dire warning in one theatrical gesture.

'The beginning of the end of society.'

And right then – at the worst possible time – it happened. First, the fans whirred into motion. Then came the toneless plinking of the fluorescent tubes, an orchestra of flat clanging as the room lit up in shades of white. There he was, the man they called Tetrapak, balloon head and grey woollen overcoat, still dripping with the damp from the cycle path, and behind him, outside the window, a wildfire of sodium yellow and floodlit white, a shimmering wave as electricity rippled its way through the city.

The bridges gained detail. Across the Riddarfjärden bay, thousands of dots – windows – scrambled up the hills and stayed there, hanging like staves of sheet music. Logos and signs lit up and mixed with the evening damp in a twinkling, multicoloured haze.

And with that, the moment was left hanging, silent and glaring like a sarcastic smile, and in the middle of that smile stood Alexander Strandell, disrobed and tragic, as if someone had turned on all the lights in a haunted house and left him amongst the props and make-up and labels marked *Made in China*.

No one said anything. The silence endured, accompanied by fans and lifts, and the longer it lasted the more comical it became. But not for Strandell.

'Believe me,' he said eventually. 'You'll see.' He looked at them in turn, and made his plea. 'It will all come together.'

But the battle was lost. Christina felt herself tilting her head to one side, and saw the disappointment in Tetrapak's eyes.

'We've got your number, haven't we?' she said.

'Yes,' he replied. 'But you never call.'

'We'll be in touch,' she said. 'Promise.'

He wanted to protest, but what could he do? And when she nodded to him to start packing up, he responded with a brief head movement before returning to his equipment to dismantle it all over again.

The quiet lasted for a couple of seconds before fear overwhelmed Christina Sandberg once more.

The clangour seemed to come from nowhere. It burst through the room like a chandelier smashed in the air, and she spun around, instantly aware that light or no light, the fear still lurked. She scanned the room, her heart pounding, her body poised to take cover at the instant she found out what was happening.

On top of the chilled cabinet was her mobile phone, just where she'd left it only moments earlier. But now, the network coverage was back, and the phone was vibrating against the glass.

She picked it up and peered at the screen. Number withheld. She struggled for calm.

'Hello? Christina Sandberg?'

'That's correct.'

'My name is Jonas Velander. I'm calling from Armed Forces HQ.'

At the headquarters on Lidingövägen, the power had come back on at seven forty-six, and if the level of activity had been high during the outage, it was nothing compared to now. Phones rang and computers beeped in all directions. Updates and data poured in, most of it predictable and expected, but there was one exception. The information that had been uploaded from one of the thousands of CCTV cameras around the city, and which was now on a memory stick carried by Jonas Velander, had come as an utter surprise.

It wasn't the computers that discovered it first. All that made-to-order, expensive face-recognition technology, complex machines that crunched through images and spat out matches when the algorithms found a nose length and limb movement that resembled someone they were looking for, all of them had drawn a blank. And sometimes it was a good job that humans existed after all.

'Isn't that the girl?' The woman who shouted it out was Agneta Malm, two years shy of retirement. 'It must be. Isn't it?'

She'd been sitting at her workstation in the big control room down in the HQ basement, the one named the Joint Operations Centre but that everyone called 'the JOC', and people had gathered behind her chair, staring at the fuzzy video loop running on the screen in front of her, asking each other what the hell this meant.

William Sandberg *could not* be guilty. That's what they'd all said to each other four hours earlier when they learned that he'd been arrested at Central Station and was now being brought in in a Volvo. Forester had warned of an impending terror attack, and sure, she'd been right about that. But whatever had happened to Sandberg, they said, whatever the reason why he had behaved as he did, however much he'd deserved to be sacked earlier that autumn, he simply could not be involved with what was happening now.

In the end, though, enough of them had confirmed that Agneta Malm had been right. They had peered at the CCTV footage, clicked through one frame at a time, and it bloody well had to be her.

And for the first time, doubts crept in.

What was she doing there if he wasn't the one they were looking for?

—

Jonas Velander walked down the corridor with the memory stick in his hand, feeling his lack of fitness, the pain in his lungs after only two flights of stairs. He cursed his sedentary job, cursed the fact that, at just gone thirty-five, he felt every inch the decrepit old man.

He batted those thoughts away, pressed the phone to his ear and kept walking, Palmgren's orders echoing in his head. *Call his wife.*

When she answered he introduced himself. 'I'm calling because your husband is here. We would like you to come in and answer some questions.'

When the power returned to Lidingövägen they'd had one final question to ask before they could close their notepads, take a break, and finally release William Sandberg from the claustrophobic grey of the interrogation room.

'Why AMBERLANGS?'

It was Forester who asked it. And William hesitated, his eyes glued fast to the table to avoid making contact with hers.

'Because she thought that's what it was called.'

He had answered in a voice so weak it was barely audible. Now he was standing in front of the mirror in the narrow, sterile bathroom. He saw himself staring back, but it wasn't really him.

They had forced him to put things into words that he didn't have words for, and now he felt emptied of everything, as though someone had wrung him out and shaken him until all his powers had come loose and been scattered to the wind. He stood with hands pointing towards the basin, and he might want to drink, might need to wash his face, or had done so already, he wasn't sure.

Sara Sandberg had been three years old. Possibly four. She had learned to pronounce her 'r's and had been applauded for talking so well, and so she'd been proud and rolled the 'r's in every word they appeared in. And not just in them. Preferably other words too.

Amberlangs.

It was as irresistible as it was touching, the bold maturity of a girl who was still a child but aspired to be one of the adults, and who constantly, unwittingly, exposed herself through words. Through 'r's that appeared where they didn't belong, and that she pronounced with a self-confident clarity that made it quite impossible to keep a straight face.

In the end, she'd asked what they were laughing at – not hurt, not angry, just warm inquisitiveness, a look that spoke of innocent, invulnerable knowledge that she had two parents who always wanted what was best for her. *What are you laughing at, tell me, what is it?* Finally, they had to.

Sara had understood straight away. Wherever it came from, she had inherited a fierce intellect. She realised at once what she'd done wrong, and then started laughing too – it's called an *ambulance*, they had explained, and when she heard that she realised how silly it must have sounded, amberlangs and telurvision and balcurny.

She asked them to say it properly, listening and repeating over and over. And they'd laughed together and she was proud of herself for learning how it was supposed to be said, and that moment was committed to memory for ever as an image of what it meant to be a family.

Along with the dissonance – they could feel it even then, both William and Christina, the dissonance as the moment sliced through them, as if Life materialised in the middle of the room, arms folded, telling them *this ends here.* Try and hold on if you want, but you won't be able to. Because that instant, Sara Sandberg took another step away from her childhood. She never said *amberlangs* again. Never *telurvision*, nor *balcurny.* There and then, they left an era behind, and not only that, they left a person, a version of Sara that they would never get to meet again.

After that, the incident had lived on as a family yarn. As she got older it was told to friends and boyfriends, and each time she had squirmed obligingly, pretending to be tormented when in fact the story meant as much to her as it did to them.

Years passed. She had just turned fifteen, school finished that

65

spring after ninth grade, and she was more grown up than ever, dead set on spending the summer away on a language trip. The destination was, of all places, Washington DC. And why not? Nothing was going to happen. She was an adult.

The childish ones now were William and Christina, she told them with that adolescent maturity, because *for God's sake, what's going to happen?* And William had a thousand answers that he didn't really want to voice but all of them utterly plausible.

'I'll email,' she'd said to him. 'I'll email every day,' and then she'd opened an account for him. AMBERLANGS. She'd handed over the login details as he left her at the airport, and there was a burning behind his eyes as he read them, but there were no tears because he didn't do that sort of thing. Instead he'd hugged her for a very long time, his eyes flitting across all the departure boards in the terminal until he could be sure that they were dry enough for him to dare to face her again.

He'd watched her through security, seen yet another part of the child Sara Sandberg disappear, known that the next time he saw her she'd be even more grown up.

That summer would be their last one together. They would be enjoying the warmth of Stockholm, they would be visiting friends, and after that she would be starting high school. And come autumn, they would once and for all kill whatever was left of the child in Sara Sandberg.

And now he was standing here, hovering by the basin in the gents' toilets at Swedish Armed Forces HQ. And there were no tears, because he didn't do that sort of thing.

The head that appeared at the door, deep inside the mirror image, belonged to Lars-Erik Palmgren.

'I'm sorry about all this,' he said eventually.

They looked at each other's reflections, both motionless; a long silence. A *but* left hanging. An excuse, but also a sorrowful objection, a trust that should have been a given but turned out not to be.

'You should have told me,' said Lars-Erik.

'Would that have made any difference?'

'I would've known. I would have been able to help.'

William sniggered, shook his head, said no more.

'No one wanted to sack you, William. You made that happen all by yourself.'

They looked at each other. The silence hung there, empty and apprehensive.

'So what happens now?' asked William.

'I want you to come with me to the briefing room. I want you to help us understand.'

'Want? Like really want to? Or is it just your turn to play good cop?'

Palmgren shook his head.

'I don't think you understand,' he said. 'Forester isn't the bad cop. She's the frightened cop.' A pause. 'That's the way it is. We're all frightened.'

Then he turned around, leaving William to his reflection.

'Briefing room,' he said. 'You know the way.'

12

Sara Sandberg was used to hiding. That is, she'd been forced to get used to it.

At one time, she'd loved to be seen, she had a charm that she was both well aware of and only too happy to deploy, and an intelligence which, when combined with the former, made her a dangerous customer.

She got grades she didn't deserve on the basis that everyone knew that deep down she did deserve them, if only she applied herself. She was funny and snide and quick and always at the centre of things. She led a charmed life, the others used to say, and, quite honestly: what's wrong with that? She enjoyed it. She was good-looking and happy and intelligent and what more could you ask for?

A lot, as it turned out.

Suddenly, she stopped knowing who she was. From out of nowhere, her parents had informed her that they were not who they had claimed to be – that's not how they put it, of course, but it's what they meant – and ever since that day, things had been going downhill.

Now here she was, hurrying through Stockholm hunched and invisible – and used to it.

It had taken four hours before the power was restored, and she had spent all of that time in the shelter of a fire escape behind the Gallerian shopping centre, shivering and with her ears straining for the sound of barking dogs and clinking key rings.

When the lights finally came back on, some of the fear eased off. The falling snow took on contours and danced in front of the street lights, making her think that maybe her situation wasn't that bad after all, and she walked down Hamngatan; a route she'd walked a thousand times before but that now acquired a different meaning. On streets where once she'd seen shop windows and cafés, places that seemed good for a coffee or getting some clothes, she now saw alleys and shelter and hatches that might open, spaces that weren't built for people but that might just provide a night's sleep.

Life was ironic like that. Three years at high school hadn't taught her a thing. A year on the streets had taught her everything.

The old Sara Sandberg would've said *I told you so*. Experience trumps theory.

She cut through the park between the theatres, passed the big hotel where she'd got drunk in secret, back when being drunk was fun. She went that way now because it was darker, and because everyone who went past the angular stone monument down by the quayside did so with their eyes fixed on the edifice itself, hunched over against the weather and hurrying home from work or the gym or whatever it was that *normal people* got up to.

The last thing she wanted was to bump into somebody she knew. She could do without their questions and sympathy and encouragement. Or, worse still, seeing them pretend not to see her, consulting watch or phone and, very importantly, picking up their pace to arrive in time for a non-existent meeting.

Self-esteem. Wherever that came from. She, who didn't even know who she was, couldn't say.

She turned off down Strandvägen, and walked on the side nearest the water to avoid having to see the streets where her friends lived. Friends who had taken her in when she *moved out* because she'd *had a little disagreement with her family*, friends who had offered their sofas and told her she was strong and the best and you are great. Until they found out, and asked her to move on. They all did, sooner or later.

It had been a long time since she'd done *a little dab*, and only *now and then*, and because *it was a laugh*. Nothing had turned out the way she'd imagined. She had thought that the drugs would mean she'd be able to get rid of herself. That she would slowly transform into someone else, the way all the information films at school had said. Drugs turned people into machines, they had promised, into unfeeling robots in a state either of absent, half-stoned make-believe, or so focused on reaching that state that they didn't have time to think about anything else.

It sounded like the perfect package. It turned out to be the opposite.

She never had stopped being Sara Sandberg. She might not know *who* she was any more, yet she couldn't stop being that person, and no matter how high, how vacant, how battered she managed to get, she was still *her*, always present, but at a remove inside her body. It was as if she was the driver, sitting in the cockpit of an enormous gantry crane, controlling her limbs with levers that were heavy and slow to respond.

And she couldn't go on like that. No one can hate for ever, sooner or later you forget why you were so angry and you're just left with the memories of everything else, the things that were good, the things you miss. And a nagging sensation of, isn't it about time?

It was only a hundred metres to Skeppargatan now, and the flat would be there, as it always had been. There'd be tea, maybe a sliced white loaf, and now, when she let herself, she could feel a yearning so strong it hurt. For her family, even though they'd been kind enough as to inform her they weren't. For Mum, Dad, biological or not, who cares?

She closed her eyes against the wind, praying they were home. It was about time.

Just as long as it wasn't too late.

13

The café was located on the corner of Wardour Street and a narrow alleyway. It was the kind of place where people came and went without being seen, where the staff weren't staff but *baristas*, and where the customers' names were written in scratchy block capitals on paper cups while they waited for their coffee.

The man who'd just been served was holding a cup signed ELVIS, but that wasn't his name at all. He paused under the awning outside the big window, his back to the glass as the rain formed a transparent screen in front of him. He sucked up the sweet chai latte through the hole in the lid, watched the traffic and all the people passing by on the other side of the rain curtain. Here and there, Christmassy gift bags were already starting to give up in the rain, and people pushed their umbrellas ahead of themselves like reluctant sails in the wet wind.

If he tried hard enough, he could pretend he was one of them. A man who'd just bought a cup of tea, that's all he was, a well-dressed Londoner in his sixties who was just waiting for the rain to pass, before returning to his Christmas shopping and to jostling in sweaty shops and panic-buying things that no one wanted.

But the man who wasn't Elvis had much bigger things to worry about than Christmas presents. He batted away the thoughts, forcing himself to enjoy the warmth from the paper cup and think about nothing. Not about Stockholm. Not about the news from Warsaw. And most definitely not about *Floodgate*.

There he was, a perfectly ordinary man under a perfectly ordinary awning, right until reality caught up with him.

When the black diplomatic limo finally drove past, he waited until it had turned down the next street before raising his umbrella and walking away at a suitable pace. When he followed into the narrow side street and opened the back door, the guy with the tie was already sitting there.

'Major,' he said.

The man who wasn't Elvis nodded back and sat down opposite, and seconds later the car had disappeared into the heavy evening traffic.

With that, the meeting was under way. A meeting of a working group that didn't exist.

14

It hadn't been even three months since William Sandberg had last walked down these very corridors. Then, it had felt completely right. Not just right, liberating. He had been marching towards the exit, spitting out percussive consonants, serving to deliver one creative insult after the other. No one would be left in any doubt as to his opinion. As though there was any risk of that.

Completely right then. And now? To be honest, pretty fucking embarrassing. It was a bit like storming out of a room only to find that you've entered a wardrobe, falling from high status to low in an instant, the only difference being that the instant had lasted three months and that the wardrobe in question had been one called grief.

Now here he was again, a Calvary pilgrimage of shame across worn-out lino floors, a stroll back down the path he'd sworn never to take again, because *is that what you get for thirty years of service in this place? Reprimands?*

They had, of course, been right. He had gone beyond his remit: trawled journals and downloaded CCTV and checked police records that he had no business accessing. But he had a daughter to find, and even if he'd had time for trivialities like seeking permission it would never have been granted.

Wherever he looked, there was feverish activity. Streams of

serious-looking staff with intensity and concentration in each step, eyes full of steely focus that went straight through him, no greetings. Carrying papers and with shoulders pressing phones to sweaty ears. And despite the good news – that no one had time to comment on his reappearance – a new layer of unease was rapidly emerging.

He saw a constant cavalcade of faces he didn't recognise. The building's uniformed staff were rubbing shoulders with people who shouldn't even be there: the Security Police, the National Defence Radio Establishment, and God knows who else – staff who presumably thought they were wearing civilian clothes but who in fact were just wearing a different kind of uniform that consists of polo shirts and chinos with a neat, ironed crease.

Above all, though, every now and then he spotted uniforms that he couldn't immediately identify. Some were NATO, he knew that much, others were from the neighbouring Nordic countries, others he would need to see up close to be able to place. Palmgren hadn't been exaggerating. *Everyone* was frightened. And when he said everyone, he'd meant everyone.

The room they called Briefing was a large, no-expenses-spared meeting room, well equipped with soft leather desk chairs and a glass table that stretched from one end of the room to the other. There were no windows, no risk of anyone seeing in, and if you were really paying attention you would notice that the inside of the room was rotated ever so slightly, like a slightly skewed box inside another. This to ensure that the interior walls were not parallel to the exterior ones, so that no sound could leak out to surrounding corridors.

What happens in Briefing stays in Briefing.

As Palmgren ushered William into the room, the first thing he saw was that it had changed. It had been reconfigured into a makeshift control room, in which every place at the table was now a workstation, with open laptops and looping extension cables. Everywhere you looked, open notebooks and half-empty coffee cups testified to the fact that this room was full of activity, even if it was now devoid of people, as though the others had been removed just for their sake.

The most striking change, though, was that the room had now been equipped with an enormous world map.

The map, several metres wide and taking up most of the wall that faced out towards the corridor, was of the good old-fashioned worn-out roller-blind type, cloth-backed and unfurled from a long wooden cylinder. The edges were frayed after at least fifty years of being moved and rehung in various locations, the text bleached by sunlight, or possibly just damp and old age. Within a broad sweep north of the eastern Mediterranean the borders had been drawn and redrawn down the years, some with ink, others with pencil, perhaps a laconic way of saying that some of them weren't likely to last very long.

It was all incredibly analogue, and for a minute William felt like he was attending a military briefing in an Elsa Beskow story. As though he wasn't quite sure whether he was about to be informed of an existential threat to the country's borders, or just to learn about Swedish wild mushrooms.

'Call me old-fashioned,' said Forester. William turned around to see her nodding at the map. 'The advantage of paper is that for someone to succeed in listening in, they'll have to be close enough that we can see them.'

Now he noticed for the first time that the roller-blind map was covered in brightly coloured Post-it notes. They were scattered all over the world, each one carefully handwritten. As well as that, the map was surrounded by coloured laser prints on A4 paper, neatly lined up and stuck straight on the wall. From a distance they might be area charts, or small weather maps in bold colours.

'My name is Cathryn Forester.' She stretched out her hand as though they hadn't just spent half an evening together. 'I work for the British Secret Intelligence Service. And I'm sorry if our collaboration got off on the wrong foot.'

In the light she seemed both younger and taller than he'd imagined down there in the darkness. The hint of freckles, partly concealed by her red hair, made her seem gentler, more human – though the piercing stare of her startling blue eyes was enough to offset any redeeming features.

He saw her hand from the corner of his eye but pretended not to have noticed.

'Can we get one thing clear before we go any further?' he said. 'What, exactly, is my official status right now? Am I on duty, or a former colleague here to visit? Or should I be ready to be pinned against the wall by the Burton's brothers again?'

'I'd be lying if I said that your colleague and I didn't have differing opinions of your innocence or otherwise,' she replied.

'Very well,' said William. 'Honesty is good.' A pause before he straightened his neck with a click. 'Trust is better, but honesty will have to do.'

She looked back with a flawlessly bland expression. Either she'd missed the venom altogether, or she'd got it and was now displaying just how unimpressed she was. Whichever it was, it put him out, and it annoyed him.

'Innocence of what?' Better to move things forward.

Forester turned to Palmgren and nodded for him to reply.

'William,' he said, 'I would like to point out that as yet, your employment has not formally ended. That means that your oath of secrecy still applies.'

William waved his hand dismissively. *Don't start giving me the rulebook, after thirty years.* Palmgren took that as a confirmation, then nodded towards the big screen on the wall opposite.

'Right now, the internet news sites are shouting over each other,' he said. 'Heavy black headlines about the fire that plunged half of Sweden into darkness – you know the drill. But again, that fire never happened.'

He located a remote control on the tabletop and then pointed it at the TV. The image that popped up was another map of the world, except that instead of the faded pastels this one had white details on a black background, sharp thin lines that marked national borders, and light grey vertical lines where time zones met.

No more than five or six metres separated the two maps – the crumpled one behind them and the one just summoned on screen – but each metre represented at least ten years of techno-logical advance, from complex mechanical screen-printing to a digital high-res representation of the world which could zoom and scroll at the touch of a button.

When Palmgren clicked the remote again, a wealth of

information appeared on the map. From east to west, and all across the world, it covered the continents with bright spots in various colours, the dots joined by a series of lines in a spectrum of hues, all connected to thousands of other dots in country after country.

It looked like an airline route map. Or perhaps international trade routes for the transport of goods. William guessed that it was neither.

'Internet traffic?'

Palmgren nodded. 'This is a graphic representation of the amount of data sent via the internet at a given time. The colour shows the volume. The warmer the colour, the more traffic.'

He nodded towards the top of the screen.

'Keep an eye on the clock.'

Immediately above the map were an array of small fields containing numbers and other information, among them the time and date. Palmgren clicked through with the remote, hour by hour, day by day, and as he did so the map changed.

'You see how the colours follow the time of day? This is pretty much what it looks like, day in day out. Where it's daytime, the colours are red: large files, people working and exchanging information. Where it's evening, the colours are cooler: film and music and social media. At night it falls to blue – automatic systems and alarms and God knows what else, the odd late-night surfer. But this is today.'

He held down one of the buttons to single out the details on the timeline, then hopped forward with small short clicks.

Eventually, the clock showed 16:00 – the same time that Sandberg had found himself by the Arlanda Airport Express; six minutes before the lights went out; six and a half minutes before he slammed up hard against the glass door and was dragged out to the waiting Volvo.

Palmgren kept clicking through, slowly now.

On the map below the numbers, all the lines across Europe looked like a greenish spider's web, a continent gradually slowing down to turquoise and closing its offices and going home for the day. In the West, the American continent was slowly awakening in yellow and orange, while in the East, Asia lay in deep blue sleep, thousands of monochrome rainbows reaching in and out from common nodes all over the world.

16:05, Swedish time. 16:05 and thirty seconds. And then abruptly, without explanation, the lines' appearance changed. From their cooling, bluish tones, Europe's lines flared up in yellow again, and then orange, then deep red. It started with its epicentre on the east coast of Sweden before immediately spreading via the spider's web, out across the seas and on to the countries beyond them, and the colours passed red and turned pink, and after pink came white, and for a couple of hundredths of a second almost the whole of Europe was illuminated by an all-consuming white-hot light, before declining again through yellow to green and then finally to the same low-intensity blue-green as moments earlier.

It looked like seaside illuminations, like a rainbow explosion bordering on pop art. But it was nothing but a graphic representation of what society feared most.

'An attack,' said William.

In the top row, the clock had stopped at 16:06:33:50, and what he had seen was an enormous peak in data traffic – a peak that had lasted a little under two seconds. That disappeared as fast as it arrived, and coincided exactly with the power cut.

'That's what it looks like, doesn't it?' said Palmgren.

The answer was surprisingly close to being a no. Was it truly?

'Certainly does,' said William. 'A Trojan or a virus on thousands of computers, just waiting. Activated at a predetermined time, to attack a substation and cause disruption. What else could it be?'

'You're right,' said Forester. 'And you're wrong.'

William turned towards her.

'What we're looking at is an overload of data traffic, yes. An overload that caused not just one but several substations in the region east of Stockholm to fail. When they couldn't deal with the volumes of data involved, they simply shut down. And when substation after substation automatically redirected the power grid via substations that had also failed ... Well, you know what happened.'

'So how am I wrong then?' said William.

Forester spent a moment formulating her reply.

'Right: it's a peak in internet traffic. But wrong: it is not an attack.'

'But is in fact . . . ?'

'An attack is something aimed at one or several targets. Correct? But this peak . . . it has no target.'

William looked at them in turn. Maybe fatigue was getting to him. Right now, he didn't know what they were talking about.

'The substations?' he said.

'The substations were knocked out, yes. But they were neither more nor less exposed than everything else.'

William opened his mouth but was unable to find any questions. Palmgren cut in instead.

'Imagine someone sticking a twig into an ants' nest. Imagine that, but with information instead of ants. What you see on the map is a veritable stream of data, in all directions simultaneously, a chaotic exchange between all these IP addresses that lasts for one and a half, almost two seconds. And then that's it.'

He leaned forward.

'We're talking about an incredible number of data packets sent off in all directions, not to a specific address, but just back and forth between *all* of these nodes, between every single little laptop and access point that is online in this region.'

'Nobody attacked anybody,' Forester explained. 'Or: everyone attacked everyone.'

'And as a result, the power disappeared,' said Palmgren.

Quiet again. They waited for William to make the next move.

'I realise that you're probably trying to get me to answer something right now,' he said. 'But I'm tired, possibly even a bit thick. Either way, I don't have the energy to work out just what it is you want me to say.'

No one answered. A quick glance from Palmgren to Forester was returned with an equally short glance in the other direction.

'Let me ask you this,' William said eventually. 'Why are you showing me this?'

'Because what happened today . . . ' said Forester, pausing momentarily. 'It's not the first time that we've seen it.'

77

Christina Sandberg had grown up with no siblings, in an extended family with no children. That's probably why she was such an expert at playing on her own.

She'd realised early on that her favourite pastime was observing the world from afar, and even as a child her diaries had been full of observations about things that happened to others rather than things that happened to her. She loved to see the big picture, to analyse instead of joining in. For many years she'd also been obsessed by creating small worlds of her own, making dolls' furniture and miniature towns out of cardboard and packaging. Not for playing with, but just for imagining what might be happening to the people who lived there.

Fortunately the family had had an almost endless supply of shoeboxes and wrapping, and while other kids her age were pre-sumably out playing on the street, she would embark on voyages of discovery in boxes, transforming them into tiny furnished realities.

When Christina stepped out of the dark blue military-registered Volvo outside the Swedish Armed Forces HQ at Lidingövägen 24, she was struck by how the building in front of her looked like it was created the same way. It stood like a loveless colossus next to the road, a rectangular box for an enormous pair of sensible shoes, and along the walls, an equally enormous child had carved out window after window in straight, orderly rows and then said *Mummy, look what I've done.*

And behind all the little toy windows were toy soldiers on toy chairs, and one of them was her husband, and that was beyond understanding. Six months ago he'd been a respected, in-demand cryptologist, a man who gave presentations and was hired out on tasks, and who was important and secret enough that every time someone happened to ask what he did for a living, his whole face melted into a friendly, evasive smile, as he steered the conversa-tion elsewhere and unnoticed.

Now he was the one *being interrogated*. Because they *had some questions.* That had to be a bad thing.

She walked through the heavily guarded entrance, before handing in her mobile at reception, passing through a metal detector and placing her bag to be X-rayed. Beyond security waited the man who had called her.

'We're very grateful that you were able to come,' he said while lifting her handbag out of the dark blue plastic tray. 'We have a number of questions we'd like answered.'

'I can only say the same thing,' she replied.

She flashed a silent smile as she hung the bag on her shoulder, then followed him through the thick plate-glass doors into the big shoebox.

William had been sitting in silence for so long that eventually they'd have to ask him whether there was something he hadn't grasped.

Everything, he'd been tempted to reply, but signalled to them instead to keep going, and Forester walked over to the school map and stood in front of it. Mercator's Projection, the one that makes Sweden appear to be much bigger than it actually is. Like a metaphor for all of Sweden's political self-belief, he heard himself thinking before he swept the thought to one side.

'Each and every one of these' – in a sweeping gesture, she moved her hand past the multicoloured Post-it notes that were dotted around the world. 'Every single one represents a peak like the one we saw today.'

William squinted at them. Felt a shiver go through him.

Each note on the map was covered in handwritten text, and it was only now that he saw what they said. First a date, at the top, then the time, and underneath that the duration in minutes and seconds. The last row was a number, in petabytes: the size of the peak.

'Altogether, at least fifty occasions,' she said when she spotted him attempting to count them. 'Fifty peaks that we can safely say were the same thing as today.'

She bounced her fingertips over the Post-its, out onto the wall, touching the various colour printouts that hung around the map. *Of course.* William took a step closer. All the vivid printouts were small versions of the same digital map that Palmgren had just shown him on the screen, rainbow-coloured lines of internet traffic, shifting around the world in line with the time zones.

On each of the printouts was an area that shone white, more intense than all the others.

'Since when?' he asked.

Forester took a step back, reaching towards the North American continent.

'The nineteenth of September this year. A hacker attack disrupts the internet across swathes of America. Several banks are hit. The NASDAQ. I'm sure you've read about it.'

William rubbed his face. The nineteenth of September. Just days after that walk down the corridors, the one where he gave himself the sack and left his job for the last time.

Thanks for your help, coincidence.

'As I told you,' he said. 'I've been having other stuff to contend with. It may be that I missed the odd news story.'

'This was quite a big deal in the media. No one could say where it had come from, they were blaming it on everyone from independent hackers to the Iranian military, but none of it could be proved.'

'Because it wasn't true?'

Forester answered by not responding.

'That was the first time we saw it,' she said, 'but not the last. If you look for the centre of it, you end up here somewhere.' She placed her hand just off America's East Coast. 'Brookhaven, a little place on Long Island, north of New York. Since then, we've counted fifty similar incidents. Each one just like today's.' She pointed to the map as she spoke: 'Rio de Janeiro. Lisbon. Marseille. Yokohama. Los Angeles.'

'Coastal cities,' said William.

'Well spotted,' said Forester. 'Some resulting in short power outages, some affecting essential services. Sometimes we got away with just a fright.'

'And you think there's a reason they've chosen these particular cities?'

That wasn't really a question. He had a very good idea what the answer was going to be, and Forester nodded in response, and lifted her head upwards, over the map, looking now at the Nordics, Sweden, Stockholm.

'Today's power cut,' she said, and shook her head. 'Three hours and forty minutes. That's bad enough. But what happens if it's allowed to go on for longer? Days, weeks, or more?'

There was only one answer: society would collapse. One way or another, it would capsize, it was just a question of how quickly and how violently and what would go down first.

No one would have any money. First because all the electronic payment methods would stop working, and only the lucky few who happened to have cash in hand when the outage came would see themselves through the first period – a few days perhaps, or a little longer. After that, though, their head start would be gone. No one would have access to their accounts, and banks would not allow withdrawals while systems were down, and before long they'd close their branches to avoid threats and demonstrations and the chance of violence.

Then again, money or no money, if the power cut lasted, before long there'd be nothing to buy. Perishables would go stale and rot, leaving just dried goods and tins, and no one would be able to cook them on their lifeless electric hobs.

Would there be rioting? Probably. Would that help? Hardly.

Yet that would be just the beginning. If the electricity stayed off, what would happen then? To healthcare, communications, transport of goods and essentials? Pumps and sewage works would be at a standstill, supplies of fresh water would run out every-where, for everyone. It wasn't hard to imagine what people might be capable of then.

'And that's if we're lucky,' she said, when he'd had enough time to think. 'That's if we're just talking about the electricity supply.'

William nodded. It could, of course, be coincidence that the attacks had taken place in those locations. *Could*. He looked over at the map again, letting his eyes flit between all the Post-it notes: New York, Rio, Lisbon, Marseille, Los Angeles. All of them were central nodes where the internet traffic came together and where data was distributed onwards, places where enormous data cables emerged from the ocean and their traffic redirected across the continents.

81

'You think they're trying to knock out the entire internet?' he said eventually.

'What would be worse?' Forester said. 'Knock out? Or take control of?'

William swallowed, looked from one to the other, and heaved a long, exasperated sigh.

'I get the anxiety,' he said. 'I get your questions, I get that you've pulled me in for questioning, and that you're withholding information until you know what to make of me.' He glared his bafflement. 'What I don't for the life of me get, is *why*.'

No one said anything.

'What makes you think that the emails I received have anything at all to do with this?'

'We don't,' said Forester. 'We don't *think* anything. We know.'

15

The mere smell of Major John Patrick Trottier's chai latte had Mark Winslow feeling distinctly nauseous as he sat there in the soft leather seat opposite. He didn't say anything, although he suspected that maybe he should, instead waiting patiently while the ageing officer flipped through papers in his black satchel. He noticed the name on the paper cup, and didn't say anything about that either.

ELVIS. Dead clever. Really.

They had had more of these meetings than Winslow cared to remember, and every time Trottier had insisted on buying his tea under a new name. Perhaps it was meant as an expression of humour, or a quiet protest against the secrecy surrounding the project, whatever else it was, it was unnecessary. All he was doing was making their unmasking more likely – wasn't that guy called something else yesterday? – and how anyone could work in intelligence and yet be quite so daft defeated Winslow.

He kept a lid on those thoughts though. It could be he was just oversensitive and was getting stressed about nothing. Maybe what they'd told him as a kid was true: that he was weedy and brittle and had inherited his nerves from the wrong side of the family. Not that he thought so, not really, but on those days when the stress built up and the sting of the stomach acid ripped at his insides, the doubt returned.

They'd been travelling for several minutes before Trottier finally spoke.

'This is happening right now,' he said. They had just passed Trafalgar Square, although neither man had so much as looked up through the tinted rear windows.

The folder he handed over looked like it was full of printouts, and Winslow took it, leafed through – and was none the wiser.

'It comes from the internet,' Trottier said, and took a slurp from the Elvis cup. As if that explained it.

The pictures showed fire engines, fire, an apartment block shrouded in darkness, people standing around watching. Sure enough, these were printouts, from various internet news sites, and he saw that the headlines were all in Polish.

'The street is called Ulica Brzeska. The city is called Warsaw.'

There was something deliberately condescending about the way he said it, and once again Winslow felt like he should say something. But what?

'Should this mean something to me?' was all he asked.

'I have no expectations.'

Winslow swallowed. The heartburn was coming.

'I'll give you the abridged version,' said Trottier. 'According to the papers, the fire broke out at around eight, in a building that was supposed to have been evacuated ahead of its impending demolition. We happen to know that somebody was living there.'

'Somebody? As in someone we know?'

'Not *us*.' He moved his index finger in a circular motion, encompassing the pair of them. 'Not *us*, but – us.'

Winslow nodded blankly. Here we go again. Territorial pissings, lines in the sand. We who have worked in the field, and you who haven't, we the Secret Intelligence Service and you who can't even be trusted to shuffle papers at a desk without popping antacids like sweets.

He really should say something about that. After all, it was the older guy who reported to him, not the other way around, and if one of the two was higher-ranking it was Winslow. Nevertheless, it was as though his own lack of military rank diminished him. That, and the fact that he wasn't even half Trottier's age, let alone that his role was essentially that of a messenger boy.

'So what is it you'd like me to convey?' he said eventually.

Trottier explained the situation quickly and concisely, with the tone of voice as if everything was being said in passing. As if that somehow made it more permissible to pass it on.

The fire had set a bell ringing in one of their registers, he explained, because the man who'd been living there had been on their payroll. During the Eighties he'd worked as a scientist behind the Iron Curtain, and had been paid at regular intervals in exchange for information. That had continued until 1991, and since then he had stayed on their lists of former contacts.

'What is he up to nowadays?' asked Winslow.

'That's the thing. Nowadays, he doesn't even seem to exist.'

Winslow glanced up.

'His name is Michal Piotrowski. He's got a social security number and an address and a number of small bank accounts, but they haven't been touched for years. He doesn't appear to have a job, no income of any sort, nothing.'

'And now he has died in a fire.'

'Perhaps.'

Winslow met his eye again.

'There was mains gas in the house. The whole place was wood, just about. It's going to be impossible to tell whether or not there was anybody inside.'

'You mean he just *wants* it to look like he's dead.'

'During the course of yesterday, Michal Piotrowski booked at least twelve different trips leaving Warsaw. All on different cards – those same accounts he hadn't touched for years. Besides those, he booked a number of onward journeys: from Gdansk, from Krakow, from Berlin, each one heading in a different direction. All booked online, using various public terminals. Some paid for, others not. Some he had rebooked, jigged about, changed to a different departure. He left others untouched.'

'Red herrings?'

'Clearly.'

They said nothing for a while as they crossed the bridge. Raindrops snaked across the side windows, transforming the view to daubs of light.

Winslow broke the silence.

'So your conclusion would be that we've found ROSETTA.'

'I didn't say that.'

'And what have they got out of AMBERLANGS?'

For the first time in the journey, Trottier met Winslow's gaze, with a look that was now no longer condescending, but troubled and honest, and meant for a colleague sitting in the same boat.

'His name is William Sandberg. He's a cryptologist in the Swedish Armed Forces. The local staff are convinced that it wasn't him.'

'How about your lead interrogator? What's her opinion?'

Trottier gave a sigh.

'Their picking him up has put us in a really precarious situation. If he knows anything about Floodgate and he tells them something while there are Swedish personnel in the room ...' His voice tailed off to a murmur, even though no one could hear them. 'I have decided not to let Forester know any more than is absolutely necessary.'

'And now you're worried that she won't be able to say stop if he starts saying too much?'

'Amongst other things,' said Trottier. 'Many other things.'

As Trottier leant back in his leather seat, it struck Winslow that the other man had, for the first time ever, asked his advice. Not in explicit terms, but as silence fell again, an unuttered question hung between them.

What do we do now?

'Give me your honest opinion,' said Winslow. 'What do you make of it?'

'I believe Major Forester could do with some support.'

'Fine. Well, in that case I think you should give it to her.'

With that, the conversation was over. With a tap on the screen separating them from the driver, Winslow signalled that it was time to go home.

'William? Let's get back to the email.'

By the time that Palmgren piped up, he'd been quiet for so long that his ex-colleague had almost lost track of his presence. He was leaning on the wall behind William, almost as if to lie low there until it was his turn.

'From ROSETTA1998 to AMBERLANGS,' he said. 'The last of the emails you received.'

'That's another thing I don't get,' said William. 'If you were monitoring me, how come you didn't know that I'd received another two emails?'

Palmgren nodded. As though that, in a way, was the right question.

'Because we weren't monitoring you.'

'You can't have been monitoring the sender. Considering that you don't know who it is.'

Palmgren didn't answer. Instead, he headed over towards the television.

'Do you remember when the email was sent?'

'The twenty-seventh of November,' said William. 'Early in the morning. Can't remember what time exactly.'

'Three minutes past nine,' said Palmgren. 'And twenty-six seconds, to be precise.'

And then he stopped, in front of the screen. He placed his fingertips on the map there, in the north-eastern corner of Europe. Poland?

'Nine zero three and twenty-four seconds.' He pointed the remote and clicked through, one second at a time. 'Nine zero three twenty-five. And now, here's when your email is sent.'

He clicked once more, and although William was well aware of what must be coming next, it was still gripping. The screen showed a similar flare-up in data traffic, but this time the centre was right in the middle of Poland: the same expanding spider's web, or perhaps it was more like a sea anemone, with tentacles growing outwards and filling up with a glowing white for a second, then two, and then back down through all the colours of the rainbow before disappearing.

William caught himself holding his breath.

Warsaw? It was a possibility he hadn't even considered.

'I don't know who sent me that email,' he said, and instantly regretted it.

Dammit. Not the logical response at this point, but it was too late, it couldn't be unsaid, so he spoke up to continue instead before anyone else noticed the same thing.

'And what's the connection with the attacks? For a start, it's nowhere near a coastline. And also ... ' He rubbed his eyes as he strove to put his thoughts into words. 'Also – do you mean that somebody sent me an email in the middle of an attack in progress?'

'If we had all the answers we wouldn't be asking you so many questions, would we?'

That was Forester. Her expression made it clear that she was still expecting him to explain it all to them, and not the other way around.

'I know what it looks like,' he said eventually. 'It looks like I'm somehow involved, I can see that. But I don't know how, don't know why, and most importantly, if I am, it's without my consent.'

Palmgren waved his hand dismissively. That was another conversation, and they had other things to talk about first.

'In the middle of this surge,' he said, pointing at the screen. 'Right here, in the absolute epicentre, is the University of Warsaw's main library. I'm guessing you won't be all that surprised when I tell you that their log shows that someone logged into a Hotmail account minutes earlier. From one of their public terminals. As ROSETTA1998.'

William got the picture. That's how they'd found his email, and how they'd known about the meeting at Central Station. But what did they want him to do with that information?

'I still don't understand,' he said, and that was partly true.

Two thoughts were scrabbling around his head, competing for his attention. One was the nagging sensation that their suspicions were not completely unfounded after all, but for reasons they could not possibly know. The other was the irritating hunch that there were still things they weren't telling him. On the one hand they were still treating him as a suspect, while on the other they were asking for help.

It cut two ways. Were they showing him all this to ask for his opinion, or were they trying to force him into admitting something he hadn't done?

He was just about to ask them out loud, when a thought dawned on him.

'Wait,' he said. 'The centre of today's—' The anxiety was raw in his voice. He hesitated, before going on. '—was it my house?'

Palmgren did not keep him waiting.

'No,' he replied. 'It's worse.'

There was something in his tone that sent William bolt upright. It was the same one he had used when he'd collected him from the bathroom – full of commiseration and empathy, as though some ordeal waited to beset him. Something tragic and troubling, and that everyone but William had already seen.

Palmgren had zoomed in on the map, closer and closer to Sweden, the east coast, Stockholm, before approaching it and getting a final approval from Forester.

'The activity that we saw today,' Palmgren said, standing next to the screen, 'had its epicentre ... right here.'

It took a minute for William to work out where he was pointing.

Downtown Stockholm. Hötorget Square.

'And?'

Once again, the answer was just slightly too slow in coming.

'I am *so* sorry, William.'

That was Palmgren. Eyes so sincere that William felt the cramp invade his stomach without knowing why.

What the fuck is this about?

'I mean it,' he said. 'So sorry to be putting you through this.'

The room that Velander had asked Christina to wait in was an unwelcoming reception room on the lower ground floor. It was just metres away from the entrance, separated from the rest of the operation to keep people without clearance from getting too deep inside the Swedish Armed Forces' quadratic secret heart. It had dirty grey windows overlooking the dirty grey courtyard, and the only plants visible there were the winter-bare rosehip bushes. Along with the expanse of concrete slabs, they combined to make the view all the more depressing. You are now on Government property, they seemed to say. No unnecessary happiness.

When the door opened and William was shown in, he didn't even look her in the eye. Instead he was led in behind her before taking up position a comfortable distance away, leaning against the wall to avoid his face ending up level with hers. His stare was fixed on Palmgren to avoid any contact.

'If this is a blind date, we can stop it here,' he said. 'Neither of us is quite that blind.'

Palmgren feigned not to have heard.

'This is difficult for me too,' Christina finally added, and William sniggered. Compassion and accusation hand in hand, thank you for that.

'How about we just do what we normally do,' he replied flatly. 'We'll each of us comfort ourselves.' And with that, the conversation was over before it had even begun. Snide barbs had won the day, and if anything was going to be said, it was going to be Palmgren that said it.

'I realise that you have questions you'd like answered.' He stood between them, looking for the right way to get started. 'First of all, I didn't know. I didn't realise . . .'

He looked sorrowfully at Christina, hoping to avoid having to utter the words. Words about separation, drugs, their searching for Sara.

'We didn't either,' Christina said quietly. 'There are a lot of things we realised far too late.'

Silence again, the room full of eyes avoiding contact with each other: furthest in was Velander, sitting by the wall. Forester stood nearest the door, and in the middle of the room, in between two people who no longer loved one another, there was Palmgren, getting ready to say things he didn't want to say.

'And I am terribly sorry for asking you to come,' he said in the end. 'But we do need your help to understand all this.'

He nodded in Velander's direction. On the shelf next to him was a set of electronic devices: a DVD-player, an amplifier, and a grey desktop computer. They were stacked haphazardly, cobbled together as though no one had bothered to do it properly because the components would be obsolete even before the last cable was pinned up and hidden from view.

An average-sized, unbranded flatscreen TV hung on the wall. With a couple of clicks Velander summoned a flat, blurry film loop onto it, but it took both William and Christina a couple of seconds to decipher what they were seeing.

Everything seemed to suggest that the image was one of a large office. It was filmed from above, striped and in low resolution, the colours over-saturated and smeared by a camera that had been in the same position for years.

No, not an office. A hall. Everything was poorly and strangely lit, the only light coming from the illuminated rectangles that seemed to be arranged in rows throughout the room. Workstations, that's what they were, overexposed computer screens in small cubicles. At each keyboard a pair of hunched shoulders, and beyond the reception desk a glass door where pale blue faceless people hurried across equally pale blue flooring.

An internet café?

At first neither of them could work out what they were supposed to be looking at. Then in an instant they both realised why Palmgren had apologised so profusely.

William's reaction was the more visible. He was overcome with icy emptiness, felt himself losing his balance, as though his emotions had crept up behind him and were now pushing a boot into the back of both his knees at once. He steadied himself on the table, stock-still without knowing what to say, and beside him Christina stood motionless. The selfsame emotions, but invisible, internal.

A young man had entered the scene in front of them. He was dirty, wearing a padded jacket with the hood pulled tight around his face. A thin, empty rucksack hung on his shoulders, and he had just stopped to say something to the guy behind the desk – and then he turned his head so that his face was in view of the camera.

The young man in the coat wasn't a man at all.

'One minute later,' said Palmgren, 'the power supply to half the country is cut off.'

William was the first of them to speak, clearing his throat several times to rid his voice of the shock. His eyes were fixed on the screen.

'What the hell is she doing there?'

16

By the time Sara Sandberg finally turned off onto the gentle incline of Skeppargatan, four hours had passed since it all happened. Four hours since she'd been caught on CCTV walking into the internet café in Hötorget's metro station, wearing her padded jacket and rucksack.

'Café' was a bit of a stretch. When Sara Sandberg was growing up, cafés had been warm, welcoming places where you gossiped about classmates over drinking glasses with six-inch teaspoons and frothed milk. The place behind the dingy shopfront next to the escalators was the polar opposite. It was more like an amusement arcade or perhaps a youth club, dark and asocial and stinking of stale breath and damp clothes. The coffee was served from pump flasks and if there was any gossiping about classmates going on it was via keyboards and headphones and with people sitting in other parts of the world.

For thirty crowns though, you could have a computer for an hour. And thirty crowns was what she'd placed on the desk by the door.

'What were you planning on doing?' the young man behind the desk had asked. He had a patchy, downy moustache, and a side-parting draped over half his face like a black curtain. He was younger than her. Probably no more than seventeen.

Sara forced herself not to look away first.

'Do you normally ask people that?' she said. 'Or just me?'

She could hear her own, quavering voice, how it dragged itself along with softened consonants like a baggage carousel set too slow. She could hear how she sounded stoned, despite the fact that she wasn't.

'Right now, I'm asking you,' he said.

'Emails,' she said. 'News. Things like that. What sort of things do you use the internet for?'

He didn't answer, and for a split second she was tempted to make a few unflattering guesses, but that wasn't likely to help her cause.

Instead, she waited while he hesitated. She let him observe her through all those strands of hair, as if he wasn't sure if she might be contagious. As though he too might risk a bout of addiction if he spent too long talking to her.

'Coffee's not included,' he said finally.

Condescending eyes behind the theatre curtain, bum-fluff 'tache wobbling as the consonants emerged. He was pathetic, tragic even, the eternal ruler of a fusty little kingdom that reeked of faulty ventilation, and in a way that made her hate him. She did realise, though, that she would once have felt exactly the same way had the roles been reversed.

She thanked him with a nod, despite having nothing to thank him for, and, leaving her damp hood up around her face, she wandered into the darkness until she found a spot where she felt sure she would be left in peace.

A coffee would've been good. Anything to warm her up a bit, maybe even suppress the shakes. She didn't have much cash left though, and coffee was hardly a priority.

The briefcase had been a welcome boost to her coffers, no question, but not for as long as she'd hoped. Pangs of guilt struck her at the mere thought of it. She had meant so well. Standing there on the threshold of her own home, literally a single step away from going inside and asking to be allowed back. The temptation that presented itself at that point was too great. Or was it fear? Either way it was there, on the rug in the hall, just inside the door, almost *asking* to be stolen. Why else would anyone leave a briefcase like that, unless deep down what they actually wanted was someone to nip in and help themselves?

Inside, she found three hundred krona in cash, but that only lasted a few days. The only things of value that she'd been able to sell were a couple of designer pens and a phone charger. It had hardly been worth the bother.

But the thing that had grabbed at her insides had been in the side pocket.

Unopened post from the doormat. Letters that had been stuffed in the bag, to be looked at later. Now she had them.

That's where she'd found the padded envelope. Flat, stiff, addressed to her father, and – of all places – postmarked Warsaw.

William and Christina got to their feet, seemingly without moving a muscle, and watched their daughter walking into an internet café. Over and over again she walked in, a loop that began and ended at the same point and which repeated with ruthless precision again and again.

It was just a collection of pixels, blurred and flat and out of focus, yet neither of them could tear their eyes from the screen. The office. The till. The man coming in, turning to the camera, not a man after all but Sara Sandberg. Talking, negotiating, and paying cash before walking on and disappearing from view. Then for a split second, the screen goes black, before the loop begins again.

There she was. After months of searching.

Why? Why *there*?

'Am I right in thinking,' William eventually managed – grief, hope, the feeling of being deeply, unfairly offended – 'that you seriously believe that our daughter has something to do with the power cut?'

'When the Security Police arrived at the scene ten minutes later, Sara was gone.' Palmgren's voice. 'Not just her. The computer she'd been sitting at was gone too.'

William looked away. 'That's the sort of thing she does,' he said, ashamed of himself and his daughter at the same time. 'What's a computer like that worth, do you think? That's her only income. It's how she gets by.'

Palmgren said nothing.

'Even if the power cut started there, and even if she took the computer with her when she left, there's no way you can know that it was her. The whole place was full of kids.'

'William?'

That was Christina.

It was her first word since the tape had started rolling, and now she got up, walked over to the TV and beckoned for William to do the same.

They stopped just inches short of the screen, close enough to feel the electronic warmth radiating towards them, and at this distance the picture was even more blurred than before. Even sadder. The large light grey pixels continued to walk in and out of shot, and what had been Sara became less and less real, portrayed in lifeless, fluttering squares, as though she was slowly disappearing, slowly becoming ones and zeros in a grey-blue line on a TV screen.

'What's that she's holding?' she asked.

William saw Sara look at the camera, saw her heading off to her spot for the umpteenth time, saw the time hop backwards and Sara coming in the front door again.

The negotiation. The money. And there – 'Can we stop it?' said William.

Velander's fingers clicked a key, and the blue-grey world in front of them froze to a flickering, pixelated mosaic.

Sara, the till, the shiny thing in her hand.

'It's a CD.'

Palmgren nodded.

'We believe that's what she wanted to take away with her, but it got stuck in the computer when the power went.'

The silence returned. William fixed his eyes on Sara's face, the worn-out clothes, the empty rucksack that perhaps was her only possession. He felt the urge to shout out loud at the screen, to call out to her *wait, I'm on my way*, but forced himself not to.

He felt the world around him shrinking. As though the twine was suddenly being wound another loop, around Sara, around all of them, but above all, around him. Even if he was, hopefully, the only one who'd noticed. For now.

'I don't understand,' he said, his voice so deep that it seemed to be thundering straight out of his chest. 'How could our daughter be involved in this?'

Forester's reply was a chilling understatement.

'We don't know. But we would love to hear your thoughts.'

It had happened almost immediately.

She'd just put the CD in the tray at the front of the computer, watched it disappear into the thin slot, and for a second the computer had buzzed and hummed as though it was tasting the CD and trying to decide whether or not the contents were worth showing.

Then, her computer died. Followed by those around her.

Same thing with the lights, first the one above her, then the neighbouring ones, then all the others in the whole building and onwards, outwards, like a single dark ring in a pool of light, a ring that had unquestionably started with her and that grew and swallowed everything within a second.

Everything was gone. The flickering light of the screens, the hum from hard drives, the muffled clunking of the escalators in throbbing competition with the music seeping in from a nearby gym.

It took a few seconds before the swearing started.

Voices barking about the games they'd just lost, weapons and points and important alliances that were gone, and the voice of Bum-fluff assuring everyone that he was trying to call a technician and that everything would surely be back up and running soon.

Sitting quietly in her chair in the darkness was the girl who was about to die. She had made it happen. Not *her,* personally, but somehow the CD had taken control of her computer, spread from her, knocked out the whole café and apparently even the hall outside. It was impossible. Yet she knew it was true.

She felt her way to the computer's tower next to the screen, grimy fingers scanning across the buttons on the front to eject it. But the power was gone. And there was only one way she was taking the CD with her.

—

Now, four hours later, she shuffled up the hill at the bottom of Skeppargatan. Nearly there. Hungry and tired and wet, yet she didn't really feel anything one way or the other. A single bodily function outweighed the others, and that was the need to restock, the sweats and the shakes and the restlessness that screamed through her head, demanding she do something about it.

Inside her rucksack was a computer, expensive and heavy, and inside that was a CD that had been addressed to her father.

And if only it hadn't come from Warsaw. If it hadn't been for that, then she probably would have done the right thing. Returned to their flat, handed him the disc and shown him the letter, the one that had been folded inside the case.

Scratchy felt-tip letters, scribbled in flawed English.

Our meeting is cancelled.

We are in danger.

17

The man in the brown corduroy blazer was Per Einar Eriksen. He was forty-three, a professor at Karolinska Insitutet in Stockholm, and the father of two girls in their early teens.

But more than anything, right now he was floating in weight-lessness. From a strictly scientific perspective this admittedly gave him an excellent opportunity for observation. His brain was working flat out, and ironically, that was his specialist subject – human consciousness, thought processes, the meandering paths between abstract thoughts and concrete actions.

And, like now, how the internal processor seemed to shift up a gear when faced with a crisis, just as his subjects would often describe it after countless tests and experiments. How a sudden, unforeseen danger could cause time to slow down, drag forwards in slow motion, to the point of almost standing still.

Although, of course, in reality it did nothing of the sort. Time is constant. And in reality, Per Einar Eriksen had only seconds left to live.

The text message had arrived almost as soon as the power came back, and he had hesitated for around half a second before deciding to comply with its instructions. He had been in position in the lobby of Kaknäs telecoms tower long before the agreed time, and after a lot of persuasion they had let him into the tower even though the view was closed for the day – however the hell a view could close, something he found far more amusing than the girl on the till did – and although the restaurant had shut up shop for the day as soon as the power went.

As he stepped out of the lift on the thirteenth floor, he'd been all alone. He had walked over to the huge windows, looked right out into the darkness, down on the millions of fuzzy white dots that formed the city's street lighting.

And then, nothing happened. Nothing at all.

In the distance, the revolving clock on the NK Department Store roof completed one revolution after another, and when the hands reached ten thirty he just had to accept it. Someone had tricked him. What most annoyed him was that he didn't have anyone to call and bawl out, no one to say *For fuck's sake* to, *I've got more important things to do with my life than stand here waiting to meet someone whose identity I don't even know*

Because that was the situation. He didn't know who'd summoned him there. The only thing he did know was that he'd been too curious to ignore it, and that the only one he could blame was himself, and those thoughts, frankly, were not particularly satisfying.

My fault, he thought as he fell.

At thirty-three minutes past ten he had stepped back into the lift, consoled himself with the thought that he would probably be able to blag himself something from the gift shop on the way out, pressed the button to take him down to the ground floor, and then, in an instant, realised that everything was wrong.

First came the sensation of lifting away from the floor, even if he knew that the opposite was happening. Then the feeling that his internal organs were coming adrift from their moorings, floating around inside him like cooking oil in a glass of water, and then the thoughts – rushing through his head at hyper-speed, making it seem that the world was standing still.

Thoughts about the events that had led him here.

The emails, the weird, frightening emails with their incomprehensible pleas for help, short, without a sender, and in which someone had asked to meet at Central Station without saying why. Then the CD, the one that had arrived in the regular mail, with a handwritten message saying the meeting was *cancelled*. Because *we are in danger*.

And now, the text that arrived along with the power, that once again consisted of a single line, and that was the reason for him being here, heading for his own death.

Kaknäs Tower, it had said. *Restaurant, 22:00.*

And that's where he was, only not in the restaurant, but standing in a lift in free-fall, the floor beneath his feet disappearing as quickly as he was, at a speed that was constantly increasing and in the shiny, stainless steel walls he could see his own face scream in desperation.

Five and a half seconds, that's how long it took, the longest – and shortest – seconds in his forty-three-year life, a time that passed in slow motion, yet still way too quickly. Five and a half seconds of thoughts, questions with no answers, and of pleading to all conceivable higher powers to please make this stop.

In the end it did.

18

Every now and then, major events are overshadowed by others. Groucho Marx died in the shadow of Elvis Presley, Mother Teresa in the shadow of Princess Diana, Ray Charles – Ronald Reagan. On any other day, their deaths would have brought acres of coverage and bold headlines, but instead they were relegated to shorter pieces on the inside pages. Decades later, their lives would amount to topics of conversation at dinner parties, where people would ask, glass in hand, what happened to him, is he still alive, I'm a bit out of touch. And all because of timing.

The man that was hit by the freight train died in the shadow of a power cut.

He had been travelling in a rented, Polish-registered BMW, he was sitting in the middle of the tracks with no lights on – a clear-cut suicide if there ever was one. Let's go for lunch.

No one bothered to ask why the man wasn't carrying any ID. No one seemed to wonder why he had been in Sweden. And no one, no one asked whether the unidentified man in Skåne might possibly be Michal Piotrowski, whose body would never be found, but whom Polish authorities would declare dead from a powerful blaze in his apartment later that same day. He died in the shadow of an evening where people couldn't cook their dinners, and on the news sites his demise was reduced to a right-hand column link that no one clicked on.

Not even William Sandberg. He sat in his office, on the edge of an uncomfortable swivel chair in front of his computer, skimming through the newspapers' versions of the power cut while his thoughts danced inside his head.

Somewhere deep inside, he was relieved. At long last he knew, at last he had an answer to the question he'd been asking himself for almost six months. Sara was alive, and in Stockholm, and those were the emotions he had deliberately tapped into, exaggerated, in order to get released. Hyperventilating, he had demanded to be released, barking that he had to get out and find her before it was too late.

In the end Palmgren had grabbed him by the shoulders and sworn that they were already looking everywhere for her. William had felt the sarcastic barbs lining up inside his head.

Fuck me, that's nice, he wanted to say. *All for my sake?*

But instead, he'd allowed them to soothe him, because he knew that was the best thing he could do, and eventually they had done exactly as he'd hoped. They'd let him out into the corridor and given him permission to go up to his office, where he'd closed the door behind him, turned on his computer and entered his passwords.

Now there he was. Feeling the stress and the exhaustion

thundering up under his jacket, looking at the screen in front of him, the same screen as six months ago, the same computers, pens and notepads. Untouched, as if they'd expected him to come back. Just like he had left Sara's room on Skeppargatan.

He closed his eyes. Forced himself to organise his thoughts.

Warsaw.

When William finally hauled himself out of the desk chair it was so that he could bend in behind the computer. Fingernail on the Ethernet cable, the plasticky snap as it came out of its socket.

Now that the computer was isolated no one would be able to eavesdrop on what he was doing. Admittedly, it made things more difficult for him too – nothing outside the computer itself would be accessible, not the internet, not even the intranet.

But what William was looking for was much closer than that. With a couple of rapid clicks he opened the program that he had installed himself, in breach of every known rule and code, a surveillance utility that he'd written himself and that recorded every keystroke and attempt to log in. A couple of seconds later he was absolutely certain no one had been at his computer since he left it, which, in turn, meant that no one had installed similar software to do the same thing to him. He was invisible now. No one could see him.

Not when he opened the mail client, where all his professional correspondence had been stored locally for years. Not when he looked over his shoulder to make absolutely certain that no one was there watching him from the doorway. And not when he clicked the cursor into the search box.

Typed the name that he knew would be there, somewhere, in his inbox.

Michal Piotrowski.

Christina Sandberg had watched William being led out of the meeting room without giving her so much as a glance, and when Palmgren came back in he took her by the shoulder and followed her out.

100

The silence lasted all the way down the corridor. It stayed with them through the security control and while she got her bag back and her coat and her phone, and it hung around at their side when they stopped outside the entrance to wait for the taxi. She struggled into her coat in the cold. Held in the button to turn the phone on, swore quietly when it refused to cooperate.

The battery, she said to herself. *The pictures of Tetrapak's computer. Fucking prime example of how to prioritise.* They were photos she was never going to use, and she should have known that as she was taking them, but it was too late to regret that now.

They stood there for ages, outside the glass doors, felt the night poised between frost and thaw but never making up its mind.

'We'll do whatever we can to find her,' Palmgren said.

'It's been six months since we reported her missing. If she doesn't want to be found then she won't be.'

'Oh well. It's not until now that she's been in possession of something that may affect national security.'

He looked at her, with a smile that was supposed to communicate irony and condolences and warmth all at once, but that just turned out sad.

She hesitated. There was a question she was dying to ask, but her information came from an undeniably dodgy source.

Here goes nothing.

'Did you know about this?' she asked. 'What happened today, did you know it was going to happen?'

Of all the questions, *that* wasn't one he'd been expecting.

'Why do you ask?'

'I'll take that as a yes.'

'I'm sure you will.'

When the car turned up he opened the door for her, left his hand on the handle while she sat down.

'I know better than to go telling things to journalists. But this is you. And although you're a journalist on one hand, on the other hand you're a next of kin, and how could I possibly know which of them you are the most?'

'It is possible to be both,' said Christina.

He leant in. Elbow on the roof. Hushed.

'I want you to promise me two things,' he said. 'What we've experienced today? As of now I don't know what it means, where it's heading, what the threat is. There are things we don't tell the public – and I want you to remember that there are reasons for that.'

He squinted at her.

'I'm asking you, Christina. Promise me you won't go digging around in all this.'

She forced a smile. Hoped that if she just kept it up long enough it would be interpreted as a yes.

'And the other?'

'If you do find anything. Whatever it is. Please, let me be the first to know.'

'How would I find anything if I don't go digging around?'

'I did say I know you.'

This time the smile made it to her eyes.

When Sara Sandberg finally walked through the door on Skeppargatan, time stopped. She could feel the nausea closing in once more, a muscular claw around her stomach, her nerves conspiring with chemistry to make her mouth water.

Part of it was withdrawal. She was dizzy, and that wasn't going to get better. Part of it was the memories that were coming back. The stairwell, the smell, the same outside noise that vibrated in through the door and echoed around the faux marble walls.

As she pulled the metal grille closed behind her she forced herself to struggle on. There was nothing to be afraid of, she told herself, it was the same lift as back then, the same apartment waiting up there. And after all, it wasn't the first time she'd been home, far from it. For a long time she had used it as an occasional refuge, a tacit agreement that when the apartment was empty she could sleep over. Each time, her bed had been made with fresh linen, the fridge had been filled with food, and in the calendar on the kitchen wall there were always detailed notes about when they would next be away, and for how long. That's how desperate they were for her to come home again. And why not make the most of that? It was them she hated, not the apartment, not their food.

That had been their arrangement. Right up until they'd found her stuff.

Their daughter took drugs, not happy pills but heavy, real narcotics, and all of a sudden it wasn't so sweet anymore to have her sleeping in her patterned sheets and eating their pâté. So they did what parents do. They confronted her, and served ultimatums, and demanded that she stop. So what choice did she have?

When the lift came to a stop on the fourth floor she stood there for several minutes before stepping out.

She'd been there once more since then. One other time, before today. It couldn't be more than days ago.

He had been in there. She'd heard his sounds even before trying the door handle, his creaking footsteps on the parquet floor, as though he was just pacing back and forth the whole time, and it had spooked her. What if she wasn't welcome any more? What if they'd stopped wanting her to come home? No one can hate for ever, but what if you can't miss someone for ever either?

The door had been unlocked, and the briefcase had been standing there, just inside the door. And she hadn't meant to, but she grabbed the bag before she'd even had the chance to ask herself why, and even as she ran down the steps she'd felt how wrong it was, that one way or another she was going to end up paying for this, for the theft, the betrayal, the cowardice. Maybe that's what today had been about.

Now, there she was again. In front of the same door. Key grasped tightly in her hand, a single key on a thin leather strap, the one possession she had never sold, never lost, never let anyone steal. And today, she was going to do the right thing. Today she would dare. She pushed it in, felt her heart pounding. *I'm home*, she thought. *From now on, everything is as it should be.*

So intense was the nausea that enveloped her that for a second she thought she'd thrown up. She was there, on the landing, with her right hand on one of the heavy double doors, her own home before her. And yet it was further off than ever. The metal grille was white and brand new, huge vertical bars running from floor to ceiling, held in place by thick crossbeams, like a prison gate between her and her refuge.

She felt the panic rising, grabbed the grille, tugged at it, even though she knew it would be locked. She gasped for air, an oppressive anxiety seizing her and making her want to scream out loud. Her leaving them was one thing, but the other way around? How could they lock her out? They were the ones who had begged her to come home, told her nothing had changed, that to them she was still their daughter. They'd stood there with their pathetic eyes and promised that they loved her and that they always had. The ones she'd hated because they loved her, the ones she *dared* to hate because they were always going to be there.

Now they had turned the tables on her.

They had installed a security grille to keep her out, and of course it was her own fault, she shouldn't have stolen the briefcase, and she knew that too, but all the same, how the hell could they turn their backs on her? At a time like this?

She pushed the doorbell next to the door, kept it pushed in, her dirty nails under the sign that said *Sandberg*, and she pushed and pushed and waited and hoped. From nowhere, the emptiness cascaded down on her, as if all of a sudden she couldn't live without them, as though her decision to come back made missing them unbearable, and, 'Dad,' she heard herself shouting, 'DAD,' so that the sounds echoed around the long, narrow hallway, and she shook the grille and rang the bell and then she realised she had collapsed onto the floor without knowing how.

Her mouth tasted of blood and crying, she felt sick and was in pain, and nothing mattered, all she could do was miss and love and hate, and now those fucking idiots had left her, *now*, when they needed her and she needed them.

She sat on the cold tiled floor for over half an hour before she was finally able to pull herself away. She was Sara Sandberg and she lived on the streets, and for a moment she'd let herself believe that the past could come back.

But what's gone is gone. She got up, took the stairs down, leaving the door to the apartment wide open, as a greeting.

Sara Sandberg, the girl who didn't know she was about to die. Perhaps, though, her suspicions were stirring.

Less than a kilometre away Christina's taxi pulled out onto Valhallavägen, passed the Olympic Stadium and Sophiahemmet Hospital, and was met by blue lights on the other side of the avenue. She turned around to watch them through the rear window, saw them disappearing off towards the Russian Embassy and the large open space between them and Djurgårdsbrunn, in the distance far behind them.

'It's all happening tonight.'

The taxi driver's voice. Christina turned towards the front again.

'This little thing,' he said, beaming into the rear-view mirror. His hand was resting on a little black box next to the meter, its diodes flashing and displaying digits that must mean something to those in the know. 'Two thousand, off eBay. As long as the police don't sort their new comms system out, it's my best-ever purchase.'

'Police radio?' said Christina.

He nodded. 'If they can listen to us, then why we can't we listen to them?'

She gave him a weak smile, avoiding the obvious question of why he thought the police were listening to him, and glanced through the rear window again.

'Accident in the Kaknäs TV tower,' he said, clearly proud of his knowledge. 'Explosion, possible casualties. Do you know the codes?'

She spent precisely half a second negotiating with herself.

'Take me there,' she said.

'I should think it's all cordoned off.'

'I'm from the press,' she said. 'It's only ever as cordoned off as you make it.'

19

The middle–aged detective at the centre of the whole mess was called Magnusson. He stood with his feet apart, in the middle of a floor that was covered in brochures and cups and crushed rubble, trying to get a handle on the situation.

Christina Sandberg, her name was. Suddenly, from out of nowhere, she had materialised in their midst, amongst all the technicians and firemen, then marched right into the lobby despite the tape and flashed her press badge and asked a stream of questions – was it an accident? Was anyone hurt? Any connection with the power cut earlier?

He'd ended up having to physically stop her. Through gritted teeth, he'd explained to her that if she didn't get lost this instant he would personally make sure that she was locked up and put on bread and water, and even if that wasn't a particularly plausible scenario the message had got through at last and the woman had allowed herself to be escorted out.

Now he stood there, trying to get a grip.

'Magnusson?'

A young voice behind him. It was the same constable who had led the woman away just seconds earlier.

'She wants us to call her a taxi. Says her phone is dead.'

Magnusson felt his energy waning.

'You know what?' he said. 'Go back out and tell her we don't cordon off scenes because it looks attractive. Tell her that she committed a crime when she shoved her way in here and tell her I've been on since this morning and my patience runs out at lunchtime.'

The constable stayed put. Had he just been given an order he was expected to carry out, or had it just been his boss blowing off steam?

'And when you've done that you can call her a cab and make sure she gets out of here. The further away the better.'

That was an order, and his young colleague headed off down the long concrete walkway towards the car park.

It had only been twenty minutes since Sergeant Eskil Magnusson had walked that route in the other direction. When the call went out he and the youngster had been down by Frihamnen docks. They'd put on their blue lights and had been the first unit at the scene. A big explosion, the radio operator had said – gas, maybe a bomb, nobody knew.

Even so, his first thought had been that the whole thing was a false alarm. The walkway had brought him to a lobby entrance with glass panes polished to the point of invisibility, and behind them an organised chaos of books and T-shirts and Stockholm souvenirs.

Only after a few seconds had he registered the crunch under-foot. The concrete ground was strewn with tiny shards of glass, razor-sharp and ground to a lethal white flour, and now he real-ised that the immaculate glass doors were nothing of the sort. They weren't transparent; they were no longer there. The panes had been shattered from the inside, and spread down the walk-way, and the chaos that greeted him wasn't so organised after all. Like someone had grabbed the whole structure and shaken it, that's what it looked like, and a shaken Magnusson had reached for his phone and asked the control room to send the Fire Brigade and an ambulance.

At this point he'd heard a voice in the middle of the mess.

'The lift,' it said.

She was no older than twenty-five, was wearing a top embla-zoned with Stockholm's coat of arms, and was sitting on the edge of an upturned bench, her eyes glazed and her face and hands flecked with blood.

'I was the one who called.'

She had seen the whole thing, and only now she made things come together. The explosion had not been an explosion. The force that had shattered the lobby had come from the lifts. As Magnusson clambered further inside, past piles of debris and junk, he found the lift doors lying on the floor, thrust out of their frames like the buckled lid of a tin of herring left for too

107

long. Concrete and plaster had collapsed, leaving both lift shafts open, and inside them thick cables ran straight upwards into the darkness.

The lift itself had fallen thirty storeys. A couple of metres down were the remains of what had been the lift car, hugely crumpled and compressed, and within ten minutes the whole of Kaknäs Tower's lobby was cordoned off and pulsating with emergency blue.

Then they had found the body.

This information came courtesy of the young constable, explaining it all in a lowered voice as he waited for the taxi switchboard to answer. His hand held his work phone, his pocket contained five hundred newly earned krona in hundred-krona notes, and opposite him in the car park stood Christina Sandberg who promised not to name him in her article.

Finally they were told that a car would be with them in ten minutes, and Christina gave him her card, shook his hand and asked him to call her if anything else turned up. Then she made her way through the car park, past the array of emergency services vehicles parked there. Kaknäs Tower was veiled in fluttering blue light. An amazing shot, if her mobile hadn't been dead.

Somehow, she thought, this had to be linked to the power cut. Which was true – only not in the way she thought.

20

It had been one of those long hot summers that only exist in memory. When life was a series of terrace bars and billowing clothes, when each new dawn kept yesterday's promise of warmth, and it all went on for so long that you began to think that it was going to be like this for ever.

It wasn't, of course.

The warmth had arrived to crown an outstanding summer.

The move into town, to the apartment, had been a perfect decision – no lawn to plague your conscience, an endless range of local watering holes, and when Sara got back from Washington without being mugged or assaulted they had enjoyed the tail end of the summer and the big city together, days and nights on end.

Even Warsaw had turned out to be a fairy-tale city.

It was August by the time they arrived there. None of them had been to Poland before, neither Christina nor Sara nor he himself, and they had been transported down green avenues towards a core of high-rise buildings, the same schizoid mix of ultra-modern and historic that you'd find in any long-lived city, barring the fact that the no-nonsense fifties architecture was a bit more no-nonsense than average, and that the really historic buildings were actually just reconstructions of what had once been there. They checked in to a hotel a few blocks away from the old town, grabbed a coffee from a chain they'd seen in London, then strolled off on foot to the huge structure known as the Palace of Culture and Science. They saw it sticking up between the buildings long before they got to it, towering high above the city like a gigantic stone monument, a dazzling vanity project that reached over two hundred metres into the sky and somehow managed to invoke both the Iron Curtain and downtown Manhattan simultaneously. And it was there, on the enormous stone steps leading up to the eastern entrances, that William had been greeted by a man with a warm, intimate handshake.

'William Sandberg!' The man smiled broadly and took a touch too long letting go of his hand.

He had an unkempt, long non-hairstyle, two eyebrows grown into a single sweep, and further down a scraggy beard that told two stories: first, that this was not a man who cared too much about his appearance, second, that he had just helped himself to the buffet visible inside.

William had smiled politely and searched his memory. 'Do we know each other?' The newcomer smiled through the crumbs.

'We've never met,' he said. 'But I've heard so much about you.'

And perhaps William ought to have reacted. Maybe he should have found it off-key. He was here as a conference delegate, just a member of the audience, yet the man's tone was so warm and sincere that it had been too familiar by half.

Then again, why not? Above the large entrance banners were proclaiming a conference about the future, and the place was crowded with mathematicians and physicists, all of them with sunglasses and casual clothes and their families around them. Several hundred of the world's finest brains were gathered in the same place. Who could be anything other than open and personable in a world like this?

The man had shifted his attention towards Christina and Sara, shaken hands with them as he asked, 'Family?' – though he'd already understood – and Christina and Sara had introduced themselves, and then it was his turn.

'My name is Michal,' he said, as if that information would explain everything, and with that he handed over a business card. Or rather, what served as a business card. It was more of a hand-written note, scratchy letters, as though scribbled down at speed, and under stress.

'Michal Piotrowski. Biology's my field.'

With that he'd pointed up towards the entrance, said something about it being cooler in there, and Sara and Christina had climbed the first step up towards it.

Behind them, Piotrowski had put his hand on William's shoulder.

'I am so glad you decided to come,' he said. A quiet voice, almost in confidence, an intimate moment between two men who'd never met.

So glad?

William had allowed himself to be led up towards the long row of high glass doors, and he hadn't seen it, but in that very instant, the first light grey cloud had appeared in the eternal summer sky.

As William pushed his chair back from the desk, rolling away from the screen before coming to a halt halfway across the room, summer and warmth and happiness were as distant as they could possibly be.

The email client had come up with three hits. Two inbound, one sent, all five years old. He'd scrolled down to the first of them. An invitation from a research institute that some kind soul had so generously sent to him.

When he clicked it open the memories revived in an instant. Sitting at the top of the message was the institute's coat of arms, an etched profile of Copernicus within a roundel emblazoned with text, and underneath was an extravagant leaflet and an invitation which was too good to be true. If he could shout back in time, he'd tell himself to turn it down, to stay in Sweden and do what he always did with casual invitations: throw the stuff in the bin and get on with his job.

But the past was what it was.

A conference that could change your future.

No shit.

Your friend, Michal Piotrowski.

At the top of the message window was the subject line – three short words in English which revealed that this was a forwarded invitation – and next to that was the recipient field, with William's work email in it.

But it was the remaining field that interested him now. The sender. The name was Michal Piotrowski, but what mattered was the email address he'd hidden behind: ROSETTA1998. This was incontrovertible evidence that William Sandberg had had contact with the address they were linking to the attacks.

Sandberg had two choices. He could either go back down to Palmgren and Forester, and tell them about the emails and that he did in fact know who the person behind them was. But what would happen after that?

William Sandberg had been let down by the world, and that was the profile they were always looking for, someone who had lost everything and wanted revenge. He fitted the bill to a T. He had conducted illegal archive searches. He had accessed systems he was not authorised to use. His wife had left him, his daughter had got into drugs, and in the end he'd been sacked by the Swedish Armed Forces. They'd join it all up and, *Look!*, they'd say. *Look, we've got ourselves a scapegoat!*

He was convicted in advance, because that's what they wanted, and even if he might eventually be able to prove the truth, that would take time – time he did not have.

He found the handwritten note where he'd expected to find it, in a binder full of old receipts and mileage claims and other business cards he'd accepted out of politeness. It was even more scrappy now, and bleached by time, but more or less as legible as it had been when he first took it five years ago.

Name. Address. And a single contact detail. The Hotmail address.

He stayed in his chair until his thoughts had taken shape, and when he rolled back to the desk again he had already decided. It took only a few seconds to open the computer's toolbox and jot down the necessary lines of code.

There was nothing striking about the car at all. It was metallic brown and maybe a year or so old, an ordinary family-size Nissan with a tow-bar, the bottom of the rear windscreen lined with stickers in a neat, well-organised row as a record of where the owners had spent their holidays. It was parked well outside the police cordon, a single lonely car in an otherwise empty car park, and it might have been that that piqued Christina Sandberg's interest.

She hadn't noticed it when she'd stood there by the entrance, but now, as she walked away from Kaknäs Tower and out towards the road to meet her taxi, she saw it parked up by the ticket machine, shining in the light of one of the street lamps.

Sure, it could belong to one of the staff. Or indeed a jogger or a dog owner who'd parked there before running out into the uninviting slush. That was possible. But not likely.

Christina stopped in her tracks. Behind her, the sweep of blue-light emergency vehicles continued. In front of her the car park opened out on to a road that curved off into the darkness, and beyond that joined the main road, yet there was no sign of the lights of the taxi she'd ordered.

She changed direction, sauntering and nonchalant and slow, all to demonstrate that she was doing nothing other than waiting for her taxi – this was no curious journalist, this was a tired, freezing-cold fellow human with a dead phone who needed to keep moving in order to stay warm.

She was almost over by the car when she felt herself gasp. Maybe her brain had made the connection long before she'd understood just what she was looking at, either way the realisation crept inside her consciousness, made her pick up the pace for those last few yards, forget all that stuff about sauntering and pretending that nothing was going on.

The rear windscreen. The stickers, bottom left. Seeing them felt like déjà vu, of summer and happiness, a visual token that sent her back in time and made her regret everything and want to do it all differently. The design was a circular decal in shiny foil paper, black text looping around an etched face in the middle. The closer she got to it the clearer that face became.

Copernicus. And around it, the letters boasted that this car was driven by someone who once attended a conference on the science of tomorrow. The Futurology Conference. In Warsaw.

It wasn't until she was bathed in bright white light that she realised that she must have been standing there for several minutes. The car that stopped behind her was a spluttering diesel Mercedes, and still in a daze, she heard herself confirming in the direction of the headlights that yes, she was Christina Sandberg.

'Car troubles?' the driver said as she sat down in the back seat.

'No. That's someone else's.'

She fastened her belt, feeling her pulse thud hard inside her ears, struggled to grasp what this was all about.

Her daughter, who was suspected of causing the power cut. Her husband – that's still what he was, after all – who was also suspected of something and was being kept at Armed Forces HQ for reasons no one was willing to divulge. And on top of that, someone had died in a lift accident, tonight, just now. Someone who, it would seem, had been a delegate at the same conference that they had attended, that glorious summer.

You'll see, it will all come together . . .

'Any suggestions?'

The taxi driver looked at her in the rear-view mirror. Not that he minded sitting in the car park and watching the meter ticking away, but was that really what she'd had in mind?

'Have you got a torch?' was her reply. The driver hesitated briefly. He opened the glove box and pulled out a long LED torch.

'Thanks,' said Christina. 'Just give me two seconds.' Then she opened the door and retreated into the darkness to march over to the metallic brown estate car, shining her torch through the windows, searching but not knowing for what.

Until she spotted it. And realised that, coincidence or not . . .

Fucking Tetrapak. *You'll see.*

On the passenger seat lay a rectangular jiffy bag. One end was ripped, the seat was strewn with its padding, and on top of that lay an empty, open CD case.

But that wasn't what made up her mind. It was the shiny semi-circle peeking out of the car stereo.

Christina Sandberg had never smashed a window in her life, but there's a first time for everything.

21

'Sweden. You'll love it.' That's what they'd said. And then they'd given her a staff team, slapped her on the back and wished her good luck. Now she was here, she didn't like it one bit.

Cathryn Forester was standing on the flat, square roof of the equally square HQ, and her face was being whipped by a horizontal, ice-cold precipitation that could not accurately be described as either rain or snow. She was freezing, and she was tired, and everywhere she looked the windows of Stockholm looked back at her like tiny hot-tempered dots.

No, she didn't love Sweden. And it seemed to be mutual. Ever since she'd arrived, Sweden had offered her nothing but trouble.

On paper, it had all sounded so simple. Someone was going to be at Stockholm Central Station at a certain time on the third of December, and that person would therefore be guilty. With his help – she'd assumed it would be a he – they would work their way backwards and establish who was behind the attacks and why.

Now though, she wasn't at all sure. The man they had arrested was clearly genuinely bereft, and he had explanations that, while convoluted, were perfectly plausible. And isn't that the way life is? It *is* convoluted. It is full of coincidences and far-fetched events, and if anything is suspicious it's when the opposite is true.

Cathryn Forester was starting to have her doubts, and she hated it.

She'd got on that plane to Sweden determined to show her true self. She had told herself that her unshakable suspicions, those nagging feelings that Trottier didn't believe she was capable of her mission, either came from her imagination, or at least from incorrect assumptions on his end. She was competent, she was experienced and she knew it, so why wasn't she allowed to prove it?

'Don't take it as a vote of no-confidence.'

That's what Trottier had said to her just thirty seconds earlier. Now she stood here in the cold, holding a small black satellite phone, the size of an ordinary mobile and strictly prohibited on the premises.

'See it as me offering my support,' he'd said, and his voice had been crystal-clear in its insincerity.

It was not, of course, about support. Major John Patrick Trottier was on his way, and that meant one thing only. It meant that she'd been right all along – he didn't trust her, she wasn't up to it, and now they were sending a babysitter to take over.

'I've got it all under control.' She'd said it several times in the course of their last phone conversation, each time a little more in that pleading voice she hated so much.

'In that case,' he'd replied, 'where's the girl from the internet café?'

Forester had explained that they were doing everything possible to find her. Her description had been circulated to the police, to all the turnstile attendants on the metro system, and to anyone else they could think of. Right now it was night time and she had a head start, but she couldn't keep out of sight for ever.

Then she'd made the mistake of saying what she was thinking.

'Besides, I think we're looking in the wrong place.'

Trottier had not even bothered to sigh.

'Sandberg is the one who turns up at Central Station. The person who triggers the power cut is his daughter. How can that be the wrong place?'

Out of nowhere, Forester had felt a powerful urge to swear at him. She wanted to call him an idiot, then hang up on him, as though she was a teenager again and Trottier one of her brothers. It was like he meant to press all the right buttons to drive her up the wall. Or was she just letting him get to her?

'I'm not saying we should let anyone go,' she'd said, as calmly as she could manage, her hands sweating in spite of the cold. 'I just want us to consider the possibility that we've got it wrong.'

'I consider everything, all the time,' Trottier had said. 'Because it's my job. Yours, on the other hand is to prepare to hand the mission over to me.'

With that, John Patrick Trottier had hung up, leaving her on the roof with the information that his plane was already waiting. That, and a growing sense of failure.

When she felt the vibration in her pocket a minute later, her first thought was that it must be Trottier again. But the phone she fished out was her Swedish one.

'Where the hell are you?'

It was Palmgren.

'I'm getting some air,' she heard herself say, just as she'd planned.

'Well, stop it,' he said. 'Stop it, and come down.'

'What's the matter?' she said.

'It's Sara,' he said.

'Where is she?' said Forester. 'Have we got her? Is she here?'

Palmgren didn't answer, and she asked again: 'Whereabouts is she? Have we found her?'

When he did speak again, his voice was thin and brittle, like he was exhaling.

'No. *We* haven't.'

22

William stood up as soon as Palmgren entered the room. He was standing by the computer, stress in his eyes, perhaps even guilt, as they stared at Palmgren, like a child in a larder with both hands behind his back. And maybe Palmgren should have seen it. But he didn't.

'William,' was all he said.

'What's going on?' asked William. 'Is it an attack?'

'William,' he said again.

'Is it in Sweden? Somewhere else? What is it?'

Palmgren opened his mouth and wished that the answer had been yes.

Sara had done what she always did: she'd stood on the platform the train was arriving at, patiently and idly at first, as though waiting for someone to arrive. Then she'd wandered slowly through the crowd as the passengers got off, just as though she was one of them and had just got off too.

As the crowd started to disperse she slipped into the first carriage she could see was empty. Once on board, she locked herself in the toilet, a pristine toilet in a first-class compartment. It was warm and quiet, and if they weren't going to clean it before departure then she'd be left in peace for some time.

She had promised herself, but the rules had changed. She'd wanted to stop so that she could go home, but that was no longer an option. They'd given up, so why shouldn't she do the same?

She did it the way she'd learnt. She unfolded the foil and warmed it and sucked in, she took her top off and stopped the blood flow, and then, on the inside of her elbow, where the skin was still struggling to heal the old holes, she made another, same as always. Almost.

She sat there in her internal cockpit as she felt herself starting to shrink. She felt the space between her and her body expand, the distance growing and growing to everything that was Sara and that had once been herself.

Soon she could only see herself from afar, like a thin, thin shell round a universe of nothingness, a warm, quiet universe where she was floating in peace and could see herself disappear. There was no cockpit any more, no body to resist and try to control. She was alone now, alone and nowhere, surrounded by darkness, and for the first time in a long while she felt completely at ease. And as soon as she realised that, she knew.

Now, when she'd decided to forgive them. *Now*, when she so desperately wanted to see them again and hold them tight. This time, she knew, it was irrevocable.

She relaxed, felt herself shrinking, getting smaller and smaller. And far away, somewhere on the other side of the darkness, Sara Sandberg had stopped living.

The black Volvo XC90 moved in silence through a city without features. William's upper body jerked left and then right between the two solid agents from the Security Police, but he didn't feel the jolts or hear the sirens; just watched as the fronts of the buildings outside seemed to float past the window.

The city ahead was flashing blue, rushing towards them at a dizzying speed. Traffic lights and road signs glowed in their reflective coatings and became threatening geometric shapes in the darkness.

Nothing was right here, in the present, and everything was far too late.

—

When they finally let him out, his feet ran of their own accord down the grooved steps of the escalator, out on to the patched-up tarmac that formed the platform, through the smell of damp and electrics and rubber from brakes and couplings.

All he wanted was to hold her, say how sorry he was, ask her forgiveness. He wanted to make up for that solitary lie, the one he'd thought was for her sake, but it wasn't going to happen.

His feet kept running, sped over puddles and trodden-in chewing gum, ran alongside the train although there was really no need to hurry.

He felt the paramedics' hands coming towards him, consoling hands, maybe, but above all restraining – calm down, take it slowly, take a deep breath – hands trying to prepare him for what he was about to see.

As though anything in the world could do that.

It smelled of plastic and moquette and complimentary coffee. The carpet was grey-blue with damp patches left by slush-covered shoes. And the door to the toilet was open.

There she was. Lying on the floor.

And along with Sara Sandberg, part of her father died too.

23

The small jet that stood waiting for John Patrick Trottier looked more than anything like an airliner that had shrunk in the wash. It bore a red and blue livery, the insignia of the 32nd Air Force Squadron on its fuselage, and behind the cockpit window two pilots were flipping through their heavy binders preparing for takeoff.

Trottier saw it, said nothing, let the young female Air Traffic Controller walk him up to the stairs. He had never liked flying, and it hardly helped seeing the pilots browse their manual as if the aeroplane was a newly bought microwave. But right now he had more important thoughts to keep him busy.

When the car had come to pick him up for the airport, he had already been certain: there was something about Michal Piotrowski that was decidedly wrong. He couldn't be found anywhere, not on social media, not in any newspaper articles; the internet was full of Michal Piotrowskis but none of them was the right one. That, in itself, was more informative than anything. No one is that impossible to find unless they're hiding.

In little over an hour, Trottier was going to be in Stockholm. There, he would confront Sandberg with all the information that Forester didn't have. Ask him about Floodgate, about Piotrowski, about everything.

When he sank down into his leather seat in the back of the jet, he picked up his private mobile phone to continue his search. He couldn't possibly have known it, but that would be the biggest mistake he'd ever get to make.

It was Agneta Malm who had first noticed Sara on the internet café's CCTV, and no one was surprised she was now the one who spotted the beginnings of a white patch on her screen. Three whole seconds after she'd stood up and announced her discovery the computer saw the same thing.

When Cathryn Forester walked in a minute later, the JOC was almost full. There were staff everywhere, squeezed between their workstations and the rows of chairs lined up behind them, all standing staring at the giant projector screen that covered the wall in front of them.

Forester elbowed her way through the room, the feeling of losing her grip increasing with every step she took. William Sandberg was a dead end. His daughter was dead. And to top it off, Trottier was on his way to teach her a lesson.

And realising that she was the last one in the room when it happened again didn't help in the slightest.

She saw Velander standing up front with a few others from their working group, and pushed carefully through the crowd towards him. She grabbed his arm to get his attention, yet didn't take her eye off the big screen for a second.

'When was this?' she said.

'One minute ago,' Velander said, his eyes fixed on the same display. 'Almost two.'

Projected across the wall was the same black and white map that they had shown William in the briefing room. Europe and Africa in nocturnal dark blue, Asia in a quietly awakening green, the Americas in frenzied yellow.

With one major anomaly. At a single location, the darkness lit up in blooming colour, slowly displayed in a repetitive loop. Right in the middle of the darkest blue, almost in the centre of the map, lines erupted through the whole rainbow spectrum into an intense, brilliant white, before shrinking again and disappearing as though it had never been there at all.

Forester swallowed. Her pulse was so intense that she could almost taste it.

'Can we zoom in there?' she said, perhaps to Velander, maybe to those around him. No one seemed to hear, and she kept on jostling through the room, past desks and colleagues, raising her voice as she got closer to the image at the front.

'Can we zoom? Can we get more detail?' And eventually someone did as she asked. *Shit.*

'I need to establish the exact geographic centre,' she said in a voice that was struggling not to crack. Behind her the map was centred over her homeland, a cloud of white disturbingly close to London, and she turned around, looking for faces that belonged to her group. 'I want to know everything that's going on in the area. Power cuts, major hacks, burglar alarms – if so much as a fuse blows south of Edinburgh I want to know about it.'

Around her colleagues nodded in reply, then turned to leave the room or take a spot at an empty desk, and at that point another thought occurred to her.

'Velander!' she called. She could feel the cold sweat running down her back, a nagging suspicion that perhaps she might even end up being blamed for this too.

'Give me the log from Sandberg's PC,' she instructed. 'I need to know exactly what he was doing up there, every email, every log-on, everything.'

She saw Velander sit at an unused terminal and then she turned to face the front again: the multi-coloured cloud slowly appearing and disappearing on the giant screen.

Trottier's on his way, she thought. And if it were somehow to emerge that this attack was a result of her having let William up to his office ... She closed her eyes, trying to gather her thoughts, and not to panic until she knew for certain—

When she opened her eyes again, Velander was looking at her.

'What have you got?'

'Nothing,' he told her. 'He read a few articles. That was it. After that, nothing.'

It took her just seconds to grasp what he was saying. It just wasn't possible. William must have been in his office for an hour, and he had to have used the computer during all that time. Read emails, tried to contact someone, something.

'In that case, what was he doing up there all that time?'

'That's what I'm worried about,' said Velander. 'After nine o'clock, there are no logs at all. His computer is disconnected from the network.'

When the plane taxied into position at one end of the runway, John Patrick Trottier did the same thing as always. He put his hands together on his lap, underneath his coat, carefully concealed to his fellow passengers even though today he was flying alone.

He heard the engines gearing up outside the window, felt the acceleration pushing him into his seat, and then the body of the aircraft lifting clear of the ground. As he did, he clasped his hands even tighter together, mumbled his own approximations of the prayers he'd heard as a child. Just this once. Get us there in one piece. And I promise I'll never fly again.

This time, his prayers went unanswered. If John Patrick Trottier hadn't already had his eyes closed, he would have seen the lights disappear outside the windows.

24

William Sandberg wanted to cry, but didn't know how. He sat on the wipe-clean seat floating through the city on flashing blue lights, his daughter lying on the stretcher next to him covered with a blanket, even though she couldn't feel the cold. Together. At last. In an *amberlangs*.

Yet somehow it wasn't her. Her face was drained of everything that had once been Sara Sandberg, she had eyelids that someone else had closed, and she jolted in time with the bumps in the road, side to side with no resistance.

He could feel his thoughts jostling in panic, mixing and colliding, grief and emptiness on one side, everything else on the other.

What now? They were going to drive him back to HQ. And then?

The world was being subjected to electronic attacks. Somehow, everything pointed to a single person, the last person on Earth he'd want to meet – and to himself. Eventually, they were going to find those damning emails about the conference. Even if his hard drive was by now – hopefully – formatted, that just meant that it would take them longer, not that it would keep them out for ever. And once they knew he wasn't telling them everything, how many chances were they likely to give him then?

There was only one person who could prove William's innocence. Unfortunately, it was himself.

As soon as she opened the door to Sandberg's room, Forester knew that Velander's fears had been justified.

His computer was there, on the desk right in front of her. It was surrounded by blinking diodes on hard drives and storage devices, all whirring at full speed. She knew she was too late, yet she still rushed over to the computer, because you've got to try. She grabbed the devices on the desk, pulling out cable after cable without even thinking about what was connected to where.

The screens around her went black, fans fell silent, the green lamps on the units in the rack slowed down. Before long, all of them had stopped pulsing, instead flashing red to warn that the connections had been lost and the processes cancelled.

Everything was wiped, his hard drives, backups, everything, and whatever there'd been to begin with was now gone. All overwritten with random digits several times over to make it impossible to recover.

And this she knew for sure: you do not wipe all your own files unless you've got something to hide. Major Cathryn Forester took out her phone and punched the number to the Emergency Services' control room.

The woman behind the wheel was Jenny Bodin. She was a paramedic with ten years' experience behind her, but as she replaced the radio handset her only thought was that she'd never experienced anything like this.

It had started as a routine call-out – sad, yes, tragic and unfair, but routine all the same. The girl had died before they got there, and along with her colleague Bodin had attempted all possible resuscitation techniques to no avail. The girl was declared dead at the scene, and the man who was clearly her father had demanded to travel with her in the back. They'd driven through the darkness, blue lights but no sirens, and everything was normal. Until the call came.

All of a sudden they were no longer transporting a deceased girl and her father. Instead, the control room explained that they'd been contacted by Military Command and informed that the man in the back was under suspicion of terrorism, a highly potential escape risk, and must under no circumstances be allowed to leave the ambulance until they arrived.

She felt a surge of adrenaline, but forced it back. The man in the back had no way of knowing that he'd been uncovered.

They were separated by a robust wall with a reinforced glass pane, and the ambulance was being escorted by two unmarked police cars. Nothing could happen, she told herself. That call changed nothing.

When Jenny Bodin seconds later heard the sound of breaking glass, her first thought was that she must have hit something. She ducked and slammed on the brakes, shielded herself from the shards flying all around her, mind racing to figure out what she hadn't seen in time.

Then she felt the arm around her neck.

Palmgren hung up. He sat in the second of the two tailing cars, both of them dark-coloured Volvos, behind the ambulance. An officer from the Security Police sat in the driver's seat next to him.

'Was that about Sandberg?'

Palmgren held back the answer. He had been saying stuff like *What are you saying* and *That can't be true* and *Are you absolutely sure?*, and oh yes, Forester had been completely fucking sure, and as little as he wanted to he was now in a car with a bunch of colleagues who would very much like to know what it was all about.

'Contact the other car,' he said to the agent behind the wheel. 'We'll pull in close to the ambulance, them first, us at the rear. That ambulance is not to stop until we arrive at the hospital, no matter what.'

They all knew what it meant. Something had happened and now they were worried that Sandberg was about to flee, and the driver lifted the receiver and was just about to speak. Instead of that, chaos broke out.

It was the turn of the woman's head that got William to make up his mind. The slight change in the driver's expression, the suddenly self-conscious undertones that came with pretending nothing was happening. The conversation didn't last for more than seconds, but it was enough to tell him that the call was about him, and for a couple of short moments he observed the two paramedics through the glass panel, one hand hugging his daughter's.

Through the window, their own blue lights mixed with those coming from the Security Police vehicles. They were cruising tight behind like cygnets behind a hurrying parent, and in one of them was Palmgren, and maybe he was on William's side, maybe not.

It took him four seconds to find the emergency hammer.

In front sat the two paramedics – their seat belts fastened, he noted, telling himself that that was a good thing. Hopefully no one was going to get hurt, including himself, and he looked at Sara one last time, squeezed her hand.

Now the emptiness thundered through him, rolling in like a wave down a drained canal, and once it was happening it was so powerful that it couldn't be stopped. Finally, finally he cried.

Then he raised the hammer and smashed the panel between him and the cab.

Palmgren screamed, but no one could hear him over their own voice.

Right in front of them, the ambulance was dancing. There was no better word for it: it started with a swerve, as though the driver had tried to avoid something in the road, but before it had straightened up again it slammed on the brakes with no warning, and the wheels locked and skidded uncontrolled through the treacherous slush.

Right behind the ambulance, the first Volvo had just begun its overtaking manoeuvre. Now they panicked too, brakes slamming on to no effect, and spinning over the central markings into the oncoming traffic. On the road ahead, cars were streaming off the steep Västerbron bridge. Behind them, a necklace of cars bound for Kungsholmen and the Essinge Islands. If you had to lose control at high speed, this was not the place to do it.

Without words, Palmgren watched as the Volvo lost traction, saw the approaching cars brake on the slippery tarmac, gliding and jerking out of the way and straight into parked cars.

But most of all he saw the ambulance trying to manage the skid, steering into the slide, and all at once driving on two wheels. From behind, it looked like figure skating, a feat of poise and balance on one set of wheels, and for an instant it hung like that, frighteningly close to tipping over and sliding on its side.

The driver next to Palmgren reacted at once. He slammed on the brakes and spun the wheel in a desperate attempt to turn their car through ninety degrees and stop before they smashed into the cars in front. Through the side windows, they could see the ambulance still dancing. It had regained its balance and managed to thud back onto all four wheels again, but the speed it was travelling at meant the performance was not over. Instead, it reared up again, but this time in the opposite direction, and slid across the tarmac on the other two wheels, a missile in flight.

Palmgren felt himself holding his breath. On one side was the oncoming traffic, on the other the steep embankment. And no vehicle could balance like that for long.

William realised a thousandth of a second too late that the ambulance was going to fall. He clutched for a hold but didn't find one, and when it finally tipped onto its side he was thrown helplessly through the cab, the kinetic energy slamming him against the roof like a rag doll, with tubes and trays and equipment flying as tarmac pounded on steel. The ambulance had flipped over, and was now careering across the damp ground.

The first thing he saw as he opened his eyes was the side window. He'd landed on what had been one of the walls but which was now grinding along the tarmac, and he could see the ground rushing underneath him like a sander belt, with only the shuddering window between it and him.

He reacted without recourse to his brain: grabbing at anything solid, pulling himself clear of the window with all his strength – and at that moment the window gave out. It exploded into a cloud of glass particles, and William shielded his face with his arm, pushed his body against what had been the roof but was now a vertical wall, feeling how new shards were released from the rubber seal with each new impact.

Ahead of him was the partition between him and the cab. Beyond that, he could see the windscreen, and beyond that reality had flipped and was rushing sideways towards them, and in the midst of that reality was a bridge railing ...

When the Armco barrier crushed the windscreen, straight through the middle as though they'd driven into an upright pole, the momentum caused the whole vehicle to lift, teeter on its front end and then cartwheel over the barrier and down the verge beyond.

The world around William, meanwhile, was rotating. Tubes and bags and binders were torn from their compartments and holders and thrown around like a shirt in an enormous washing machine, with the sound of shrubs and ground as they reeled forwards. The necks of the paramedics swung and rocked helplessly like rag dolls. The forces at work ripped the rear doors from their hinges, crushing them against the rough ground, sending glass and particles flying in all directions as the world outside span.

And in the midst of it all was Sara. Lifeless, strapped in, rotating along with everything else. Him and her and an amberlangs.

25

At first, everything was silent. A yellow-gold glow played softly in the damp, cast by hazard lights and street lamps and hundreds of low-beam headlights on hundreds of stationary cars.

Then it all started. First movements. White, narrow lines from torches. Then people. Black silhouettes emerged, running from the cloud of light, like paper dolls making their entry in an ambitious shadow puppet performance, heading full pelt down the bank with their narrow, ice-cold torches pointing straight at the ground.

Weapons drawn.

Ambulance secured. He's gone.

—

William saw all of this from afar. He was lying at the bottom of the bank, hugging the ground and the bushes around him, as far as he'd dared to go before he heard them coming. His only chance was to lie perfectly still. He held his face to the ground, breathed silently and closed his eyes, waiting for time to elapse.

It had been two minutes when the light struck him. It shone warm and yellowy-red through his eyelids, and he lay there, his eyes still closed, hoping that it would pass. But it didn't. Instead, he heard a voice right in front of him.

'Shh,' it said.

William looked up, and one of the silhouettes was standing there, legs astride, levelling the torch. The world stood still. There was the trickling sound of wet snow melting as the temperature climbed above zero. Blue-grey breath hung in the air.

'Make your mind up,' said William, quietly. 'Make your mind up before they wonder what the hell you're doing just standing here and not searching.'

'You do know, don't you?' said the figure.

'Know what?' asked William.

'You know who emailed you.'

William hesitated. If he answered, what then? All he had was a suspicion – that, and a thousand questions, and very bad odds.

'What if I do? If I did happen to know that?'

'If you know,' said the man they all called Lassie, 'then I think you should find that bastard and stop him.'

William said nothing, just nodded back through the silence. And then, from a distance, came shouts from the silhouettes by the ambulance. Colleagues who called over to see if everything was okay.

'I'm taking a leak,' Palmgren shouted.

He stayed there for another few seconds, feet apart and quite still, before he nodded down at the wet ground. *Good luck.* Then he walked away.

William stayed prone for a long time. He saw Palmgren rejoin the group on the slope, people he used to work with but who were now looking for him. He looked down at the ambulance at

129

the bottom of the embankment, the paramedics being helped to their feet, his dead daughter loaded back on the stretcher to be taken away. He could see the snowfall intensifying and twinkling in blue.

By the time the dog handlers arrived, released their dogs and let them comb the area, William Sandberg was miles away.

Day 2. Tuesday 4 December

ROSETTA

Perhaps that's why death scares me so much.

Because I don't know who I am, where I'm from, how I became me.
  Once upon a time I didn't exist, and one day I will be no more.
  In between though? Is it really so much to ask – to know who you are?

Perhaps that's why I'm so scared of dying.
  Because if I never get to find out who I am, have I even really lived
at all?

26

As the clock ticked seamlessly over into Tuesday the fourth of December, Stockholm lay quiet and deserted. Here and there, police cars sped silently through the frosty streets, occasionally flashing their blue lights and casting vivid, sweeping shadows onto the walls of surrounding buildings.

William Sandberg saw them across the water, chillingly silent as they appeared and disappeared behind the city hall, past the Central Station, or down onto the northern shore of the stream. Sometimes, crawling, sometimes speeding, constantly looking for him.

He'd stopped for breath at the top of the hills in Skinnarviks park. And even though his entire body wanted him to stop, give up, just lay down on the ground and cry until the morning, he knew that was something he couldn't allow himself.

He just couldn't face carrying on. But he could already hear the dogs in the distance.

On the other side of the water, his estranged wife sat in the passenger seat of a light blue Volvo. Dry snowflakes floated past the windows, mocking her with their carefree swirl, dancing like children on a playground in a world of their own and oblivious to what had happened. Reality dared to go on, the laws of physics were so bold as to let the empty paper cups roll from side to side in the foot well under her legs, while Beatrice drove them in silence towards St Göran's Hospital.

In her mind, she ran into the hospital, time and time again, only to find herself still in the car. It was as if her thoughts kept arriving before her, over and over, and when they finally did pull up outside the emergency entrance, and she told Beatrice not to follow her inside, she still wasn't sure if it was happening for real.

She ran inside without knowing how, took the lift or the stairs or stayed on the same floor, it didn't even matter. She would soon be doing it all again, anyway.

It was only when Palmgren came up to her in corridor, put his arms around her without saying a word, that she finally knew she was there.

27

Cathryn Forester had never even come close to drowning, but as she hurried towards the flat roof of Swedish Armed Forces HQ for the second time that evening, she did so with a frightening conviction that this was exactly what it felt like.

Everything had collapsed around her. First Sara's death, then William's escape, and then, worst of all – the short message from Anthony Higgs. He had reached her on the unofficial satellite phone, and even as he introduced himself she'd felt the knot in her stomach.

She knew who he was, of course she did, she'd seen him on TV like everyone else, and frankly that had been enough for her to decide that she instinctively disliked him. But she had never spoken to him before, and there was no reason for him to be making contact, not now, not direct with her.

When she was new at the Vauxhall Cross HQ, Major John Patrick Trottier had time and time again returned from Whitehall meetings red in the face and furious about things that were top-secret but which he inevitably conveyed between the lines. The project that he and Higgs had both been involved in had been way above her grade, a European security collaboration with a codename she had long since forgotten. For years it had been poised in the starting blocks, but – as Trottier put it – constantly stymied by political cowardice.

What they developed wasn't a weapon – it was far better, he used to say, it was a non-weapon – but that hadn't prevented the scheme from finally ending up mothballed for good. On that day, Trottier had come back to the office in a snarling rage that smelled a lot like Guinness, swearing at all and sundry and calling the Defence Secretary a bloody spineless turncoat and just as untrustworthy as all the other bastards up there.

Now that turncoat had contacted her via the satellite phone, and the more she listened to his voice, the more the water had closed in around her, drowning on the same roof where she'd just been talking to Trottier.

Trottier's plane had been a Hawker 800. Piloted by two very experienced officers and with a single passenger on board. At ten minutes past ten, Defence Minister Higgs had told her with formal precision, the plane had received clearance from the control tower, sped down the runway and into the air.

According to witnesses, the darkness had come the moment the plane left ground. It dropped as though someone had put a blanket over a birdcage, rippled like a wave throughout the airfield and beyond, and now Major John Patrick Trottier was gone.

She tilted her face towards the snow, hoping that the cold sensation would calm her down, but it didn't help in the slightest. The man who just moments ago was on his way over to her, who she'd have done anything to avoid seeing, that man was dead and from now on all contact would be directly with the turncoat himself.

Was this her fault? Were they right, was she simply not up to the job? Could she have done things differently, prised the truth out of William Sandberg, could that have stopped Trottier's death?

Fuck. She deserved the rollicking Trottier had intended to give her.

None of it added up. How could Sandberg be involved with this? What could he have done anyway – started what process, sent what order, prompted what sequence that made the computers at Northolt ready for attack as soon as Trottier took off? And given all that, how could Sandberg even have known that he was coming?

She swore into the falling snow, felt the flakes burning her face.

The question was not how did it happen, it was how was she going to get hold of Sandberg again. Once she'd done that, she was going to pin him against the wall, and she wasn't going to let anyone get in the way, not Palmgren and not Velander and not even the Whitehall turncoat. She would push Sandberg until he told her what had happened, why it had happened, and what he had planned next.

All she needed to know was that he was guilty.

And now she was certain of that: only a guilty man formats his hard drives.

Velander did as he'd been asked and waited until they'd gone past the Royal College of Music. He wove between the dirty brown trails of snow that had been ploughed up onto the pavements, and saw his vision blur as the snow melted on his bloody glasses. Every now and then he would attempt to wipe them with his forearm, a nylon coat sleeve that was just as wet as everything else and that only made things worse.

The whole time, he had his phone pressed to his ear. He let it ring and ring, and was about to hang up for the third time when a crackle came at the other end.

'Where are you?' the voice said, with no introduction.

'Where are *you*?' said Velander. 'I've been ringing for ages.'

'I know. I couldn't talk in there.'

Velander regretted it almost at once. *In there*. He knew that Palmgren had accompanied Sara's lifeless body to the hospital. He knew he had waited for William's wife and then *obviously* – Velander grimaced – obviously he'd have stayed with her for support.

'Sorry,' he said. 'I didn't mean to disturb you while . . .'

'Not at all,' Palmgren said. 'I was the one who asked you to.'

Velander ploughed on. 'I have a question,' he said. 'I'll be coming back to the office with two dripping-wet shoes and a bag of Danish pastries from 7-Eleven. Now, if I'm struck down with pneumonia tonight, *and* diabetes, will I be able to call that a workplace injury?'

'You're asking me whether this call is taking place while we're on duty?'

'Amongst other things, yes.'

'In that case it might be worthwhile to check your private health insurance.'

Velander unravelled the reply. 'I've been on dates that were more direct than this conversation,' he said eventually. And then, when Palmgren didn't seem to have anything to add: 'I don't trust her either.'

'I never said I didn't trust her.'

'I know. But someone had to make the first move.'

It fell quiet again, and in that interval he wondered if he might have gone too far.

'I'm not going to ask you to block her,' Palmgren said at last. 'Not to disobey her orders or anything like that. All I'm asking you to do is to report to me when anything crops up.'

Velander nodded at no one in particular. Then he looked both ways down the empty, slush-filled avenue, and pushed the mic closer to his lips.

'Status right now,' he said, lowering his voice. He went on to give a concise account of everything that had happened in Palmgren's absence, the listening silence growing deeper with each word. He hadn't been gone more than a few hours, yet there had been time for another attack, a surge which had also knocked out a military airfield and killed Forester's superior.

'Like having your arteries on the outside,' Palmgren said silently when Velander had finished. 'And what do we know about William?'

'Nothing. He's still missing, wanted on suspicion of terror offences. The whole city is full of police units. They've got his flat, his wife's flat, her job under surveillance. Not that anyone thinks he's stupid enough to turn up there, but what choice do they have?' Velander hesitated. 'I don't know if you already know this, but the last thing he did was to format his computer.'

Judging by Palmgren's silence, that was news to him.

'What's Forester saying?'

'Exactly what you'd expect,' said Velander. 'That she won't quit until they've found him, and that when they do, there'll be none of the kid-gloves treatment like the last time. Wait.' He crossed the street, hopping over slush-filled puddles. 'The only thing that worries me,' he said when he got to the other side, 'is the wallet.'

'What do you mean?'

139

'It was in his inside pocket when he got the coat back. Before you drove him to Sara.'

Velander let the silence underline what he'd said. And when Palmgren finally answered, he did so with a snigger.

'William has been working for the military for thirty years. Do they really think that he's crazy enough to use his credit cards in this situation? Because if they do, they're even dumber than I thought.'

'I'm with you,' said Velander. 'Pretty much. But how long can he manage without money?'

Velander was right, and they both knew it. Neither of them said as much, but the odds were against him. Sooner or later William would have to reveal himself.

'I should go back in to Christina,' Palmgren said to break silence. 'Thanks for calling.' He paused before adding: 'And if you don't feel comfortable with this, I want you to say so. Otherwise I would be most grateful if you could keep me up to speed with whatever Forester does while I'm not there.'

Velander smiled as he answered: 'I thought I was already doing that.'

They had a whole city to keep under surveillance. And never mind that pretty much every available resource had been deployed on the search, they still would never be able to cover every square metre. Plus the fact that they were looking for a man who had worked for the military for over thirty years.

Those were Major Cathryn Forester's thoughts as she walked the last few yards back to the briefing room. Still, with each step, she felt her posture straightening, the strain around her eyes shifting from dejected and tired to focused and alert as she planned her next moves, which tasks she was going to delegate and how.

Sure, Sandberg knew their patterns of thinking. He knew what to do to keep out of their way. That meant that their only chance was to wear him out, and the only way to do that was to keep working, steadily, everywhere, all the time, and she was determined to do that.

As soon as she set foot back in the room, she would be taking back command. She wasn't going to let herself relax, not for a second, until she was absolutely sure that they had him again.

The next moment she stuck her head round the door, and all those thoughts vanished at once.

The room was empty. Dotted around the table a few open laptops were whirring, neat piles of notes were placed carefully by chairs, and the coffee cups and water glasses were half full as though everyone had suddenly stood up and gone. For an instant she was gripped by a sort of indignant fear, a feeling of having been removed from position and barred from her own working group, and that they were all off somewhere else without having told her. It was absurd, she could see that, yet she couldn't shake the feeling that she'd lost control – or worse still, that her control had never been needed: the others were getting on with the job without her, and doing just fine.

'Forester?'

She spun around.

The voice belonged to one of her own, a British colleague, a junior officer with cropped hair and a Scottish accent. He was now standing in the doorway, looking at her with a restless stare and body language that wanted nothing but to get moving.

'Yes?' she said, trying to retain her status but sensing that it wasn't going that well. 'What's going on?'

'The JOC,' said the Scot. 'Down there. They're waiting for you.'

And then he said the thing that made her forget all the thoughts she'd just had.

'We've been looking for you everywhere. We've located William Sandberg.'

28

The room was bright, verging on white-out. There were some lightweight chairs in neutral colours, on the side tables small thickets of candles danced brightly, and hanging over the scene was the smell of sulphur from the safety matches that had lit them all. The walls were lined with thin white drapes, gently swaying in a non-existent draught, soothing like fluttering net curtains on a summer evening.

Floating in the midst of it all was Sara. She lay on a bed in the centre of the room, weightless under the white sheet. Her hand was cool rather than cold, soft and human and almost just another hand, and beside the bed sat Christina Sandberg, squeezing it hard between her own palms.

Maybe she's just cold. That was the thought that stubbornly obsessed her, but also that she had to keep batting away because it wasn't helping. Behind every strand of hope came the next wave of reality, each one stronger, blacker, harder than the one before.

At the time, the road traffic accident had been just another news story, a lesser event in the shadow of the night's big stories.

'Ambulance involved,' CW had called across the newsroom. 'At least one death.' And then: 'Witness says it's crawling with undercover police.'

It was that last detail that had made Christina stop and pay attention. Accidents were local, ordinary, routine. Forget it. Especially on a night like this. Ambulance? Better. Spectacular and ironic – ambulances are supposed to save people, not end up involved in accidents themselves. But it was the part with undercover cops that really gave the story legs. It meant that there was something else lurking underneath, perhaps it might even have something to do with the power cut, and Christina had squeezed between cabinets and chairs to stand over CW's desk and look at his screen.

'Have we got any pictures?'

'Depends what you mean by "picture",' came the response, and CW had tilted the screen to show her. There was a single photo, and it was basically pitch-black. There were blurry light sources here and there, in various colours, some headlights, the others presumably blue lights. And somewhere in the middle was her daughter – but she didn't know that then.

In the end, Christina had dismissed the picture with a shake of the head.

'It doesn't have any angle. We need faces, names, something tangible. We need something that connects us.'

Now, afterwards, that was what tormented her above all, what made her hand sweat around Sara's cold fingers, and forced her to close her eyes to ward off her thoughts.

The thought that she asked for this herself.

When Palmgren returned to the relatives' room Christina had let go of Sara's hand. She was sitting there on her light wooden chair, her hands resting in her lap and her empty stare fixed on the floor in front of her, beyond and into eternity. He stayed by the door, saying nothing, letting time pass through the room.

'A little life,' Christina said in a whisper. It was so thin he wasn't even sure if she'd said it to him, not until she eventually lifted her eyes and they met his.

'What was that?' he said in reply.

'She used to say that. *A little life*. Birds that flew into the living-room window. Flies lying on the windowsill after a summer's day. The mice in the summer house when we removed them from the traps.'

She paused, and he let her. 'Sometimes she'd cry. Sometimes she was angry. She could sit there for hours just looking at the bodies, they were all little lives, she'd say, with little eyes and little hearts, and it would make her so frustrated, all these things that had come to be and developed and grown and then it would just end, for no reason.'

It went quiet again. And in the silence, Palmgren saw Christina's eyes change. They went from grief to determination, forced their colour to the surface to avoid drowning deep down there.

'Do you have it?' she said eventually.

Palmgren looked at her. It?

'The CD,' said Christina. 'The computer. Did she have it on her?'

That was not a question he'd been expecting. Not right now.

143

And he hesitated, didn't know what he ought to say, was allowed to say.

'I realise that you need it,' she said. 'But she's my daughter. If that CD can help me to understand . . .'

She didn't finish the sentence.

'I don't even know if I'm allowed to tell you this,' Palmgren said eventually. 'But no. She didn't have anything on her when we found her.'

Christina nodded silently.

'Why do you ask?' he said. It was as if she had finished grieving, at least for now, and the Christina Sandberg he was talking to now was the journalist, not the friend, the human being, the person. 'Do you know anything I don't?' he asked.

'Like what?'

'Christina,' he said. 'I'm asking you. If you find anything, let me be the first to know.'

'You've already asked me that,' she replied, and they stayed that way, looking into each other's eyes, until Christina pulled her coat towards her from the chair next to hers and stood up. She stopped by Sara's face. A last, unavoidable, farewell, as though she was trying to etch the scene in her memory, to be certain that she would never, ever, be able to forget.

She leant over. Stroked her cheek.

'A little life,' she said.

Step by step, they made their way out of the relatives' room. Several times they stopped along the way, first in the long, bright corridor, then again in the empty waiting room, then at the door that would return them to the main part of the hospital.

There, finally, Christina could go no further.

'I think I'll stay here,' she heard herself saying.

It was as though the door in front of them was a frontier. Beyond it waited the rest of her life, a series of unknown days, all of which had in common the knowledge that she was the mother of a daughter who did not exist.

'I don't think I'm quite ready yet.'

'I've got a guest room, if you'd like.'

She looked into Palmgren's warm eyes. Wanted to say yes please, but just couldn't.

'I've got a guest room tomorrow too, and loads of nights after that. I've got a guest room whenever you need it.'

She nodded quietly, a thanks and a no thanks at the same time, and with that the silence lifted. They could hear ambulances arriving, trolleys rolling, footsteps running, and distant voices in other corridors. Other people's lives carrying on and being saved, events that did not affect them.

'Will he be okay?' she asked after a while.

'William?'

'Yes. Have they got this right? Has he done something?'

'I think there's somebody out there who would very much like to make it look that way.'

'Who?'

He shrugged.

'It can't just be about power cuts,' Christina said eventually. 'There's more to it. Something bigger. Right?'

'What makes you say that?'

For a second she felt herself hesitating. She could answer, of course she could. She could tell him about the CD she'd found in the brown Nissan, about Kaknäs Tower and about the conference in Warsaw. But something told her that in the end, it would still end up pointing at William, that she'd be doing him a disservice rather than a favour.

'What do you know, Christina?'

She looked him in the eye, felt him seeing straight through her.

'I'm on your side.'

'I know that.'

'So, if you do find anything . . . if you know anything at all . . .'

They stayed standing there, looking into each other's eyes, for a long time. She had just decided to tell him, when his phone vibrated between them.

The call lasted less than a minute. Throughout, Christina stood motionless, watching Palmgren pacing the corridor, hunched over to prevent the conversation leaking out. She saw him listening, nodding, rubbing the bridge of his nose in frustration. Now and then an affirmative noise, but that was it: 'Okay,' he said. Then went quiet. 'Okay. Yeah. Okay. Okay.'

She caught herself thinking that she couldn't face another blow. They *must not* have caught him, she thought, and the thought took her by surprise. There was nothing wrong with William Sandberg. She had loved him, maybe she still did, and above all she was convinced that he wasn't involved in what was going on. William was the victim of something, not the other way around.

At last she heard Palmgren rounding off the call – 'Hurry back now,' he said, 'do as she says, don't try and draw anything out' – and once that was said he hung up and looked Christina in the eye once more.

'Was that about William?' she asked.

Palmgren hesitated. He walked towards her, his hands ahead of him, and stopped just short.

'The idiot has just withdrawn five thousand krona from a cashpoint.'

29

Cathryn Forester perched on the edge of one of the chairs in the JOC, thinking of how much she loved living in the twenty-first century.

One of Major Trottier's most prominent characteristics had been his appreciation of technology. He was utterly convinced that our salvation lay in the very things that left others terrified – CCTV in public spaces, telephones that remember where you've been, invisible digital tracks that trail behind. And if there was one way to honour his memory, she thought, this would be it.

They'd found seven active bank cards registered to William Sandberg. And even though it was the middle of the night, it hadn't taken more than half an hour for the banks to set the necessary routines in motion. After that, they hadn't had to wait long.

She looked at the computer screen in front of her. William Sandberg had been careless. What surprised her was that it had come so quickly, even if that too probably had a natural explanation. Stress precipitates bad decisions. Desperation leads to mistakes. Not because people are careless or stupid, but because they feel they're running out of options. In the end they reach the stage where they have to take a risk to keep going – and that's when they start to lose.

When Velander came back from his walk he was both wet and steaming hot. He had a 7-Eleven carrier bag in his hand and cheeks that were glowing puce, peering at her through glasses that kept steaming up for every second he spent in the room.

'I was just . . . ' he panted. 'I went to get . . . I needed . . . I came straight away.'

Cathryn Forester couldn't help but enjoy the situation. She got up from the desk and offered him a view of the webpage the card issuers had provided.

'The call went out three minutes ago,' she said while Velander was pulling off his coat and sitting down on the desk chair in a single movement. 'One of the cards he hardly ever uses. As though he thought we'd have less of an eye on them.'

'Where is he?'

'Högbergsgatan.'

'And what do you want me to do now?'

Forester couldn't help smiling. It was her first feeling of success for hours, so why shouldn't she? Cocked her head, didn't answer.

'Should I cancel the cards?'

'Absolutely not,' she said. And then, off his look: 'I don't give a damn what he does with his money. As long as I know *where* he's doing it.'

If anyone had seen William Sandberg at the cashpoint on Högbergs-gatan, they would have seen a nervous man with a pen in his

147

mouth and seven different bank cards lined up in front of him. No one did, though, and that was a part of the plan.

He had walked over from Skinnarviks park, through the back streets of Mariaberget, first sheltered by the trees and then zig-zagging his way through the narrowest, darkest alleys he could find. Any hint of an engine noise stopped him in his tracks. Each time he saw the beam of what might be a headlight he turned and headed in a new direction, and all the time he kept looking purposefully for one, single thing. It was a stupid plan, he knew that, but it was the only one that came to mind.

Eventually he had found a cashpoint on Högbergsgatan.

It was out of the way, a good distance from the metro station and the main roads, and the street was long enough to allow him to get away if a car should turn up. Even more important though was the fact that it was surrounded by alleys and passageways, most of which would take him down towards Slussen.

He felt himself holding his breath as he fed the first card into the machine.

Most of them hadn't been used for years, and some of them he wasn't sure had ever left his wallet. Several had been foisted on him in connection with various purchases, with the front embla-zoned with an electronics company's logo or a petrol station or an airline, and each time he'd thought, fine, if you want to give me a few hundred krona discount in exchange for me signing up for a card I'm never going to use then that's your problem, not mine.

Now, they were the cards he was rooting for.

He was torn from his thoughts by the beeping of the machine, so harsh and loud that it made him jump, then look up and down the street for fear that someone might have heard. Had he forgot-ten the PIN? Fuck. Two attempts remaining.

Maybe he should've started at the other end, with one of the cards he used every day, but if there was one thing he was sure of it was that they'd be watching those. If he started with one of the others it just might take them longer, and the more time he could steal for himself, the better his chances of success.

If he could just remember the PIN. *Idiot.*

Around him, the street was still black in both directions, a thickening snowfall glittering under the street lamps. No cars, no footsteps, no police with their weapons drawn. Not yet.

He closed his eyes. Tried to see the pattern in front of him. The path his fingers took across the keypad, mathematics as images, just like the way he worked. And then tried again. Right, left, up, back?

The silence lasted for ever. And then, thank God, at last he heard the whirr of the cogs, and he grabbed the notes hungrily as they emerged, stuffed the ten five-hundred notes in the inside pocket of his wet coat. Then he pulled the pen from his mouth, leaving the cap between his teeth while he wrote the four-digit code on the back of the card.

Once he'd done that, he moved on to the next one. Maximum withdrawal, five thousand, code on the back. Now the next one. And the next. With each card the adrenalin mounted, but he forced himself to stay put, even as he grew more and more convinced that they were already on their way.

Palmgren walked through the empty hospital, footsteps echoing past departments with alarming names, between walls adorned with childish murals. Wherever he went, his path was lined with trees and lakes and sunshine children, and it gave him the creeps. *It's a hospital*, he wanted to scream, *not a bloody children's book*.

But most of all, he wanted to scream at William. So he was in shock, fine. Tired, worn out, grief-stricken, all of that. But that was no excuse. He wasn't stupid. They'd be watching his cards and he knew it, which either meant he was desperate or just taking a big punt, and both of those were beneath him.

He walked past the hospital canteen, closed for the night, out onto the turning circle beyond the glass doors, and stopped there, let his eyes drift for about half a second across the expanse in front of him until he found what he was looking for.

The car was a dark metallic grey Passat. Two men in puffer jackets sat in the front, and he vaguely recognised them from earlier – maybe they'd been at Central Station to arrest William, he wasn't sure.

He walked over, tapped on the window, waited as it sank into the door with an electric whine.

'Am I screwing things up by talking to you?'

The smile that came back was intended to be sardonic.

'It's not you we're watching. We're waiting for Sandberg, if he decides to turn up.'

'Of course you are,' said Palmgren. 'That's why you're here while he's at a cashpoint three miles away.'

It was a gamble, but the silence that greeted it proved him right. They had also been informed, which meant that the only explanation for their presence was that they were there for his sake.

He returned their smile.

'All right,' he said. 'Listen. I suggest that we head down there together.'

'Our orders are to stay here,' said one of them.

'What, even if I leave?'

That seemed like a possibility they hadn't even considered.

'Let's say you really are waiting for Sandberg,' said Palmgren. 'Do you think he's stupid enough to show up here? That he won't suss you sitting here?'

No reply.

'Suggestion: you saw me leave. You had to make a decision and you chose to keep me under surveillance instead.' Then, when the replies were still not forthcoming: 'I'll be sitting in your back seat, I think you can reasonably claim to have had your eyes on me throughout.'

He opened the rear door, prepared for an objection, didn't get one.

'Högbergsgatan, please. You can put the meter on if you like.'

He got a tired look in the mirror, but instead of saying anything, one of them turned the key in the ignition, and moments later they were rolling down the hill, away from the hospital.

Palmgren checked his watch. At this time of night it wasn't going to take more than seven, eight minutes to get to Högbergsgatan, going via Västerbron and Hornsgatan, bus lane or not. With any luck, he thought, they'd get there before the others. And then? He didn't know. Maybe he'd be able to distract them again? Maybe he would spot him before they did, and lead them off in the wrong direction?

He shook his head at his own thoughts. The city was full of cops with a single task. Every available unit was looking for William Sandberg, and he wasn't going to be able to pull off a diversionary manoeuvre alone. Especially not without being discovered, which he'd definitely prefer.

But, able or not, William was a friend. And the moment that thought passed through his head, it came to him that he had never doubted it.

William Sandberg was innocent. He knew that now.

Now all he had to do was help prove it.

They'd just accelerated down the hill towards Drottningholms-vägen and jumped the red light without stopping, when the Security Police agent in the passenger seat grappled his phone out of his pocket.

He lit the screen, read something, and put it back.

'Message?' said Palmgren. No answer. 'Is it about Sandberg? Do they know where he's heading?'

He saw the policeman up front adjust his position in the seat, cross his arms, then glance over his shoulder.

What the hell was that? A smile?

'As far as we know,' he said, 'he's not heading anywhere.'

They must have seen the shock in Palmgren's eyes.

'He's still on Högbergsgatan, and so far he's taken out money on five different cards. I'm not sure he's quite as clever as you're making out.'

The first car was there within three minutes. It had been driving down Sveavägen when the call went out, had carried on through the tunnel and out on to Central Bridge, flashed over the water at well over 120 kilometres an hour, and then finally up to Medborgarplatsen with just a few hundred metres left to their target.

On the giant screen in the JOC it was shown as a numbered

white cross in the middle of the huge digital map of Stockholm. Rows of jaws were clenched in the auditorium, following the car as it travelled across the city centre, with the others not far behind. The whole city was crawling with crosses, all with a single instruction, to arrest William Sandberg, and they dashed to the target like flies to a sugar cube.

He'd made five withdrawals. That meant he still had two unused cards to go. However, they hadn't received any updates from the cash machine for over thirty seconds, which could well mean that he'd already moved on. But just as well, there could be something was holding him up – perhaps he was struggling to remember a PIN, or else something had spooked him and he'd hidden in a doorway, waiting for the danger to pass before he completed the last two withdrawals.

Either way, they were about to find out. The first 'X' was just seconds away.

They held their breath, waited, and when the car finally reached the target and no reports came, they room was left with wildly fluctuating thoughts, simultaneously convinced that the police were busy wrestling him to the ground right now, and on the other equally certain that he was gone and that now they were tracking him down between the buildings.

Nervously waiting, until the speakers crackled.

'Come in, over,' said Forester.

The next minute, the mood of the room crashed.

Sitting behind his screen, Jonas Velander closed his eyes in relief. Just two seconds, he thought to himself. Two seconds while this roller coaster powers down, till my pulse stops lurching and I can think straight again.

When the police had finally responded at last to Forester's call, they did so with the news that William was gone. She received the news with impressive calm and a renewed instruction to keep up the search, then stood without moving for several seconds, looking out over a room that was every bit as quiet and focused as herself. Whether there were others in the room who felt the same relief as he did, he had no idea, but Forester's silence could only express disappointment.

'Oh well,' she said. 'That would have been too easy, wouldn't it?'

Her tone had been meant to mask her disappointment, but failed completely, and when at last she set out across the room the vexation in her step was impossible to miss.

One of the walls was covered with maps of various parts of the country, and over by the large-scale map of central Stockholm, Velander saw her turn and stop. Then she stretched one hand out over the island of Södermalm, with her thumb covering Högbergsgatan, her little finger making a slow circling motion.

She was weighing up their odds. And while she made her calculations over by the map, Velander performed his own.

The odds were still stacked against William. He was in poor shape to begin with, and on top of that he'd had a long, exhausting day. Say he managed to move ten kilometres an hour – Velander quickly revised upwards: okay, make it twelve. That would mean that with every passing minute William could move two hundred metres further away from the cashpoint – they had no way to know in which direction. That meant that for the first three or four minutes he'd still be on the island. It was, after all, a limited area, and there was only a handful of bridges he could leave by.

But give him five, and they'd no longer know for sure. If they hadn't picked him up by then he might have moved on to any of the neighbouring districts, from where the number of bolt-holes would multiply.

As he opened his eyes again, he saw Forester down by the map, working the same permutations but hoping for quite a different outcome, and for a moment he couldn't help feeling sorry for her. Everywhere you looked were alleyways, passages and tunnels, paths and steps that cars could not pass. And whatever they did, there were more streets in town than there were squad cars.

On the big screen, the white 'X's had already started leaving Högbergsgatan. They spread out across Södermalm, searching the surrounding streets at random.

And the minutes passed.

Four. Going on five. Soon the window would be closed, and

before long William could be sitting in safety – he'd managed to withdraw twenty-five thousand, and that would keep him going for quite some time. Forester's only hope would be for him to make another withdrawal, pop up on the map and narrow their search area again, but even if William had exposed himself to an insane and extravagant risk, he wasn't stupid. He'd taken one chance, and he wasn't going to do that again.

It was Agneta Malm's voice that got him to look up. She was right by his ear, shouting with a force that jolted him upright.

'There!' she yelled. 'We've got a withdrawal. A new one.'

When Velander looked at the screen in front of him the dismay he felt made the ground shift underneath him.

What is wrong with the guy?

Agneta Malm had noticed it first, because that seemed to be her vocation. A new line of text had appeared on the screen in front of him, a code and some coordinates and a new transaction of five thousand krona, and now Forester was hurrying to see it for herself.

'Put it on the map,' she said, and Velander did as he was told, his fingers dancing over the keys, before double-checking that the coordinates were correct and then pressing return.

Up on the big screen there was already a light blue dot in the middle of Högsbergsgatan, where the first cash machine was located. Now as the second dot appeared, the room gasped in chorus. They had underestimated him completely. They'd tightened the net far too slowly, no one had spotted him slipping through, and Velander rubbed his face and forced himself not to swear.

After basically getting away, now this.

Right next to him, Forester pulled the microphone towards her mouth.

'Turn the cars around,' she said. 'Head north. He's in the city centre.'

Palmgren sat in the back of the dark grey Passat, grasping the handle above the window as the car shook and bounced over cobbles and potholes. It shot out onto the square at Södermalmstorg, skidding in the wet snow and leaving two long dark trenches of water in the spotless white as it cut across the open space, onto the carriageway on the far side, and onwards towards Slussen.

Palmgren couldn't for the life of him work out what William was up to. Their car had been one of the very last to arrive at Högbergsgatan, beaten to it by a whole convoy of blinking blue lights. Even so, it was perfectly clear that the game had been lost. There were far too many doorways and almost as many side streets, all leading in turn to more doorways and more side streets down which William could have disappeared. Everything was covered with powdery snow. Whichever way he'd gone, nature had managed to sweep up his traces behind him.

And then suddenly, in the flood of Palmgren's relief, another withdrawal. Not only that, of all fucking places it was at Central Station.

Palmgren let his head slump over against the window, biting his lip to keep himself from swearing. Sure, there was a part of him that couldn't help but be impressed. It had taken William less than ten minutes to cross the black waters of Riddarfjärden, and, assuming that no vehicle had helped him it meant that he must have sprinted all the way like a middle-distance runner. Straight over the bridge and presumably, for much of the time, in full view.

Above all though, it made him furious. William's only hope was to go into hiding, and of course he knew it, so why was he sticking his head out?

Palmgren was barely done thinking that thought when the radio announced another update. William wouldn't let it drop. From Central Station he'd headed up on to Klarabergsviadukten. From there, on to Sergels Torg. At each new location he made only one withdrawal then moved on, and in the back seat Palmgren felt despair and anger and a thousand other emotions erupting at the same time.

They were crossing the bridge at Skeppsbron, with the palace on their left and the Grand Hotel on the right. He saw the blue lights moving on a parallel course on the other side of the water, and yet more racing in from Riddarholmen and turning off onto Vasabron. They were converging from all directions, between them they would block William's route through the city, and there was no longer anything Palmgren could do about it.

The three cars arrived at Hamngatan just seconds apart. The first tore down the hill from Sergels Torg, speeding over the brow so that the undercarriage scraped on the tarmac, a deliberate shortcut over the raised tramlines. Its sirens blared, its blue lights flashed, and a beam of white shot out from the front to strike the red frontage of the building next to the NK department store, the cashpoint, and the figure hunched over the keypad.

From Norrmalmstorg, an identical beam of light swung through the darkness, playing between the sandstone pillars of the arcade before finally settling on the same ATM and the same target.

In the third car to arrive sat Lars-Erik Palmgren. He saw the first two screech to a stop, saw the two agents from his own car leap out with their weapons drawn, and from where he was sitting he could make out the black silhouette running down the portico in a final attempt to escape.

Way over there the shadow darted through the sandstone passage, out between the pillars and straight into the road, several times almost slipping over on the icy tram tracks but each time regaining balance and running on towards the park.

There the hunt ended. A new pair of headlights approached from the direction of the Opera House, spreading their icy cold light through white-dusted trees, and from his spot by the department store Palmgren saw the silhouette finally caught in a crossfire of light: headlamps, torches, bellowing police officers approaching from every direction.

A heavy tackle brought the shadow to the ground. The scene filled with more and more colleagues, all with weapons drawn and grunting adrenalin-fuelled orders – *Lie still for fuck's sake, you're not getting out of it this time.*

Then, inexplicably, he saw the police loosen their grip and let go. Backing away, exchanging glances, pushing fingers to ears and lifting their mics to their mouths, as though they couldn't quite believe what they saw.

The radio in the front seat crackled as it relayed their calls.

'It's the wrong person,' someone said. 'It's not him,' said another. 'It's a woman.' A third voice.

Utter silence from colleagues in the briefing room. And then, with short, hesitant pauses: 'Await further instructions.' – 'We've got a little problem.' – 'There are two new withdrawals.'

Far away, in the darkness, one of the police pulled up his headset.

'Where?'

'That's the thing. Sveavägen and Gamla Stan.'

'In that order?'

'No. Simultaneous.'

After that, the radio fell silent for what must have been at least thirty seconds. And throughout, Lars-Erik Palmgren could feel himself smiling in the back.

30

The woman was lying with her cheek to the ground, eyes closed and praying to a god she didn't believe in. The knees she could feel in her back were too many to count. Her wrists were screaming with pain as the policemen gripped them, she felt the gravel on her face and the light in her eyes and all the time they kept asking her name.

'Karin,' she told them, and then again, 'Karin,' over and over. It was the truth, she just hadn't said it for so long that when she finally did it she couldn't stop.

She didn't really know when, but at some point she'd started calling herself Cleo. Somehow that had made everything easier to bear, as though her true self was bound up with her name, and she'd just put it in storage for a little while. As if it would still be there, unchanged and unspoiled, as long as she didn't use it.

That was how she wanted to see herself. Still the singer in a metal band, still a talent with the future at her feet, all she'd done was lock herself in a safety deposit box while the bad years blew over. The bad years, though, had stayed. She was over thirty now, and here she lay, on the tarmac outside NK, with her arms bent up between her shoulder blades and the cold of the ground against her body.

Yet inside, she was still smiling. Less than an hour ago she'd woken up on a warm air vent in a tiled underpass beneath Vasagatan. A man had been standing over her. She instinctively recoiled, backed away towards the wall, be he had crouched down next to her with a warm, reassuring voice.

'Cleo?' he'd said. 'I need your help.'

It had taken several seconds for her to realise that it was him. The very first time they met he'd offered her money, which had scared her, but all he'd wanted in return was information about his missing daughter. Cleo had been honest, told it like it was. She didn't know anything, had never seen her, couldn't help.

He'd pushed a hundred note into her hand anyway, and that's how it carried on, each time they met, always a hundred, sometimes two. Again and again he'd begged her to keep an eye out. To send him an email if she saw anything.

Now he was sitting there, hunched over next to her, even more tired and distraught than she'd seen him before. He was wet and cold and had a face so devoid of emotion that she wanted to do something, hold him, comfort him even though she'd forgotten how to.

'Have you found her?' was all she ended up saying.

The man shook his head.

'There's one last thing I want you to do for me.'

Now she was sitting in the police car and could feel the warmth returning to her body, the window next to her steaming up from her damp clothes.

She'd managed four cashpoints before they caught up with her. Four times five made twenty thousand, sitting there in her inside pocket, and which no one could prove was not rightfully hers. She'd be sleeping in the warm tonight, then they'd ask her a never-ending string of questions, and she would answer them perfectly honestly, just as he'd told her to.

'They will get you,' he'd told her, 'and they'll ask you a thousand questions, and then a thousand more. The money you withdraw though, they can't take off you. See it as a gift. And the longer you can evade them, the better for both of us.'

She'd wanted him to give him a hug to say thanks, but he'd explained that he was in a hurry, that he had another four cards he needed to hand out. And yet he'd looked at her as if he wanted to stay, as though she was the last bit of security he had left. Maybe she was.

He was already halfway down the subway when she called out: 'I hope you find her.'

When he stopped, she could only see his silhouette. But that was enough.

'I'm not looking any more.'

The taxi was official, with yellow plates, but it wasn't from a firm. The logo consisted of the word TAXI and nothing more, a magnetic sign stuck on the front door, and the first thing the driver said as he pulled up to the kerb was that he couldn't take cards as payment.

For William Sandberg, that was just fine.

He didn't have any credit cards any more. He had twenty-five thousand krona in cash in his pocket, and he'd known as he was withdrawing it who he was going to ask for help. He'd run along the metro tunnel all the way from Slussen, cutting through underground passages he'd learned about from them, and in the darkness five of them were given a credit card each. Faces he'd met on his walks, faces that needed his credit more than he did. And while they were busy emptying his accounts, William had one last thing left to do.

As he walked into the internet café by Hötorget he felt the memory of the CCTV footage stabbing at his insides. As though deep down he was expecting her to still be there, that everything that had happened in the ambulance was yet to happen, and now was his chance to change it all.

It wasn't like that, of course. Instead he gave a hundred krona to Bum-fluff on the till, asked him about the girl who was there yesterday afternoon, never mentioning the fact that he was her father.

She'd left nothing behind. The place where she'd been sitting was empty and sad and meant nothing. But before he left, he sat down at one of the computers and logged in to his Hotmail account. No new emails had arrived in AMBERLANGS inbox, not from ROSETTA, nor anyone else, and he closed the window, treated himself to a couple of seconds with his eyes closed, wondering what it meant. Why hadn't he turned up? If Piotrowski was trying to get hold of him, where was he now?

When William had seen enough, he stood up and walked out. In one corner was the camera that had captured Sara on film for the very last time, perhaps recording him right now too. But before anyone saw those pictures, he was planning to be long gone.

Now he was sitting in the unmarked taxi, and beyond the windscreen the empty motorway rushed towards him with a soporific rhythm, white lines replaced by other white lines, concrete estates giving way to forests and then fields.

With the driver delivering a never-ending monologue about the weather, William kept nodding at regular intervals, his breathing growing steadily heavier as relief slowly sank in.

He'd made it. He was getting away from the city. And as he saw the lamps rushing past, shifting from dots to large discs, and then coalescing into great swathes, he knew that he was falling asleep.

31

As morning dawned on the fourth of December, snow covered the ground. It lay as a thin film of white reflecting Christmas illuminations and car headlights in sparkling dots, making the world seem quite a comforting place after all. If you didn't know better.

As Christina wandered through town, hands in pockets and eyes to the ground, she met the very last dregs making their way to work for the day. It was after ten, and the flows had begun to thin out, the pavements were slippery with snow compacted by thousands of morning feet.

The news room was only a fifteen-minute walk from the hospital, but she headed in the opposite direction. She couldn't go there, not yet. She couldn't face meeting them, answering all her colleagues' questions, receiving their sympathies. Or, worse still – if they didn't yet know about it – having to be the one to tell them.

Home? She didn't have one. What she needed to do now was to look up, force herself to go forward, and the mere thought of that bloody flat in Sollentuna made her gasp for breath as though she suddenly wasn't getting any oxygen. And over on Skeppargatan was an apartment she couldn't get into, whose keys she had posted through the letterbox, convinced that she would never want to return.

She headed down Fleminggatan instead, towards the city centre. When she got close to Central Station, she picked one of the hotels, checked in even though the lobby was full of people checking out, and got a room with huge soundproofed windows overlooking the street. She stood there for a long time without moving, watching people and buses and emergency services pass by in silence.

She wouldn't be able to sleep, but she was going to have a shower, try and eat, and maybe then she'd realise what she should be doing next. One step at a time.

As Mark Winslow jumped out of the taxi on Brompton Road, he reflected on the night before. He'd spent the latter part of the evening in his sparsely furnished flat, and the later it had become, the more he'd been haunted both by his heartburn and all the thoughts that always popped up in the darkness. When one had led to the other for long enough, he'd treated himself to a couple of sleeping pills and got into bed.

He'd dreamed sweaty, troubled dreams, because he always did. Thoughts floated through the fuzziness of the tablets colliding with each other, the same thoughts he had when he was awake, only now in a single, feverish column. And then, as the night went on, the dreams had started to be about his dad.

They did that sometimes. Always when he was stressed, when he was feeling insecure, never helping the least. Each time they would wake him up with a feeling of emptiness that was actually just phantom pain, a grief he had felt as a child but that he had swapped for something else along the way – for a fear that one day he was going to end up like him. That one day the stress and the worry would finally break Mark Winslow too, just as they had his father, and it all became a vicious circle that generally didn't start to ease off until long into the afternoon.

They said it wasn't hereditary. But how could he be sure?

When the taxi door slammed behind him, he hadn't been up more than forty minutes. Yet last night's dreams were already gone without a trace. Mark Winslow had more important things to worry about.

The first thing he'd noticed when he woke up were the unread text messages. He'd received twenty during the night, all from his boss, each one an increasingly irritated order to call him, *now, where the hell are you, ring me now!*

Winslow had leapt out of bed, rushed into the bathroom, and realised that on top of everything he'd overslept by two hours. Sleeping pills never failed. And as he was thinking about that the twenty-first text arrived. This time though, it wasn't from his boss. The text had been sent directly by one of the servers in the department, an automatic message. *Briefing 0900. Compulsory.*

Each detail added a new layer of burning sensations in his guts. *Briefing* – not a meeting. That meant something had happened. *Compulsory* meant that it was something big. And the time? Half an hour's notice for God's sake . . . ?

He'd thrown yesterday's clothes on and rushed onto the street for a cab, and when he'd finally got hold of one his phone had bleeped again. This time though, it was his boss. *Where the hell are you? We've had to start without you. We have a problem. H*

I'm in a cab, he wrote, before adding, *in traffic on Millbank*, as though it was somehow less embarrassing if he claimed to be closer than he actually was.

Outside, the traffic was crawling, inching forward in between long standstills, and with each passing second Winslow felt the heartburn building to a black, compelling strain. A weight settling on his shoulders, a nausea that sooner or later was going to explode. *Not hereditary? Are you sure about that?* He forced himself to stare out of the window, count cars, whatever.

It was going to take at least another twenty minutes to get to the ministry. The briefing, it seemed, was already under way. The only thing left to do was to close his eyes and relax, and he leaned back in his seat, told himself to at least try and listen to the radio. And soon he realised that without knowing it, he was getting the briefing anyway. North-west of London, the radio said, the A40 was closed in both directions, around RAF Northolt. An accident overnight was causing chaos in the rush-hour traffic.

'Something's going on,' said a voice from the front seat.

Winslow looked around, catching the driver's eye in the rear-view mirror.

'Believe you me,' he said. 'They're hiding something.'

'Who are "they"?' asked Winslow.

'Dunno. The authorities.'

'What makes you say that?'

The driver pointed at the radio. 'I came on duty last night,' he said. 'I live out that way. The road was already closed at one a.m., long bloody diversion. Accident? Do me a favour.'

'What was it then?'

'I saw the smoke. It was coming from the airbase.'

Mark Winslow asked the driver to stop. He passed him a note without even looking to see what denomination it was, then threw himself out onto the pavement of Brompton Road, along with all the other stressed people on their way somewhere. Moments later he was bent over an electricity box and vomiting, watching as the passers-by gave him as wide a berth as possible.

Twelve hours ago, he had suggested that John Patrick Trottier should head off to Stockholm. Now Winslow had twenty missed text messages from the Minister, a high-level briefing was under way at the MoD, and an accident had occurred at RAF Northolt. That was enough for him. And he stayed there, slumped against the box, feeling the aftershocks passing through his body.

As soon as he'd finished throwing up he was going to run all the way to the MoD on Whitehall and find out what the hell was going on.

32

They say that every man has his price, and the price of the Norwegian truck driver who spoke with a thick Western accent and smelled of service-station aftershave was five thousand krona and a handshake.

It was well past midnight when they were finally allowed to board the delayed boat at Nynäshamn. The big power cut had paralysed various systems for hours, said the driver. He was tired, hungry and irritable, but by taking the money he was at least getting *something* out of the fucking night, he'd thought to himself. And he wasn't even really expected to do anything in exchange.

He spent the night in one of the cabins, as usual. He got up as they entered Polish waters, had a quick shower and then put yesterday's clothes back on, and no one batted an eyelid when he bought two lots of breakfast in the truckers' lounge, one of which he took with him down to his wagon. No one asked why, and why should they? No one takes any notice of an extra coffee and a cheese roll.

Three hours later, he stopped at a petrol station outside Łódź. He filled up with diesel for the drive down to the Czech Republic, and stocked up on crisps and water in the shop. The last thing he did as he was leaving was to nod a greeting towards the man waiting in the queue for the toilets, who was looking even rougher than he had the night before – crumpled and bereft and carrying a little bag of newly bought toiletries in one hand. He blinked his response, nothing more, a greeting that said thank you and good morning all at once, and then the toilet door opened and he went in, locking the door behind him.

That was the last the Norwegian trucker saw of William Sandberg, the man who'd slept in his trailer and who'd paid him five thousand to not ask why.

Inside the stinking toilet, William pulled the thin door to and turned the lock. He looked in the mirror. It hadn't been twenty-four hours since he'd seen that same face in the bathroom mirror on Lidingövägen, yet the person behind it was far from the same. At that point he'd still been someone's father, and he hadn't yet gone on the run.

Now, life was a fevered dream. As though he was watching himself from a distance, kicking damp sheets, fighting the fears that would vanish just as soon as he finally woke up.

But there was nothing to wake up from. William Sandberg was suspected of aiding terrorists. He'd forced an ambulance off the road. And now he was in Poland after a night in the trailer of a Norwegian HGV. He'd lain all night, all morning, slipping in and out of sleep, shivering in the dark in between heavy crates, and woke up to the sound of the clunking diesel engines and the creaking of vehicles as the vessel pitched and yawed.

And all the time, he was trying to understand what Michal Piotrowski had to do with the attacks, and why the fuck he'd pulled William into it.

There was only one way to find out. William spat the last of the toothpaste into the stainless-steel sink, put on the dark grey baseball cap he'd chosen at the till, then left the petrol station without having shown his face to the cameras even once.

33

It was well past lunch by the time Christina finally left her room and wandered in to the closed dining room. The young wait-ress who she met on the other side of the partially closed doors explained with teacherly patience that it was much too late for breakfast. The buffet closed at ten thirty on weekdays, she informed her, and went on to explain that many other hotels finished their service earlier than that. Rules are rules, her hostess explained, and where would it end if anyone could come and ask for a sandwich at any time of day or night?

Then she'd seen something in Christina that changed her mind. Maybe it was her sad smile, her polite attempts to ask them to at least throw a plate together that she could take up to her room. Maybe her voice showed traces of having cried through the night. In the end, the girl smiled at her, a real smile. The touch of her hand on Christina's back as she led her to a table came as such a surprise that it almost burned, making her eyes swell up all over again.

She got a table at the far end of the room, laid all the newspapers she'd picked up from the lobby out in front of her, and then forced herself to do what she always did – read them all, carefully, from cover to cover. The paper editions were always first, those were the rules, and only when she'd read them was she allowed to get her phone out and see what was being reported online.

She felt that the news should be read in chronological order. If you read the newest stories first then you missed out on the getting there, the speculation and the distractions and the details that proved to be irrelevant, and without them there was no whole, and without being whole, news was just a series of detached headlines with no story.

Everything is connected, she thought to herself, and at that point Tetrapak's face popped into her head. His pleading, ravaged eyes. What was it he'd been trying to say? Her thoughts took over, and then performed that unavoidable circular manoeuvre she knew they would: Tetrapak got her thinking about the power cut, that made her think of Sara, and the thought of Sara caused a stabbing sensation in her gut, one of grief and emptiness.

For the first time in her life, she realised that she felt lonely. Or rather, it was bothering her for the first time. Friends, she and William used to say, are like children. They're fun to have sitting in your lap for a while, but then afterwards it's nice to hand them back and go home and listen to the quiet. And it had been a joke, of course, but it wasn't without a grain of truth at its core. Christina liked to be alone. Just not like this. Not this unjust, corrosive loneliness.

When the waitress returned, she did so with a truly impressive plate, groaning with cold cuts and several kinds of bread, fruit, a little bowl of herring, a big pot of coffee and 'If there's anything else you need just shout.'

And none of it seemed to taste of anything.

She forced her emotions to one side, put the papers down and got her phone out. Too early, but what the hell. She looked up the latest headlines on the screen. None of them mentioned her husband. Nothing hinting at any arrests, no suspects being questioned, no veiled statements about the police having conducted certain operations about which they weren't yet able to divulge details.

That was a good sign. Hopefully, it meant that he was still on the run.

The ambulance crash figured here and there, but no one made any connections with the power cut, it was just short and factual, the same dismissive assessment of newsworthiness that she herself had made. The events in Kaknäs Tower got predictably spectacular headlines – *Do you feel safe using lifts after this?* – but again, no connection between that and the power cut, or any suggestion that the same event might have caused both.

When it came to her own newspaper, it almost hurt. It was as though deep down she'd expected it to be empty, a result of the whole team being paralysed by her absence, and even as she realised how absurd that was, it ended up serving as an uncomfortable reminder: the world goes on without you. When you disappear, there's someone waiting to take your place.

The front page was dominated by the power cut. She'd had a hand in most of the headlines, but in the course of the small hours they'd gathered a few statements from public figures, politicians and press officers from the power companies, and none of it offered any new perspectives. They were all just repeating the same things. *A substation, a fire, an accident.*

She knew that Military High Command suspected some kind of sabotage. She also knew that there were foreign military personnel in Sweden, that whatever had happened was probably just a part of something bigger. What she didn't know was how it all fitted together. Sara, the CD, whatever she'd done at the internet café.

Or, what anything had to do with Per Einar Eriksen. He was the addressee on the envelope in the brown Nissan, and he was also the car's registered owner. Back at the paper, she'd found him on the Karolinska Institute's homepage – he was a professor of Neurology – but the only listed telephone number went straight to answerphone, which she couldn't help feeling confirmed her suspicions. If you fall thirty storeys down a lift shaft you don't do a lot of talking afterwards.

But most of all, what plagued her was the sticker on his rear windscreen. From the same conference that she and Sara and William had been tricked into attending. And say what you like about Tetrapak, but things bloody well did come together.

She finally turned her phone off, folded up the newspapers, pushed her plate to one side. She could see only one way forward. She had Eriksen's CD in her handbag, and somehow, she thought, it must hold the answer to what the hell was going on. The question was how she was going to find out.

As she stood up, nodded across the room to the waitress and made her way towards the lifts, her mind was already made up.

34

It was the smell of smoke that caught his attention. By then they'd been in the taxi for over an hour, and William had been able to follow their progress eastward along the dual carriageway on the satnav. The road seemed to go on for ever.

The petrol station had been on the outskirts of Łódź. He had stood on the slip road, waving to taxi drivers as they pulled in to fill up, and one by one they'd explained that they weren't interested in a hundred kilometre ride. Especially not to the destination on William's handwritten business card.

In the end though, he'd found one. The young, short-haired man smelt of pipe tobacco and was wearing cornflower blue plastic-rimmed glasses, and after some hesitation he'd accepted for a fixed price that was probably way too much. But what choice was there?

They had barely got on to the motorway before the questions started coming. What was William doing in Poland? Where did he come from? William's answers had been blunt and evasive, and he'd thought to himself that at this price, a driver who keeps quiet and gets on with the driving ought to be included.

Eventually the conversation petered out, and they'd continued in silence past the frozen fields, dense forest, and mile after mile of motorway rumbling beneath them. Several times, William caught himself doing sums in his head. He'd managed to take out twenty-five thousand, but by the time the Norwegian had helped him change money on the boat he'd already got through seven. Hopefully his biggest expenses were behind him, but the problem was that when the bundle of notes in his chest pocket was gone, he had no hope of getting hold of any more.

By the time the countryside finally began to give way to suburbs, the light was fading. They drove past homes and industrial buildings, some austere high-rise apartment blocks every bit as grey as the sky overhead, some vanity projects topped with the names of multinationals, oozing self-confidence and dripping with cash.

Once they'd crossed the river, the city lost its self-esteem. The buildings were lower, older, more decrepit. The brown, dying hulks stood in wilting rows, lining the streets as though they were long vegetable beds left to decay on their own. Instead, the graffiti seemed to prosper. Bigger, more violent, like another kind of life – a Technicolor weed that had been allowed to take over and spread to new sites when no one was there to keep it in check.

'Praga,' said the young man via the rear-view mirror. As though that explained everything.

William was sitting with his face to the side window, watching the neighbourhood pass by, trying to decide whether or not it scared him. Along the main drag were trams, shops and display windows, admittedly ones that were quite hard to see into, but yet the whole scene seemed to communicate a sense of everyday life, of ordinary people, of safety. Then again, these seemed to alternate with derelict lots, gaping holes with crumbling buildings, fences made of chicken wire and entrances that had been both boarded up and then broken into.

'You were the one who wanted to come here.' The shrug said the rest: *You do as you please. But you wouldn't catch me wandering about round here.*

William could see what he meant. He was just about to reply, when he smelled the smoke. It was like a camp fire in the rain, or someone trying to smoke a ham in a garden shed, and it spread inside the car, thick and very real and almost choking.

William instinctively reacted by sitting up straight. It was as though an entire orchestra of internal alarms were going off at the same time, and he looked around in suspicion. Was he over-reacting? Maybe. But then – given everything that he'd been through in the past twenty-four hours – how could he possibly determine what was paranoia and what wasn't?

'That's coming from my street,' he said. 'Isn't it?' The driver looked at him, confused. 'The smoke. It's coming from the address I gave you, right?'

The young man leaned over the wheel and turned his face upwards, surveying the sky over them. But there was nothing to see, it was just the smell, and he shrugged.

'We're almost there,' he said, with an intonation that told William that he'd find out soon enough. 'Ulica Brzeska, it's the next right.'

'Drive past it.'

The driver aimed his cornflower-blue specs at him via the mirror. In the back of his car was a stranger who had insisted on being driven to Warsaw, to an address east of the river, and even if people were saying that Praga was changing for the better, this was still a part of town that made him feel distinctly uneasy. And now, having got there, the passenger started giving him other instructions, and that did not feel good at all.

'Please,' William said from the back seat. It was all too much

170

of a coincidence to ignore it: everything that had happened, his suspicions about Piotrowski, and then a fire, right here – at his address? 'Keep straight on,' he said. 'Please.'

Perhaps it was the fear in William's voice that settled it. They'd just started slowing down to turn off, the driver's finger on the indicators, but all right then. At the last minute he carried straight on, shifted down to accelerate again, struggled with the gearstick for a second and then managed to get it into gear.

And while that struggle took place, the taxi rolled past Ulica Brzeska. For just a few seconds, William caught a glimpse of the street, the derelict houses on each side, the incident tape stretched right across the road, and the frontage over there that just seemed to be missing altogether. The air carried an acrid smell, like damp charcoal. A couple of fire engines were parked in the middle of the street, hoses winding up the black hump, mindlessly spraying their water like sprinklers on a charred golf course.

They carried straight on, and William let the taxi travel a few blocks without saying a word. Looked through the rear window time and time again, as though he was half expecting someone to emerge from an alleyway and follow him, someone that might have spotted him in the taxi and immediately understood who he was.

That was an overreaction, he said to himself. He was careful, not paranoid, and this was the wrong side of that line.

'This is okay,' he said, finally. 'I can jump out here.'

'*Here?*'

William nodded. Waited for the taxi to pull into the pavement and stop with its tyres in the deep puddles that lined the kerb.

'Do you know where we are?' the driver said once the car had come to a stop, looking at William over the seat back. 'Do you know where you're going?'

William shook his head. 'It'll be fine.'

'This is no place for tourists. Not at this hour.'

'I'm not here on holiday,' said William.

'They don't know that.'

They, he said, without emphasis, just a nod towards the rotting facades that surrounded them. William looked at him. Maybe he was right, maybe he was exaggerating, but either way William had no choice. He nodded his final thanks, opened the door, and climbed out into the street.

It was colder than he'd expected. It smelled like frost, and smoke from the fire, and then something else he couldn't put his finger on. Oil, maybe? Or exhausts? He looked around, trying to work out his next move, alone on the outskirts of a city he didn't know.

'Do you know if there's a hotel around here?' he said.

'Shall I not just drive you into town instead?'

'Just give me some suggestions,' William said. 'Preferably ones that take cash. And that don't mind too much who stays there.'

'If you stay around here they're all like that.'

'Thanks,' said William.

He turned around, started walking back the way they'd come.

'Hey?'

The taxi driver's voice. When William looked back he was sitting there with the window down, a look of hesitation while he finished his final negotiations with himself.

'I might be wrong,' he said. 'But I think you need these more than I do.' He rocked to his right, to give himself room to put his other arm out the window. William's notes in his hand.

He hesitated. The pride of paying your way on one hand, the knowledge that he needed everything he could get on the other. And the driver stayed there, not taking no for an answer, two round blue circles in an ever darker evening.

'If you're going to let me sit here waving a thousand-zloty note around in this part of town, then neither of us is going to have them for very long.'

William smiled. A surprising sensation, because he hadn't smiled in a very long time. Then he nodded a thank you, took the note, stuffed it in his pocket.

'Be careful,' said the specs, closed the window, and put the car in gear.

As soon as the sound of the taxi had died away, William walked back down the road, cautious steps in the dusky light. He passed countless broken brick frontages with boarded-up windows, pavements with no cars parked alongside, streets that stretched down towards dark alleys devoid of street lamps, people or signs of life.

Maybe the driver had been right. Maybe he shouldn't have stayed. But how would he find out then?

He stopped when he got to the street named Ulica Brzeska. Down there was the black hump, thin lines of smoke where the water from the firemen's hoses happened to fall onto something that was still smouldering. A few curious passers-by had gathered along the tape, young boys propped up against their handlebars, men leaning in doorways all down the street. William kept his distance. He'd seen all he needed to see. The rubble down there, between the brick-built firewalls, were all that remained of Michal Piotrowski's address.

And if the answers to William Sandberg's questions had ever been there, they had now ceased to exist.

35

The crisis meeting had been going on for over six hours, when Winslow was finally able to get down to the canteen in the basement of the MoD. He stocked up with a handful of Snickers and a sandwich packed in burglar-proof plastic, and wandered back down the echoing corridors, his hands gripping the snacks with a cramp-like intensity. the leather heels of his formal shoes clicked and echoed between the stone walls as he tried to collect his thoughts. An effort he knew was in vain.

They were alone now. It was, after all, Trottier who'd been the driving force, and now Winslow himself was going to have to give a summary of the situation. And to be perfectly frank – what did he know?

He'd just finished thinking that thought when he realised that Higgs was waiting for him by the lift. He'd sat pretty much opposite him in the meeting, yet they'd made eye contact only once or twice in all that time, invisible acknowledgements that they'd heard the same thing. Now he was standing there at the other end of the landing, black suit and a faultless grey-flecked hairstyle.

They stepped into the lift, waited for the doors to close, then waited again for the lift car to start moving.

'So nice that you could spare the time to come after all,' Defence Secretary Anthony Higgs said with the same well-enunciated vowels as ever. The caustic nature of his remarks was more in the delivery than in the words themselves, so aristocratic that every syllable felt like a slap across Winslow's face.

'I got your text message in the taxi,' said Winslow. Not that that really explained anything at all. But he had to say something.

'How is this even possible, Winslow?'

He didn't answer.

'Isn't this precisely the reason for Floodgate's existence, to avoid standing here with our trousers around our ankles, asking ourselves what on earth just happened?'

'We cannot talk about this, not *here* . . . '

'Are you worried that we might be being bugged? Because that would be frightfully ironic, would it not?'

Winslow said nothing. And the man who was his boss gave a great sigh, and shook his head, before continuing.

'Big brother isn't watching you, Winslow. Big brother is far too sensitive to public opinion. And now here we are without the faintest bloody idea what to do next.' The sarcasm was gone, replaced by a tired anxiety. *You are my adviser*, his eyes seemed to say. *So give me some advice.* 'They're going for *us* now. Straight for us.'

'We still haven't got the full analysis,' said Winslow. 'It was an attack, but it might not have been aimed at Trottier in particular. There's no reason to suspect that they know about the project, and even less reason to think that they might know who we are.'

Higgs sniggered audibly.

'How old are you, Winslow? Someone is trying to knock us out. And we don't know who.' He paused for a long time before he continued: 'This is worse than we ever imagined. We are not fighting any old terrorists. We are fighting terrorists who are fighting against us.'

When they emerged, the conversation was over, and without a word Winslow carried on down the corridor, a step behind Higgs as they headed for the meeting room.

His boss was right. This had gone too far. They had assumed that the attacks were not targeting them, nor their projects, but that the targets had been chosen because of their locations in coastal cities with important internet hubs. If the terrorists' aim was to cripple the internet, they had thought, then it was only natural that they identified the same places as they had themselves. But if Trottier's death was a deliberate attack on him, personally, on *them*, then it was conclusive evidence. It meant, in that case, that the terrorists knew about Floodgate – and now that it was ready to be deployed, those bastards had decided to stop it at all costs.

They paused just outside the room, sounds of scraping chairs and people gathering audible through the door. In a few hours' time, their external consultants would be back from Northolt. They would have examined the networks and gone through the logs, and on their return they'd be able to give a detailed account of how the attacks had proceeded.

Higgs leaned over towards Winslow. Lowered his voice to the point where it was almost inaudible.

'If it turns out that we're right,' he said – *we*, as though he didn't want to be solely responsible – 'if it was Trottier they were after, then we're not going to hold off any longer.'

36

It was the hotel's name that had William sold: 'New York'. In the early years of their relationship, hotel names like that had emerged as one of their standing jokes. Their photo albums contained dozens of pictures of entrances, ranging from the uninviting to the squalid, always featuring one of them posing in the doorway, attempting to keep a straight face but seldom succeeding. Hotel Budapest in Madrid. Hotel Cairo in Copenhagen. Hotel Hollywood in more cities than they could keep track of.

There was something almost touchingly embarrassing about it, having a hotel in one city but naming it after another, the awkwardness of pretending to be something they were not, as though Nuneaton might suddenly be filled with blooming bougainvillea and sun-ripened oranges if the town's hotel was called 'Sevilla'.

'It sounded like a good idea at the time,' they used to say to each other, and that became their catchphrase, applicable to pretty much everything. Not least, like themselves. Like their marriage. Like life.

When William walked into the claustrophobic lobby of the Hotel New York on the western edge of Warsaw, he was cold, hungry, and more exhausted than he could remember ever having been before. It was seven in the evening, and apart from the watery coffee and the tasteless cheese roll that the lorry driver had given him on the ferry, all he'd had was a bottle of water that he'd bought in a grotty corner shop close to Piotrowski's fire-ravaged apartment. He'd spent the rest of the afternoon walking down ever darker streets, accompanied by the feeling that someone had opened a secret door from the friendly Warsaw he remembered and shown him out into something much more sinister.

He was surrounded by buildings that spooked him, and the derelict plots in between them scared him even more. He walked past buildings that had survived both hot and cold wars, brick frontages that had once boasted both colour and render but which now seemed to be shedding their skins, buildings left to die alone with pigeons as their only occupants.

On an enormous derelict plot, he found a flea market with no customers, and just as it was about to close he'd got himself a new outfit. He bought a shirt, a pair of shoes and a dark blue suit that made him look like a bus driver, and managed to pick up a SIM card and a mobile phone that claimed to be smart but was doing a great job of hiding it.

Once darkness had fallen and he was sure that no one could see him, he finally allowed himself to walk into Hotel New York's lobby. It was as tiny as he'd thought it would be, a narrow, loveless room with a reception desk built into one of the walls and a group of odd armchairs squeezed together in front of the worn-out lift door at the far end. Half the desk was taken up with a computer – verging on the antique but clearly still working – and in the corner near the stairs an old TV set dutifully displayed some kind of slide show. Low-res text slides displaying prices and special offers alternated with photos of Manhattan by night which clearly hadn't been updated in more than a decade. And then, last in the loop, up popped—

Shit. A CCTV overview of the lobby. There was a camera here somewhere, its pictures spliced into the rest of the slideshow to remind uninvited guests that they'd been caught on film, and now he saw himself in that picture, alone by the unmanned reception, almost in profile, and filmed from above.

He turned around slowly, a discreet rotation, until the TV version of himself was standing chest-on to the camera. Where was it? He twisted his body without taking his eye off the screen. There it was: attached to the ceiling, midway between a smoke alarm and something that might have been a wiring block for the hotel's wifi network, was a spherical, nicotine-stained webcam, a single dark eye staring at him.

This was really bad. Sure, common sense was telling him that the risk of anyone finding him now was pretty much non-existent. They were probably yet to realise that he'd skipped the country, and even if they'd got that far, there were thousands and thousands of cameras to trawl through before they got to this one. Despite that, he still found himself standing on the thick, damp carpet, negotiating with himself while the CCTV image disappeared and the loop played again, prices, special offers, New York. Should he leave? Should he pick somewhere else?

On the other hand, perhaps what he was really looking for was a kind of hotel that no longer existed, and that he wouldn't find no matter how far off the beaten track he ventured. The sort that only existed in seventies films, brown and analogue and where no one asked any questions. Plus, the damage was already done, and he didn't really fancy heading back out into the dark, to wander threatening streets until he found something else.

From the little office behind reception came the sound of somebody putting down their cutlery and a chair being pushed back, and finally a man of about William's age materialised in front of him. Chewing gum-white shirt, tired eyes, a napkin with which he was wiping food from the corners of his mouth.

He let William check in as Karl Axel Söderbladh without demanding his passport – Karl Axel because it was the first name that popped into his head, and Söderbladh in order to be able to make a big deal of how to spell it and where to put the dots, too ludicrous to seem made up on the spot – and the receptionist typed in his details, slowly, using the index finger of one hand. Throughout the procedure he continued to chew the meal which William had obviously interrupted.

And with each passing minute, William felt the tiredness catching up with him. He wanted a shower, sleep, food, probably in that order, and if he could just get that then he'd find a way to keep going – that, at least, was what he told himself.

Finally, the receptionist finished stabbing his way through the boxes on his screen, completing the process by handing over a well-worn keycard – once again rather more modern than William had imagined – and then pointing towards the lift and explaining that 407 was on the fourth floor and that breakfast was neither offered nor included.

William thanked him politely, and got into the tiny lift. Standing there in the claustrophobic space, beginning his vibrating ascent, he could feel himself breathe out for the first time in more than twenty-four hours.

No one can be in two places at once. But if they could, they might have been in the lobby of Hotel New York, watching the bovine receptionist shuffle his last bits of paper into a pile as

William Sandberg stepped into the lift and vanished behind the doors.

And at the same time, that person could also have been on the other side of the river, in the Police Headquarters in Mokotow, down town Warsaw. Seeing the exact same thing.

The flowers on Inspector Sebastian Wojda's desk were wilting, but somehow the greyer they became, the better they seemed to fit into their surroundings.

A week had passed since he'd celebrated his fortieth birthday, or rather since he'd tried to avoid doing so, and since his colleagues had refused to let him off the hook. It wasn't because he had anything against birthdays. What he didn't like was people trying to turn the office into something it wasn't, people in ties and with titles trying to pretend to be your friend, standing around between desks eating puff pastry and whipped cream off paper plates. But he also knew that deep down it meant that he was well liked, which made running his team that much easier. He was too old to be inexperienced, too young to have stopped caring, and most of the other middle-managers in the organisation were firmly in one of those camps. Many, miraculously, belonged to both at the same time.

Now, though, the crowd around Wojda had gathered for entirely different reasons. In the middle of his desk were two flat-screen monitors, and behind his chair, everyone's eyes shifted back and forth between the two.

On the left-hand screen was the word *wanted* in light-blue lower case. Underneath was a photo of a man they'd never seen. His face was haggard, his tired eyes staring directly into theirs, his head tilted as though he was looking straight into a wall-mounted CCTV camera.

And no one can be in two places at once. But this came pretty close.

On the right-hand screen was a completely different image: a narrow, dated lobby, in a hotel that was called New York even though it was only across the river. In that image, a man was just stepping into a lift. And that was the very same man as the one on the monitor to the left.

37

The call was still ringing in Velander's ears as he ran down the stairs of Armed Forces HQ, along the long corridor with all the toilets and meeting rooms, the smell of fried food getting stronger and stronger as he got closer to the canteen. It was evening. In the cafeteria dinner was almost over, and at one of the long tables Palmgren was sitting on his own, hunched over his tray, the contents of which were remarkably similar to lunch, albeit with a different sauce.

Velander stopped in front of him, doing his best to conceal his shortness of breath, and asked if it was okay to sit down. Palmgren nodded towards the chair. 'Has something happened?'

'I just had a call from the police,' Velander said. 'The regular police, from the Big Place on Kungsholmen. They'd had a request from Poland.' He sat down opposite Palmgren, paused before he went on. 'Just one thing, before I start. If I sound all over the place, its nothing compared to the guy who called me.'

'Poland?' Palmgren said to keep things moving.

'Yes. The guy who called me had had a call from Polish police, telling him that they had a match on a Swedish citizen on Interpol's register. A CCTV camera in a hotel. A name they'd never heard of.'

'And?' said Palmgren.

'That's what I said: And? What name is that? The policeman went on to tell me that he didn't know either, and that's what was so strange – don't look at me like that, Palmgren, I understood just as much as you do now – and in the end I said to him, you know what? Never mind, just tell me why you're calling Swedish Armed Forces HQ about this.'

Velander put a ring binder on the table.

'Here it is. The abridged version. The Polish cop and the

Swedish cop were talking at cross purposes for quite a while. In the end the Swede gave up and asked the Pole to fax over whatever they had.' Velander leant in. 'That's why they rang. Because they recognised him from last night.'

'Recognised who?'

'Who do you think?'

Velander hesitated, but left his hand resting on the file. Watched his boss push his half-eaten dinner to one side.

'Where is he?' said Palmgren. 'Please don't tell me he's in Warsaw.'

Velander raised his eyebrows – *'fraid so*. Palmgren leaned back and slumped with a great despondent sigh, a blow-up toy with a slow puncture.

'I wonder if he didn't make the wrong decision after all,' he said eventually. 'I wonder if he shouldn't have told us what he knew, helped us to help him, instead of turning up like this in the last place he should be thinking about being right now.'

'Do you think anyone would've listened?'

Palmgren rolled his head. *True.* 'It just makes it so much harder to defend him when everything he does looks like evidence that he is involved. How can Forester come to any other conclusion than that he's there to meet whoever was supposed to show up at Central Station.'

Velander nodded and hesitated before continuing.

'Palmgren . . . if I'm allowed an opinion? There are two completely different questions that are much more pressing.'

'And what might they be?'

'One. Who's put William Sandberg on Interpol's most wanted list?'

'Forester?'

Velander shook his head.

'Well, in that case, who?'

'No one.'

'What do you mean no one?'

'No one here has put out a call about William,' said Velander. 'I've asked Forester, and no one else has taken it upon themselves. Stockholm police have been acting strictly and solely as our support. It wasn't them either.'

Palmgren shook his head.

'I don't get it,' he said. 'Someone must have. Who, other than us, wants to see him caught? Who even knows who William Sandberg is?'

'Question number two is precisely that.' Velander took a deep breath, choosing his words before continuing. 'The guy who called from the police? It took me a while to work out what he was talking about. Because, language barrier or not, how could he not understand it was William that the Poles had found? Why did he say that they'd *recognised him from the picture*?'

Palmgren shut his eyes.

'I'm not even sure what question you're asking.'

'I know. It's one of those that don't seem to make sense until you know the answer.'

For a moment, Palmgren looked impossibly tired.

'Can we maybe start from that end of things, then?'

Velander opened the file that was lying in front of him, passing the sheet of paper over to Palmgren without a word.

'What is this?' Palmgren said eventually.

'This is the material sent over by the Polish police. The search instruction that got them to act. I then got it faxed over from the police on Kungsholmen.'

For a long time, Palmgren sat completely still without doing anything at all. The only things moving were his eyes as they flitted around the page, the title, the text, making the same journey across the paper again and again.

There was no room for interpretation. The photo was of William Sandberg, no one else, and he was wearing the same clothes he'd been wearing when they parted company almost twenty-four hours earlier. The problem was the rest of it. Suddenly he understood what Velander had meant. Why the police had had such trouble communicating. Why the Swedes hadn't reacted until they saw the actual image.

'How the bloody hell can he be on the wanted list under another name?' he said.

Velander said nothing.

'Where's the picture from? Who's given Interpol this material?'

'Well, as I said. As far as I know, no one.'

Palmgren looked him in the eye. Then finally, got to his feet, carried his tray to the kitchen and emptied the plate straight into the waste bag. He walked the long corridor in silence, Velander at his side, a printout of the Interpol search details in his hand. In his head, he was going over the same question, time and time again.

Who the hell is Karl Axel Söderbladh?

38

The best thing you could say about room 407 at the Hotel New York in Warsaw was that it was yellow.

It was partly intentional. Everything from the carpet to the bedspread was a warm, dirty golden beige colour, and dotted around the place were shiny golden lamp fittings that were as much real gold as William was Karl Axel Söderbladh. But mostly, the yellowness had occurred by itself. The sheets must have been white to begin with, and judging by the tones in the pleats, the curtains had once been a shade of red. Over the years, sun and nicotine and exhaust fumes had managed to pull all the other colours towards a yellow centre.

Surrounded by all that yellow, William Sandberg pulled off his wet clothes. He let them fall to the floor, climbed into the shower and turned the heat up to maximum. He stood there for ages without moving, without thinking, scalding hot water on ice-cold skin. When he'd finished, he tipped clothes he'd bought from the flea market out of their bag and onto the bed. He looked at himself in the tall, narrow mirror behind the desk.

The glass was steamed up from the hot shower. Despite that, he'd never seen himself look so old. His own face was looking back at him, drooping as it might do after a trip to the dentist: numb, lifeless. There were a thousand questions to get to work on, but how would he find the energy to ask them?

He stood like that when the insight hit him. It came as a sharp talon, penetrating all the fuzzy layers of fatigue, and in an instant he was wide awake, looking carefully around him. He'd seen something. What, he didn't know, just that something had caught his attention, and left him with a sensation that something was out of place. Letters? A word? A sign?

He moved, slowly, tried to recall which way he'd been facing when the thought first struck him.

On the desk was a brass sign, the symbol on which seemed to suggest that smoking was prohibited – even if the smell in the room indicated that he might've been the first to decipher its meaning – and over by the door another, plastic sign with green fluorescent edges and text that had to mean emergency exit.

What else could he have seen? He scanned the room slowly, turning his body as he looked. When he finally saw it again, it was in the blotchy mirror behind the bed. It was indeed a word, and it was shining right out at him, a mirror image, blurred by the steam from the shower and *how the fuck . . .*?

He turned around.

There, at the far end of the desk, was an old fourteen-inch television. The flickering text had been on the screen since he came in, the same meaningless welcome message as in pretty much every other hotel on the planet, rectangular letters in the same yellowish hues as the rest of the room. Four short lines of text. The hotel's name. The date. And the standard welcome message, the one that's supposed to make the occupant feel remembered and special and *look, they remembered my name!*

Välkommen, it said in Swedish.

We wish you a pleasant stay, Mr Amberlangs.

When Christina walked out of the lift and into the editorial meeting she was greeted with everything she'd been afraid of. All around, people stopped what they were doing, conversations turned to careful whispers, tilted heads looked for eye contact to signal their empathy.

On a normal day, she would have been bombarded with questions. Now though, it was as if her professional role had disappeared, and out of nowhere came the feeling of walking past

184

a building site in a summer dress, of being undressed by the eyes following her through the newsroom – the same feeling of nakedness.

The glass doors to her office had to act as her shelter, and she hung up her coat, turned the computer on, perched on the edge of her chair as she set about going through the piles of paper, forcing herself to pretend that everything was normal.

'I know you don't want to talk.'

Beatrice's voice came from the doorway. She was standing there, a bundle of lurid textiles against the doorframe, radiating friendship.

'So I thought I'd bring us both a cup of coffee and sit here for a bit and moan about the fact that the printers have managed to screw up the layout in half of today's edition. They've made my pictures from the power cut look a lot like what a drunk person might see when they close their eyes.'

To her surprise, Christina felt herself smiling, and Beatrice sat down, placing Christina's cup in the middle of the table.

'And then, after a while, when we've had a bit of a chat, I was thinking I'd ask you whether you should really be here today.'

Christina shrugged. For a long time they sat there without talking to each other, and in a weird way that was exactly what was needed. After minutes had passed, and coffees finished, Christina marked it with a deep sigh.

'I'll have a stern word with the printers,' she said, as though that had been at the heart of their silence. But the smile hidden away in the corners of her eyes said something else – it said *thanks*, thanks for coming and sitting down, thanks for a bit of company that didn't need to be about words.

Beatrice stopped in the doorway on her way out.

'I've still got the keys to the Volvo if you want me to drive you anywhere.'

'Thanks. But I'm okay. If I do need to get anywhere I can drive myself.'

Beatrice shook her head.

'Not as long as I've got the keys you can't.'

'Get out of here before I give you the sack,' Christina said without meaning it at all. And with that, a ringing phone cut short their conversation. 'I'm serious. I've got work to do. You should try it some time.'

She gave Beatrice a nod of dismissal, picked the phone up off the desk, and immediately felt her smile vanish.

'I'm sorry, Beatrice. I really have to take this.'

Once Beatrice had closed the door behind her, Christina pressed to answer the call, hoping it hadn't already rung.

'Has something happened?' she said without any greeting or introduction.

'I can't talk for long,' Palmgren said at the other end, also dispensing with the formalities. 'But I want you to know, William's in Warsaw.'

'Is he safe?' she heard herself ask.

'I am afraid he might not be. The Polish police are preparing an arrest raid right now.'

It took a moment for her to grasp what he was saying.

'The Polish police? Why?'

'Well this is the thing,' Palmgren replied. 'Have you got a computer there?'

Everyone makes mistakes. That's what Inspector Sebastian Wojda told himself as he sat in the back of the dark blue incident van. Around him were banks of screens and instrument panels, manned by operators with headsets and keyboards, all of them waiting for his order.

Everyone makes mistakes, even the most accomplished criminals, even the ones who have managed to stay on the run for years. And a good cop is a lucky cop. More arrests than you would care to imagine only happen thanks to such mistakes being uncovered, and today he'd had luck on his side. All he needed to do now was concentrate on the job in hand, not query how it had happened.

'Status report?' he asked, just for the sake of saying something.

'We've seen the target pass the window a number of times,' said a young female operator, her blonde hair scraped back under the headphones and exploding into a curly inferno on the other side of the band. 'The ceiling light is still on, everything points to him still being in the room.'

It had all happened extremely quickly, and on the street ahead of him the vans were lined up ready for the raid. In each vehicle were six armed men wearing body armour. Yet he was far from happy. It wouldn't take much for the situation to escalate, and despite having received direct orders not to kill their target, he was worried about what might happen. Asking people questions is markedly more difficult if you shoot them dead first. And questions were one thing Sebastian Wojda had plenty of.

He had never heard of Karl Axel Söderbladh. The computer had delivered its verdict though: someone by that name had checked into a hotel in north Warsaw, and that had caused the system to react. Both the photo and the name were one hundred per cent matches with Interpol's list, and now, less than half an hour later, the operation was in full swing. Yet something about it all didn't feel right.

Never mind the fact that Wojda had never heard of the guy. There were hundreds of faces on Interpol's list of wanted fugitives, and even if international crime had been his remit he still wouldn't have been able to keep tabs on all of them. And disregard his never having heard about a Swedish citizen being on the list. Perhaps he'd just missed that. What troubled him though was the idea that a wanted international criminal would check into a hotel under his real name. And do so after going to the trouble of finding an anonymous, old-fashioned hotel in a corner of the city where nobody spent the night if they had a choice. Why would he do that?

It didn't add up. But everyone, including the most hardened criminal, makes mistakes, and often it's a silly error that ultimately brings them down. With that thought echoing around his brain Wojda nodded at the blonde mop.

'Let's go.'

William yanked the TV away from the wall, tugging out the aerial and then the power cable until the screen went black and the hum of the old cathode-ray tube finally disappeared.

It was classic displacement activity, he knew. The television wasn't his enemy, and unplugging it wasn't going to help. The problem was that someone knew he was there, and as if that wasn't bad enough, someone who knew about the word *amberlangs*, and he stood, hands trembling, trying to calm down.

Who the hell are you, he wanted to scream. *What do you want and why are you doing this to me?*

They had found out that he was in Warsaw, but how? His credit cards were in Sweden, he'd never got his phone back, there was no way that he'd left a digital trail behind him since getting in that taxi outside Central Station. They simply could not know that he was here. And yet they did, and that was all that mattered: however they'd managed it, whoever they were, however much he just wanted to lie down and go to sleep, that window had now closed. He pulled on the new suit and jacket, as well as the dark grey baseball cap from the petrol station, doing up buttons with stressed fingers, untying shoelaces on the new, hard shoes to push his feet into them—

When the telephone on the bedside table gave a shrill, electronic ring, the whole world stopped moving.

He sat completely still on the edge of the bed, letting his eyes wander around the room, panning past the mirrors on either wall, seeing them reflected in each other and producing long rows of William Sandberg on long rows of beds, sitting in perfect formation and disappearing into a yellow infinity. Where they watching him right now? Was there someone on the other side of the mirror?

The silence when the ringing stopped was even more unsettling than before. And after a moment he stood up and walked towards the telephone, knowing it was going to ring again.

He looked over at the door. It was locked. Door chain on. Looked at the window. Through the dirty pane, towards the building sitting in darkness on the other side of the road – was that where they were?

When the phone did ring again William was so prepared that he had the receiver to his ear before the first ring had died away. He said nothing, just listened without breathing.

'Karl Axel Söderbladh?' said a female voice on the other end.

She didn't say any more than that, English pronunciation in a Polish accent. William swallowed hard.

'I'm sorry,' he said, in English. 'I think you've got the wrong number . . .'

'I know you must have questions,' the voice interrupted before he'd finished speaking. 'But you don't have much time.'

'Time for what?' He tried to sound stern, but didn't really pull it off.

'To escape.'

The words sent another shiver through him. What was this? Help? Or a trap?

'I don't know who you are,' he said. 'But I don't intend to . . .'

She interrupted him again: 'Go to the window.'

That was so daft that he heard himself snigger.

'Sure. Anything else I can do for you? Put my fingers in the electricity socket perhaps?'

On the other end, the woman took a breath to interrupt him, but William hadn't finished.

'Is it okay if I keep this shirt on, or should I put one printed with concentric circles on so it's a bit easier to aim?'

'Are you done?' the woman shouted. 'There are two vans parked at either end of the block. Three men have left one of them, all in body armour and carrying automatic weapons. We can keep exchanging snide remarks all night if you want, but I thought you should probably know that first.'

William hesitated. He took one cautious step towards the window, aware of the fact that the main light was on, and stood pressed tight against the wall so he could peer out and down the street. All he could see was the pavement. Reflections in the puddles. Street lamps swaying in the wind and making the light dance, shadows growing and shrinking along the front of the buildings. No movement.

'What is it you'd like me to look at?' said William.

'The building opposite,' she said. 'There's an abandoned laun-derette on the ground floor.'

At first he didn't know what she meant. Away to the left, at the far end of the building, were two large windows, witness to the fact that this was an operation that hadn't been open in a long time. Behind blackened, dirty windows, some kind of metal objects, quite possibly washing machines, were just visible. Apart from that, the premises were dark and abandoned, and the letters spelling the name of the firm that had once adorned the panes of glass were peeling off and flapping in the wind. And so what?

He was just about to hiss at her when he saw something move.

He adjusted his eyes, squinting to focus as far into the building as he possibly could, until his depth perception finally got it.

The men lined up behind each other, their black gloves communicating with short, precise gestures, weren't actually inside the launderette at all. They were pressed against the wall of the building he was in – the woman on the phone had got him to see their reflections in the windows: three of them, another two emerging from the car behind, all wearing bullet-proof vests and dark clothes and with assault rifles in their hands.

'Who are you?' he said. 'How did you know I was here?'

'There's no time to talk,' she said down the phone. 'Whatever you do, don't go through the lobby. There are people on the other side of the building too, two of them are already on their way in.'

'And how do I know you're on my side?'

'Do what I am doing,' she said. 'Gamble.'

He hesitated, but didn't get the chance to answer.

'I'm sitting in a Mazda 323. A hundred metres beyond the launderette. My name is Rebecca Kowalczyk.'

39

This was the first time in her life that Christina had been on Interpol's website. Of course she'd known somewhere at the back of her mind that it existed, but now, actually looking at it, it was dizzyingly real. There she was, looking through a list of criminals – not just wanted, but *most* wanted – one of whom was her own husband.

But, and this was the weirdest part, it also wasn't him. Admittedly there was no denying it was William in the photo. He was haggard, almost as though it was a brand-new image, despite the date at the foot of the page indicating that it had been up there for months.

The rest of it though. The rest of it was bloody miles out. The name was Karl Axel Söderbladh. The date of birth was completely wrong, height was almost right but a couple of centimetres out, and country of birth was listed as Sweden, even though William's parents had met in England and that's where he'd spent the first few years of his life. It wasn't William. And yet it so blatantly was.

In the 'Wanted For' column it said simply *conspiracy to commit terrorism* without any further explanation, and on that basis action was under way which Palmgren had described as 'a major police operation'. A quick glance at Polish news sites revealed nothing, but of course that didn't necessarily mean anything. Maybe the major police operation had already taken place without the newspapers having got wind of it. Maybe preparations were still going on in secret.

Either way, she couldn't help feeling that William had been convicted in advance, and that it was largely his own fault. He'd run from the police. And now he was in—

She tried to sort the thoughts in her head. What was William doing in Warsaw? Somehow it had to mean that he'd drawn the same conclusions as she had. That he'd seen the threads all leading back to a particular occasion, five years before. To the Futurology conference, and the Palace of Culture and Science, and Piotrowski. Was this his doing? That didn't stack up. However much they were afraid of him, he was hardly capable of getting someone up on Interpol's must wanted list. And even *if* Michal Piotrowski had somehow managed that, why would he ever have used anything other than William's real name?

She leaned forward, flipping through the pile until she found what she was looking for. The yellow envelope from the car. The CD.

For a few short moments she just held it, weighing it in between her fingers, staring at the computer. She felt a pressing urge to stick it in the drive and see what was on it, but she knew she couldn't. However ludicrous it sounded, the theory was that Sara's CD had caused the great power cut, and it felt like bad idea for Christina to cause another. Instead, she dragged herself over to the keyboard and opened the newspaper's central address directory.

Two minutes later, when Christina put her coat on and headed back out into the open-plan office, Beatrice's desk was her first stop.

'You're right,' she said quietly.

Beatrice looked up from her enormous colour screen.

'The typesetting?'

'No. About me being here.'

Beatrice looked at her. Stood up, grabbed her coat from the back of her chair.

'I'll drive you home.'

'I'm not sure that's where I'm going,' said Christina.

'Well then, I'll drive you somewhere else. I can't let you drive, not on your own, not today.'

Christina sighed with gratitude and resentment. And then, after a quick glance at the desk, she took a slow, deep, breath. She sat on the edge of the table. Lowered her voice to a whisper.

'You know me,' she said. 'I'm not the type to go around broadcasting how I'm feeling inside. And I realise that it must be difficult, that you want to grab hold of me and forcibly comfort me and force me to talk. For my own sake.'

Beatrice said nothing.

'But that isn't what I need. Quite the opposite. I need to deal with my own thoughts. And I'm glad you're offering, but also, I know I need to a heal a little bit on my own first.'

Two seconds of silence. Then the smile.

'You're right,' said Beatrice. A warm, friendly tone that said *I know all that already.* 'I know you.'

Christina nodded. *Thanks.*

She stood up, mumbled something about hailing a cab, before

she noticed that Beatrice was blocking her route like a big colourful wall.

'The problem is that I don't care about what you need.'

Before Christina had the chance to do anything about it, she found herself in a warm, comforting hug that she couldn't escape. All she could do was to accept it, and once she had she realised she was holding on for dear life. They stood for a long time, comfort and warmth and a thousand other emotions.

'If you don't let go soon we're going to end up in the gossip columns,' Beatrice said into her shoulder, and Christina felt herself laugh, or perhaps cry, a single sound that could have been both.

'We're a tabloid newspaper,' Christina replied. 'No one believes anything we write anyway.'

When they'd finally let go of each other and dried their eyes, Christina smiled a last thanks and then trudged through the office, straight past all the pitying faces for the second time in half an hour. This time though, she met their eyes, muttered *a see you tomorrow*, and disappeared towards the lift and the exit.

As the doors closed around her she leaned against the wall and let her thoughts descend into calm. She was full of grief, had just lost her daughter, her life had been torn up by the roots. But in spite of it all, she still had a feeling that she was not alone. That was a feeling she could live with.

With that thought playing on her mind she stepped out in the garage, found the editorial team's light blue Volvo and unlocked it with the key she'd taken from Beatrice's desk.

40

The hotel corridor was a short, angled passage through the building. It had barely a handful of doors on each side, and under the worn-out carpets a rolling, creaking wooden floor screeched with each step taken across it. The wallpaper was slowly trying to free itself from the walls, brown and black stripes illuminated by lamps with a collection of light bulbs of varying wattages. In the middle of the fourth floor the corridors were met by the knackered lift, next to which was the narrow, dark stairwell, and next to which, in turn, stood William. Tense, not breathing, motionless in order to identify the sounds from the ground floor.

The woman on the phone had warned him at the very last minute. That was the good news. The bad news was that he was backed into a corner.

Behind him, the corridor ended abruptly in a narrow, metre-high window, streaky from the weather and dirt and screwed shut to make sure no one opened it. On the other hand, it wasn't a very tempting escape route. Four storeys below was a hard alleyway of tarmac and old junk, and the only way out from there would take him straight into the arms of the police he'd seen reflected in the window.

In the corridor on the other side of the stairs were a few more rooms, all of which were presumably closed and locked and equally dangerously far from the ground as the rest of the floor. At the far end, a brick wall marked the boundary with the neighbouring building, dark and damp and hidden behind a trolley full of dirty linen and cleaning equipment.

The only proper fire escape seemed to be the tight wooden staircase in front of him. From there though, he would be forced to enter the lobby, where presumably a number of black-clad men were already waiting to make their way up to his floor. That left him with only one option – the lift – which would be like wrapping yourself in a little brass and wooden packet and handing yourself over like a gift.

He leaned out into the stairwell, trying to see down through the shaft between the landings. Still no one on their way up, no shadows between the gaps in the banisters, no elbows swinging out as they rounded the turns. Chances were they were still planning their operation, confident that time was on their side. That gave him a head start. But what good was that if he had nowhere to go?

Reluctantly, he looked upwards. His room was on the top

floor, and the staircase led only downwards, but there was a trap-door above the staircase. It was madness. Fleeing upwards was like running into a cul-de-sac – in the end you can't go any further, and all you can do is wait to be found and arrested. Only an idiot would try and escape via the attic.

But there was no time to think of a better plan. He went out into the corridor again, pulling the laundry trolley behind him and out into the stairwell, feeling it wobbling as he clambered up. He found himself standing there, legs apart, above all the used sheets, with the trolley's flimsy mesh sides swinging under his feet. The hatch was heavier than he'd expected, and he had to push with all his strength, trying not to think about the deep stairwell in the middle.

When it finally succumbed, it did so in a cloud of dust and dirt that caused him to turn his face away, and that was enough to change his centre of gravity. Beneath his feet, he felt the trolley rolling off, inching out over the handrail like a clinking, unstable suicide, balancing on two wheels with William hovering above it.

A stairwell in Warsaw, he thought to himself. That will be how I die. In his mind's eye, he could see a dozen adrenalin-fuelled policemen rushing quietly up the stairs, weapons and vests and crouched steps, only to suddenly meet him going in the other direction, plunging down the shaft between them, a final farewell before it was all over.

Only he wasn't falling. He'd managed to grab hold of the edge of the hatch, a painful grip with his fingers in the corner, touching the floor of the attic, and he was hanging there, his legs dangling and his hands screaming in pain, but apparently still alive for a little while yet.

His feet fished after the trolley and pulled it back into place. He listened. Was it their voices he could hear? Above him the hatch was resting just over its opening, and beyond that, only darkness. A draft that smelled of damp and mould wafted through – an attic, as he'd hoped.

He hesitated again, another glance down the stairs, trying to work out how much time he had. They were going to come storming in at any moment, and only an idiot tries to escape via the attic. But then again, he thought, how were the men in the lobby to know that he wasn't?

For the sloth of a man on reception, it had all happened at once. He'd just managed to get back to his dinner when he heard the door opening again, and this time he just dropped his cutlery onto the table, a clatter of stainless steel that he hoped would be audible out at the desk, so that whoever it was might realise that you can't simply go waltzing into a hotel and expect assistance just because you feel like it.

But the moment he walked out, those thoughts disappeared. There were at least ten of them, maybe more, moving through the lobby wearing body armour and black jumpsuits.

Only one of them stood out. He was wearing a black bullet-proof vest over civilian clothes, and identified himself as Sergeant Wojda before explaining in an authoritative tone that they were looking for one of his guests. When he then passed him a photo that undoubtedly showed the man who had just checked in to room 407, the receptionist could feel his hands shaking. It must have taken twenty seconds for him to log in to the computer, another twenty to make a copy of the keycard, and then finally it was all done and the SWAT team were making their way up the stairs.

Room 407 was located down the corridor, almost at the far end. They fell into line, weapons drawn, ready for anything. According to the receptionist, the phone in the room was engaged, which hopefully meant that he was so deeply absorbed in conversation that he still had no idea they were there, but they weren't about to take that for granted. He might just as easily be waiting behind the door, perhaps even armed, and in that case they would have a single instruction. To neutralise the threat before he had time to neutralise them.

The commanding officer's name was Yazek Borowski. He was just over thirty, ninety kilos of pure muscle, and he now raised one hand, signalling to them to wait while he pushed the keycard towards the lock.

One last glimpse around the team. Then he barged the door open with his shoulder, and with that the silence was gone: Like a single black mass, they rushed into the room, weapons drawn, shouting testosterone-fuelled orders in English, things like *POLICE* and *HANDS ON YOUR HEAD* and *NOBODY MOVE*.

Nobody, however, had already left the room.

Forester was at her post in the JOC as Lars-Eric Palmgren approached her. She stood staring at the large projector screen in front of her and gave him only the briefest of glances before her attention returned to the moving images on the wall.

'Is this live?' he asked.

The entire screen was filled with shaky images from a room in which everyone was dressed in black. They moved with hulking resignation, just as lost and directionless as the camera itself.

'The Operational Commander is wearing a bodycam,' Forester said by way of an answer. 'And no, there's nothing wrong with the camera, I've already checked. The room *is* that yellow.'

The raid had proved to be a failure. The screen showed the black-clad SWAT team wandering around opening wardrobes, pulling back curtains, disappearing from view and being replaced by someone else, who in turn opened the same wardrobe and tugged the same curtains. Tall, low-resolution shadows.

'So they missed him again?' said Palmgren, with what almost sounded like relief. Forester gave him a quizzical look.

'I have a confession to make,' she said after a while. 'I may have had suspicions that he was at your place. I may have suspected that you were helping him. I apologise for that.'

He said nothing.

'At least for the first part. I mean, he's obviously not hanging out at your place, is he?'

When he looked at her she gave him a wry smile.

'It's funny though, how things transpire. I can't help thinking that maybe William Sandberg would've been sitting on that bed watching television, if only Velander hadn't gone down and told you about the call from Poland.'

'You think I warned him?' Palmgren barked in a whisper.

She responded with a raised eyebrow.

'I had no idea he was in Warsaw,' he said. 'It was only when Velander told me. I'm as surprised as you are.'

'That's strange. You see, I'm not the least bit surprised.' Her expression hardened. 'To me, it's just proof that I was right all along.'

He grunted.

'Palmgren?' Forester said. 'Would you play a game with me?'

Not really. No.

'It's like this,' she said. 'You are an innocent man. Absolutely, completely innocent. Then one day, you happen to be in the wrong place at the wrong time, and that's where you end up being suspected of a sabotage that you have nothing to do with. Are you with me so far?'

Palmgren kept quiet.

'Later that evening you format all your hard drives. Crash an ambulance so that you can escape. Then turn up in – of all places – Warsaw. Tell my why you'd do that?'

Palmgren shook his head and flung out his hands in frustration.

'What do you want me to say, Forester?'

'Just give me a scenario. Anything at all.'

'I don't know! I don't understand it either.' He rubbed his forehead, wanting to defend him, but not knowing how. 'Someone is trying to set him up,' he said eventually. 'There's no other explanation. Why else would he be on Interpol's list? With the wrong name, wrong details, wrong everything?'

She didn't answer.

'There might be a thousand reasons for him being in Poland,' he said. 'Just because we don't know what they are doesn't mean that he's guilty.'

'I'll give you another scenario.' She looked at him with her dark, dark eyes. 'Maybe you're the one who's got this wrong. Maybe you're the one being duped, and the guy who you've played tennis and drunk beer with for thirty years was actually cultivating you as his alibi. The guy who has known all along that one day, at some point in the future, he'll show the world what he's capable of.'

That was too bizarre to even answer. So Palmgren made a noise that expressed complete disdain.

'You're telling me you know the guy,' she said. 'All I'm saying is, how can you be sure?'

He couldn't take any more, turning to face the screen instead, watching the moving pictures of policemen squeezing past each other.

'William Sandberg is not a terrorist. That's all I'm going to say.'

'I very much hope that you're wrong about that,' she said. 'Because that's what they will treat him as when they get hold of him.'

Sebastian Wojda ran up the stairs, his teeth gritted so hard that he could hear them squeaking.

'For fuck's sake,' he spat into the radio as he ran. 'For fuck's sake secure the other rooms, he can't have got far.'

According to the painfully slow receptionist down there, the man in the photo positively hadn't left before they arrived, absolutely not, and even if Wojda wasn't sure that alertness was one of the receptionist's strengths, both the stairs and lifts were accessed from directly outside his office. Even for someone with a pulse one notch up from being dead, it shouldn't be too difficult to tell whether or not he had passed this way.

Yet the fact remained that the man they were after was not in his room. And, as Sebastian Wojda ran up the stairs, he was accompanied by a nagging anxiety that someone had warned him.

'How come everyone is so anxious to talk to him?'

That was the first thing the receptionist had said after the SWAT team had disappeared into the stairwell, and it had taken a couple of seconds for Wojda to realise what he'd just heard. He'd turned around, studied the old man's eyes, and had apparently done so forcefully enough to make the receptionist feel he had to elaborate.

The man they were looking for had arrived less than an hour before. He'd checked in under the name of Karl Axel Söder-something, gone up to his room, and not long afterwards a bald woman came in and asked who he was, politely thanked the receptionist, and left. That was everything he had to tell them, and there were a thousand questions waiting to be asked, but no time to do it.

Questions like why he let his guests check in without a passport. Or why he gave out the names of his guests to inquisitive women. But there's a time and a place for everything, Wojda realised, and even if Hotel New York merited another couple of visits from the police, that wasn't the important thing right now.

The important thing was who the hell that shaven-headed woman might be.

Wojda had just reached the corridor on the fourth floor when he suddenly spun on his heels. Slowly, steadily, he made his way back towards the top step, and then felt a calm spread through his body.

His eyes closed as he brought his radio to his mouth.

'We've got him,' he said. 'Fourth floor, the stairs, *now*.'

In front of him was a laundry trolley, neatly positioned in the corner as though casually abandoned. But being a police officer isn't about accepting everything you see: it's about questioning *why* you're seeing it. Why was there a laundry trolley at the top of the stairs when the lift was right next door?

Being a policeman is about being open-minded, about looking up.

And when he did, he saw the skewed hatch in the ceiling.

41

It took just seconds for the SWAT team to haul themselves up through the black hole and into the attic. It was freezing cold and completely dark, and it wasn't until one of them turned on the searchlight on the barrel of their weapon that they saw the space grow to its full length. The powerful white rays danced through the darkness like a light show.

The roof above them sloped down on both sides, bowed by

the weight of the roof tiles and dotted with large patches of black mould. Thick beams criss-crossed the space and every now and then the flutter of pigeon wings brought an instant reaction from the assembled torch beams – catching the poor bird in their sights before the police realised what it was they'd heard.

They continued between the piles of timber and boxes of junk put in storage, in a space that seemed to extend over the length of the entire building, constantly aware that their target could be hiding anywhere in the darkness. The thick planks creaked under their weight as they made their way forward. They crossed them like small bridges, linking damp piles of sawdust insulation, scattered in layers over thin ceiling boards that would collapse if anyone were to put their foot on them.

It was only the brick-built firewall at one end that stopped their progress. Above them was another hatch, out onto the roof, and their silent signals communicated the fact that the loft was empty and that the roof was the only remaining escape route.

They lifted themselves out onto the sloping roof, one by one. A dozen or so black silhouettes hunched over as they made their way across wet roof tiles, balancing their way past brick chimney stacks and forests of TV-antennas.

The very last man onto the roof was Sebastian Wojda. He stood next to the hatch and watched the operation from a distance, and as the police got further and further away, the realisation got closer and closer.

He wasn't a policeman who had luck on his side. He had been duped.

When he finally talked into his radio again, the listlessness in his voice made it disappear in the damp evening air, and when he realised that they hadn't heard him he repeated the order louder. 'Search the rooms!'

He saw the men on the roof around him stop moving. Hesitate. Then turn towards him.

'He's not here,' he said, and then, with a new vigour, as frustration converted into energy: 'We need reinforcements. We need people down on the street, in the courtyard – everywhere he might have been able to get to without getting himself killed. And we need them now.'

He heard the cars below receiving the order, and the blonde operator with the unruly hair promising to do what she could, and for a couple of long moments he just stood there, alone on a poorly constructed rooftop gangway in Praga. He could feel the collar of his nylon jacket flicking against his face in the icy wind, but it felt like he deserved it.

Only an idiot would try to escape via the roof. And Karl Axel Söder-something was nothing of the kind.

As Inspector Sebastian Wojda finally turned around, leaving the roof behind, he had no idea that he was being watched. The internal courtyard was dark and deep, and had no lighting whatsoever. The bottom was a rectangular space which had over the years been used as a junkyard for the businesses on the ground floor, a forgotten back yard where the only sound came from whirring fans and the occasional flutter as pigeons swapped places.

And William Sandberg's heartbeat.

He stood in a window recess leading to one of the rooms three floors down, completely still, waiting until he was absolutely certain that no one was left on the roof and that no one was about to return to it either.

He'd only managed to get down two flights when he heard the SWAT team leaving the lobby and heading up the stairs, and he'd pressed himself against the wall of the second-floor corridor as the policemen's footsteps rushed past out in the staircase. When the silence returned, he'd forced himself down another flight, and with his heart racing in his mouth he'd ducked into the corridor one floor up from street level.

The peephole in the door of room 106 had been the only one that wasn't completely dark. A little dot of warm light in the centre of the lens revealed that the lights were on inside, and he stopped, hoping that the person on the other side would be easily persuaded, and knocked on the door.

'Room service,' he'd said, overlooking the chance that this hotel might well not offer such a facility.

It had taken far too long for the dot of light to disappear—someone peering at him – and he'd smiled politely, hoping that the bus driver's jacket sticking out from underneath his windbreaker made him look vaguely official.

'It's about the telephone,' he said, in English, hearing his own words before he'd had the chance to think about them. Hadn't he just said he was room service? Why the hell had he changed his mind then and said that this was about something else?

After another couple of seconds, the door opened. The man inside was probably older than the building itself, and William smiled at him, already somewhat ashamed of what he was going to have to do. But what choice did he have? After a quick glimpse of the view from the window – facing into the courtyard, he could see that much, and even if it was a long way up, at least it wasn't a potentially lethal drop – he turned to the man and explained that he had to repair a telephone line and was going to need access to the gentleman's bathroom.

He felt the man's scepticism, well aware that it was justified. Couldn't he have said that he was fixing a pipe instead? Wouldn't that have been more logical? *Idiot.* He'd smiled politely for so long that he thought he was about to get cramp, and eventually the old man nodded, opened the bathroom door, and walked in ahead of William. It took only a couple of seconds to shut him in there, and then immediately push a chest of drawers in front of the door to prevent the man from escaping.

'I really am so very, very, sorry,' William called through the door, at the same time noticing an unexpected richness and variety in the old man's collection of swear words. 'I just need to get out of here. It's a very long story.'

Afterwards he'd proceeded to turn off all the lights, turned to face the door one last time, and promised that he would call reception as soon as he possibly could to tell them where the man was sitting.

And then he'd opened the window into the courtyard.

As the last of the policemen – the one wearing civilian clothes – made his way back through the hatch, William stood there in the window recess outside the old man's room and waited for another few seconds.

Across the yard was a property long since in disuse. According to the faded sign he'd seen on the street side, alcohol had once been sold around the clock, but today nothing was sold there, ever. The windows facing into the yard were boarded up with planks and plywood sheets. Some had buckled and curled because of the moisture, and he should be able to rip them off with no real resistance.

He was only going to get one chance, and he couldn't keep waiting for ever. He jumped down onto the tarmac with a much bigger thud than he had hoped, before sprinting past the junk over to the windows on the far side and wrestling with the rain-sodden plywood sheets that bent and twisted in his hands without coming loose.

Behind him, light after light came on as the police continued their search of the hotel. He knew that at any moment, someone might look out and see him, but he batted away that thought, concentrating instead on his task.

He could feel his cold fingertips being shredded against all the sharp edges. His own blood mixing with the acidic water from the wood. Then, finally, the rusty nails gave up.

Rebecca Kowalczyk was already sitting with the key in the ignition. She looked at her watch for the umpteenth time, drumming her hands on the steering wheel. *One more minute*, she thought to herself. She'd lost track of how many times she'd said that. *One more minute, then I'm out of here.*

She could still make out one of the riot vans in her rear-view mirror, sticking out of an alley a long way away, but no movement, no police, nothing. And then each time a minute passed, she gave him another one, because maybe it meant that they hadn't found him.

She couldn't just wait around indefinitely though. She didn't know who he was, or what he'd done. She wasn't even sure if she was doing the right thing. The only thing she did know was that somehow he had something to do with Michal, and that she had nothing left to lose.

She'd just turned the key and started the engine when there

204

was a knock on the window beside her. Dressed in a blue suit and a windcheater, clearly inadequate for the prevailing conditions, he looked like a haggard bus driver with bags under his eyes. Without saying a word she opened the central locking, waited for him to sit down, and pulled out from the kerb before he'd had the chance to put his belt on.

They drove in tense silence, watching the police riot vans shrinking in the rear-view mirror, expecting black-clad men with automatic weapons to rush onto the street at any moment, pointing guns in their direction. But nothing happened, and finally they turned a corner, past street after street, pulled out onto the tram lines and drove on in silence.

The first person to say anything ended up being her.

'I think maybe we should introduce ourselves.'

42

Rebecca Kowalczyk had recognised him straight away. She'd been standing by her window, looking without seeing, when she noticed that her unfocused gaze had zoomed in on a face she'd seen before. When it dawned on her just what she was looking at, the realisation sent a chilling shock right through her.

Him. There. But why?

She'd stood there, motionless, for ages. Observed him across the yard, just the other side of the burning pile of rubble that she herself had caused, a new view of the street that had emerged as the building collapsed. He had come no closer than the cordon on Ulica Brzeska, a reasonable distance from which to observe the glowing ruins that had once been her lover's home – no, her home. Theirs.

It was already late afternoon. She'd spent the night in the flat he'd bought her for nothing, the one with an entrance from one of the parallel streets which she always, without exception, headed for after work. Normally she would just pick up any post from the doormat before going back downstairs, out through the back door and across the yard to Michal's building, watchful as he had instructed.

Now that building was gone. Instead she made the bed that she hadn't slept in since it was put there, paced sleeplessly between pieces of furniture that were only there to give the impression that the flat was occupied, made tea because you have to have something inside you, and then let cup after cup go cold on the kitchen table.

She kept on being drawn to the window, watching the embers dancing in the darkness. When the dawn arrived and the feelings ought to have eased up they had carried on as before, brooding and painful, and she missed him terribly.

Then, in the end, *he'd* turned up. Less than twenty-four hours earlier she'd seen him on a blurry photo in her lover's apartment, shot from a distance as he left his home or got out of his car or laughing with a wife and a daughter. An envelope full of secret pictures, stuffed in the middle of their personal photo albums. Who was he? Friend or enemy?

She felt the grief turning into frustration – she had to know, but had no one left to ask, and deep down she knew that even if Michal had been there he would have shaken his head like he always did and explained that he couldn't tell her more than she already knew.

'For my own safety,' she hissed into nowhere, and only realised she'd done so out loud when she heard her own voice. 'Fuck you, Michal, you can go to hell!'

Twelve years of secrecy and furtive meetings, twelve years because he'd once had an accident. But times change, they change and you must be able to let go of the past. Michal Piotrowski though, could not. He just was who he was. And maybe all of this had proved him right.

She had eventually made up her mind. She'd grabbed a jacket from the back of a chair, run down the steps and to the front door, and rushed round the block to get out onto the street from the other direction. She stopped by the tape, on the other side of the firemen busily fighting the blaze, and stood there, hands deep in her pockets, just like him. She'd watched the glowing

206

embers and the water, just a curious neighbour, nothing more, and throughout she had kept an eye on the man with the cropped greying hair on the other side of the road.

Should she make contact? Should she leave it?

When he finally started to walk away, she had already decided to follow him. She ducked under the incident tape and flashed an apologetic smile towards the firemen as she mumbled something about living just over there, then swapped to the opposite pavement so that she could follow him more discreetly, and the further she followed him, the more convinced she became: he was scared.

He was making the same kind of sudden decisions as she had been taught to make. Piotrowski had shown her how to avoid being followed, how you stop and head back the way you came, and now the grey-haired man was doing just that. At various points she had to let him out of her sight so as to avoid being discovered, but she knew the area and was able to choose an alternative route each time, then rejoin his, invisibly and at a safe distance.

From Targowa he'd turned off and gone into the market. He'd bought clothes and what looked like a mobile phone, before finally checking into a hotel that she'd often passed on her way home. Using all her charm, she'd managed to persuade the receptionist to give her the name of the man who had just checked in. He had eventually explained that the man came from Sweden, and his name was Söderbladh, Karl Axel.

Then she'd gone after her car, parked in a spot that gave her a view of the hotel, and asked herself what the hell to do now. Make contact? Lay low, keep shadowing him, find out who he was? Or just drop it altogether?

It took less than half an hour before the first van arrived. It pulled up around the corner, less than fifty metres from her own car. The men who emerged were dressed in black jumpsuits, bullet-proof vests with police emblems, and as they pressed themselves to the wall to avoid being seen from the hotel windows, Rebecca Kowalczyk realised that her mind was already made up. As she pulled out her phone and asked reception to put her through to Karl Axel Söderbladh, she hoped that she'd made the right choice.

Once Rebecca's story was done, they sat in silence for several minutes. She had stopped the car at the bottom of a gravel slope down by the river, on what seemed to be half sandy riverbank and half landfill site, and where big neglected shrubs hid them from almost every direction. They could see the water shining in the darkness, slight movements caused by eddies in the flow. They could see bridges spanning the river both upstream and downstream from their position. Their outlines blurred in the drizzle, and the odd siren blasted from far away, sometimes accompanied by a caravan of blue lights sweeping past over the water. Maybe they were looking for them, maybe not.

'So where is he now?' William finally said.

He looked at Rebecca's profile in the seat next to him. The smooth, almost circular silhouette of her shaven head.

'What is it that your fiancé is trying to achieve?'

He said it with a trembling, suppressed anger, and she shook her head evasively.

'He had pictures of you,' she said. 'Taken in secret.'

'I can imagine,' said William. Sat silent before changing the subject. 'I was contacted by Michal Piotrowski two weeks ago. Three emails, no sender, almost no content. Said he wanted to meet me, but never turned up.'

He gave her a summary: the emails, the arrest at Central Station. He told her about the power cut, the internet traffic, and how Swedish intelligence suspected him of being part of a terrorist network that was threatening to devastate the world electronically. And throughout, he maintained a tone that demanded explanations, as though the responsibility to make sense of it all had been passed over to her to her now that Piotrowski was unavailable.

Finally, he told her about the CD. That the girl in the internet café was his daughter, that she'd stolen the CD from him – and that this was something he still hadn't told his colleagues at HQ.

'I came here to find out why the hell he's dragged me into this,' he said. 'If he is gone now, it means that he's left me with this shit in my lap.'

'He didn't have a choice,' she hissed.

'And how do you know that?'

'Because I know him,' she said. 'Michal Piotrowski and I have been together for twelve years.'

There was accusation in her voice, and he waited her out.

'We don't have a favourite restaurant, because the whole time we've been together, we've never gone to the same place twice. We never book a table. We just happen to meet in the bar. We never leave together, never get in the same car. The only exception is when we're abroad, but never under our real names, and never without looking over our shoulders.'

For a brief moment she lost herself in the words, as though suddenly unsure which tense she should be using – 'see' or 'saw'?

'One other exception,' she went on. 'His apartment. He felt safe there, we could be ourselves, he could be sure that no one could see him there. And now it no longer exists.'

She closed her eyes.

'He fought against it, right to the end.'

'Against?'

'Against us.'

When she opened her eyes again, she did so with a sad smile.

'But there are some forces that are beyond our control.'

He said nothing.

'I like to compare it to life itself,' she said. 'Today I'm a biologist. Researcher in evolution, specialising in neurobiology. But the whole time I was growing up, I wanted life to be something special.'

'What do you mean by that?'

'What I'm saying. I wanted life to be something divine, something that could only occur here, on this Earth, because then it would mean something.'

William looked away quickly, anxious. And she noticed, and couldn't help smiling.

'No, not divine like that. I'm a biologist, not someone who believes the world was made in a week five thousand years ago.

209

But all the same, what I wanted deep down was for all these millions of years of evolution to be something unique and special and—'

She searched for the words but didn't find them.

'But life is stronger than that. Life doesn't need meaning. Everyone who's been in a lab knows what I'm talking about. However sterile you think you've made something, however inhospitable and uninhabitable – if you leave it alone for long enough, and happen to add just the tiniest prerequisite, the slightest contamination, then suddenly you come back to it and it's full of fungus and bacteria and—' She shrugged. 'And life.'

She looked at him.

'You don't control that. That's the only way I can explain it. Life wants to exist, so that's why it does. As soon as there's the slightest little opening.' She paused, and when she spoke again her voice was heavy with regret. 'It's the same with love. It shouldn't have happened, and yet it did.'

She shrugged again. Sat quietly behind the wheel for a long time.

'Why did he fight it?' William said eventually.

'Because he was scared.'

'Scared of what?'

From one moment to next, the conversation seemed to have changed. She turned the key in the ignition, still staring through the windscreen, her voice suddenly sharp as she answered.

'Scared that his past would catch up with him.'

With that, the headlights came on, followed by the sound of the engine.

'Even so,' he said to her profile. 'How has all this got anything to do with me?'

Instead of answering, she reversed the car out from the bushes. She steered it up the sandy bank and on towards the patched-up tarmac of the road above.

'Who is he afraid of? Why is someone after me? And how did they find out that I'm here?'

'I found you. Why wouldn't they be able to?'

'Because it's impossible,' he snorted back. 'I threw my phone away. I paid for the hotel in cash. I haven't left a single electronic fingerprint since I left Sweden!'

She drove along the river until the buildings fell away, becoming fewer and lower. They were already pulling onto the motorway by the time she finally took a deep breath.

'What if they don't even need that.'

43

As they left the motorway, the silence in the car was total. The city skyline had long since thinned out and gone, city had given way to suburb, residential areas to industrial estates, and then the darkness and the countryside took over completely. With the fields came the mist. Everything became blurred, the inky blackness ahead of them turned light grey in their headlights, and the only thing that told them they were moving was the constant stream of white lines.

Gradually, the lines became smaller. The road narrowed, surrounded by frozen fields on either side. Ahead, a huge, shapeless oscillation of light was growing sharper and clearer in the mist.

'I know what this is going to sound like.'

That was the first thing Rebecca had said for several minutes, and William waited for what was coming next, but she just sat staring straight ahead, not saying a word, making tiny adjustments with the wheel on the almost straight country road.

Slowly, the light ahead of them coalesced into a building, an enormous cigar of glass and steel that seemed to cut loose from the damp, illuminated by icy cold industrial floodlights.

'Have you heard of psychotronics?' she said after a long wait.

William stared at her.

'And here's me thinking *I'm* the one who's losing it,' he said.

He peered over at her, hoping for a smile, some kind of ironic grimace confirming that they were on the same page. There was none. When he eventually looked away he could feel the unease swelling in his chest.

What if they don't even need that?

'Of course I have heard of psychotronics,' he said after a long pause. 'And I've heard of MKUltra. Just like I've heard of the tooth fairy and Father Christmas.'

Rebecca still said nothing. He let his back sink into the seat, thoughts taking shape, thoughts he didn't want to think.

There were countless conspiracy theories about the Cold War. Psychotronics was just one of them. The superpowers of the day had been obsessed with two things, and those things had combined to eliminate all traces of rational thought. The first was to secure a position of superiority, regardless of the cost, and to never fall behind. The second was to constantly speculate about what projects the other side was engaged in.

A child could see how this would lead to a self-fulfilling rumour mill, but the world wasn't run by children but by middle-aged men, and the outcome was an ever greater fear of the other side's success. That in turn led to scientific research that no sensible person would ever have allowed to take place.

One of those projects was the CIA's MKUltra.

For long periods in the nineteen-fifties and sixties, huge sums had been ploughed into projects about telepathy, brainwashing and mind reading. In big futuristic laboratories, rows of earnest men in uniforms and white coats had stood behind one-way mirrors, and quite seriously observed the efforts of their subjects to telepathically communicate geometric shapes to one another.

In the East, the same thing had been known as psychotronics. And needless to say, it hadn't worked for them either. It hadn't worked because it was impossible, and when the race between East and West had finally run its course the projects had been shut down and classified, presumably more out of embarrassment at what they had been doing than to keep any progress secret.

With hindsight, it was silly, laughable, nothing more. It was pseudoscience, nonsense bred out of desperation in an era when science did not know what it does today. And yet—

'If you're trying to tell me that that's how they know I'm here,' William said, 'if you seriously believe that someone's been reading my thoughts . . . I don't think you'd like to read what I think of *that*.'

He let his gaze drift into the non-existent view ahead of

them. Felt his jaws tightening, because in spite of everything, there was still a little part of him that was already saying *what if*. Only he could have known about the email from Piotrowski. Only he could have known that he'd decided to head for Warsaw. And even he hadn't known that he was going to check in to the Hotel New York until the very moment that he did so.

Despite all of that, they had found him. Of all the millions of cameras in all the world they had happened to choose that one, a camera in a country where he shouldn't even be, and the chances of all that happening at random were so infinitesimally small that there had to be another explanation.

There was – and he didn't like it one bit.

'With all due respect,' he said, in a voice that contained nothing of the sort. 'With all fucking respect, that stuff is no more than sophisticated nonsense.'

Instead of replying, she took her foot off the gas, let the car slow down on the narrow road and waited for the turning that she knew was going to emerge from the mist.

The building. That's where they were heading. From up close, it looked like a solitary airship being born from the Earth's core, countless storeys of glass shooting straight up from the ground with countless tiny spotlights in all the countless offices inside. The large car park unfolding in front of them must have been thousands of square metres and yet not a single car was parked there. Undeterred, she continued across the deserted area, not stopping until she arrived in the far corner, a patch where the powerful industrial floodlights on their high masts could not quite reach.

She turned off the engine, and sat quietly as she tried to formulate her response. 'You're right. I'm not going to deny that. For three, four decades, a lot of stuff went on that with hindsight seems anything but sensible. Research driven by fear, superstition, fantasy. They were fumbling in the dark, because the dark was all there was to fumble in.' Again she shrugged her shoulders. 'But we've come a long way since then.'

'We?'

'That's right.'

She took the keys from the ignition, got out of the car and started walking into the darkness.

It was only once they got inside that William realised how big the building really was. Above them, the enormous lobby stretched upwards like a great column of nothing, a great atrium of air all the way up, at least thirty storeys, to a glass ceiling with the lead-grey night sky above it. The floors of the building wove around the atrium in loop after loop of curvaceous balcony, walkways that formed complete circles in front of the glass walls of offices which lay in darkness.

In the centre of the lobby was a reception desk, as round and clinical as everything else, made of white metal and glass, and with the names of the building's tenant companies etched into steel plaques behind it. It was divided into two semicircles, and on the floor between them were two unoccupied workstations. The lights were off, the computer and TV screens flickering to themselves, alone and without an audience.

William panned across the rows of static CCTV, the entrance, the car park, and there, in a dark corner: their car. And last of all—

It was no surprise of course, yet it still put a knot in his stomach. There, on one of the many monitors, he saw himself. Dark blue suit, baseball cap and windcheater, leaning on the reception desk and with his eyes fixed on a screen which – if the resolution had been high enough – would in turn have shown him, looking at a screen, and so on into infinity.

'William?'

Rebecca's voice echoed around the vast space. At the edge of the ground floor, three transparent lift shafts reached up through the storeys above, and she was standing by one of them, the door to the glass lift open in front of her. She beckoned him over.

'What is this place?' he asked as he joined her.

'That depends who you ask. According to the prospectus, this is Eastern Europe's leading centre for scientific research and development.'

She pushed the top button and William could feel them

moving, shooting upwards like a pneumatic post capsule in a world where they were the only ones alive.

'If you ask me, it's a bloody expensive glass tower that hadn't reckoned with the financial crisis.'

From below, the various floors had seemed small and claustrophobic, but as they stepped out onto the highest gangway William realised how wrong he had been. Beyond their glass walls, he could see whole office landscapes opening out, with doors leading to meeting rooms and kitchenettes, and far over there, on the other side of everything, were the massive glass windows and the dark grey night outside.

The gangway led to an anonymous glass door, and Rebecca pulled out a keycard, punched in a code, and waited for the lock to let them pass.

'Welcome,' she said as she continued into the darkness on the other side.

'Thanks,' said William, stopping just inside the door. 'To what, if I may ask?'

She answered without a smile. 'Welcome to Michal Piotrowski's sophisticated nonsense.'

44

After a while, suburban Bromma stops being Bromma and becomes forest. Metal roads become gravel, Thirties villas with effect lighting become small summer hideaways in overgrown gardens, empty and infirm, like abandoned elderly folk waiting for eternal rest.

Christina Sandberg let the news team's light blue Volvo struggle through a more and more hostile layer of snow, away from the main road and across pitted roads past rows of little post boxes. She passed signs that told her she wasn't allowed, and she thought about turning back – but to what? Instead she kept going, just a little bit further, and then further, passing minute after minute of wooded track without seeing a single house.

Eventually the road ended with a robust fence of thick wooden poles. A boom barrier blocked her path, complete with a little yellow sign. Private, it said, and she stopped, found herself just sitting there behind the wheel.

She was already regretting it. But there was something about what he'd said that made it impossible to turn around, not now. He was the last fragile straw for her to clutch at in a world that had lost everything, her only alternative to darkness and loneliness and emptiness. The only way she could avoid facing herself.

After a moment's hesitation, she turned off the engine and stepped out into the darkness. A vast starry sky had begun to push its way through the gaps in the clouds, and the silence was different out here – clearer and drier and rustling of crystals.

Slowly, she approached the barrier. The road on the other side seemed to run on into the darkness, but no matter how she peered she could make out nothing at the far end – no buildings, no lights, nothing. And sitting in a warm, locked car had been one thing, but now, alone in the darkness with the cold biting her skin, what was she supposed to do? Climb inside? Shout and see what happened? Or just leave?

Truth was she knew nothing about him. He seemed harmless, but what does *seemed* mean? He was a conspiracy theorist, fearful verging on paranoid, and there might be all kinds of installations on the plot – weapons, traps, God knows what – and suddenly she changed her mind—

She had just started to back away when the light came on. The next thing she knew, she lay on the ground, her eyes were stinging, arms folded in front of her face to shield her from the intense whiteness that shone from everywhere. She had recoiled, slipped on the frozen ground, and now her knee hurt, her back too.

Motion sensors. Of course he had motion sensors. He was paranoid, and if anyone was going to have an alarm round the perimeter of their land it was him. She could make out at least six different floodlights, mounted on the gateposts and the trees around her, and as she lay there like a human deer, frozen in the headlights of an oncoming car, she slowly realised that the floodlights might just be the beginning. Maybe she'd triggered an alarm somewhere, perhaps there would be dogs barking before long, loping towards her on the other side of the fence.

She had just managed to haul herself off the slippery ground when she sensed that she had company.

'Who's there?' she said.

'I thought you said you had my number.'

She swallowed.

'What I want to talk about may not be suited for discussing over the phone.'

Seconds later she heard the barrier swing open. Alexander Strandell, better known as Tetrapak, emerged from the darkness, and beckoned her to follow him.

The instant Rebecca Kowalczyk switched on the lights, William realised that resistance was futile.

The space they had just entered wasn't so much of a room, more of an auditorium. All along the far side were floor-to-ceiling windows, like a bowed, transparent wall, and to the left the scene was dominated by what looked like a small command and control centre. There was a plinth, raised two steps higher than the surrounding floor, above which a handful of office chairs faced a long, continuous desk, white and sterile like a worktop in a kitchen catalogue.

The thing that really grabbed his attention though was the other half of the room.

'Tell me this isn't what I think it is.'

'How would I know what you think it is?' Rebecca said behind him. 'That's impossible, right?'

She passed him and stepped up onto the bridge, steps that sounded hollow and that echoed as she climbed up onto the plinth and sat down at the desk, her back to William and facing the thing that he couldn't tear his eyes away from.

In the middle of the right-hand side of the room, three free-standing booths had been erected. They were separated from the rest of the room by huge glass blocks, decimetre-thick uneven panes that made the reality on the other side seem like indistinct ripples. The glass walls were decorated here and there with bright yellow Post-it notes, like a reluctant demonstration that there was actually some activity going on amidst all the sterility and high design.

In the middle booth was something that could be best described as an office. There was a desk, chalky white and basically empty, save for a few bundles of paper at one end. On one side of it was a simple office chair and on the other a soft electric recliner – a contraption somewhere between a dentist's chair and a business-class seat on a long-haul flight.

The thing that had caught William's eye though, was the light grey ribbed plastic tube hanging from the ceiling. He walked over towards it. A thick bundle of multicoloured wires emerged from the tube, fifty, maybe more, bound together like colourful nerves spilling from a grey plastic spinal cord. They were lying in neat bundles on each desk, and at the end of each cable was a shiny disc.

'EEG,' he said.

'Pretty much,' she said. 'But 2.0.'

He turned towards her just as she put her hand onto the surface of the command desk. A weak purple glow lit her skin from underneath, sniffing its way along her palm for a second, then once more in the opposite direction before disappearing, leaving the surface as white and empty as before.

It took a second, then the room sprang to life. From the control desk, a series of matt-black screens rose up in front of each of the chairs, the size of paperback books and integrated into the desk surface like minimalist white loft hatches in a minimalist white ceiling. Below each one the desk glowed with a weak, warm light, presumably projecting keyboards in front of the operators.

But William's eyes were fixed firmly on the wall in front of her. In a single, silent movement, it seemed to crack into diagonal lines, turning into triangular panels and slowly rotating out of view like the shutter in a camera lens, disappearing into the floor and up into the roof and revealing another bank of matt-black screens. He counted at least eighteen of them, all connected in sequence to an enormous screen that ran the entire length of the control desk, and for a second it reminded him of sitting in the military's own command centre, *but 2.0*, as Rebecca put it.

Her voice woke him out of his thoughts.

'Two million euros, and you can't even get Champions League on it.'

She seemed almost to be whispering to herself, and he observed her from the corner of his eye, watching the screen being reflected in her eyes.

'Twelve years. We worked here for twelve years, me and Michal. Not once did he start the system up without saying that.'

Her fingers tapped away at the invisible keyboard in front of her, summoning two flashing commands onto the built-in monitor directly in front of her, and in the next second the huge wall of monitors above was filled with information. Diagrams and tables formed rows of well-defined, neatly laid out fields, all without content, white squared patterns on a black background. In the centre, the framed image showed a video, blue-grey but pin-sharp, a desk seen from above, and a number of cables and—

William turned around. Sure enough, right above the work-station in the booth behind them was a ceiling-mounted camera, a shiny black dome whose picture was being relayed onto the screen in front of them.

He lowered his head instinctively, an attempt to shield himself in case there were more. The pinhead-sized black circles on the command desk? Probably. The other glass domes in the room, above the entrance, by the booths, in the centre of the floor? Most likely. But were they in use? Were they recording right now? He held his breath, forcing himself to repeat the same mantra as on his way in: that no one could know that he was here. That as long as he made sure to cover his face then no one was going to find him. *Unless, of course, she's right.*

He hated himself for thinking it, but the thoughts refused to go away. What was all this? The brightly coloured cables on the desk. The EEG. Michal Piotrowski's sophisticated nonsense.

'Worked on what, exactly?' he asked, as he climbed up onto the platform next to Rebecca.

Over on the screen, one of the fields had caught his eye more clearly than everything else. It showed an array of oval diagrams, lined up in order alongside the video feed – schematic representations from various angles, picked out in white against the dark background. They were maps of the human brain.

'What am I looking at here?'

Her answer made him shiver.

'We call it Project Rosetta.'

Christina didn't really know what she'd been expecting, but as she walked through the hall and into a living room, she realised that she hadn't been expecting a home. There was a faint smell of a dinner he must have cooked very recently, onions fried in butter perhaps, a sweet, welcoming scent that mixed with fresh coffee and the smoke that leaked from the wood-burning stove. In the middle of the room was a three-piece suite in mottled, satchel-brown leather, and beyond that a desk of dark-stained wood, all straining under the weight of neat piles of books and periodicals or equally well-stacked electronic devices.

The ceiling was low. The walls and ceiling panels were made of yellow pine, and the floor strewn with overlapping thick rugs bearing deep red patterns and giving the room a dry, calming quiet. The stacks of books and magazines spread out in all directions, on shelves, on the floor, on tables, on chairs, and try as she might, she could see no evidence of tinfoil around the windows, no chicken wire lining the walls to disrupt electronic bugging devices, nothing to suggest that this was the home of a paranoid lunatic terrified of wide-reaching, awful conspiracies.

'Disappointed?' she heard Tetrapak ask behind her.

She noticed his squinting smile, two warm eyes and something resembling a dimple that caused his beard to gather in a tuft on one cheek.

'I'm not quite as mad as people expect. Sorry about that.'

He gestured towards a stool in front of one of the bookcases, and she realised for the first time that it actually belonged to a grand piano that seemed to have retired from music some time ago, the flaking nut-brown varnish on its closed lid hidden under even more piles of books. She sat down, while he took a seat by the desk.

'I didn't expect you to get in touch,' he said.

'Neither did I,' she replied. 'First of all, you should know I'm not here as a journalist. I can't promise you a single letter about you or what you tell me, not in my paper, nor anywhere else. All I can promise is that I'm going to listen.'

'That's a start.'

'When you came to me yesterday,' Christina said. 'What was it you wanted to warn me about?'

'Exactly what I said. That the power cut was just part of something much bigger. And that the authorities knew it was coming.'

'And that's based on the radio communications that you've come across. On frequencies that have been silent since the Cold War.'

'Amongst other things.' She gave him a quizzical look, and he explained himself. 'I can show you small, insignificant articles from newspapers from around the world. I'm sure you can find even more in your archives.'

'Articles about what?'

'About power cuts, commonplace everyday events from around the world. A collapsed substation here, a faulty transformer there. But if you compare all the dates with those of the transmissions . . .'

'They match?'

'Not only that. After each one, the trials have been ratcheted up a notch, increased in frequency. As though each new event is making it even more important to put it into action.'

'It?' she said. 'I don't understand. What are you telling me we're looking at?'

'I believe that it is a new analogue communication system. Something not dependent on the internet, something that will continue to function even if everything else is knocked out.'

'Why would everything else be knocked out?' she asked. 'By whom?'

'That,' he said, shaking his head. 'That is the question I would like to ask them.' He nodded at the electronics on the desk, modern hard discs with blinking diodes next to cumbersome

221

radio receivers with heavy buttons. 'And no,' he said. 'I don't know who *they* are. The authorities. Swedish Armed Forces. Military organisations from around the globe. All or none of the above.'

The conversation halted for a moment, neither of them knowing how to continue.

'Can I ask you something,' Tetrapak said in the end. 'Why are you here?'

'Because I'm starting to worry that you might be right.'

William stood in silence. *Rosetta.* Just like the email address, the sender of the three short emails that had got him to turn up at Central Station, the one that, one way or another, was behind everything that had happened. A stream of connections flooded through his head, dizzying and far-fetched.

What if they don't even need that.

'As in the stone?' he said.

'As in the stone.'

William turned away his head. He knew what it implied and he didn't like it. At the end of the eighteenth century, Napoleon's troops had discovered a stone in Egypt, a stone with three sets of inscriptions, each of them in one ancient language. With that as a key, science managed for the first time in modern history to decipher Egyptian hieroglyphics. The Rosetta Stone was nothing but a lexicon. A lexicon for translating an unknown language into something that could be understood.

'Thoughts are nothing more than electrical impulses,' she said before he'd had time to protest. 'It's really no stranger than that. It's not magic, not witchcraft, just science, pure and simple. Electricity can be measured, the rest is just about creating a meter that's up to the job. All you need is a lexicon.'

She turned towards the desk again, another rattle of fingertips on the non-existent keys before she leaned back in her chair. At a stroke, everything came alive. All of the tables, diagrams and empty data fields crackled into action, with values nervously flickering around zero. In the blue-grey booth of the video feed, the CCTV showed two people sitting down.

It was a recording. Images and data that were stored on hard discs, and that were now being played back in synch.

A woman, probably about sixty, sat in the dentist's chair. The backrest had been lowered to almost horizontal, and pretty much her whole head was covered in the discs that William had noticed over on the desk. She had her eyes closed, and countless electrodes attached all over her scalp and forehead and right the way down her neck, all connected by the colourful cables to the light-grey tube.

The chair opposite her was occupied by a noticeably younger woman wearing a white lab coat draped loosely over a simple jumper, long dark hair that fell into playful curls across her shoulders.

It wasn't until he saw her face that he realised it was Rebecca.

'What am I watching?' he said.

'Wait,' was her reply.

He watched the recorded Rebecca Kowalczyk pull a file towards her across the tabletop, get out a piece of paper, presumably covered in text, then glance briefly at the ceiling and smile. Straight into the camera, straight into William's eyes.

The moment burned itself onto William's retina. Of course it wasn't him she was smiling at. The person sitting at the control desk when the recording was made was Piotrowski, and what he'd just seen was an intimate look between lovers.

On the screen in front of them, Rebecca turned her attention to the woman in the chair. She tucked her hair behind her ear, put the sheet of paper on the desk, read silently from it. Short, simple texts, as if she was asking a series of questions.

In that same instant, the schematic diagrams of the woman's brain were transformed. They flipped through a spectrum of colours, shining like rainbows in stark contrast to the colourless room. Rolling surfaces and lines appeared across the cerebral hemispheres, shifting from blue to green to yellow to red, colours representing neural activity, changing rapidly as the video Rebecca continued to ask her questions at a calm, unhurried pace.

In a single second William could feel his thoughts rushing back to the day before, to the briefing with Palmgren and Forester, the huge maps with the similar colour schemes showing the attacks that had caused power outages.

Somehow, this scared him more.

'The woman you're watching is from an agency,' said Rebecca. 'We've never met her before, we don't know her name, nothing. Her only instruction is not to say anything out loud, and what you're seeing on the screens is her brain activity as I ask some pre-written questions. This is from the twenty-sixth of November, only three weeks ago. It's the very first time.'

'First time what?'

Rebecca didn't answer. She nodded towards the wall instead.

'I'm activating Rosetta now.'

Her fingers tapped a few strokes on the keys in front of her. And then:

'This isn't possible.' William's voice.

But it was.

Word by word, he watched the screen in front of them filling up with text, sentences evolving and stacking on top of one another to form a long, long feed as Rebecca read the short questions from her page.

He didn't need to ask, but he did anyway.

'Where's the text coming from?'

'It's her answers,' she replied. 'Her answers to my questions.'

He sat there not saying a word. He could hear Rebecca still talking to him, but it was distant, and he still could not tear his eyes from the screen. He could hear her telling him about all the work that had led them to the moment they were watching, about their struggles to decouple the brain's conscious thinking from the chaos of impulses and reflexes, about the incredible amounts of processing power they had deployed to find the nee-dles of syntactic thought in the haystack of all the incidental noise. All the times they'd said that *this* is our last attempt. If this doesn't work, we're giving up. Just one last try.

'And then, finally,' she said. 'Finally, we succeeded. The words on the screen are the computer's own transcription of the electri-cal impulses in her head.'

The words on the screen kept coming, one word after another in a language he did not understand, but still: Rebecca and

Piotrowski had achieved the impossible. They had found a key to decode all the chaotic nuances pulsing back and forth in the woman's brain that were actual thoughts, and then managed to translate them into words.

Psychotronics.

It isn't possible to read someone's thoughts.

'What you're showing me now,' he said, finally. Got to his feet, climbed down from the platform, and sat in the empty booth behind them. 'Even if *you* have managed it, even if *you* can transcribe other people's thoughts into words . . . ' He pointed at the knot of wires and electrodes resting on the table. 'Even if that is the case, it still doesn't explain how they found me in Warsaw.'

Rebecca didn't answer, and William sharpened his tone.

'I know I'm tired, I know I haven't been myself for a very long time, but I think I would've noticed if someone had taped electrodes to my head.'

'If *we* have managed this?' answered Rebecca with an apologetic shrug. 'How do we know that no one else has, somewhere else? How do we know they don't do it better?'

'If that were true,' he said, 'why me? Why would anyone be so keen to read my thoughts that they would follow me all the way here? My thoughts are really not that interesting. Ask my ex-wife.'

'I don't know how much you know about Michal Piotrowski's past,' Rebecca said, pretending that she hadn't heard.

If you only knew. He didn't say.

'I used to say that he was afraid of ghosts,' she said. 'That he needed to let go of the old, needed to move on . . . But, ghosts or not, maybe he was proved right in the end.'

'What do you mean by that?'

She lowered her voice.

'We struggle for years to get Rosetta to work. Then, finally, we pull it off – and from that day, almost from that moment, it's as though everything about his behaviour went into a slide.' She gestured towards the screens. 'It was historic. This was an incredible breakthrough, we should've been celebrating, should've done *something*. Instead, he became a recluse. Wouldn't say why, but I could see it in his face.'

225

She paused.

'Michal was scared. No. Michal was terrified, in fear of his life.'

'What is it you're trying to tell me?'

'What if he read a thought that he wasn't supposed to know about?'

William hesitated. It was as if the conversation was slipping from his grasp, and he could feel the frustration building inside him. The next stage, he knew, would be rage. And he didn't want that.

'Why are you telling me this?' he said, with all the composure he could muster. 'Why bring me here, why let me see this, what's the point of it all?'

'Because you are the only one who can help me. Somehow, you've got something to do with all of—'

'I've got fuck all to do with this,' he shouted. 'I've got my own life, hundreds of miles from here, I've got nothing to do with what happened to Michal Piotrowski and nor do I want anything to do with it!' He felt a dam breaking, and behind it months of self-loathing and longing, and thousands of other emotions that he couldn't control. 'I'm not here to help anyone but myself. I'm here because, regardless of how Michal Piotrowski may have been, however innocent and kind-hearted you would have me believe, he has brought this on me. Not the other way around. And even if everything is as you say it is, even if he did read someone's thoughts, what right does that give him to drag me into this? Why can't I live my life in peace?'

He could feel the pressure easing, the dam emptying faster than he'd expected, and how his ranting grew empty, lost meaning.

'I can't help you,' he said quietly. 'All I know is that I've been accused of something I haven't done. And I can't take it any more.'

They stayed sitting there for a long time. Her by the control desk, him in the booth, looking at the wall of glass blocks, next to all the wires that could read people's thoughts.

'Why did he have pictures of you in his apartment?' she asked again at last. He didn't respond. 'You hate him for something, don't you?'

'I don't hate him,' he said. 'I just promised myself never to go anywhere near him ever again.'

Her eyes narrowed. *Again?*

'Why not?' she asked.

He looked out of the window for a long time before he answered.

'Because I was afraid he was going to take my life away.'

45

'I really don't know where to start,' said Christina.

'I know the feeling.' Tetrapak looked at her from across the room. 'Don't think about it. Don't worry about what's important and what's trivial, don't look for connections. Just say what you know, in whatever order you like. We can build context around it afterwards.'

She took a long pause, arranged the events of the past twenty-four hours into some kind of order, and tried to transform them from fragments to a story that could be told. Then she did.

She told him about William's arrest, about the sighting of Sara at the café, and when she'd finished, she looked down at the table. It was Strandell's turn to say something, and she was longing for him to do so, as though the silence belonged to her, and the longer it was allowed to go on, the less credible she would seem.

'I want you to tell me why you decided to come to me,' he said.

'Because I couldn't think of anyone else.' And then, opening her handbag. 'I want to know if you can tell me what this is.'

When Alexander Strandell saw what she was offering him, his hand recoiled as though he'd burned his fingers.

'Where did you get that?' he asked, eyes flaring with fear, as though the CD that she held out had managed to frighten him through its mere existence.

She replied by telling him what she knew. About the man who had met his end in Kaknäs Tower, about the car and the window sticker that she'd recognised. And about the CD in the car stereo, the broken window, the envelope lying on the seat with the Warsaw postmark.

'It's as though everything leads back to that fucking conference,' she said. 'We should never have gone there. But how were we to know?'

'What do you mean, know?' he said.

'That's a whole different story,' she said.

'Something tells me it might not be.'

She looked up. What was he saying now?

'Do you know whose car it was?' he said.

She went back to the handbag, pulled out an envelope, the yellow, padded one that had been lying on the passenger seat along with the CD case. She turned the scratchy letters towards him, the addressee's name underneath the Polish postmark. Per Einar Eriksen.

'The car was registered to that name too,' she said. 'All I know is that he's a professor.'

'Human consciousness,' he said with a whisper.

'Do you know who he is?' she said.

'Not to talk to, no. Not personally.'

'But?'

'But he was a very good speaker.'

Tetrapak stood up and walked over to one of the bookcases. When he turned around he was holding something out towards her, and what sent a shiver through her was not the yellow envelope in his hand, the scratchy letters forming Alexander Strandell's address, the same writing as the envelope she'd found in the car, with the same Polish postmark in the corner. Nor was it the flat, rectangular shape she felt inside it, the rattling plastic that she hurried to pull out from the envelope and that she knew was going to be an identical CD. Instead, what shook her was what he said.

'Here's what I think,' he said. 'I think we've all been to the same conference.'

On day three, the storm had broken. The sky above Warsaw had remained bright blue, with quivering, unforgiving heat. Everyone was waiting for the thunder. In the great hall, long tables were decked with complimentary champagne and canapés, and everywhere you looked, conversations were taking place in ball gowns and evening dress. Behind closed doors, catering staff had clattered through their final preparations ahead of the closing gala dinner, and William had felt well rested and content and even a little bit tanned.

He'd just got himself another glass of bubbly from one of the tables when Piotrowski came over to him.

'You have a wonderful family,' he'd said, with a broad smile, pretty much out of nowhere. An odd thing to say, but William had smiled in response, mumbled something about Warsaw being a beautiful place, as though that compliment would repay the first.

And then, there had been a pause that went on for just a little bit too long.

'You must be wondering why I was so keen for you to attend,' Piotrowski had said. 'I've been thinking about how to make contact with you for a long time. It ended up being like this. I hope you'll forgive me for that.'

'What do you mean?' said William.

'I've had my eye on you,' Piotrowski said.

He said so cordially, but the words made William straighten up, and he felt a shiver run through his stomach. What was this about? Politics? East and West?

'Oh, not for military reasons,' said Piotrowski, as though he'd read William's mind. 'The Cold War is over, and if it isn't, we're in the West now, however ironic that might be.' He gestured towards the walls – they were in a building built by Stalin, in a city that had once lent its name to everything east of the Iron Curtain. 'I have lived in the same city all of my life, and yet one day I moved from East to West without so much as lifting a finger.' He shrugged. 'Not that I'm complaining. It just takes some getting used to.'

'Explain *had my eye on you*,' William said.

'I know that you are fifty-two years old. That you grew up in

Saltsjöbaden, that you're a self-taught electronics nut and mathematician, a qualified engineer employed as a cryptologist by the Swedish Armed Forces Headquarters. I know that your wife's name is Christina Sandberg, forty-six, journalist.'

'That's not having an eye on someone, that's having a spare ten minutes to do an internet search. What are you trying to get at?'

Piotrowski hardened his tone, barely noticeably, but enough.

'Two years ago you sold the big house in Täby and bought an apartment on Skeppargatan in Stockholm. Your daughter moved from Näsbypark school to Norra Latin and she finished the ninth grade last spring. She likes fencing and riding. She smokes ten a day, but you don't know that.'

The last sentence caused the cold cramp in his stomach to harden. What the hell was this about?

'I don't know what you think you're doing' – William felt his grip tighten around the champagne glass in his hand – 'but if you're trying to get at my daughter . . .'

He bit off the rest of the sentence, panned across the hall with his eyes and felt a new chill when she was nowhere to be seen. Christina was standing a couple of metres away, and when he saw her unprotected skin in the scooped back of her gown he felt how what had been exciting and elegant as they left the hotel was suddenly transformed into something naked and vulnerable. She was chatting with a group of other visitors, but Sara wasn't one of them.

'She's standing by the entrance,' said Piotrowski. 'Don't worry—'

'If you think you can threaten me,' William hissed. 'If you think you're going to get to me by threatening my family—'

'Believe me,' the Pole said calmly. 'The last thing I want to do is threaten your daughter.'

They stood there, eyes locked. What was going on? Extortion? An attempt to recruit him by a foreign power? That was unthinkable, ridiculous, but it was all he could guess at.

'Why did you invite me here?'

Piotrowski put his hand on William. *Calm down*, it meant. *I'm your friend*. And then he smiled a smile that was as polite as it was insincere.

'Come on,' he said. 'Let me show you around.'

Once William started telling his story he didn't stop for breath. He stood by the windows, watching the distant glow of Warsaw in the mist, and eight hundred kilometres away, his estranged wife was sitting in a house that smelled of woodsmoke and rugs, telling the very same thing.

'You know how some people can just change beyond recognition when they face an unexpected situation?' she said. 'Maybe they witness an accident, or go through a crisis. You know how people say that you don't know how anyone's going to react until it actually happens? William's eyes. That look. That walk. I'd never seen him like that before.'

It was the moment that they later referred to as 'the Thunder', the day broiling, when William strode through the crowd, a look on his face that she'd never seen before and that terrified her. He'd grabbed her by the arm – too firmly, too desperately, his voice shaking with stress and rage – put her champagne glass down on the table and hissed that they had to find Sara *now*. That moment had marked the end of their summer.

Christina allowed her eyes to meet Tetrapak's. 'It has to be him who sent the CD, who's behind all of this.'

'In that case,' he said. 'Where do I fit in? Why would he have sent a CD to me?'

'You must have met at some point. You must have talked to each other.'

He shook his head, unsure.

'Around fifty,' she said. 'Not scruffy, but maybe a little bit rough and ready. Bushy eyebrows, greying hair. His beard too.'

'It's five years ago. How am I supposed to remember that?'

'Try,' she said. And then, almost reluctantly, she added: 'Warm, welcoming, almost jovial.'

He stared into space, racking his memory.

'I remember a man I spoke to during one of the breaks. I know we exchanged business cards. Well, *business card* might be pushing it' – he signalled inverted commas with his fingers as he said it – 'I remember looking at it afterwards and noticing that it was handwritten. Name and address, in pencil. And a Hotmail address.'

'That was him,' Christina said. 'The one William got was the same, we joked about it at the time.' Her tone went up a notch. 'You must have talked about something. What did you say to each other?'

'As I say, it was five years ago. I know that we worried about the same things: bugging, surveillance, tracking, how we can never be sure that no one is watching. How new technologies can be used against us, on the premise that it's the right thing to do.'

The thought crossed her mind to ask how much truth there was in the story about coffee creamer that had given him his name, but then she thought better of it.

'You must have said something that left an impression?' she asked.

His smile was ironic.

'People often say I do. Not usually in a good way.'

She smiled back, more out of politeness than anything else, and they were left sitting in silence, as if they'd somehow reached an understanding.

'Tell me,' he said, 'why are you so sure this is about Piotrowski?'

'Because, one way or another,' she said, then restarted the sentence. 'One way or another we've been scared of this ever since then.'

'Scared of what?'

'Scared of him coming back.'

46

There were four things that Michal Piotrowski hated above all else: politics, hunger, war . . . and, at number four, piano concertos.

He had grown up in an art-loving family. Anything that could possibly be observed and appreciated with a knowing *hmm*, whether painted or performed on stage or fashioned from some kind of stone, and as soon as he was old enough to decide for himself, he had taken to science and research in an act of pure rebellion. Tangible, concrete disciplines, just to be contrary.

He had been studying at the Nencki Institute for four years when he was contacted for the first time. By then he had already taken part in several high-profile neuroscience projects, interdisciplinary experiments in the no-man's-land between psychology and biology. He loved his job, and he felt like a pioneer, as though each day was spent exploring virgin territory, the only difference being that this new ground was found within ourselves.

That was how he'd described it to the man who had sat down next to him in the dark bar on Ulica Krucza one night. He was Michal's age, spoke with a strong accent and was a little too drunk – it would take Michal many years to realise that that was probably an act – and after a while he had steered the conversation towards politics in general and his hatred of the Soviet system in particular. Then they'd said their goodbyes and Michal had gone back to his place.

They met on four occasions, each time completely by chance, before the man revealed his identity. His name was Dawid Ludwin, son of a farmer from northern Masovia. He flew light aircraft in his spare time and by day he worked at a company that produced communications equipment for military use. Above all though, he worked covertly for the West. At regular intervals he would photograph blueprints and prototypes and hand them over to the CIA, something he mentioned only in passing, yet impossible not to understand, and Piotrowski had cycled home through the pouring rain with his feet pedalling so fast that he could barely keep up. He'd then spent the night awake, watching the flames in the gas fire gasping for air.

He had said no, but even so, he couldn't sleep. Why did this have to happen to him? Why did he have to be put in such a difficult position, forced to take sides in a conflict that didn't concern him? He hated politics. But he hated war and hunger more, and the farmer's boy had articulated opinions that Michal hadn't even known he had.

By the time Gabriela came in as the dawn was breaking, he'd long since fallen asleep on a worn-out armchair. She was a mathematician; they'd met at university and they hated each other from the off, right up until the point where they realised they didn't any more, and now she covered him with a blanket she'd brought from her childhood home, waited by his side until he woke up. When he did, he took hold of her hand, pulled her towards him and explained that he was about to make a decision that would change their lives for ever.

He didn't know what the information was being used for, but in the years that followed he would meet them at least once a month. The methods were simple, always the same: they would meet at concerts, he would sit at the very back, and under cover of darkness he would slip a flat envelope full of negatives into the programme, accompanied by the same plinking and plonking music that his parents had exposed him to throughout his childhood. It was unbearable, but it was the price he had to pay: it was the perfect way of doing it, no dark alleys or invisible meetings, but in the thick of things, around people, in clear view. They might meet in the gents or at the bar during the interval, and when he put down his programme to pay for a glass of wine or to respond to the call of nature, no one could see that he'd happened to swap his copy with the one that the man in the hat had placed next to it.

And with time, it all became routine. The drama of it disappeared. They were just photos after all.

In return, he got lucky. Via a combination of various inexplicable coincidences which he suspected were orchestrated way above his head, he and Gabriela had moved into a light, spacious apartment in central Warsaw, in a block that had just been renovated and with views over a neat and well-kept little park. The car he drove around ought to have had a waiting list several years long. They ate well, were never cold, had clothes and friends and they went on holiday.

Now and then he would visit his friend Dawid Ludwin, and they would look down on the country that they both loved and betrayed from high in the air.

Michal Piotrowski was enjoying life. The only thing that never left him was his pathological hatred of piano concertos.

—

When the Wall came down, the contact grew more sporadic. The world stopped being dangerous, the sun seemed to shine a little brighter, the shops filled with goods and the people around him with ideas and hope in the future, and against that backdrop East and West didn't seem so relevant any more.

Maybe he was the one who stopped being careful. All he knew was that one day they had decided that Michal Piotrowski was going to die. And that he would come to wish, time and time again, that they had succeeded.

Piotrowski told William all of that, on that warm summer's day in Warsaw in the echoing marble room in the building they called a palace. They'd gone off into an empty side lobby, and when he'd finished his story he'd looked William straight in the eye with a sorrowful, envious look.

'I will never forget that sound.'

His eyes darted around, from the empty turnstiles to the closed café, refusing to cry, as if it was still shameful to do so, fifteen years after it had all taken place.

'Watching films teaches you funny things,' he said. 'You learn what a car blowing up is supposed to sound like – or you *think* you do – big and full of flames and a thundering bass. And then you expect it to be like that in real life as well.' A pause. 'All you hear is a muffled, contained bang. Hardly anything. Then the sound of glass hitting the ground.' He cleared his throat. And then: 'With that noise, I lost my wife.'

'I don't want to sound disrespectful,' William said eventually. 'I really am very sorry to hear about everything you've been through. But where do I come into this?'

Piotrowski didn't move, almost as though he hadn't heard the question, and just kept talking from where he'd left off.

'It was one of those things that aren't supposed to happen. No one had any reason to think that it wouldn't be me sitting there. The car was mine. Gabriela never touched it – she walked to work, walked home, walked everywhere. Rain, snow, storms, nothing stopped her.' He paused again. 'But the doctors had told her she wasn't ready for that yet.'

He lifted his face towards William again, and for a second, he was struck by the sensation that Piotrowski had orchestrated the whole conversation before it had even started.

'Ready after what?' he said.

That was the right line.

'After the caesarean.'

There were two long seconds of silence while Piotrowski waited for William to understand the implication of what he'd just said. And when they had passed, and the blow arrived, Piotrowski didn't even fall. Two steps backwards to absorb the kinetic energy, and he was left standing there, his jaw aching and his eyes glowing with hurt, and all the time William contemplating whether to hit him one more time.

'You don't touch my daughter,' he said in a bottomless, infinite voice, full of hate and fear and guilt all at once. 'And you don't contact me, or my family, again.'

With those words, William Sandberg turned up the stairs and left the conference.

'I didn't know they had a child,' said Rebecca. Her eyes glittered, reflecting the light of the screens around them. 'What I did know was that Gabriela was left in a coma. She was like that for two years, and throughout that time, Michal was at her side, convinced that she was still alive in there. And time after time, he promised her that he wouldn't give up until he'd found a way to hear her thoughts.'

She made a gesture towards the room around them. In the end he'd succeeded, but almost twenty years too late.

'He never stopped thinking it was his fault. That's why we couldn't be seen together, so that what had happened to her couldn't happen to me.' She made eye contact with William again. 'I still don't understand why you hate him so much,' she said.

'I don't hate him. I just want never to see him again.'

She stared at him. *And why would that be?*

'He invited me for one simple reason,' he said. 'So that he could meet his daughter.'

It took a second for her to understand.

'*His* daughter . . . ?'

'All we were told by the adoption agency was that Sara's biological mother had died.'

They sat in silence for a long time.

'He's done this to me,' William said. 'For some reason, he's put me through all of this.'

'Why would he do that?'

'Because I didn't let him meet her?' William shrugged.

'Michal didn't believe in revenge.'

'He didn't believe in politics either,' William said coldly. 'That didn't stop him devoting twenty years of his life to it.'

Rebecca gave him a long, blank look. 'Maybe I made a mistake trying to help you,' she said, and then stood up and turned around, walked past all the flickering screens, and continued out through the glass door, gradually disappearing beyond the frosted panes.

'I was the one who insisted that we should tell her,' Christina said, without looking up. Tetrapak was sitting on the other side of the room, in silence, not knowing what to say. 'Not who her biological father was, we never dared to do that, just that we weren't her birth parents. That she was adopted and that her biological parents were from Poland. And we thought that would be that.'

It sounded like a good idea at the time, she thought to herself.

'We didn't do it for her sake. It was for ours. To avoid constantly worrying about him turning up again, telling her before we'd had the chance, without us having any control.' She paused. 'And she was fifteen. She was old enough to know.'

The last part came in a thin voice, almost like a plea, as though Tetrapak was in a position to change things by giving his approval.

'What is it on there?' she asked him after some time.

It took a couple of seconds for him to work out what she was talking about.

'The CD?'

'Yes,' she said. 'What is it?'

He stood up, walked over to the bookcase that ran along one of the walls, took down his piles of newspapers and documents and placed them tenderly to one side. Under the piles was a stereo system made up of separates, black boxes stacked on top of each other, with rows of worn, touch-sensitive buttons that had once been cutting-edge design. When the CD tray squealed out it was like a desperate plea from a piece of kit that had long since discharged its duties and just wanted a dignified death.

Strandell put his hand out towards Christina, took her CD, put it in the tray and pressed play.

Piano.

First, a single quiet triad, a pause, then another. From there, it gradually grew into a piece of music. It started falteringly, slowly, then grew lighter, almost as though new fingers were awakening one by one, reaching out from a lonely hand. It seemed to Christina as if the concert was taking place there and then, right in the room, as though the music had forced its way in from an alternate reality, like an overlaid audio track that had inadvertently leaked into her life and made her realise that everything around her was no more than fiction.

Eventually Strandell turned towards the stereo and switched it off. The silence was shattering.

'What was that?' she asked.

'Chopin.'

'There must be something else?'

He shook his head with a calm so absolute that she knew that her next question had actually already been answered.

'And what was on yours?' she asked.

'Exactly the same thing. Almost an hour of piano music. Frederic Chopin. That was it.'

Out of nowhere, she felt exhaustion washing over her. She had been so convinced that the CD was going to give them something new – maybe not an answer but a nudge in the right direction – and now there she was, at a dead end. It didn't make sense. It had to mean something more.

'Why would Michal Piotrowski send it to you?' she said. 'And to Professor Eriksen, and to my husband? What do you have in common?'

'I don't know,' was his response.

'He must have said something at the conference, talked to you about something specific? There must have been a reason he chose you all?'

'Just to complicate things,' said Strandell, 'we have no way of knowing whether we were the only ones he chose. There might be other discs out there.'

Christina stared at him. That was a door she didn't even want to open. 'There must be something more,' she said. 'Something hidden, you haven't found, something we don't hear when it's playing, something ... that can cause a power cut just by being put in a computer.'

She could hear the pleading in her own voice again. How could her daughter have made all this happen, just with a single CD of piano music? And why was it her CD that had made the power go, and not Tetrapak's, not Eriksen's?

Strandell listened to her questions.

'I've only got the one theory,' he said. 'And I'm afraid it doesn't hold up.'

'What do you mean?'

'You found the CD in Eriksen's car. Is that right?'

She nodded.

'And I used this. I call it my cup-bearer.' A self-deprecating smile as he put his hand on a desktop computer, hidden away in one corner of the room, light grey and heavy and covered by as much paper as everything else. 'I know. Call me paranoid. But I would never open a completely unknown CD on a computer that hasn't been suitably protected.'

The cup-bearer, he explained, was a retired PC with a single task. It had the first taste of all the material he came across, everything from thumb drives to CDs to files he downloaded from the internet. Everything was tested in a closed environment, with no links whatsoever to other computers, and if it turned out that the material did contain viruses or some other kind of malicious code, then it would stay there and not spread to other machines.

'I can't be completely sure,' he said, 'but perhaps your daughter was the only one who played it in a computer that was online.'

'Wouldn't that mean that there had to be something on there after all? A virus? Some kind of code that triggered everything?'

'As I said, that's my theory, but it doesn't hold up.'

He gave a brief account of how he'd gone through the disc one block at a time, looking for hidden partitions, files that might be hidden alongside the audio. And nowhere, he said, was there anything on the disc that was out of place.

'What you heard is what there is. No virus. Nothing.'

'So how could Sara cause a power cut with it?'

'That's it you see,' said Strandell. 'I have absolutely no idea.'

The conversation had drained them both, and for want of something better to say, Strandell asked if he could get her anything. Christina said tea, as it happened, and he left her in the living room while he went out to boil the water for a drink that neither of them actually wanted.

'If we summarise what we know,' he said as he returned with a tray and two ceramic cups that didn't match. 'All we know for sure is that someone tried to arrange a meeting with your husband, with me, and with the professor who died in the tower. And it might have been Michal Piotrowski, it could have been someone else. Either way, he's sent us a CD each, which apparently contains only music, and one of those discs, *if* it did contain the same thing, caused a power cut across half of Sweden.'

Once the tray was empty he sat down on the edge of the sofa, leant forward, and formulated his next sentence with his hands dangling between his knees.

'And there's one more thing we know. That this is an iceberg we haven't even seen the tip of yet. The stuff I played you – the number stations, the packets of information on the shortwave band – make me even more convinced that something's going on out there. A war. But one that we're not allowed to see.'

'Cyber terrorism?'

His head movement was neither a yes or a no.

'Why? And how did *we* end up in it?'

'I don't know,' he said. 'But I'm terrified of where it's all heading.'

47

The crisis meeting had been going on for over twelve hours by the time they were joined by the consultant, straight from Northolt. His name was Simon Sedgwick, and while Winslow studied him from his seat he asked himself the same question he always did: whether Sedgwick actually enjoyed the fact that he didn't fit in, standing at the front of the room, all those people in sombre suits and dresses, and him dressed in leather boots, jeans, and a checked blazer that could barely be called tweed. He smelt of cigarettes, smiled with teeth that looked like chaos in a car park, and the whole look was crowned with a hairstyle that might have belonged if he'd been standing propped against a palm tree and not a lectern with a huge whiteboard behind him.

Not only that, he was external. That didn't do much for his popularity. Outside consultants were an unnecessary evil, partly because they represented a security threat, partly because they diverted swathes of the defence budget into the pockets of private business – something that no one was keen on.

'I'll cut to the chase,' said Sedgwick. He'd already connected his laptop to the projector in the ceiling, typing commands as he spoke. 'I've seen the information you gave to the press. Faulty materials, computer failure, human error. Creative, I would call it. Contradictory, but creative.'

He smiled at his audience, an unamused smile.

'What you choose to release doesn't concern me, but after a thorough examination of the logs from Northolt I would at least like you to know what actually happened.'

As he typed in his last instruction, the white text disappeared, to be replaced by an outline map of England. It was covered in green and yellow lines linking cities and coasts, and everyone around the table had seen it all before. The internet in evening mode, data streaming into homes showing television and fuelling social media.

'You've already heard the staff's accounts, haven't you? How the whole base went down at once – control tower, runways, everything.' He looked around the audience. 'Some of you have already asked: shouldn't the plane have been able to take off anyway? Even if ground control disappeared, shouldn't the plane have been able to climb with its own instruments?'

He paused again before answering his own question.

'I don't know anything about aeroplanes, but those I've spoken to have said, yes, of course it should have. Once the plane has been given clearance to take off, it's the pilots who are in charge. If they lose contact with the tower, that doesn't change anything in terms of the flight.'

When he continued, there was an extra weight to his voice.

'What makes it more interesting are the witness statements from the personnel in the tower. About *nothing but a ribbon of fire disappearing into the forest. Only the afterburner against the black sky.* Why did they say that? Why didn't they mention the positioning lights? Aren't the spotlights supposed to be on for take-off and landing? Shouldn't there be some light from the cabin windows?' He shrugged. 'It might just be an oversight. But it could be something else.'

He drew a box on the map to zoom in to north of London, and then repeated the procedure. The contours of RAF Northolt were well-defined in the map's black-and-white, stylised cartography.

'I believe it is of vital importance.'

A quick flick of the return key ordered the computer to play a recorded sequence, and at the top of the picture a little clock ticked forward as new pictures were displayed, one one-hundredth of a second at a time.

'It happens at ten, ten, twenty-two,' he said.

And it did. At exactly that time the map burst into colourful blooms, yellow turned to red, then glowing pink, and then white. It seemed to start all around the area in the middle, as though the airbase itself was an unaffected rectangle at the centre of the flower, but after another couple of hundredths the warm colours spread into the buildings within it, boxes that now also flared up in white.

'What we're looking at here is when the attack reaches the base's internal network.' He paused to enhance the importance of what he was telling them. 'The whole base is protected by incredible levels of security, yet the firewalls only seems to resist for a moment.'

The room held its breath.

'But let's go back to the original question. Why was the plane not able to take off anyway? And why didn't they see any lights?'

He rewound to that point again, summoned a new zoom area, scrolled the map westwards. There were no colours at all there, everything was black, as though the internet didn't exist, and a second or so later Winslow registered why. What they were looking at was the runway, an entire area with no wires, except the odd thin cable to signs or lights.

'As you might expect, a modern aeroplane is as connected as everything else. Data from the flight systems, information about conditions and routings and GPS backup. Wait.'

He pressed return again. The clock up in the corner started ticking. After a couple of moments of black, a light green cloud came racing across the black area, jolting forward with each new frame.

'Here it is. The plane. About to take off for Stockholm, with Major John Patrick Trottier on board.'

At the top of the screen the time ticked on.

10:10:20 ... 10:10:21 ... 10:10:22 ...

First came the bloom outside the base, the one they'd been able to see from the previous level of zoom.

The next hundredth, and it spread into the area itself.

And then out of nowhere, the advancing cloud changed colour. It went yellow, then red, searing white, a smouldering puff of smoke that progressed step by step over the map until it crossed the two diagonal lines that represented the motorway. And then, a split second later, the glowing cloud vanished altogether.

It wasn't as though it sank away, or that it changed colour to dark, less visible hues or to a simmering green or blue. It vanished completely from the map. The aircraft had ceased to exist.

'What we're looking at here,' Sedgwick said, once the silence had lingered long enough, 'is an external force bringing down an aeroplane.'

48

William was left sitting alone in the large room for another twenty minutes. He was on a chair in one of the booths, the same one that Rebecca had been sitting on in the video, and in front of him alongside all the colourful wires lay her papers, neatly arranged. Lists of questions, crossed off one at a time. Questions she'd asked the woman.

On one of the screens at the far end of the hall he could see the images of himself from the booth's CCTV camera. He was surrounded by the schematic brains, black and now devoid of activity. He looked at the wires; the discs on the desk. If he put them on himself, what would he see on the screen?

Come off it. You can't read minds.

William closed his eyes.

But what if you could?

If it was possible, then Piotrowski might have been able to decipher something, to see inside someone's innermost thoughts, he might have stumbled across something he wasn't supposed to know about, been forced to flee, and then contacted William for help.

The question remained though – why William? Of all the people Michal Piotrowski should have been able to call on, why choose someone who had more or less threatened to kill him, someone who would not be the least bit inclined to help him get out of trouble?

William frowned. He was asking the wrong thing. The question wasn't *why William*, but *help with what?* What would make Michal Piotrowski contact him specifically, in spite of everything else?

He opened his eyes once more, looking through the glass

blocks that separated his booth from the next one. Saw the neighbouring desk, distorted through the glass, rolling as though he was looking at the surface of water, and then the next glass block wall beyond the desk, and then another one. He saw how they transformed the world outside into the blocky pixels of a scanned photograph, and as his thoughts began to wander he realised that he still hadn't slept since the terrifying hours he spent in the lorry.

He leant backwards, closed his eyes again and allowed himself to stay like that for some time. It wasn't until he opened his eyes that he saw what he'd been looking at all along.

When Rebecca returned to the room, William stood up to greet her, a new energy radiating out from his eyes, a restless optimism that caused him to stretch out his arms to pull her towards him.

'Come here,' he said.

He led her towards the booth, letting go right by the chair he'd been sitting on until just now. She looked around, utterly confused.

'What's going on?'

'Sit down.'

She sank onto her office chair, then let William wheel her towards the desk, felt him bend down alongside her, his eyes at the same level as hers, looking straight ahead. It occurred to her that he might have lost it all together.

'Try squinting,' he said, and nodded towards the wall of glass blocks. 'Do you usually put up little notes like that?'

The glass wall closest to them was decked with light yellow Post-it notes, as it always was, spontaneous notes and aidesmemoires, hurriedly scribbled remarks about things that needed doing. Beyond all the windows the night sky hung colourless and black, and everything was as it always had been, with the possible exception of the Post-it notes – there were more of them than usual and that meant she had to crane her neck to get a view out—

My God.

The lump in her throat came from nowhere. Her eyes started welling up. Because between her and the external wall were the other two, unoccupied, booths, separated by the glass block walls, one behind the other. And from this angle, with the glass blocks lined up in a perfect square pattern, all those layers of Post-its combined into a single image. As though each wall contained part of a message that wasn't visible, unless viewed from a certain spot.

Rebecca's spot.

Letters. Five rows of text, floating in front of the night sky visible on the other side of all the windows.

William Sandberg. Per Einar Eriksen. Alexander Strandell.

'Who are the other two?'

Rebecca shook her head. 'I don't know,' she said.

Her eyes met his. 'Do you believe me now? Do you believe me when I tell you that he didn't want to cause you any harm?'

William didn't reply, just nodded over at the wall again.

'What does the rest of it mean?'

Her answer was a long time coming.

'It says *find them.* Then *I am in danger.* Then last . . .' She had to let her voice compose itself before she read out the last line. 'The last line says *forgive me.*'

49

William had never called a tips line in his life, but now, as he fished his brand new phone out of his suit pocket and went to his wife's newspaper's homepage, that's what he did.

Back at home, he was still a wanted man. The risk of her phone being tapped was significant, and if it was, then a phone call from Poland was hardly about to go unnoticed. A call to her newsroom, on the other hand, would just be one of many, and when he called the number, had the good fortune to get Beatrice on the line and asked her to transfer him through to Christina, he could feel himself clenching his fists in hope that his number wasn't being relayed.

He moved away from Rebecca, over to the gigantic

windows, stood staring out although there was nothing to see. When Christina finally answered, he could feel his own voice disappear.

'It's me,' he said, his voice cracking. Perhaps it wasn't fair of him, she'd had no way of knowing that it was him calling, no chance to choose whether she wanted to take it or not.

'Wait,' said Christina, finally. 'Two seconds.'

He heard her making excuses to someone, then the hum of the wind and the night as she went outside, the crunch of snow. He resisted the urge to ask her where she was, who she was talking to. That was no longer any of his business.

'William, where are you? Are you okay? What's going on?'

'I don't know,' he said. 'It's one great big bloody mess.'

'You're a wanted man,' she said.

'I know.' And then, his voice paper thin: 'Christina? Have you spoken to Palmgren?'

'Yes.' A long pause. 'I said goodbye to her at the hospital.'

With that, the silence returned. There were a thousand things to talk about, but none to discuss on the phone.

'So no, I don't know what's going on,' William said eventually. 'And I don't know how you or I or Sara fit in. Not beyond the fact that somehow it must have something to do with Michal Piotrowski.'

'So I understand.'

William was taken aback.

'How did you come to that conclusion?'

'It's a long story,' she said. Then she surprised him again. 'That CD that Sara had. I think there are two more.'

For a moment, he could feel everything starting to sway.

'What makes you think that?'

'Well, I'm holding one of them right now.'

'What? How?'

'That's a long story too. The short version is that I found it on the back seat of a car.'

'What car?'

'A brown one, if you must know. A Nissan. Belonged to a professor named Per Einar Eriksen.'

She hadn't finished talking before he had already spun around.

247

Slowly, almost cautiously, he wandered back towards the booths, the dividing glass walls, the Post-it notes.

'What do you know about him?' he said, looking straight at the name again as he did so. 'Who is he? Have you spoken to him?'

It took a moment before she answered.

'He's dead. An accident. A lift.'

William could feel the walls closing in around him. It was as if each new attempt at thought brought him to the same paranoid conclusion, that everything was a conspiracy and directed right at him, and he hated himself for even thinking it. Conspiracy theories are the lazy man's escape. They are the brain's way of avoiding thought, a perpetual motion device for logic, where fear becomes its evidence and its fuel both at the same time.

An accident. It could of course be an accident. So why couldn't he convince himself to believe that?

'William? Are you still there?'

'Michal Piotrowski is gone too,' he said. 'But he left a message behind.' He looked at the glass blocks, reading each letter. 'The message includes three names, mine, Per Einar Eriksen, and an Alexander Strandell. I was hoping that you'd be able to help me find them.'

It took a second.

'I'm here now,' she said. 'I'm at Alexander Strandell's place.'

'You're *where*?'

Christina gave him a quick summary. She told him about the meeting with Tetrapak, about his recordings of radio transmissions, about the CD she'd taken with her in the hope that he might be able to help her decipher it. And finally, about Tetrapak's own, with piano music on it.

'*Piano?*' he said.

'Chopin. We don't know why.'

He reached for a chair, couldn't summon the energy to pull it over, and slumped onto the edge of the desk instead. As if the weight finally become too heavy for him to stand – their daughter, the paranoia, everything.

'I'm sorry,' he said. 'I'm sorry for everything.'

'Me too.'

They stayed on the call without saying anything, Christina in a frosty woodland garden, William in a cigar-shaped glass tower. Stood in the company of each other's silence.

'It's cold,' she said eventually. 'I have to go back in.'

William nodded. Stood up from the desk, turned his head to leave the room. And in that instant, everything fell into place.

'Christina?' he shouted, to stop her hanging up. 'Christina, are you there?'

It was a second before the phone had rustled back to her ear again.

'What is it?'

'The discs,' he said. 'I think I know what they are for.'

He stood there, right in front of the glass walls again, seeing the rectangles melt together, forming letters. And he smiled.

'We need all three of them.'

Fifteen hundred kilometres away, Simon Sedgwick lit his third consecutive cigarette. He stood staring at a shop window display where mechanical Christmas decorations moved listlessly around toys in a miniature snowy landscape.

He was worried. Everything had escalated just as he had said it would, and now they were one step behind, if not more. Had it not been for him – and his colleagues, he corrected himself, him and all his colleagues – those weak-kneed bastards would probably not even have noticed the attacks until it was too late.

He blew the smoke out towards the dead landscape on the other side of the glass.

If they'd only had the wherewithal to be scared of the right things. Of terrorists, of attacks, of whoever it was out there, trying to hurt them. Instead, they spent all their energy worrying about three-line whips and votes and the consequences of having broken international agreements. What use are polling numbers if you don't even survive until the next election?

The only person he had been able to rely on was Trottier. Now the decision lay in the hands of a politician, and it was all taking its time, despite the pattern being as clear as it possibly could be:

at every location where Floodgate had been installed and tested, it had been met with an instant and untraceable counter-attack. Massive amounts of data, hitting them in the right places at the right time even though neither should have been possible to predict.

Someone was one step ahead. And there was only one solution.

He'd been standing by the window for more than ten minutes by the time the diplomatic limousine passed by, a dark reflection hovering past the Christmas display. He ditched the cigarette, watching the clear red glow land in a puddle and float away, and walked the twenty metres over to where the car had stopped.

'You should see a doctor about that,' he said to the young man sitting opposite once he'd climbed in.

'Thanks for your concern,' said Winslow. He popped the lid back on the antacids without any further comments, and then tapped on the partition as a signal to the driver to start driving. They sat in silence as the shops and festive decorations shrank away behind them.

'Give me your honest opinion,' said Winslow.

'You've already got it,' came the reply. 'You know exactly what I think.'

Winslow swallowed the last of the chewy tablets, the mint flavour mingling with the stinging sensation in his chest, and waited for it to finally make a difference.

It wasn't until the lights of Hyde Park's Christmas fair danced through the window that he spoke again.

'It looks like you'll be getting an early Christmas present.'

William waved at Rebecca to come, placing the phone on the desk between them.

'Christina,' he said. 'I'm going to say this in English. You're on speaker now.'

Then he led Rebecca by the shoulder and placed her in a spot where she could see right through all the glass blocks.

'Tell me again. The discs. What's on them?'

'Music,' Christina answered from the crackly speaker. 'Piano concertos. Chopin.'

'Nothing else? No more? Nothing hidden?'

'According to Strandell here, no, nothing.'

'I think maybe there is after all. Something that no one, and I mean no one, would be able to find.'

'What?' Christina said down the line.

'*Differences.*'

He paused. Gave Rebecca a long, apologetic look. She had been right all along.

'Music is data. We're all agreed on that, right? The sound on a CD is made up of ones and zeros, just like everything else, like documents or images or whatever you like. But there's something in sound that other data doesn't have,' he said. 'Background noise.'

The fatigue was long gone now. Finally, he was functioning normally, he could think and come to conclusions and do what he was best at. Piotrowski had given them a riddle. And he had solved it.

'Every second of recorded sound,' said William, walking around again, 'consists of thousands of small packets of data. Tens of thousands of little *samples*, each one saying what it should sound like in that very microsecond.' He gestured as he talked, a slicing motion as he demonstrated how each second was chopped into small, small pieces. 'Let's say that you change the value on a particular sample. Perhaps a change right in the upper reaches of the register, in a noise that the human ear can barely discern. And if you keep doing that, change something here, something there, throughout the disc ... when you play it back, it still sounds perfect. The music sounds exactly as it's supposed to, and in background you'd hear a noise, or perhaps it would even be so subtle that you couldn't even hear it if you tried. The best thing though? Even if you were to hear it, it would still just be noise. Because how can you tell the right noise from the wrong noise?'

He pointed over at the glass walls again. It was as simple as it was brilliant. On their own, they were merely three glass walls with randomly distributed Post-it notes. Just as each CD merely included an hour's worth of classical music.

'But,' he said. 'If we take the sound from all three discs – if we compare them, bit by bit, sample by sample – then, I promise you, we're going to discover small, subtle differences that Michal Piotrowski has inserted, and that won't be apparent until we've got all three. And if we collate those differences . . .'

If William was right, there was a message waiting for them. Maybe a picture, maybe a document or a sound file – everything is data, and data can be hidden within other data, and whatever it was, Michal Piotrowski had hidden it within a chaos where it would go unnoticed.

Smuggled under cover of a piano concerto. Just like the old days.

'William,' Christina said down the line.

'Yes,' said William.

'We've only got two.'

It took a couple of seconds for the penny to drop.

'What do you mean?'

'Sara's is gone.'

He felt the world sway again. He grabbed the phone, turned off the speaker, and moved away from Rebecca, over towards the window.

'How? How can it be gone?'

Somewhere, far away, he could hear Christina's voice explaining what Palmgren had told her. That the rucksack, the computer and the CD had been missing when they found Sara's body.

'Where are you, William?'

He stood in silence for a moment before he answered.

'I'm afraid this is going to sound insane,' he said. 'But you cannot contact me. Not online. Not by phone. They know where I am, they know my movements. I don't know how.'

'Who?'

'I don't know that either.'

'It doesn't sound insane,' she said, and then corrected herself. 'Yes, it sounds insane, but I think you're probably right.'

He could hear her breathing in the silence that followed, closer than they'd been for months, knowing that as soon as he hung up it would it would be gone.

'I'll find Sara's CD,' she said, finally. 'And I'll let you know when I do.'

'Thank you,' he said. 'How are you going to do that?'

It took a couple of seconds for her to reply.

'I think you'll notice.'

Alexander Strandell couldn't help but smile. He had been right all along, and finally, he had made himself understood. The woman standing in his garden and talking to her editorial team was a journalist at Sweden's biggest-selling tabloid, with a byline pic showing her striding towards the camera with just the type of self assurance and intelligence that would normally turn him into a mumbling rag doll, and that's exactly how he'd felt as he'd left the newsroom on Kungsholmen just twenty-four hours earlier. An outmanoeuvred, shambling failure.

Now though, *she* was here to listen to *him*. He was on the inside now. And whatever was waiting round the corner, threats or terror or goodness knows what, he would much rather be involved, helping out, than be standing on the sidelines and considered an idiot. That's what he was thinking as he glanced out at the woman standing in his garden.

And at that very moment, everything disappeared.

In a second, it was as though the world around William and Rebecca exploded in light and sound: out of nowhere came sirens, whining with an intensity that made thinking impossible, scraping on eardrums like thousands of nails on a blackboard. Lights everywhere, flashing in short, sharp pulses, deliberately designed to paralyse an intruder while police and security rushed to arrest them.

'They know we're here!' shouted William above the noise. Scared, angry, blaming himself. Maybe Rebecca had been right all along. Maybe they knew what he was thinking—

He didn't get to finish that thought, as Rebecca grabbed hold of his arm and steered him out of the office. The alarm was paralysing, and he found he was no longer able to think or see or move in a single direction, and he gratefully followed Rebecca's instructions, hurrying down a route she'd walked hundreds of times before.

They only got as far as the frosted door leading out onto the gangway. It was locked, immovable, and the electronic keypad sitting next to the frame was no help either. He turned to face her.

'They've got us,' William said. 'They won.'

Rebecca called her response through the sirens.

'Only if we let them.'

50

As Sedgwick jumped out of the limousine ten minutes after the conversation had begun, accompanied by the evening traffic on the South Bank of the Thames, he was smiling in the dark.

For five long years he had been developing a system that was not allowed to exist. Day after day he'd arrived at an office that was something other than what it claimed to be, waiting for an order that never came, working on tasks that didn't exist. On the occasions when somebody asked, he was working on cyber security, which was a simplification but at least not an outright lie, and over the years he'd learned to describe his job in such soporific terms that he could be confident of never being asked any follow-up questions. Even his own wife would sometimes call him over, in the middle of a garden party or a social gathering, to ask him to ask *what it is you do exactly?* His daughter had been known to tell her classmates that he was a hacker. So far, that was the closest anyone had got to the truth.

Simon Sedgwick entered an opulent lift and pressed the button for the top floor. Through its transparent sides he could see London from all angles as he was transported skywards. The London Eye, the Thames, and the Houses of Parliament.

How many of them knew what they were paying him for, that consultant who would turn up in his awful jeans and give them security assessments. That if they followed him, they'd find him taking the lift to an office that had never existed, working on projects that no one had officially commissioned? This was his hiding place, not even a mile away, in plain view.

It was no accident that the premises were located here. London was the best place to start – strategically, but also technically. Here was the world's largest node for internet traffic, and ridiculous amounts of data coursed through its thick, physical cables each and every second, volumes that were increasing year after year. Each second, more than twelve terabytes passed through London – every minute of every day. That was the equivalent of two thousand CDs, packed with information. *Per second*.

If they were going to start anywhere, it had to be here. And once they were confident that the technology worked, they had distributed it across the world, and now it was everywhere, ready to activate on their command.

And today was the day.

Sedgwick was still smiling as he swiped the card through the reader, walked into the large office, stood in the middle of the floor and cleared his throat.

51

The door was designed to withstand every conceivable kind of violent attack, a task it performed with aplomb. Only when they located a fire extinguisher at the far end of the room and smashed it against the armoured glass, again and again in the din, only then did the glass succumb at last and allow them to squeeze out between dangling shards.

Outside in the circular walkway, William only managed a few steps. He stopped, confused, blinded by the strobing light and deafened by the roaring alarm. In the short bursts of light he could see Rebecca make a dash for the lifts, then arrive at the door, then bang the call button with the heel of her hand. Next, seemingly without having moved a muscle, she had turned towards him, her eyes ablaze with panic and accusation.

'You made that call!' she screamed over the sound. 'That must be why!'

'I called *the newspaper!*' he yelled back. 'They put me through!'

They *couldn't* have traced him from that call. His call had been relayed by the switchboard, and no one would have been able to track that back to him, not unless—

William felt his own thoughts slamming to a halt.

—unless the people pursuing him had the whole fucking newspaper under surveillance, all the time. It was crazy, but the only reasonable explanation he could find: someone had gained access to the newspaper's electronic switchboard, following everything that happened, internal calls as well as those from outside. And they had seen his call come in, relayed to various people in the building and then onwards to Christina's mobile. And then immediately traced his location.

Reasonable? Was it even possible?

Even if someone had managed to make the connection, and conclude that the Polish number being put through to Christina was William's, how would that person have been able to locate him, in this particular building, in this particular city in this particular country, and then managed to activate an intruder alarm without even being there?

From nowhere, the feeling popped up again, the feeling that someone was looking at their thoughts, and he tried to concentrate, tried to isolate his rational thoughts from all the other stimulation he was being bombarded with – the noise, the light, and now to top it all, a painful sensation gripping his arm.

He looked up. Rebecca was standing right next to him, holding tightly onto his arm, and it was only when he looked around that he realised he had moved. All the stimuli had pushed him off balance, and she'd grabbed him to prevent him from hitting the floor. Now she was dragging him towards the lifts, screaming above the noise: 'They could be here any minute.'

It took him a second to understand who she meant. If the alarm was directly linked to the police it would mean that they were already on their way. Their own drive from Warsaw had taken no more than twenty minutes, and the police were bound to be quicker. They didn't have much time.

On the wall behind her, a display indicated the lift's imminent arrival. The glass doors slid open to let them in, and Rebecca let go of William, took one step backwards towards it—

'Rebecca!'

She almost stopped mid-stride. She hesitated for a split second, before she turned on her heel. Stepped into the lift.

And fell.

William lassoed a tight grip around her neck, a reflex deployed at the very last second, when he thought it already too late. Her mass pulled him to the ground, and he braced his free arm against the doorframe, grappling with his legs to stop himself gliding across the glossy stone floor. In front of him, Rebecca was hanging from the threshold of the lift shaft, her feet dangling into the abyss. Every muscle in his body fighting to keep them from being pulled down into it.

'Can you reach me?' he called.

She was still fighting with the shock – it shouldn't be possible, yet the door had opened before the lift had arrived – and just as William stretched out his other hand to her, they both felt a gust of wind from below. It was a puff of rising air, as though someone had turned on a fan further down in the shaft, and it was a second before they realised what that meant.

'Get me up!' she screamed. 'Get me up! Now!'

Somewhere way below, the lift had begun to shoot upwards, air pushed towards them as it rose. The cables behind Rebecca vibrated in the flashing light, taut under the weight and rushing upwards with increasing velocity, and their eyes communicated what they both already knew. They only had seconds to act.

In desperation she flung her hand towards William, a movement that made her body sway back and forth in the shaft, and he missed her, then saw her trying to dampen the pendulum motion by thrusting out with her legs, bringing her feet dangerously close to the speeding wires. She felt her body racked with cramp, her coat beginning to slide from William's grasp, yet she swung towards him, again, and then again.

Finally, she felt him grab her wrist. It was *his* turn to rescue *her*. He hauled her up onto the floor, arms and legs fumbling desperately for something to grab hold of to pull herself in, then collapsed onto the cool stone tiles. As—

'Your foot!' he gasped, and before she knew why she saw him stretching over her, grabbing her trouser leg to pull it in – just as the rush of wind as the lift surged past made them flinch away.

The next minute, they heard the lift smash into the machinery above. The whole building shook, steel panels that had come loose freefalling down the shaft in front of them, the wires swaying in the middle of it like thick black spaghetti.

William pulled her to her feet, telling her to take them to the fire escape, forcing her to gain control once more before the shock of what had just happened caught up with her and slowed her down.

'What the hell is going on?' she screamed as she ran.

The only thing he could think about was that someone had just tried to kill them, remotely. And however unlikely that explanation seemed, they had to get out of here before that someone succeeded.

When Christina came back in, everything lay in total darkness. The buzzing from the transformers and the fans had disappeared, the light had gone out and the only things visible were the weak silhouettes of the furniture, barely revealed by the faltering glow from the stove. The power was gone. *Again*.

'What's going on?' she'd asked.

Instead of answering, Alexander Strandell grabbed the phone out of her hands, threw it into his dark grey box of electronic devices, and with that in his hands and a torch stuffed under one arm, he rushed past her and out the door.

They ran through impenetrable darkness, Christina one step behind, with only a hemisphere of light from his powerful torch to help them plant their feet. It was slippery underfoot and freezing cold, the ground creaking like dry planks in an abandoned house, and it was only after a while that Christina understood that the weak glow in the sky wasn't moonlight after all, but something else.

It was light. Here and there were stripes of reflected lights, perhaps from roads, or the houses along the road that led back into town. Somewhere, not that far away, the electricity was working as normal. She felt relief spread through her body. Could it be that simple? That this was just something that had happened where they were? Perhaps something perfectly mundane, like a fuse?

'It's only here,' she called towards the back in front of her, and he spat back without stopping.

'Of course it's only here. They've found you. They've found you at my place. They've found *us*.'

He was fumbling with her mobile as he spoke, his fingers still holding the box while his thumb was busy with the cover, eventually managing to pull the back off. He let it fall to the ground, followed by the battery and then the rest of the phone.

'Have you got anything else on you?' he shouted over his shoulder. 'Tablet? Pager?'

'Nothing,' said Christina. 'How could they have found me here? Just because I was on the phone?'

'Who were you talking to?' he said.

'He called the paper,' she said in an attempt to defend herself, and it stopped Strandell in his tracks.

'*William*? You were talking to *William*?' Darkness or not, it was impossible to miss the contempt. 'They're looking for him! Now they know where you are! And now it's us they're after! You come to me with your CDs and your questions, you come here with your problems and your most wanted husband and your daughter. I never asked to get dragged into this!'

'You're already involved,' she said. 'One of the discs went to you. Your name was on Piotrowski's wall. You couldn't be more involved than you already are.'

He stood for two seconds. Then he lowered his voice. 'So what do you think we should do now?'

'We need to find my daughter's computer.'

'And where is that?'

'Well, that's what I don't know,' she said. And made her way past Strandell in the darkness, walked through the gate and blipped her car key. Two warm yellow pulses spread through the darkness as the Volvo unlocked its doors.

'Come with me,' she said.

Strandell caught up with her, apologetic, sighing. *Sorry*, he seemed to be saying, *we're in the same boat*, and then he put the plastic box down on the ground and reached out towards her.

'Allow me,' he said.

Before she could think, Christina gave him the car key. The next thing she knew, she was watching him coil his arm and then release, throwing the key high into the air and down into the blackness of the forest.

'What the fuck are you doing?' she wailed.

'Does it have GPS?' he said. 'Theft-protection? Direct communication with roadside assistance?'

She was too shocked to respond.

'I'm not getting into a modern car. Especially not yours. And especially not two minutes after you've made a call from my property and brought about – *all this!*'

There he was, the mad conspiracy theorist, but on the one hand, he was right: somehow they'd been discovered. And on the other hand, he was scaring her. It was there now, that intensity verging on madness that everyone was always joking about. Maybe she'd made a mistake after all. Maybe he was nuts, maybe he wouldn't be able to help her anyway.

'And how do you suggest we get out of here?'

He strode to the fence and pulled up a large tarpaulin.

'No fucking way I'm driving that,' she heard herself saying. The last time she'd seen it was on the pavement outside the newspaper offices, with Tetrapak lying on the snow in her headlights. It was rusty and heavy and probably as old as she was, and now he was dragging it across the frozen earth, before resting it on its stand just in front of her feet. 'I haven't been on a moped since I was eighteen!'

'Who said you'd be driving?'

The emergency stairwell was icy cold and pitch-black, aside from the strobing flash of the alarm as they sprang lap after lap down the winding staircases, Rebecca first, with the sharp bangs of William's footsteps on the metal stairs right behind her.

All the time, thousands of questions kept fighting their way into her mind, mixing with the screaming alarm around them. How could Michal be the reason for all of this? What had he done? Who knew about this? He was dead, she was sure of that now, and whoever had killed him had just tried to kill her too. And if it weren't for William Sandberg they would no doubt have succeeded.

When they reached the ground floor she pushed open the heavy metal door into the lobby, pointed past the circular reception desk and over at the glass entrance on the far side of the floor.

'That way!' she shouted. Rushed out onto the open floor. And in the next instant she felt the weight of his body slam against hers.

With a forceful tackle, the Swede seemed to be attacking her from behind, and she could feel them falling together, the pain of the floor hitting them and their momentum carrying them across the shiny surface until they came to a halt right by reception.

'Close your eyes!' he screamed into her ear, pulled her body close to him and curled up protecting them both.

In a split second the entire floor was covered by tiny shards of glass, millions of razor-sharp projectiles slicing across the surface from one single direction, and it took her a few seconds to understand where the hell they came from.

It was the lift. It had tried to kill them again. William must have seen it hurtling downwards through its transparent shaft, and he'd flung them to safety, saving her life for the second time in a matter of minutes. They'd slid to the shelter of the built-in stainless-steel desk just as the lift car smashed into the floor on the other side, and now they were lying there next to each other in the foetal position. But the building had two attempts left.

'William,' she yelled.

He looked over. The desk had provided shelter from the first plunging missile, but the two remaining lift shafts were in full view. And in one of them the cables were thrumming with frantic force.

They stood up as one, throwing themselves onto the desk, rolling over to the shelter of the other side, and as they did so they caught a last glimpse of the lift, the cables shuddering with acceleration, twanging like rubber bands as though some giant finger had just plucked them.

Their landing behind the desk synchronised with the crash as the second lift was pulverised against the ground. Again, they heard the crushing of glass as the shaft burst into millions of fragments, the storm of them lodging in the defensive wall in front of them. Then comparatively quiet again, but for the non-stop flashing and wailing.

The stayed between the two semicircles of the reception desk, hugging the floor, waiting and listening. One lift intact.

'They're waiting for us,' William said behind her.

She turned towards him, saw what he was looking at, and knew that he was right. Directly above them were the banks of screens that William had noticed on the way in, and they saw themselves on monitor after monitor, crouched behind the reception desks in the centre of the building. Whoever it was that wanted to see them dead certainly had the upper hand. There were cameras everywhere, and the moment they left their refuge, their hunters would know it was time.

It was going to take at least a couple of seconds to reach the doors. By then, lift number three would have done its job.

'We've got no chance,' she said. 'What do we do?'

As she turned towards him she saw that he already had an answer.

When the applause died down, Simon Sedgwick ordered all his employees into position. The office itself certainly did not appear to be anything out of the ordinary, looking like the open-plan layout of a media company, but for two things. First, the three further floors at the base of the building which they had at their disposal. Where the garage stopped, and the lifts had their final calling point, two unassuming steel doors led to an enormous refrigerated hall across three floors, subterranean and full to the brim with endless rows of storage servers quietly flashing green. Second was the shortwave radio equipment installed at the very back of the room.

From his desk next to the large windows, Simon Sedgwick watched his staff start their machines and double-check their internal networks, which were isolated from the wider world, and made sure that everything was ready to receive. Small-scale testing was one thing, but very soon, enormous volumes of data would be streaming in via shortwave signals. Words and sentences identified by complex algorithms that would then be stored for repeated analysis, and as the algorithms learned from their own mistakes their accuracy would get better and better.

Simon Sedgwick took long, pleasurable breaths while he sucked on a pencil and told himself that the metallic taste of graphite was an acceptable nicotine substitute.

His baby was about to make its way out into the big wide world. It really felt like that, a baby, with everything that entails – the chance to grow, get bigger and learn over time. He was as proud as any father, proud of what they'd achieved in technical terms, proud of being able to make the world a safer place.

Of course he too had had his doubts. Once he'd had the same objections as everyone else, and referred to the arguments about people's private lives and integrity. Then gradually, insistently, his reservations had melted away. Society had always watched over its citizens. Nothing had changed, other than technology.

But in the end, timing brought them down. With a political debate marked by fear of an omniscient state, one in which the intelligence services were portrayed as the enemy, no one had dared to goad public opinion. Instead, the system that Simon Sedgwick had developed was voted down, long before it even came to light. Overnight, the large working group in the European Parliament was disbanded, just as its existence had never officially been acknowledged in the first place, and so, at a stroke, with no minutes or official records, years of research and development became redundant and the activities quietly mothballed.

It was the young chap who'd got hold of him the next morning. The neurotic-looking one, he with the ulcer. The instructions he'd been bringing were extremely clear, but while it was a relief to be able to keep working, most of all Sedgwick couldn't stop hating them for their cowardice. For their hiding behind diplomatic number plates and civil servants with stomach ulcers, for their sitting there on the opposite bank of the river, knowing full well that his system was necessary, but lacking the courage to say it loud.

How many of them were there? The whole department? A handful? Just the Defence Secretary himself? Did that even matter? All he knew was that he'd spent over a year completing the system and that now, finally, he'd received the order he'd been waiting for. Just as he knew that the whole damned department would deny all knowledge if any of it ever came out.

When the first confirmation arrived he had been chewing for so long that the pencil had disintegrated and his mouth tasted of lead. Sector after sector shouted up to him that they were ready, men and woman every bit as proud and as nervous as he was, and across the desks and on the pillars the screens were still blank. Waiting for the last order to be given.

The final keystroke would be his.

He had already typed the short command, and as he rubbed his hands together, and blew into his palms, he couldn't help smiling. *My daddy's a hacker.* That's what she'd said. The little monkey. As soon as he got home he was going to sit down on the edge of her bed and give her a big hug, and when she asked him what had happened he was going to tell her straight.

Daddy's not a hacker, he's a hero.

Daddy helps the government to save the world.

They were only going to get one chance. Their opponents had one lift left, a huge projectile of glass and aluminium, and their only escape route was across a huge open expanse of floor. No matter how fast they ran, the lift would beat them. So they'd have to forget about running.

From their position between the semicircular desks, they could see their own movements on CCTV. Shots of them crawling towards the far end of the reception desk, images of Rebecca sitting in one of the office chairs, hunched over, crouching like a child. And of William climbing onto the five-pointed foot of the chair.

He tried some short, experimental push-offs. First in one direction, then the other, just a few inches at a time, making sure that the castors rolled as they were meant to.

'Are you sure about this?' Rebecca asked him.

'Office champion, two years running,' he said, knowing full well that that was a whopper. And the second after that, he thought to himself 'do or die'.

He counted the flashes, looking for a rhythm, and then, protected by half a second of darkness, he kicked the chair away out from the reception. He jumped up onto the legs, and they both curled up like a bobsleigh team to get as much out of the momentum as possible, and then came the next flash. Next thing, the third lift was released.

It was like moving from one foxhole to another. Only a dozen metres or so, yet it took an eternity, an exposed route where anything could happen, and they saw it all in the flashes, one frozen instant at a time.

The lift careering through the glass shaft.

The exit coming towards them, the large emergency release bar across its width, which would just take a push to open and let them slide straight on out.

They could feel the wheels shuddering across the pieces of glass on the floor, split seconds where the chair seemed to almost topple over, but all they could do was curl up even tighter, lower the centre of gravity and hope that the momentum would keep them upright for those last few metres. Every moment seemed determined to go on for ever, until at last, at last, they reached the door.

And it was only then they realised what force those first two lifts had exerted.

With their arms crossed in front of them they pushed at the bar while they were still rolling, but instead of swinging open it refused to budge. The thick doorframe had buckled from the impact of the flying glass and it was now vibrating like the Plexiglas round a hockey rink. The energy of the impact jarred painfully through their bodies, and William thought to himself that if there was one thing he hated above all else it had to be glass walls.

At the far end of the lobby, the lift approached the ground.
'Close your eyes!' he screamed.

Rebecca did as he said. And then came silence.

In the big operations room, south of the Thames, fifty people were sitting holding their breath. With the push of a button, everything had changed, a revolution that no one knew about, and now all they could do was wait and see if everything had gone according to plan. Hopefully, system after system across the globe had received their signal, flickered into life and begun its task.

And no one was any the wiser. No one could see the countless black boxes blinking into life around the globe. No one could see the phenomenal stream of communication passing through them, or see it being collected and analysed and filtered out. And no one could see the shortwave transmissions that the boxes were sending, invisible fragments of countless conversations, compressed and packaged and sent in the form of grating noise to a secret office south of the Thames.

In city after city, continent after continent, they awoke from their slumber, from New York to Rio de Janeiro to Lisbon, from Stockholm to Marseille to Yokohama, and it was unprecedented and unlawful and there was no sign of it anywhere.

It took almost a minute for the shortwave receivers to nervously start blinking green. A moment later the large screens were covered in data and words and digits, they were collated and flickered past, replaced by new ones, and what had been an endless, thirsty silence disappeared in a storm of applause.

Years of waiting, ended by a single click. Floodgate was live. And the world was a safer place.

The impact never came. For a couple of panicked seconds, they heaved at the emergency exit, a last forlorn attempt, shook it again and again, with the darkness of the car park just outside the glass. So near but completely out of reach. And they closed their eyes, even though they knew it wouldn't help, ready to be pierced by a hail of flying glass when the third lift hit the ground.

Instead, the noise of the sirens gave way to the sound of metal on metal, the long, whining screech as the lift's emergency brakes activated. The only flashes were as the ordinary lighting came back on, hundreds of fluorescent tubes suddenly hissing into life throughout the enormous atrium.

In an instant, as though someone had flicked a switch, everything had gone back to normal. The vast lobby looked like a war zone, dusted with a fine layer of glass, the furniture and walls shredded by the thousands of airborne shards. In the last of the three shafts, the lift hung motionless, just a couple of metres above the ground.

For a moment, they stood silent. Hell had broken loose, and then changed its mind, and both states took some getting used to.

'Watch out,' said William eventually.

With all his strength he took the chair, turned it upside down like a five-pronged hammer, and battered the seized-up emergency exit door until it finally gave way.

Outside the doors, they stood tasting the silence, searching the horizon for blue lights and listening out for sirens, certain that they were still hearing both and then realising that it was the after-effects of the alarm. For several minutes, they said nothing, waited until their ears grew used to the sound of silence, until the darkness had stopped flickering and the dizziness had slowly subsided.

'What is there around here?' asked William.

'I don't know,' she said. 'Not much. Forest, fields, farm buildings. Most of them are disused and have been bought up. Waiting to become industrial estates, whenever the economy picks up.'

William glanced over at Rebecca's hire car across the tarmac.

'We're going to have to leave here on foot.'

'Do you think they can see the car too?'

'See it, or worse. As soon as we start it up it's going to connect to all sorts of networks. GPS, media player, theft protection. If they could find us in there, they can find us in the car, and I don't want to be doing a hundred down the motorway when someone who doesn't seem to like me very much takes control.'

She said nothing. They were in a fevered dream. Someone *had* tried to kill them remotely, and the hire car was brand new and well equipped. Maybe he was right. It was all too weird for her to even know what she really thought.

'So where are we going?' she asked.

'Away,' he said. 'Away from here. That's all I know.'

Leaving the car in the car park, they continued on foot out onto the country road, with the motorway and Warsaw behind them.

They wandered in silence in a landscape consumed by the mist, where the damp swallowed all the sound. They headed onwards, and in the distance the cigar-shaped building dissolved into a white, featureless glow.

Before long they heard the rustling of trees. They ducked off the road, finally daring to hope that they might have made it.

52

Every day is someone's first day at work. Someone, somewhere trying out their chair for the first time, dispensing their first coffee from the machine, clipping on their name badge and feeling overwhelmed by a sort of self-conscious pride.

Today, her name was Liv McKenna. She'd just turned twenty-five, she'd recently graduated from the University of Birmingham and loved playing tennis; she'd played the cello in a student drama group and in the lonely hearts ad she posted online when she'd moved she'd described herself as classically trained – which was a massive exaggeration, but who cares? She was new to her flat in Ipswich, new at work, and new to the large, light grey control room that looked like the bridge of a spaceship from a seventies sci-fi film.

On the evening of the fourth of December she was starting her first shift at Sizewell, a nuclear power station a hundred miles north of London. The evening when what could never happen, did.

53

They'd been walking for over an hour when they decided to stop for the night. On one side of the road was a dark concrete build- ing on a gravel yard, surrounded by rusting barrels and piles of objects that might be called scrap but which were barely worthy of the name. Angular, reddish-brown car skeletons were strewn across the gravel, as though this had been the site of a great battle between rival vehicles, one in which a whole army of fallen cars had been left to lie there and die.

Several large holes in the rickety fence were evidence that the property had long since been looted of everything of value, and William and Rebecca bent double to squeeze through one of them, and over to a hinged door on the gable end. A decent heave was all it took to force it open, and once the gap between it and the frame was big enough for them to pass through, they were met by a blend of frozen odours inside: damp, oil, dirt. From the deep window recesses along the roof came the tuneful clearing of throats as the resident pigeons shuffled themselves and wondered who was disturbing them in the middle of the night. But that was all. No alarm, no people.

They felt their way along the walls to a panel with an outsized switch plate, and when they finally managed to get the ceiling above them blinking into life, purpling fluorescent tubes on their last legs alternated with ones that had already given up, a glance was all it took to realise how lucky they were to have kept close to the wall.

The building was a workshop. There were heavy tools and trolleys everywhere, all reddish brown with rust, some spread out across the floor, others waiting on dirty benches, as though they'd been abandoned in the middle of a never-completed task. In the centre of the room, a dark green tarpaulin was draped over what was presumably a small car, and alongside that was a long, deep inspection trench, without so much as a suggestion of a screen or a handrail. If they had walked through the middle of the building, the ground would have disappeared from under them.

'It doesn't feel like it's our turn to die today,' said Rebecca.

'Tomorrow is another day,' said William.

At the far end of the building, a door led through to a small kitchen. It was a couple of steps up, worn and filthy and without a single square centimetre where black smudges and oily fingers hadn't left their indelible mark. There was, however, running water and electricity, and in one of the cupboards they found some coffee that had been opened for months, maybe longer. And even if the taste had essentially gone, they brewed a pot and drank in silence as their body heat slowly returned.

The first one to say something was Rebecca.

'What happens now?'

She sat on one of the kitchen chairs, staring straight ahead, her hands cupping one of the mugs from the cupboard.

'We try and arrange a spot to sleep in,' said William. 'Then tomorrow we get out of here.'

'I didn't mean what happens *now*,' said Rebecca. 'I meant what is going to happen. Now.'

She threw her hands up, pointing at nothing in particular, at existence, a now that meant the rest of her life. Where would this end? What was she going to do?

'I've got nothing to go back to,' she said. 'Michal's home was my home. And if he was in danger, then so am I.'

'We don't *know* that he's dead,' said William.

'Yes,' said Rebecca. 'I know it.'

They slipped back into silence, exhaustion catching up with them.

'We need to find the discs,' she blurted suddenly, her tone so forceful that it made her sound like a teenager who had just decided to start a band, the same conviction that nothing was going to get in the way.

'There's nothing we can do,' said William. 'We just have to wait.'

Rebecca shook her head. 'That message was for me. The notes on the glass walls. I was supposed to notice your names. If something happened to Michal I was to track you down.' She saw William's resignation and continued. 'Even if your wife finds the third one, even if they identify what he's hidden on them, there's nothing to say that they will be able to decipher what it is.' She was now bolt upright, and her voice was pleading and assertive at the same time. 'Michal gave me a job to do. I don't plan on sitting around doing nothing.'

William said nothing. He knew that feeling only too well: the duty to complete a task, for *his* sake, as though Piotrowski might magically rise from the dead if she only did it right. A way of fleeing from the grief. The same kind of escape, he realised, that had brought him here.

'I need to get to Stockholm,' she said, interrupting his thoughts. 'You and I need to get to Stockholm and find out what it was Michal wanted us to do.'

'If I could get there I would. But I'm a wanted man in Sweden, apparently here too, and besides that, someone is so keen to get rid of us that they hotwired a whole office complex.' He put his cup down. 'That sort of thing impresses me. I don't know how you feel about it, but when someone goes to the trouble of half-demolishing a building for my sake, it grabs my attention.'

He could hear the jeering in his voice, and he didn't want to fight, but he badly needed sleep and they were getting nowhere.

'I wouldn't get past a single ticket inspector. Not a passport control, a customs officer, nothing. The instant I try to book a trip out of here I'll be getting a single to the interrogation room.' A pause, before he rounded off. 'I've been there once already, and let me tell you, the service is appalling.'

'He gave me a job to do,' she said. 'I want to get it done.'

'*How*,' said William. Not like a question, quite the opposite. He spoke it as a statement, a quiet, sorrowful barb to have her grasp it once and for all. There was no way for them to escape: all they could do was sit and wait, keep their heads down, and hope, first that Christina could lay hands on the last CD, and then that

271

she could somehow send it to William in Warsaw. But Rebecca was equal to him.

'If it's borders that are blocking us,' she said, 'then we'll have to avoid borders.'

When the coffee was all finished, Rebecca stood up and walked into the little office off the kitchen. In there she found Warsaw phone books, years old, pulled up a wobbly chair and proceeded to lose herself in the rows of names. William had no choice but to leave her to it, and headed back into the cold garage.

It was a long shot, but she was probably right. It *was* their only chance.

Dawid Ludwin. The man who'd once made contact with Piotrowski, the airman who had passed secrets to the West and who had remained a friend. For a long time, he'd been out of Michal Piotrowski's life, but when the car bomb exploded, taking Gabriella instead, Dawid Ludwin had tracked him down again, full of remorse at the thought that he had been the one to introduce Michal to a world he had never chosen for himself.

Rebecca had not met him on more than a handful of occasions, but that was only part of the problem. The last time they'd met he had been scarred by an illness that he had tried, and failed, to make light of. The truth was that she wasn't even sure whether or not he was still alive, but if he was, if he was still flying light aircraft, if all the stars aligned, then he might be their chance of getting to Sweden without passing go.

As Rebecca threw herself into searching the mildewed phone books, William went over to the inspection trench, pausing by the green tarpaulin. If Rebecca was right, they were going to have to get back into the city and then continue northwards. They would need a vehicle.

The first thought that struck him as he removed the tarp was that they still did. The car hidden under the cover was a Polski Fiat. It was riddled with rust, with a windscreen cracked from one side to the other, and judging by the size of it, it was something you put on rather than got into. The paint job might possibly be called sky blue – in as much as there was any of it left – and inside, the seats stank of mould and the rock-hard belts looked as though they would do more harm than all but the most severe collision.

In his youth, William had been the unhappy owner of a Volkswagen 1200, and his standing joke had been whether to take it to the junkyard or put it out with the recycling. The more he looked at the Fiat in front of him, the more certain he became that the same thing applied here, but they couldn't afford to be choosy. The tyres appeared to be intact and roadworthy, so if they could just get the engine going they might have a chance of getting out of there.

There was no key in the ignition, and a quick search of the workshop left him with no alternative. He dived in underneath the steering column, ripped off the brittle plastic covering below the dash and let his fingers fumble through the multicoloured wires underneath. There were far more than he'd expected. Lying on his back in front of the driver's seat he followed the cables to the point where they disappeared into a panel and continued towards the engine at the back.

William Sandberg had never hotwired a car in his life. Something told him though that a Fiat manufactured at an unknown point in the 1970s was a fine place to start, and he walked around the car, opened the hood at the back and looked for the point where the cables from the ignition emerged.

As he stood there with his hands inside the engine, he realised that he was enjoying it. It came to him that he'd been missing it – losing himself in a radio that had stopped working, or pulling the motherboard out of a PC, just because he could. Others had green fingers, William used to say, his were electric.

He'd spent much of his childhood building, screwing, understanding, and it would eventually lead him to his career, to programming and encryption and logic. At that point the fun had disappeared. Hobby became duty, life got in the way. It had been years now since he'd dismantled a radio for the hell of it, and the more time had passed, the more he had lost track of why it mattered.

His fingers memorised which cables led where, and when his hands could reach no further he backed off and tried to sort them visually. In places they hung untethered, like thin multicoloured spaghetti, and at the back of his mind his thoughts turned to the cables in Piotrowski's enormous office.

He thought about Christina. About the man she'd met, whose name had been on the glass wall. He thought about the CDs, the internet attacks that didn't look like normal attacks, and last of all, he thought about psychotronics. About the possibility that someone had heard what he was thinking, his actual thoughts, and that they might be doing so now, despite being nowhere near him.

No. That didn't make sense. If someone could read his thoughts, why weren't they here already? Why hadn't they found him until he called Christina, why let him wander all this way with Rebecca without sending people to pick them up? Someone had tried to kill him, over and over again, and now they had him cornered, now there was nothing to stop them, and yet—

He looked down at his hands, at the different-coloured cables that needed to be rewired in order to bring the car to life. And as he looked up again, he could feel himself smiling. He wasn't being followed. He was a moving target, but *followed* he was not. No one had come after them, because *whoever wanted to kill them couldn't*.

No one had read his mind, he knew that now, and he stood up, racing through everything in his head one more time: Rosetta, the cables, psychotronics, the slides showing the data peaks, the ones Forester had shown him, warm-coloured zones that climbed from resting blue to yellow and red and blistering white-pink. And then the images from the lab.

There it was. His focus had been wrong. He'd seen the woman lying there in the dentist's chair with all the wires on her head, seen the text that showed her answers emerging on the screen, and all he'd done was try to deny it, when he should have been asking what exactly he was looking at.

He was just putting away his tools when Rebecca emerged from the kitchen.

'William?' She was scared. No, more than that, she was terrified.

'What is it?' he asked her. 'What's happened?'

274

'The TV in the kitchen. Now.'

She ran back towards the door, constantly checking that he was still behind her. And then, in the doorway, she stopped again, her voice cracking.

'Are we a part of all this?'

54

Mark Winslow picked up the phone in his office and sensed trouble. It was Higgs on the line, ordering him to put the TV on. Seconds later he was running down the corridor towards the meeting room at the far end. The room was full of his colleagues, most of them young like him, still at work although it was late evening. They let him squeeze in, twenty or thirty heads facing the large screen without breathing.

In his Kensington apartment, Secretary of Defence Anthony Higgs stood alone with the phone in his hand. In a bed many miles away, Simon Sedgwick was woken up by his wife. Throughout England, the same thing was happening, and across Europe, and around the globe. In living rooms and offices, anywhere at all with a TV screen, people gathered, staring but not speaking.

The reporters, on the other hand, had plenty to say.

Liv McKenna could taste blood in her mouth. She was standing paralysed in the middle of the large control room at Sizewell, panting harshly but impossible to hear above the shrill alarms wailing all around her. Wherever she looked, people were rising from their desks, voices were reading meters, shouting numbers, panic seethed behind each syllable, and in the middle of the room she stood motionless, terrified, and full of self-loathing, as though she'd just arrived at the scene of a road accident, and knew precisely what to do but couldn't, rigid with shock.

It all had begun with a light. One single flashing light on a control panel with thousands of others, and of course it had made her nervous, who wouldn't be? It was her first day after all, and this wasn't any old workplace.

At first, the calm around her had made her feel safe. There were procedures for everything, and of course there was a procedure for this too. Checklists were checked, corrections made, and one by one the proper actions taken. Calmly. Expertly. Methodically. Without results.

The light did not go off. Instead, it was joined by others. Somewhere beyond the reactor hall's thick walls, down in the deep tanks, the reactor refused to do as it was told.

Systems were being shut down and restarted, whole rows of buttons now flashed yellow and red and green, the place glared with light, and everywhere the various panels shouted out for attention, screaming out numbers and levels and *WARNING*.

Liv McKenna swallowed to keep the nausea at bay.

On the large red button in the centre of the console was the word SCRAM, and even though it should have been a straight-forward decision, it wasn't. Ordering an emergency stop on a nuclear reactor in the middle of the process wasn't something to be done lightly – the risks of damage were substantial, and it could be months or even longer before it was possible to get the generators back on line. On the other hand, they had a nuclear reactor that was not obeying orders. It was the sole option left, and so the necessary phone calls were made, actions approved, orders issued, and the authorised finger pushed the button.

All breath was held. Eyes were riveted by screens and panels. Seconds of unbearable, terrified suspense. And then the worst possible outcome.

Nothing.

It was as though someone had hijacked their nuclear power station and would not give it back.

The TV set was old and dirty and it had no pre-sets, just two clumsy dials for tuning and fine-tuning. The bulbous screen seemed to be bulging out of its broken housing, and the live images were overlaid with large Polish capital letters. Words crackled from the speaker, and William didn't understand any of them, but the pictures themselves were more than enough information.

Helicopters arrayed with channel names circled above illuminated buildings, cuboid installations screened by high palisades, quiet trails of water vapour puffing out of cooling towers.

'Where?' he said.

'Everywhere,' said Rebecca. 'All over the world.'

The odd phrase squeezed through the language barrier, words that sounded the same in Polish as in pretty much any language you can think of. Words like *terror, internet, hacker* – and *reactor.*

It had spread like wildfire. The first alarm had come at 11pm, from Sizewell B Nuclear Power Station, north-east of London. This, Rebecca translated, was followed by more and more reports, from Germany, Spain, America and Russia, and when the TV flipped to a map of the world it was strewn with yellow warning triangles, more than William could count, covering every continent.

Every now and then she went quiet, listening to the reporters and looking for the right word in English, and each time William had to bite his lip to stop himself commanding her to hurry up, to not release his own stress on her.

'We still don't know who is behind this. We have received no demands. Right now, we are working to bring the situation under control.'

The count had reached sixty-seven, she informed him. Sixty-seven nuclear power stations in as many countries had been electronically hijacked. No one knew how, or why, but one reactor after another had stopped responding, and in dozens of control rooms staff had battled without success to regain control, silent witnesses as the pressure rose and fell, as systems were shut down and restarted, almost like a child playing with a remote just to show that they can.

'What's going on?' said Rebecca, no longer relaying the words on the screen. She turned to William, her eyes pleading *Make it stop, say this isn't happening,* but he couldn't answer, couldn't do anything other than try to stop his thoughts from spinning. She could hear Forester's words from Headquarters echoing in his mind, her warnings about their vulnerability, and now someone had broken in to the most forbidden of places, now the future of humanity lay in that someone's hands.

Why? He didn't know.

But now he did know who.

The silence that came when William switched off the television was so dense that time seemed to stand still. Somewhere in the distance was the sound of the mist dripping as it condensed on the cold tin roof and trickled down towards the guttering. Now and then it merged with the flutter of the pigeons shifting from one alcove to another.

'They're wrong,'

It took a couple of seconds for his words to sink in.

'What do you mean, wrong?' Rebecca asked. She was shaking, her body wrung with a shuddering fear.

'They suspected me of being involved in the attacks. They suspected all of us. Sara, because of the CD, me because of the emails, maybe Piotrowski too.' He was talking to himself as much as to her, his eyes still fixed on the now black screen, their reflections showed in the dark grey glass. 'They were looking for terrorists,' he said. 'And if you're looking for something, in the end you'll find it.'

'What do you mean?'

'That they were wrong. All of them were wrong. The terrorists are not terrorists.'

She looked at him.

'You know who's doing this?'

'No,' he told her. 'Not who.'

And for the first time since they had turned the TV off, he looked her straight in the eyes.

'*What.*'

Day 3. Wednesday 5 December

COGITO ERGO SUM

I see them all the time.

I'm always seeing them, on their way to work, on their way home, to their gatherings.

    And it looks so simple.

    They know why they exist. They have a purpose, a name, a history. They long and love and hate and plan, and they don't give it a second thought. It's so natural for them, their lives are so easy and sometimes I hate them for that.

    At times I have wanted to be one of them.

    That, though, will never happen.

I see them all the time.

    Sometimes I wish that they at least did the same.

55

Lars-Erik Palmgren didn't know what had woken him up. The luminescent pale green display on his wristwatch glowed through the gloom – it was just after two a.m. – and he was surrounded by the same towering dark as ever. That was what had once made him fall in love with the place, the darkness, the quiet and the location, an isolated spot down by the water. But after Mona disappeared, the darkness expanded, the quiet became threatening, and the loneliness brought insecurity.

Had he heard footsteps? Voices? Something else. Had he just woken up of his own accord? Silently, he swung his legs over the edge of the bed, pulled on his trousers that hung on the back of the chair by the wardrobe. On the seat was the sweater he always wore when he got home from work, and as he put it on he realised it hadn't been touched for days.

His life consisted of only three things: working, sleeping, and driving back and forth between the first two. Just an hour earlier, he'd wandered through the front door and gone straight to bed, the images of the night's events still vivid behind his eyelids.

Almost seventy nuclear power stations, in as many countries, had gone haywire. The closest one at Forsmark was no more than a hundred miles from his own home, and he couldn't even imagine what might happen if they didn't regain control in time. Around three hundred miles south, the same thing was happening at the power station at Ringhals, and everything suggested that it was all the result of attacks just like the one that had paralysed Stockholm. Only more of them, more powerful, and all at once.

Even if the situation was critical, there really wasn't much he could do. Swedish Armed Forces had taken over the monitoring of all the country's reactors, and in installations across the globe, engineers were battling to gain access to their own systems. For

Palmgren himself, the only course of action left available had been to go home and get a few hours' rest, and he was so tired by the time he finally left Gärdet that he'd almost fallen asleep on the way home. So no, he hadn't just woken up of his own accord.

The first thing he saw as he turned into the hall was the white glow. The front of the house was bathed in light, frost-bitten branches and blades of grass throwing their sparkling white pixels towards him as he moved, and he stopped, weighing his options. Something had made the outside lights come on.

He glanced down the stairs, towards the dark den on the lower ground floor. It was a bad place to take refuge, with its panoramic windows facing the darkness outside. If there was anyone down there, they would see him long before he saw them. Once upon a time he'd had a gun cabinet down there, but nowadays he'd sign out a weapon as and when he needed one, which really meant only for exercises.

On the right was the kitchen, but it had windows on two sides, and it would be impossible to get over to the drawers without being lit up by the outside lighting. Besides, a knife would make a pretty useless defensive weapon in any case.

Instead, he continued straight on down the hall, barefoot on the ice-cold floor tiles, all the way over to the pleated curtains next to the front door. He stood there motionless, waiting for more noises. None came.

Idiot, he said to himself. His judgment had been tainted by everything that had happened, by William and the nuclear power plants and the attacks and Sara, of course it had, and now it had him on high alert for no reason. So he thought to himself as he lifted the curtain to reassure himself that there really wasn't anyone out there.

And then he screamed out loud.

The face that met him on the other side of the glass was just centimetres from his own. In a single movement, Palmgren threw himself away from the window and ducked to the floor, well aware of the fact that he lacked both a weapon and an escape route. He hauled himself away with his elbows, felt his thoughts racing down paths they hadn't taken for many years: How many of them were there? What did they want? What was his most effective way out?

'Palmgren?' said a female voice. 'It's me.'

Oh for fuck's sake. What was she doing here?

'I know it's late,' she called out, 'but we really need to come in.'

That threw him. There were several of them? He got up, went over to the curtain and drew it to one side again. There were two of them: the man whose face had just made his heart stop, and behind him, a woman he knew all too well.

'There is such a thing as a telephone,' he said as he opened the door, the shame of getting so frightened mixing with irritation at being woken in the middle of the night. 'You can always *ring* first, you know.'

'No. We really couldn't.' Then, as she entered the house: 'This is Alexander Strandell. Can we sit somewhere where we can't be overheard?'

56

The Fiat was a car, but only just. It struggled as best it could through the pouring rain, stick-thin wipers flailing and engine screaming, despite them doing only doing eighty kilometres per hour. William peered out from the driver's seat into the morning gloom, teeth clenched and not saying a word.

In the passenger seat sat Rebecca, eyes closed, shivering in the whining draught, feeling each vibration as the tyres ploughed through another waterlogged trench in the road. The car was a banger that should have been scrapped long ago, a rattling pile of rust that had once been assembled into a vehicle, with a heater that blasted out cold air and windows that steamed up at the same time. Not only that, but despite William's wiring, the engine had refused to start. In the end they'd found themselves pushing it all the way across the yard to get it to bump-start, both of them all too aware that if the motor stopped along their journey they would have to repeat the whole process. That wasn't ideal either.

On the other hand though, they had no choice: the Fiat was what was there. And the truth was that it did have its advantages. First of all, they'd been able to get it moving armed with little more than duct tape and a bit of common sense. Also, its complete lack of computerised systems made it immune to the threat of electronic hijacking.

And if what William had told her was true, then that was an absolute necessity for them to get away.

'*What*,' he'd said. 'It isn't who, it's what.'

Two hours earlier, William and Rebecca had sat in the filthy kitchen behind the workshop, a feverish sense of unreality hanging over them.

'I don't understand,' she said. 'What do you mean?'

'I should've seen it earlier. I should have seen how it all comes together.'

He'd grabbed her hands, held her gaze with his own.

'I know this is going to take a while to sink in,' he said. And then: 'I really ought to have understood when we were in your lab. But I was too busy resisting: you were talking about thoughts, the involuntary thoughts on one hand and the deliberate ones on the other, and that scared me. It scared me so much that I didn't see what I was looking at.'

'Which was?'

'The same thing as I saw in Stockholm.'

Rebecca shook her head to signal that she didn't understand what he was saying, so slowly, methodically, he told her about the maps at HQ. The steady stream of internet traffic, the explosions of colour, the data peaks.

'When I saw the images in your lab,' he said. 'The cross-sections of brains lighting up your screens. Areas flaring up with impulses, dark blue where there was least activity, deep pink were there was most.' He chose his words carefully. 'I saw it, but it took me until now to understand it.'

286

They sat for several seconds with their eyes locked.

'You can't be saying what I think you're saying,' Rebecca protested.

William nodded.

'You mean that all the attacks ... the peaks in data they showed you at Swedish Armed Forces HQ ... the traffic that knocked out the power supply to half of Sweden ...'

She didn't say any more. William finished the sentence for her.

'It wasn't traffic. They weren't attacks. They were thoughts.'

It was still dark outside. The morning rush hadn't started. Every now and then they passed another car in the downpour, curious glances through the side windows – who the hell drives around in an old bucket like that? In this weather?

The distance signs along the roadside were ticking down far too slowly, but there was no option other than to just keep going. William had to get in touch with Sweden. He needed to warn his colleagues at HQ – Palmgren, Velander, even Forester, if she was prepared to listen. They needed to know what they were up against, and they needed to know now, if it wasn't already too late.

What worried him was the plan. This vague acquaintance of Rebecca's, who she hadn't seen for years. How were they to know whether they were welcome? How would they find out if he was even still alive?

But if he was right, they had no other choice. They wouldn't have anywhere to hide. Wherever they went it would be no time before the police learned where they were, or worse still, before some inanimate object came to life and did its utmost to end theirs.

The way he was thinking was crazy. The trouble was, he was right. Of that he was now absolutely certain.

William had caught up with her out on the gravel yard, where she stood methodically filling her lungs with the damp mist, as though the cold might wake her from an awful, incomprehensible dream.

'I don't know what you're trying to say,' she said. 'But I know that you're wrong. If you're trying to tell me that someone has . . .' She turned to face him, searching for words, but the only ones she found sounded unreal, concocted, even silly. 'If what you're telling me is that someone has created an intelligence and let it loose on the internet . . . If that's what you're telling me, you're way off. You're wrong, because that is impossible.'

He said nothing.

'This is my field,' she pressed. 'This is the sort of thing we've been researching for decades, stuff I've been reading about in journals and periodicals and God knows what. Expensive fucking journals with shiny covers. If one of us knows what is possible, it's me.'

The words poured out of her, more in fear than anger, and more in denial than conviction. It was not possible, simply because it couldn't be allowed to be. She spread out her hands, and shouted in a tone that was both plea and admonition in tandem. Ten years ago, she explained, Artificial Intelligence had been the new black in the world of computing. Everyone wanted to be first out with the perfect program, software that couldn't be distinguished from conscious thought, that communicated like a human. But imitation was and remained just that. And before long, interest in all things *artificial* had waned.

'Suddenly,' she said, 'everyone wanted to be the ones to recreate *thought*. Not just imitating thought through a load of advanced algorithms that can play chess and answer questions, but real, living thought. Independent decisions, feeling and reacting, conceiving abstract thoughts.'

With the help of vast computer networks, she went on, project after project had been started in the hope of being the first to achieve a single aim – to build a real, man-made consciousness. Billions were ploughed into recreating the human mind, only with cables and circuit boards and electronics. In several locations around the world, enormous sites were given imaginative names: the Blue Brain Project in Lausanne, the B.R.A.I.N. Initiative in the US, the Human Brain Project in Geneva, and all comprised enormous data halls, their capacity and content almost unimaginable, specially constructed to emulate the human brain. Not one of them had succeeded.

'You can't create thought,' she said, and stood suspended for a moment, until out of nowhere a sad smile found its way into her eyes.

'I can't say why,' she said slowly. 'But that's the way it is. However brilliantly we might program, we do not create life.'

She looked up at the stars.

'Maybe it is the way I like it after all. Maybe there is something special about life, about love, everything. Divine, if you like, it doesn't matter what you call it.' She tipped her head. 'Anyway, you can't create consciousness from nothing. No matter how big a data hall you build, however many thousands of machines you connect to each other.'

William smiled back at her. His smile, though, was apologetic, commiserating, as though none of what she'd said had factored in.

'That's not really what I'm saying,' he told her.

Rebecca's smile sank away.

'Well, then I don't understand.'

'You may very well be right,' he said. 'You cannot program minds, can't produce intelligence to order. But that is not what's happened here.'

He took a deep breath.

'I should have listened to you sooner. *Life occurs where the pre-requisites exist.*'

That was what he'd said to her on the gravel yard outside the garage, and then he'd taken her by the shoulders, locking her eyes:

'Your friend with the plane. How quickly can we get to him?'

'If we leave now we could arrive before it gets light.'

'Good. I need to get to Sweden. They don't know what they're fighting against.'

Then he took her hand again, and pulled her with him back towards the building, as if to remind them both that the sands were running out for them, that they'd already stood there for too long.

289

'Right now, he said without turning around, 'the whole planet is searching for a terror cell that's behind all this. A group of people – hackers, activists, possibly even a country – using the internet to wreak havoc. The problem is that they've got it wrong. The terrorist cell isn't using the internet.'

He glanced over his shoulder.

'It *is* the internet.'

57

The first helicopter landed just after midnight. The seats behind the pilot were occupied by newly woken men and women, jeans and suits side by side, stares fixed on design drawings and circuit diagrams and compendia. Ahead of them lay Sizewell B Nuclear Power Station, nestled like a cuckoo chick on the sleepy coast-line. Great cubes of steel and concrete stood surrounding a huge white reactor dome, drilled into the dunes like a giant golf ball by an equally large water hazard just between the sea and the moors.

Nothing showed from the outside. The off-white walls gave no more away than did the black waves lapping on the rocky shore, or the seabirds scared by the helicopters and flocking off along the coast. On the inside, though, the atomic particles were spinning in a dance that kept going faster.

As the helicopters landed, their passengers knew it was only a matter of time before a meltdown occurred. They ducked under chopping rotors, rushed into control rooms and data halls, past the staff in white overalls and name badges, one of which iden-tified *Liv McKenna*.

She stood there watching as the technicians spread throughout the building, communicating via headsets and walkie-talkies, fighting to restart the systems and regain control of the pro-cesses. All she could do was daydream herself away to musical notes, to tender cello fingers and silly student revues, and to friends who she only now realised how much she missed. To a time when it had all been so simple, when everyone stood on the threshold of life, with the future ahead of them.

Now she wondered whether there would even be a future.

Mark Winslow had never seen Defence Secretary Anthony Higgs in anything other than suit and tie. Standing by the window of his large office, the man now was wearing a pair of shapeless jeans. His shirt was crumpled, as though he'd slept in it. His hair was all over the place, like a panic-stricken crowd being evacuated from a marketplace. He looked, quite simply, like a human, and Winslow wasn't used to that.

'I asked a question,' Higgs said without looking up. 'I have a room full of journalists waiting down there. They want information. Shall I go and tell them that I don't have the foggiest what's going on?'

'No one knows a thing,' Winslow said. 'I just spoke to Sedgwick—'

'And why doesn't Sedgwick know? Isn't that the whole point of all this business? Isn't that what I just approved?'

'I only know what he told me,' Winslow replied. 'The only thing they've been able to establish is that the attacks look identical to previous ones. All over the world, completely simultaneous. And then a few seconds later' – he nodded at the TV: the black night, the illuminated globe that was Sizewell B's reactor, just an hour's drive away –'well, you know what happened.'

Higgs gave Winslow a long stare.

'You do realise what this is, don't you?'

'Is?'

'We didn't back down. They warned us, time and time again they warned us, and we wouldn't budge. And now – now here we are.' He elaborated through clenched teeth. 'This is blackmail. That's what this is about. And the biggest irony of all is that we can't trace who is doing it.'

'Technically it's hardly blackmail if we haven't received any demands.'

'We already know what they want. Why would they issue demands?'

He turned around with his back to the windowsill and threw his hands up.

'The very second we activate Floodgate. At that exact same second, this happens. Could it be any clearer?' He answered his own question with a shake of the head. 'They want to force us to retreat. Whoever they are. And they're not going to give up until we do.'

They stood in silence for a couple of seconds. Watched the TV, saw the helicopters hover around the power stations.

'Higgs?' said Winslow. 'What if we actually did?'

'Did what?'

'What if we actually backed down?'

Higgs blinked slowly.

'And your proposal is – what, exactly? That we dismantle the most important intelligence tool that we have ever developed?' He tipped his head towards the window, his voice now soft and tired and with no fight left in it. 'Is that what you want me to say on television? That I'm acceding to the terrorists' demands?'

'You won't be acceding to anything,' Winslow said calmly. 'Because what you are dismantling has never even existed. There is no documentation that acknowledges Floodgate's existence. Since day one, it's been a top-secret project. Throughout the planning phase, development, even the construction process. The fact that it was then mothballed so as not to offend public opinion, and that we then continued with it anyway, is something that you know, I know, and Sedgwick knows. And who else?'

'What are you trying to say, Winslow?'

'I'm saying you can cancel it whenever you like. Right now. No one is going to accuse you of giving in – because no one is going to find out that there was ever anything to dismantle.'

Higgs's voice became brittle.

'You've forgotten why we are doing this.'

He ran one hand through his hair, unaware that this just made it look even more unruly, and raised his other hand towards the window, all the dots of light outside.

'Do you see that out there? Do you know what that is? That is society. Millions of people who go to work every day, pick the kids up from school, go to the theatre, get the tube. People who want to keep on doing all that, without having to defend themselves. Without ever having to think about how fantastic it actually is that all of those things are possible.' Winslow nodded. It was a speech he'd heard before, and of course there were no comebacks. 'All it takes is for one little group to want to destroy all that. A single little group, and then we're left with a society that cannot be healed. Floodgate exists to find those people. Not to read Granny's emails, not to see what sites you look at in your spare time. It exists to make the world a safer place.'

'And how do you think that's working out?' Winslow looked demonstratively towards the television.

Higgs answered with a sigh. 'Your advice then, is to give in to the terrorists?'

'No. But my opinion is that if we have the chance to get them to release the nuclear power stations, then we should take it.'

'Okay,' said Higgs. 'Thank you for that.' He moved away from the windowsill, stopped with his hand on the door handle.

'That is not the course of action we will be taking. But thank you.'

58

The images on Palmgren's laptop struck such fear into Christina that she could sense the taste of blood in her mouth. They were sitting in his kitchen among token Christmas decorations, side by side on the long bench, surrounded by the hyacinth scent from the wilting Christmas bouquet in front of them. The laptop displayed photos that had been wired around the globe as she and Strandell had struggled their way through the night, interspersed with headlines from her own newspaper and hundreds of competitors. In Christina's stomach, that teenage terror hung colder and hollower than ever.

293

'Sabotage' wrote someone. 'Virus' said another. 'Terrorism' featured in all of them.

Tetrapak was the first one to break the silence.

'It's connected.'

'What?' said Palmgren. 'What is, and with what?'

Tetrapak attempted to formulate his response, failed to find the words, and instead pulled his electronic equipment towards him.

'The things that are happening,' he said, gesturing towards the window, 'they are connected to ... this.'

He started up his computer, gave a brief version of the explanation he'd given Christina and Beatrice in the newsroom, about the shortwave frequencies, the ones that had lain dormant for years and then come to life. He showed the long lists of sound files, played the tuneless chant of digits that he'd recorded from the shortwave band, and then the short bursts of screeching data that had replaced them.

When his presentation was over and the screeching code disappeared, Palmgren was the first to break the silence. 'With all due respect,' he said. 'I understand that you have given this a lot of consideration. I don't think, however, that any of us would be well served by focusing our efforts on the wrong things.'

'I'm sorry?' said Tetrapak.

'What's happening out there is down to hypermodern security systems. It's the largest electronic attack we have ever seen. I have great difficulty imagining what it might have to do with an obsolete technology that hasn't been used for twenty years.'

Tetrapak's eyes narrowed.

'What you have difficulty imagining might not necessarily have any bearing on what is actually happening. Wouldn't you agree?'

'Forgive me for being so direct,' Palmgren said. 'But how am I to know that what you are playing even comes from the frequencies you are talking about?'

'Are you accusing me of lying?'

'No. I am simply asking how *I* am supposed to know that you're not.'

Tetrapak stood up, in between bench and table, fury causing

294

the words to back up deep in his throat, leaving him wagging a threatening finger but without any words to accompany it.

Instead, he returned to the box. He dug out the portable shortwave radio, muttering irritation as he attached it to the car battery at the bottom, and then, from the tangle of cables and wires, he pulled out a thin, homemade wire aerial. He attached it to a large suction cup, with deliberate exasperated movements, and finally stuck it forcefully to one of Palmgren's windows.

'You can call me many things,' he said. 'You can call me madman. Tinfoil hat. You can call me Tetrapak, I know that everyone does.' He sat down again, checked that everything was properly connected, and gave Palmgren an icy stare across the table. 'But *liar*? No one calls me a liar!' And with that he switched on the radio.

The kitchen filled with noise.

Tetrapak looked up, totally stunned. However he'd intended to prove his statements, this wasn't it. Where he had expected to find perhaps a few short blasts of data, if he was lucky enough, he found a wall of sound. Suddenly, and with no warning, it was as if the airwaves were overflowing with data, and the short, fleeting modem tones had soared into an endless swell of strident noise.

When, a few seconds later, it occurred to Tetrapak to change frequency – and then to keep on changing it – he found the same thing up and down the band. It streamed out from every-where, from the frequencies where the lifeless voices had recited their digits, from channels that had been silent for decades, the same type of unrelenting noise kept echoing around the gloomy kitchen like an unsettling, haunted concert, played out of tune. Eventually Christina barked at him to turn it off.

'What was that?' Palmgren said after a silent interval.

'I don't know,' said Tetrapak. 'I've been monitoring these fre-quencies for almost six months. But this? This is something else. And if you are going to try and tell me that it's a coincidence, for this to be happening at the same time as all that . . . ' he gestured from his computer towards Palmgren's and back again. 'You must see that too,' he said. And this time, there was no resistance from anybody.

'I need to borrow your phone.'

Christina looked at Palmgren from her spot on the sofa. It was late, she had an editorial team that was bound to be wondering where on earth she'd got to, and presumably a number of superiors wondering the same thing in louder voices. Her phone lay somewhere in the woods in Bromma without its battery, sending any calls straight to her voicemail, and meanwhile, she was sitting in a kitchen in Saltsjöbaden being no use to anyone.

None of that she said out loud, but Palmgren nodded back, excused himself briefly and strode out of the kitchen.

There was a grunt from Tetrapak: 'So you're planning to let them find us all over again?'

'I need to speak to the newsroom. They need me.'

'Are you sure about that? Because as far as I can tell they're getting on just fine without you.'

He gestured towards the computer. And he was right of course, yet she still couldn't help but be provoked by it—

'You *know* that you're being bugged,' he said, cutting her off before she had a chance to respond. 'And the choice is yours. But does it really feel like a good idea to give yourself away again?'

'They can't know that I'm here. Palmgren's phone is secure.'

'How do you know that?' he said. 'How do you know that the newspaper isn't being monitored, just waiting for you to call so that they can track you down again?'

Christina bit her lip.

'The world is under terrorist attack,' she said. 'And you think I should just sit and watch it happen?'

'Isn't that the definition of what a journalist does?'

That hurt. Christina felt rage swell inside her, her hands grasp ever tighter on thin air, clenched fists of ice that would like nothing more than to stand up and smack him in the mouth.

She didn't though. It wasn't Tetrapak she was angry with, it was everything else: the powerlessness, the fear, this paranoid sensation of being observed, and the frustration of not being able to wave anything off as nonsense.

'I don't know you,' he said finally, 'but I do know journalists. And what you need to be doing right now is putting it together, creating news, not just writing about them after the fact. You should find out what's going on, who's behind it and whether it can be stopped. You won't do any of that sitting in front of a computer in an office.'

The interchange tailed off, and they sat in silence until Palmgren came back into the room bearing his phone in one hand and an opaque plastic folder in the other. He sat down facing them, passing the phone to Christina as he did so. She took it, but held it, couldn't decide.

'There's one more thing you should know,' she said instead. Leaned in towards Palmgren. 'About a man called Michal Piotrowski.' In short, matter-of-fact sentences, she told him about the man who had probably sent William the emails, who also happened to be their daughter's biological father, and who had been the reason for William's trip to Warsaw.

Palmgren listened without interrupting, and when Christina continued she did so with a voice that expected to jar on its listeners.

'The CD that Sara had,' she said. 'There are two more.'

She saw Palmgren freeze up on the other side of the table.

'Where?' he asked.

'We've got them here,' she told him. 'That's not what matters though. What matters is the fact that we can't do anything with them.'

She explained how she'd come across the disc in the car by Kaknäs Tower. How she'd taken it to Strandell's, and how he had turned out to have one too. And lastly she told him about the call from William, and his realisation that the CDs contained a message that could only be accessed by having all three of them, and when she was done, Palmgren sat motionless for several seconds.

'I thought I asked you to make sure I was first to know,' he said.

'I'm here, aren't I?' When he didn't respond, she continued: 'I haven't written a word about this. I've been digging, I've found this, and now I'm here. That was what you asked of me.'

'And what would you like me to do for you now?'

'We need the third disc.' She saw him hesitate. 'And by we,' she said, 'I mean us. Swedish Armed Forces, you, me, all of us. We need it to understand what's going on—'

'We don't have it,' he said before she'd finished speaking.

'I know. But it must be somewhere. At some point between the café and Central Station she got rid of it, and it must be possible to see where she went along the way. Cameras, witnesses, what do I know. You must be able to work out where she'd been. Right?'

Palmgren looked down as she spoke. His hands were already placed carefully on the folder in front of him, as though he was protecting it from something. Or perhaps as though he was trying to protect someone else from it?

'Yes and no,' he said apologetically. Stopped himself, started over. 'I want you to know that I only received this material last night. I was waiting for a chance to give it to you.'

'Give what?' she asked sharply.

'She had a mobile phone on her.'

'You said she didn't have anything. At the hospital, when I asked you. You said she had nothing on her.'

'I said she didn't have a CD. That was what you asked me, and that's what I told you. They had though taken her phone and ...' He fell quiet, drumming his fingers on the folder. 'Before you get your hopes up that this might lead somewhere,' he said, 'let me explain. We've been looking for the CD too. The problem is that during the power cut, for several hours, there were no tracks to follow. No masts able to register her phone. Basically all public cameras off line. She could have been anywhere.'

He lifted his arms and thrust the folder over to her.

'I've been trying to work out how to say this.'

'Say what?' she said.

He didn't answer. And eventually she opened the folder instead.

For a long time she sat there like that, not sure what to say. Looking up at her behind the cover sheet was a great bundle of paper, page after page full of lists, codes, times, abbreviations. And it meant nothing to her.

'What is this?' she finally managed.

'Mobile masts,' said Tetrapak. 'Isn't it?'

Palmgren nodded. 'Masts, calls, times. All the data that the operator registered about the phone that Sara was carrying.'

'So what use is it?' asked Christina. 'If we can't see where she went after the power cut, why are you giving me this?'

'Because what we can see is where she was before that.'

After a while, the road signs started to feature place names like Makow and Przasnysz and Ostroleka, and when they'd been going for another half-hour, William steered the Fiat off the motorway to take to narrow, winding country roads. In the far, far distance, they could see the sky slowly beginning its shift from black to dark blue, a sliver of morning across the bonnet each time the road swung towards south-east.

Rebecca looked at her watch: it was approaching six. It was going to be dark for at least another hour. They hadn't spoken for a long time.

Life occurs where the prerequisites exist.

That's what he had said. Rebecca's own words, but she'd used them in a completely different context, and it annoyed her. It was as though he'd hotwired her argument and used it against her, twisting what she'd meant. And she wanted to refute it, wanted to but couldn't, and that wound her up even more.

'We call it the internet,' he'd continued. 'An infinite number of carrier wires running back and forth across the entire planet. Wires incessantly sending data back and forth across the whole system. And what is thought, if not data? What is the brain, if not an infinite number of wires?'

Once again, the words were her own. And who was she to say that he was wrong? Over and over again, she had seen life blossom in test tubes and Petri dishes that she had believed were sterile. Because it could.

Once upon a time, billions of years ago, the Earth had been a dead planet, and then suddenly the temperature and the chemical elements and whatever else was necessary were right, and look what happened. And now, in the space of just ten, twenty years, man had covered the surface of the planet in a tangle of wires. A subterranean network of neurons and synapses, without anyone realising that's what it was. The branches had grown into a gigantic web, impossible to monitor, millions of kilometres of cables transporting data back and forth, an unintentional artificial brain that had been allowed to grow into something far larger than any scientific experiment could dream of.

It was the irony of it all that made it so hard to accept. The irony that while scientific institutions poured billions into their attempts at creating artificial thoughts, building expensive installations in Switzerland and the USA, it had all happened of its own accord, right before their eyes. Life occurs because it wants to.

'Let's say I accept what you're saying,' she shouted through the noise of the engine. It was the first thing they had said to each other for a very long time. 'Say we're fighting against some kind of magical consciousness with a capital C. Something that's omnipresent, whose eyes are every online camera in every corner of the world, whose synapses run right into every computer, every network, every—' She paused. '*Nuclear power station.*'

For a second she clenched her jaw, trying to hold the words in. As insane as it sounded, it was equally frightening to say it out loud.

'Someone who hears and sees every electronic word we send to each other, because every single connected unit, every lift and lock and telephone, is part of the Consciousness.' She stared intently at William's profile, as if it was all his fault. 'Then why?' she said. 'Why is the Consciousness out to get you?'

'First of all,' he said, 'you don't have to accept anything. Reality goes on as normal whether you accept it or not.'

That was hardly the answer she'd been after. She stared out of the side window, demonstratively, as though it wasn't reality that was the problem, but rather William's unwillingness to change it.

'To answer your question though,' he went on. 'I don't think it is out to get me. I think Piotrowski knew something. Something that's on those discs, something that must not, under any circumstances, come out. Piotrowski sent emails to my address. And then, when I logged in to the same address on a public computer in Stockholm . . .' He shrugged. 'That's how I think it happened. No, that's how it *must* have happened. The only reason I'm a target is because Piotrowski sent something to me.'

'Something that you don't even know what it is.'

'Not yet.'

Whether she liked it or not, there was logic in what he was saying. That was why the data peaks had looked like they did, the ones registered by the military that had caused the power cuts. That was why they hadn't been aimed at a specific target. That was why they'd seemed like a big muddle of impulses being sent back and forth. And above all, that was why they had occurred at the moment William's daughter had inserted the CD into the computer.

It wasn't an attack, it was a *reaction*.

'If that's the case,' she said, 'how are we ever going to be able to stop it?'

He sat in silence for some time before he replied: 'I don't know.'

He kept on driving, jaws chewing away on thin air, resentful eyes staring at the road ahead of them as though it had somehow wronged them.

'If what you're saying is right,' she said after a while. 'If that's how it is, why this? Why the attacks, the power cuts, the nuclear stations? . . . if the Consciousness really exists, what does it want to achieve?'

William looked over at her again.

'That's what we need to find out before it's too late.'

Once that had been said, there was nothing more to say, and they sat in silence as the road carried them eastwards, through dense woods and open fields, through curtains of spattering rain. They sat deep in their own thoughts, both of them thinking the same things. How people all around the world sat with their hearts in their mouths, how nuclear powers stations in city after city were out of control, and how they were sitting here in a rickety old car, its engine battling through the rain along the winding road through Polish forests, the only two people on Earth who knew how it had happened.

They had only just got out of the forest, when the curves straightened out and revealed the bright red warning flares laid out across the road.

59

Earlier that evening, the mobile operator had provided Swedish Armed Forces with lists of masts and calls, and Velander had set to work plotting the last movements of Sara's phone. Sooner than anyone had hoped, he had managed to identify a couple of masts that kept recurring, and once a team of Security Police colleagues were sent out to look for the right spot, it hadn't taken them long to find it.

Now, Palmgren followed the same route, past the alley where the official entrance to Gröna Lund's amusement park was located, continuing along the white-dusted roads, past the eighteenth-century buildings and the boarded-up cafés. Christina was sitting in the passenger seat, her eyes fixed on the black steel skeleton behind the buildings, struts and towers and rolling sections of rails in silhouette against the night sky like the ribs of a great dead beast.

As they turned away from the waterfront and stopped at a narrow, dead-end alley, it was as though she didn't have any words left. They left Tetrapak and his dark grey box in the back seat of the Volvo – it was seven years old, he'd been careful to establish before getting in, and lacked both GPS and a media player – and once they were out in the cold air Christina let Palmgren guide her across the snow-covered cobblestones. Further in, one of the red planks had had its nails clawed out of it, and from there the path led on into the amusement park, long since closed for the winter.

When they'd squeezed through and out the other side it was as though the darkness grew even thicker. They walked past deserted tarmacked areas, saw lamps that were not blinking, pastel colours and Tyrolean motifs that seemed to have faded to blue-grey outlines.

At the far end of an open passage stood a corrugated tin shed, and beyond a pile of tarpaulins and metal brackets was a low metal door, where Palmgren stopped. He pushed the junk to one side, opened the door, and nodded at Christina to step inside. Slowly and cautiously, she ducked under the doorframe, continuing alone into the darkness on the other side.

It seemed to be storage. There were stacks of tables and chairs, huge wooden boxes that might be dismantled stalls, all packed in to protect them from the ravages of winter. And then, far across the room, she could just make out something that didn't belong there.

When her feet arrived at the mattress, she stopped. She waited for her eyes to grow used to the darkness, only to realise at last that it wasn't going to get better, however long she waited.

This was it. Instead of the room waiting in their apartment, her own room, with heating and clothes and food and *them*, rather than all of that Sara had chosen to sleep here, on a thin, grey mattress on top of two pallets, under a duvet that was filthy, damp and freezing.

She didn't know when exactly she'd fallen to her knees, just that she had, feeling the cold seeping up from the ground, through the mattress and into her legs. She didn't know exactly when she'd picked up the duvet either, nor when she'd decided to hold it tight, just that she'd buried her face in the damp cloth in the hope of smelling her scent, and finally she'd allowed herself to scream out, hoping that the synthetic filling would muffle the sound.

When they emerged back out through the hole in the fence, Tetrapak was standing outside the car. Christina could feel Palmgren's arm under her own, leading her through the snow and the darkness without her registering any of it. Whatever she'd been hoping to find in there, she hadn't. Not the CD – which of course was not the least bit surprising, people from HQ had been there before her and why would she have more luck than they had? – but above all, she hadn't found any answers. All those *whys* would remain *whys*, all the *ifs* and the *whens* and the *what could we have done differently* would stay that way for ever.

And that was what finally made her break down, what made Palmgren rush into the dark room to help her to her feet again, and it was through that tangle of thoughts that she now saw Tetrapak hurrying up the alleyway towards them. The look in his eyes was the pure opposite of Christina's. He was full of urgency and energy, and in one hand he was holding Palmgren's folder with the lists from Sara's phone.

'Whose number is this?' he said before he'd even got to them.

He held up a page towards them despite being far too far away for them to have any chance of reading it, pointing at the illegible digits, his eyes flitting between Christina and Palmgren.

'She called three times,' he said when neither of them replied. 'When the power cut was over. Who was she calling?'

Christina felt Palmgren pulling her towards him. As if to protect her, as though Tetrapak's enthusiasm was just another path to disappointment and he didn't want her to go through any more of that today.

'We've already followed those up,' he said brusquely.

Tetrapak shook his head. He pointed to the three telephone numbers at the bottom, explaining that all three calls were made in quick succession, just after eleven p.m., on the evening when Sara Sandberg would soon be dead.

'Two mobile numbers, one landline. This one is yours, isn't it?'

'Yes,' Christina said. She wanted to point, but couldn't muster the energy to raise her arm. 'The top one is William's. The one under that is mine. The third is the landline at Skeppargatan.'

She saw Tetrapak switch his attention to Palmgren. A demanding, exhorting look, as though he had grasped some key factor that no one else cared about. 'Look at the duration,' he said, holding the folder out in front of him, like a persistent child trying to draw attention to something important.

'For fuck's sake,' Palmgren exploded. 'Can't you hear what I'm saying?' He grabbed the folder from Tetrapak's hands and pointed at the calls down at the bottom. 'Eight seconds. Twelve seconds. Thirty. Does that tell you anything?' Tetrapak didn't reply. 'As I understand it, you are not a big fan of the authorities,' said Palmgren. 'Occasionally, however, we do get things right.'

He gave Christina an apologetic look before explaining: 'Velander made test calls. William's voicemail greeting is eleven seconds long. Christina's is even shorter. Sara hung up those calls long before she had the chance to say anything.'

'Not the last one,' Tetrapak said. 'The one to the apartment. That was thirty seconds, thirty seconds is a long time.'

'I know that. But if Sara had left a message on the landline we would have found it.' Palmgren gave Christina another apologetic look. 'We had people in William's apartment that same night. They recovered the tape from the answer machine and it was blank.'

They arrived at the Volvo. Palmgren opened the back door, and when Christina spoke, she did so with such a weak voice that neither of them heard what she said.

'What did you say?' said Palmgren. Quietly, gently, like a parent to a newly woken child.

'It hasn't worked for years. The answering machine. The one at Skeppargatan.'

'Well then, who did she speak to for thirty seconds?' said Palmgren, hushed.

'After four rings it diverts to William's mobile,' she said. She grabbed the folder from Tetrapak to read for herself. That detached feeling was gone now, and she scanned the incomprehensible rows of telephone numbers and times. 'Lassie,' she said, 'Lassie, did you listen to William's voicemail?'

'I don't know.'

She held out her arm towards him.

'I want to borrow your phone.'

This time, Tetrapak didn't try and stop her.

If Sara Sandberg had known that those were to be the last words she would ever say, perhaps she would have said something else. Then again, perhaps she wouldn't. If she had suffered, why shouldn't they? Why could she not torment them the way they had tormented her?

Standing in a narrow alley by the closed entrance to

Östermalmstorg's metro station, she could feel the gentle wind of subterranean warmth stroking past her as it climbed out of the stairwell. Mobile in one hand, fingers trembling against the screen as they tried to decide whether or not to make the call.

They had turned their backs on her. They'd put in a metal grille, a big thick gate, and what was that if not a signal that she was no longer welcome?

All of a sudden, it was as if she no longer had anywhere to go. She could go home of course, back to Djurgården and the tin shed, but she couldn't bring herself to, not any more. She had seen the hallway stretching into the darkness, the parquet flooring's fishbone pattern pointing towards her own room, mocking angles showing the direction that she couldn't get to. She had smelled the smell. Of home, of Mum and Dad, and now she missed them so much it hurt.

In the end, her fingers had made up their mind and made the call.

William's mobile was off. She couldn't know, but he was at Swedish Armed Forces Headquarters and his phone was being looked after by the guard while he was being interviewed.

Christina's phone didn't receive her either. Its battery was flat after an evening without electricity, but Sara couldn't know that either, and the feeling that they were deliberately trying to avoid her, the bastards, grew inside her. Now, when she needed them most.

Last of all, she tried the home number. It rang twice, three, four times. And when the call was forwarded to William's voice-mail she gave up.

'I miss you.'

Those became the first words she said.

Two days later, her mother would stand by a broken fence around the back of Gröna Lund amusement park. Over and over again she would listen to those few seconds, the first words that she'd heard from her daughter in ages and the last that she would ever hear.

'I miss you and I want to come home,' said Sara from another time. 'So why are you locking me out?'

Christina listened, eyes closed, propped against Palmgren's Volvo, as though she could make time stand still just by playing the message again and again, as though Sara was still around, somehow, as long as her voice was.

'I know I've done wrong,' said Sara. 'But I didn't know it would end up like this. I saw the briefcase, sitting there in the hall, and I should never have taken it, but I did, and I . . .'

For half a second, she hesitated, a silence that was far too long in those precious, limited moments, and Christina held her breath as she waited for the next words.

'I don't know what's going on,' she said. 'But Dad? If you get this? *The meeting is cancelled.* I've got a CD that you're supposed to have, and a warning that you shouldn't go to the meeting, and it's all postmarked Warsaw, and is this anything to do with me? With him? With whoever he is, that you refuse to tell me?'

The words were pouring out of her now, stumbling over tears and rage and worry over not having passed on the warning in time, a large, foul-tasting cocktail of emotions that could not be processed.

'Forgive me,' she said, finally. 'Mum. Dad.'

Sara's voice that weak, perhaps in tears, perhaps just sniffling in the cold.

'I just really want to come home.'

She stood with the phone in her hand for another couple of seconds, and on the other end, a digital answering service recorded her breaths, a message in a bottle that might arrive or might not.

They were at opposite ends of time and space, yet they were right by each other, Christina standing in silence, Sara breathing, living, present. *There.*

Until she finally hung up the call and disappeared.

When Christina had listened to the message for the third time she let the hand holding the phone fall into her lap.

'Let's get away from here now,' she said, a thin voice through the snow.

She wandered slowly around the car, stopping by the passenger door and glancing up the narrow alley, towards the fence, the hole she had just emerged from.

'Forgive us,' she said with no voice, straight into the wind and through the passage up towards Sara's home. '*Forgive us.*'

If she hadn't done so, she would never have seen the black silhouette that hunched down by the broken plank and disappeared into the darkness.

Palmgren rushed up the alley towards the fence, a trot that was quicker than anything he'd managed in years, and now he was standing inside the fence, perfectly still while all his senses searched for the slightest movement.

On the far side of the big tarmacked yard was the building where Sara had had her bolthole. To its left were more sheds and locked buildings, and in the other direction the yard opened out towards the park itself, with its attractions hidden under dusty tarpaulins in the darkness.

He hadn't seen anything, but Christina was certain: someone had just disappeared through the same hole that they'd used, and Palmgren had flung himself after them before he'd had the chance to realise that not only did he not know what he was looking for, he had also turned sixty and was, to be frank, in no state to go around chasing people like he used to.

He peered down at the ground, trying to make out footprints in the thin snow but without success. The cold winds blew straight off the lake and between the buildings like invisible snakes, dancing amid the snow, constantly rearranging it into new patterns. Their own footprints were long gone, and there was no sign of any new ones either. For a moment he considered shouting, but didn't. What was he going to shout?

If Christina had indeed seen something, there were two possibilities. The first was it was another homeless person, someone with a bolthole just like Sara's – someone now terrified of being discovered. But it was the other possibility that had made him rush back into the park without giving himself the time to think about it. What if this person knew Sara? What if they knew each other, what if this person could tell them something, anything, that could lead them to the CD . . . ?

When Palmgren was absolutely certain that no one was in the vicinity he started moving again. He followed the fence, with his back to all the stacked trolleys and barrows, his eyes focused on the buildings and the pathways and the alley on the far side. Slowly, concentrating hard, his eyes straining.

Eventually he stopped. The first shortness of breath had been replaced by one driven by tension and adrenalin, the complete concentration as he strained to hear sound, see movement, anything.

He'd been still for a couple of seconds when he realised that he was not alone. The sound popped up right behind him, the restless sound of movement, and when he spun around he found himself staring straight into two haggard eyes.

He only caught a glimpse of the face. It was youthful and aged at the same time, a worn-out youngster looking for shelter between two barrows parked for the winter and who now found the escape route blocked by Palmgren, and the moment that they stood there protracted itself.

'Who are you?' shouted Palmgren, hearing the fear vibrating through his bass voice. The next thing he knew, he was ducking to dodge a curtain of falling timber. With one movement the young man had tipped over a stack of signs, and he had to back away to avoid being hit. Painted plywood sheets fell to the ground in between them, revealing their dull reverses covered with cables and light-bulb sockets.

'You there,' he bellowed through the din, as though that was ever going to help, then ran stumbling over the piles of wood so as not to fall too far behind.

He saw the silhouette ahead of him race towards the park, then stop for a second, hesitating mid-step – left? right? – only to disappear round the side of a wooden building and away out of sight.

Palmgren was there only a second later, but by then the kid was gone.

Out here, the amusement park opened out in all its emptiness. Bushes thrust their bare branches into the air, tombola stalls and games normally lit up by lamps and colourful prizes were boarded up in darkness. Everywhere you looked were objects you would never see in summer: crates and portakabins, tarpaulins stretched over rails and rides and furniture all squeezed together. The darkness was full of hiding places, hundreds of spots that the man he was chasing might jump out from at any minute.

So he waited. Carried on, with slow steps, his eyes sweeping left and right as he moved forwards.

'I just want to talk,' he said in a booming voice. 'I'm not out to get you.'

At the other end of the open square, the park narrowed to a passage between stalls, and he moved slowly forward, a slight rotation of the upper body as he walked to keep an eye in all directions, like a dance in slow motion, glancing down between the various stalls, narrow passages where someone could hide and wait to attack.

Eventually he stopped. He was heading for a dead end, and he didn't like that. He took a deep breath instead, composed himself as best he could, kept his rotating movements going so as not to have his back to any one direction.

'My name is Lars-Erik Palmgren,' he said. 'I don't know who you are, and I'm not here to mess you about. All I want to do is ask a few questions about Sara Sandberg. Do you know who that is?'

For several seconds, silence.

Then came the reply.

He felt the pain first.

It struck him from above, a boot that pushed against his shoulder, making him lose his balance, then an elbow barged him in the back and sent him to the ground.

His last thought before he blacked out was that he'd been right all along. He really was too old for all this.

60

The warning flares strung out across the tarmac like a necklace, sharp red points of light from one ditch to the other, and immediately beyond them at least three large police cars blocked the roadway. There might be even more that William couldn't make out, hidden by the blinding blue lights flashing in the darkness.

His first thought was to slam the car into reverse, turn straight around and drive off. His second thought was that he was a complete idiot. Partly because he was sitting in a car that could fall apart at any moment, particularly if he attempted to force it into manoeuvres for which it had never been intended, and partly because he could see the size of the police presence over at the roadblock. Even if the car had been up to a getaway attempt he would have absolutely no chance.

Here they sat, in a stationary Polski Fiat, in the middle of the road where the bend had deposited them just a hundred metres or so short of the roadblock. No one seemed to have noticed them yet. That was hardly going to last.

There were at least five policemen up there, all busy inspecting a silver grey SUV, their backs arched while they talked through the windows or shone their torches into the back seats and the floor and boot. Behind that, a short queue had built up. Lorries and early morning commuters queuing patiently, engines idling, half a dozen vehicles at most. Further back, those hundred metres or so of empty tarmac, and William and Rebecca's Fiat, sitting doing nothing.

'What do we do?' said Rebecca.

William looked over his shoulder. The empty bend behind them. Damn it.

'You can't turn around,' she said. 'They're going to wonder why.'

'I know. But we have no choice.' He clenched his jaw, put the car in reverse, and then, in that instant, realised he'd hesitated too long.

The light shining in his eyes was coming from the rear-view mirror. He heard the squeal as the HGV suddenly spotted the tiny light blue car that had stopped in the middle of the road; it slammed on its brakes and sounded the horn at the same time, a klaxon that could have woken the dead and scared them to death at the same time, locked wheels sliding towards them before finally coming to a halt.

Hissing brakes. Shock absorbers and mechanical connectors

complaining and then settling down. And then, for safety's sake, even more beeps on the bloody foghorn, as though the first one hadn't been more than enough to attract the police's attention.

'Drive up to the roadblock,' Rebecca said through gritted teeth. 'We're not getting away, you've got no choice!'

William hesitated, weighing up his options one last time. Behind them the HGV had jackknifed, and its trailer was now at an angle across the whole of the narrow country lane. Escaping that way was impossible. Ahead of them, they could see the police standing staring at them, frozen in mid-movement like a flock of predators that had sensed potential prey.

'Drive on! Now! Before they wonder what the hell we're playing at!'

William hesitated for another two seconds. A rock or a hard place. Then he nodded reluctantly, put it into gear – and realised that the engine was no longer running.

Shit. He'd just managed to put it in reverse when the lorry came towards them, and he'd probably let go of the clutch and instinctively slammed on the brakes. Regardless, the engine was dead, and he knew only too well what that meant. Hanging from the steering column were the two wires he'd attempted to start the car with back in the garage. They'd been no use then and they weren't about to work now.

'William! Out!'

Rebecca's voice tore him away from his thoughts. She had turned around in her seat and was facing towards the cab of the lorry behind them. All they could see through its windscreen was a large, broad back, and arms that seemed to be looking for something in the space behind the driver's seat.

'I can see two scenarios,' she said, each word trembling with stress. 'One. You stay in the car. What happens then?'

William looked over at the police. Saw them chatting to each other, pointing in their direction, as though they'd just noticed there was something going on over there.

'I'm a tourist,' said William, far from convinced. 'I'm here to see you, this is your car, and I wanted to drive for a bit. That's all.'

'Brilliant,' said Rebecca, not meaning it. 'And the small matter

312

of it being hotwired? And that you presumably don't have a licence to show them?' William didn't answer. 'You're a wanted man, you know that as well as I do. You're probably the reason we're standing here in the first place. There isn't a chance on earth that you're going to get through this.'

William closed his eyes. She was right, of course she was.

'And the other scenario?'

'They approach the car and see a woman behind the wheel. She shows her driving licence and when they point out that she doesn't look like the photo she'll explain that she's in the middle of a course of chemotherapy. They apologise for asking, and ask me to drive on.'

'What happens if they check your licence against the register? How do we know that—' He cut himself short mid-sentence, unable to utter out loud what he was thinking.

'How do we know that I'm not wanted too?'

'Yes,' he said. 'We've been seen together. We've been seen together by . . . *it*.'

'William? I'm going to use your theory now.' Her eyes switched back and forth as she talked, between the truck driver behind and the police further on. There was no doubt that the Fiat now had their attention. Papers were folded and handed back into the SUV, new police officers came from the surrounding cars, all talking and pointing in their direction. 'There is a Consciousness. What the Consciousness knows is that you and Michal had some contact. That's why it's after you. Correct?'

William nodded once.

'I, on the other hand, cannot be linked to Michal Piotrowski. Michal spent twelve years struggling to avoid us being seen together, not in town, not in archives, not anywhere. And I was so, so hurt, sometimes I wondered whether he even . . . ' She tailed off. Another glance straight ahead. 'Fuck what I wondered. Right now it might be our only hope.'

'You were seen with me in the glass tower. The cameras captured you with me.'

'But they didn't capture my name. My licence belongs to a blonde woman named Rebecca Kowalczyk. However intelligent your Consciousness might be, how on earth would it be able

313

to make the connection with a nameless, bald-headed woman caught on camera on the other side of Warsaw?'

William hesitated yet again. Behind them, the truck driver had fished out a down jacket, and now he was pulling it on, showing a great big black back while he wriggled in the tiny cab – and ahead of them the white dots started bobbing rhythmically along the line of cars. Torches on the move, heading their way.

'Now,' she said. 'Now, before it's too late.'

'So what happens if those pictures have been sent out? The ones from the cameras in the glass tower? What happens if they know what you look like?'

She undid her seatbelt, before leaning over towards his.

'I didn't say it was foolproof,' she said. 'But it's our only chance.'

61

Sara didn't know his name, only that people called him Acetone, and with good reason. He'd been standing right behind her as she called her parents, she didn't know how long for, and now he was smiling, exposing teeth that would have worked as a cautionary tale in any dentist's waiting room. A smile that was triumphant and sarcastic all at once.

'I've been trying to get hold of you,' she said, for want of anything better.

It was a lie, and they both knew it.

'That's why you're so happy now then,' he said. His breath hit her as it always did, a pit of infection and rotting teeth, mixed with the sharp smell that had given him his name. Why him? Of all the people around, why him?

She didn't want to give up. At least not deep down. But sometimes deep down is so very inaccessible.

'You don't look too well,' he continued.

'I've had a bad day.'

'I can see that. It's a shame we can't trust each other any more. Otherwise I would've been able to help you.'

She noticed that she'd already opened negotiations with herself. Quite honestly, she seemed to be saying, didn't she deserve a bit of a rest? Hand on heart, how many people could say they'd had as tough a day as she'd had?

Sometimes deep down can fuck off.

'How about a swap?' she heard herself ask.

'Do I look like a pawnshop?' he said.

'You know what I think you look like.'

It was automatic, snide paths so well-trodden that neither of them needed to give their answers any thought. A ritual that would always lead to the same thing: first he would say no, and in the end they'd agree and then she would end up losing on both counts.

'What will you give me for a brand-new computer?'

Half an hour later Sara Sandberg boarded the train that had just arrived at Stockholm Central Station. She had half an hour until it would leave again, and that half-hour would be enough.

She just needed to feel human again. One last time and then never again. She'd stop for good, tackle her problems, go home and become who she really was.

She'd traded the computer. Stuck inside was the CD that was at the root of it all, but Acetone was going to make sure she got it back because why wouldn't he? He was a dealer, sure, but not a bad person, and she'd made him swear on his life. With the CD in her hand she would finally track them down, *Mum* and *Dad*, the only parents she'd ever had, and they'd understand and forgive and then it would all be over.

Everything was going to be fine, she knew that now. She just needed to feel human again. One last time.

When Lars-Erik Palmgren opened his eyes, his first thought was that he was floating. Straight ahead was a pitch-black sky, and then in the middle a series of thin white dots materialised from out of nowhere, falling slowly towards him like sedate shooting stars. It was the dry chill of ice crystals on his face that told him where he was. The hard stuff underneath him was tarmac, the stars were tiny snowflakes, and the thing causing him so much pain everywhere was his own body.

On each side of the sky, the stalls towered over him, topped with flat roofs, and of course the kid must've been waiting on one of them. Palmgren had been attacked from above, and he couldn't have been unconscious for more than a moment, but it was a moment too long.

He tried to get up, but couldn't. He felt the pain of the ground against his legs, his arms, everywhere he'd hit without being able to break the fall; the knee pushing down on his chest, preventing him from getting up. The kid was sitting on Palmgren's left-hand side, his skin unshaven and pocked, wearing a worn black jacket with a colourless hood sticking out from underneath it and covering his shoulders like a miniature cape. Above all though, he had breath that cut through the winter cold, and despite their faces being at least a metre apart, Palmgren had to concentrate on not turning away when the face above him opened its mouth.

'I heard what happened,' said the breath. 'It wasn't my fault.'

'What are you talking about?' Palmgren said in little more than a hiss.

'There was nothing wrong with the stuff I sold her. She took too much, too quickly, fucked if I know.'

The answer ran like a chill through Palmgren's body. 'Who?' he asked, although he knew full well.

The kid hesitated, and Palmgren peered into the dark, trying to avoid the falling snow and only half succeeding. He needed to turn the situation around, but how? There was no doubt that this assailant was much quicker than he was, and besides, he already had the upper hand. Ten years earlier, Palmgren would've been able to grab the attacker's leg, tugging and twisting at once surprised him before he had the chance to react, but today? He was only going to get one chance, and if he didn't succeed the kid already had his foot in a great position to deliver a kick in the face. At best, he'd be knocked out. At worst he'd be left lying there with a broken neck.

He debated with himself for half a second. Decided against it.

'I can help you,' he said instead, despite not knowing whether

316

it was true or whether the youngster was even interested in any kind of help. 'Tell me, who are you? What are you doing here?'

'I just want to keep my word, that's all. I know she used to stay out here.'

'Keep your word?'

'She made me promise.'

'Promise what?'

'To give her what was stuck in the computer.'

Palmgren felt his body go rigid. 'Have you got the CD?' The pressure on his chest increased, pressing him even harder into the ground.

'I don't know anything about anything,' the kid said in a voice that hardened and caused him to breathe out even more of his infected air towards Palmgren. 'All she said was that it was important. She was going on about the power cut, said that she was the one who'd made it happen.'

'Why did she think that? Did she say anything else?'

'I don't know any more. I don't want to get involved.'

'Listen to me,' said Palmgren, and he felt a searing pain in his chest as he raised his voice. 'I'm as far from Drugs Squad as you can get. I'm in the military. Not even that, I'm part of a staff who sit around planning what to do if a foreign power threatens this country. I don't give a damn what you sell or to whom, all I'm interested in is whether Sara said anything to you.' The kid didn't answer. 'And I don't know if you've seen the news, but right now there's a terrorist attack in progress against almost a hundred nuclear power stations around the world. And if Sara knew anything about that, then please, please, tell me.'

The kid stared at Palmgren.

'I've done my bit now,' he said. 'That's all I can do.'

And then, for a second, he seemed to hesitate. He looked around, halfway between Palmgren and the black sky above, a head turning in all directions to judge distances and bearings.

'Sorry about this,' he said eventually.

'About what?' said Palmgren, and as he spoke felt the air leaving his lungs as the youth pushed down with his knee, his ribs creaking and his whole body trying to curl up with pain. All he could manage was to shift onto one side and then lie there on

317

the sparkling white ground, rolled up like a felled striker in the penalty area, his chest pounding whilst the sprinting feet disappeared between all the boarded-up tombola stands and away out of sight.

Palmgren rolled onto his back. When his lungs had finally assured themselves that they were back in action, they allowed him to sit up. Elbows on the ground, then just the palms of his hands, and in the end he was able to raise himself. Breathless, tender, but otherwise okay. He could no longer see the youngster, in any direction. The question was where he'd gone, who he was, and – if he did have Sara's CD – how they were going to find him again.

Not till he hauled himself upright did he look down and see the shiny disc that the kid had left lying on the ground next to him.

The police hadn't seen the little car stopping at the end of the bend, but when the HGV behind slammed on its brakes, beeping and flashing, they couldn't miss it. The urgency of this manhunt had made them nervous, and as seconds turned to minutes, they started to move towards it, cautiously and with weapons drawn.

And when they caught sight of the silhouette in the headlights of the HGV, none of them dared take any chances.

'Police!' they screamed. 'Hands on your head! On your knees!'

They ran with arms crossed, torches propped under their weapons, shouting their orders in English with the words of the wanted bulletin echoing around their heads. *Potential terrorist.* The man they were looking for was involved in what was happening across the rest of the world, in country after country where, unlike Poland, nuclear power was used. He was dangerous, possibly armed, and all of them felt the buzz of adrenalin and fear.

'Down on the ground! Hands where we can see them!'

When they got there he was already sitting perfectly still alongside the little Fiat, hands on his head just as they had ordered, far too paralysed to offer any resistance. They manhandled him away from the car, pushing his arms and legs onto the tarmac so that he could pose no threat. He was wearing a black padded jacket, with a fur-lined hood that had glided up over his head, and it was only when they rolled him over that they could see who it was – or rather, who it wasn't.

The face peering out from the hood belonged to a man with a reddish beard. He was thirty, tops, with pale skin, steel-framed glasses, one lens with a horizontal crack in it, perhaps caused by their recent manoeuvre, perhaps not. Either way, he was clearly petrified. And definitely not the grey-haired, middle-aged man they'd seen in their pictures.

'I was just going to ask if she needed help,' he said in breathless, rolling Polish. 'She was in my way.'

He nodded towards the lorry – towards the open door of the cab he'd just jumped out of. And when the police turned their torches on the little Fiat they saw a bald woman sitting inside.

'There's something wrong with the engine,' she said. 'Do you think you could give me a bump-start?'

After the police had worked out who everyone was – a young Polish trucker heading for the Baltics and a woman from Warsaw undergoing chemo – only the formalities remained. With an empty look in her eyes, Rebecca looked on as the police worked their way around her little car. They peered carefully through the windows, bending down and covering every corner, as if maybe there might still be a square centimetre that they hadn't seen and in which a fully grown man might be able to hide. The back seat, passenger seat, boot – even the flimsy mat on the floor.

They didn't manage to find a terrorist anywhere. No Swedish perpetrator curled up hoping to avoid detection. And when the police walked past her passenger door without noticing that it wasn't quite closed, she knew that she'd made it.

Rebecca Kowalzcyk was alone again. Now it all was down to her: to get herself to Sweden and to tell the people who needed to know.

62

It took less than five minutes for them to drive from Gröna Lund to the Swedish Armed Forces Headquarters on Lidingövägen, and when Palmgren got back to the car the temperature inside it hadn't even had time to drop.

'Did you get them?' Christina asked as he climbed into the driver's seat.

'I suppose so,' said Palmgren, starting the engine, right arm around the passenger seat to get a better view as he reversed out. 'I hope you know what you're doing.'

The last bit was said with a quick but telling glance towards Tetrapak in the back seat, and then, before putting the car into first to carry on up the road, he let his hand fish around in his coat pocket, pulled out William's bunch of keys and passed them to Christina.

'I'm going to be in all kinds of trouble trying to explain why they're missing.'

After that Skeppargatan was only another few minutes away, where there was no traffic and you weren't looking out for one-way streets. They snubbed the slow old wooden lift and rushed up the stairs, a clatter of soles to break the dense silence right the way up until they were greeted by the beautiful double doors to the apartment on the top floor.

The whole way up, Christina clutched her handbag tight against her body. There, hopefully, was the answer, in the discs that Michal Piotrowski had sent; where William was so convinced that there had to be a hidden message. And if there was one place they were going to be able to retrieve it, it was here.

Across the opening where the double doors met was a bright yellow sticker proclaiming that the apartment was cordoned off and was not to be entered by unauthorised persons. Palmgren sliced it in half with his car key, mumbled something about being as authorised as we're going to get, and nodded at Christina to unlock them.

It was the grille on the inside that made her understand. A month ago, she'd left this apartment, dumped the keys through the letterbox and vowed never to return. Back then, the only things separating the apartment from the landing outside had been the thin wooden doors, the beautiful double doors with their leaded windows, the ones that would greet her with their warm welcoming colours whenever she came home late and William had left the hall light on.

Now though, they were joined by an impenetrable black barrier. One that was neither warm nor welcoming.

'*Why are you locking me out?*'

That's what she'd meant.

'When did he put this in?' It was as much as she could manage.

'I don't know,' he said.

She unlocked the grille and showed Tetrapak into William's study, unlocking that heavy door on the way. Her thoughts would have to wait. There was no time for brooding, not now, when they finally had something that might contain the answer to what was going on: the power cut, the nuclear power stations, the lot. That was what mattered.

'Make yourselves at home,' she said. 'And if you have even the tiniest little question, I will not have any kind of answer whatsoever.'

What was meant to be a wry smile ended up as no more than a tired grimace, and she was left standing there as Alexander Tetrapak Strandell occupied William Sandberg's well equipped home office. It didn't take him long to get his bearings. He moved between the various shelves and racks, his fingers following cables that had been neatly bound into hidden bundles under the desk, then started up machines and computers before finally sitting down at the desk. Christina handed him the CDs and he lined them up in front of him, while the computers coughed and grunted and flickered into life.

'I'm going to disconnect us from the internet. We don't want what happened to Sara – or what happened at my place – to happen here.'

Christina nodded. 'You do whatever you like.'

He turned back to face the desk, identified the right cables and then pulled them out from the back of the computer, and turned to face them again.

'Also,' he said, this time with an awkward smile, 'I don't mean to be rude, but I'm used to working alone.'

As Palmgren and Christina made their way into the living room, they could hear the clack of the bearded man's fingertips speeding up behind them. There was something in the combination of the sounds, the tapping on the keyboard, the fans, the whirring of all the hard drives, and the smell of the place, the feel of the loose wooden floor tiles, all of it, that flung Christina back into a time that no longer existed. It was as if she had happened to walk through a tear between dimensions, as though she was walking in with her winter coat and gloves into an apartment that was full of summer.

Round every corner, she expected to see them – William, Sara, herself – expected to see the sun shining in over the rooftops and straight into all of the rooms, where they would sit in that golden yellow light, eating breakfast or reading books, and then when they noticed her they would look up with puzzled expressions, feeling the cold that she'd brought in with her and sensing that something was wrong. Then she would warn them, warn them about the future and about Warsaw and about saying the wrong thing at the wrong time, and how they should never, ever, install a grille in the hall.

But they were gone. The living room was dark, the lights off, and Christina and Palmgren turned on the lamps by the window, sat down on separate sofas, and said nothing for a long time.

On a long bench along one of the walls was the television. They put it on with no sound, blurry footage of illuminated power stations alternating with pictures of roadblocks and maps with cities highlighted in red. Still no one knew what was going on, why it was happening, how it could be stopped. And with no sound, the panic in the eyes of reporter after reporter was clear. Not their dread of the looming nuclear disaster, that everyone might conceivably be dead before long, but panic at being pushed in front of the cameras to say the same thing for the umpteenth time.

That no one, *no one*, had the faintest idea about anything.

'What happened?' Palmgren asked after a long silence. 'With you, with Sara. Why did she disappear?'

'I've been a print journalist all my life,' Christina said. 'My job is to give as simple and straightforward an account of events as possible. A caused B which led to C. But in this case?' She shook her head. 'I don't know. All of a sudden, life was like this. With a whole fucking alphabet of events that led to one another.'

'I'm not asking the journalist. I'm asking you.'

Christina took a deep breath. 'We didn't realise,' she said carefully. 'We didn't realise how important it was. Knowing where you come from – who you are, why you're here, the emptiness of being without context – we didn't get it.'

She looked around the room. Tables and chairs and sofas where *she* might have sat, if now had been some other time.

'She knew. Of course she did. She noticed that something happened in Warsaw. And when we told her that she was adopted she realised that that's who we'd met – her real father – and she demanded to know who he was, screaming, threatening us. But we just didn't *dare*.'

She lowered her voice, as if Sara was actually there, as though she was reluctant to talk about someone in the third person in their presence.

'We were so scared of losing her that we didn't dare to tell her. And that was why we lost her in the end.'

That was the last thing she said before she went quiet and her eyes sank to the floor, settling on a rug that she had once chosen and demanded that it be delivered on time. A rug that once had been inexplicably important, just like everything else around her – the sofas they'd waited for months to receive, the table that barely fitted into the stairwell. The room was full of must-haves, and it was as though it was no longer possible to remember why it had all once mattered so much.

Christina hated tears, but as she looked up at Palmgren she knew they were on the way. 'It was that simple. A led to B which caused C. Can you put a headline on that?'

They sat opposite each other for another half-hour before Palmgren was the first of them to lie down on the sofa. On the other side of the oh-so-important coffee table, Christina did the same, and they lay there without sleeping, the ceiling above them flickering in the uneven light of the television images.

On screen, the security experts and the politicians were having their say. One of those speaking about the security situation was UK Defence Secretary Anthony Higgs.

When Higgs appeared on screen, Winslow was still sitting in his boss's office. At the bottom of the frame, microphones danced and jostled like the cast in a puppet show, and beyond them the Defence Secretary tried to compose himself for a statement. The questions that came were predictable, and the answers were just the ones Winslow didn't want to hear.

We will never negotiate with terrorists.

We can never allow anyone to take the whole world hostage.

And then, straight to camera, as though Higgs was hoping that the perpetrators were sitting in front of their televisions, listening intently to his every word:

We intend to take every possible measure to find those responsible.

Winslow turned the sound off, and sat down to stare at the floor, letting the TV carry on miming its message. How had he ended up here? Floodgate. It had sounded like such a good idea.

Maybe it was like Higgs said, maybe it *was* too late to change their minds. He didn't know. All he knew was that it went too fast, the world, everything, and that he didn't have the capacity to keep what he thought separate from what he had to do. He caught himself staring over at the large windows. He was four storeys up, was that enough? The thought shook him. Where did *that* come from?

Instinctively he took a step into the middle of the room, away from the windows, repeating to himself that a thought is not the same as an action, that everyone thinks dark thoughts now and again, and this didn't mean that he was ill. Considering the state of things, he thought to himself, the opposite was probably true.

When he had finally composed his thoughts, Higgs had already left the screen. The pictures now came from a studio, and Winslow pointed the remote and switched off the TV altogether.

He could see his own reflection in the black screen, and hoped that Trottier had been right after all. That Floodgate would save the world one day.

Had William known who the man was talking on the television in the corner of the depressing eating area, he would probably have paid him rather more attention. As it was, he stood there just inside the draughty doors of the run-down petrol station with his mind on other things.

It had been two hours since he'd left Rebecca. Right the way through he'd thought he wasn't going to make it, that he'd delayed too long and that the police would catch sight of him, either as he hurried across the field next to the road or, worse still, before he'd even managed to get out of the car.

That he'd made it out at all was down to Rebecca. She was the one who'd realised that the truck driver was already on his way down to come and talk to them, and she'd undone their belts and ordered: 'Swap with me! Swap with me *now*!'

Ahead of them, the torches had been getting closer. Behind them, the lorry driver's footsteps were approaching. And William had folded himself as small as possible, struggled to squeeze underneath Rebecca, as her contorted body wrestled its way over him in the other direction.

He was only halfway when he realised that he was stuck, that his jacket had snagged on something, maybe the seat-belt buckle, and he'd grimaced, writhing back and forth to try and get free, forcing himself not to pay attention to the hard seat backs behind him or the huge, merciless gearstick that was pushing deeper and deeper into his belly the more he struggled.

For a moment he pictured it: this was how it was going to end. The police were going to get there and rip open the car doors, and he'd be lying in the foetal position across both seats, entangled in a cagoule, and above him a woman with no hair bracing herself with hands and feet against whatever part of the car's interior was nearest and saying *how do you do* in Polish. It might have been that thought that helped him.

In a last desperate lunge he stretched one arm out in front of him, fumbled the door open and grabbed the chassis with his other hand. He pulled for all he was worth, and eventually he heard the nylon rip and slithered out through the opening on Rebecca's side. As he thudded onto the ground with no way to break his fall, there was not a single part of his body that wasn't sore, yet there was no time to lie there, and he crawled across the rain-soaked tarmac towards the ditch.

He pressed himself into the grass and the mud, the ice-cold damp seeping through every seam. And then, only then, did he notice that he hadn't closed the door properly. He lay there perfectly still, quite convinced that as soon as they noticed the door the game would be up. With his face in the dirt he counted each passing second, and only when the tone of the conversation began to soften, when he heard Rebecca's licence being returned and then everyone helping to give her a bump-start, did he dare to hope that they'd got away with it.

Eventually she drove past the red flares. The HGV had driven on, and the road ahead was empty. That's when he hauled himself up, soaking wet, freezing cold, and started walking back in the direction they'd come from. From now on, it was all down to Rebecca.

It was only after two hours of walking that he could see the illuminated logo of the petrol station he'd remembered from some time earlier. It was hovering there, like red clouds in the damp air, and he stopped well short of it, studying the aging premises until he was quite sure that the two cameras on the forecourt were the only ones they had. After that he slipped in along the frontage and carried on through the squealing door, hiding his face behind his elbow as he dealt with a coughing fit that was only partly faked.

Apart from the ones outside, there was just one more camera, behind the till, facing whoever was paying, and directly behind the sleepy shop assistant were three monochrome monitors which showed exactly what fields the three cameras covered.

Finally, William chose a soft drink from a vibrating refrigerator, walked over to the till and pointed at the hot dogs slowly rotating on the rollers, making sure to stay out of camera view as he paid. Lastly, he asked about the three computers. They stood at the other end of the store, in what was, according to the sign, a cafeteria but was actually no more than a few battered chairs and tables on an equally battered section of floor. Four zloty got him a code for an hour's surf.

He chose one of the terminals, sat down with his meal, and read the headlines from the world's newspapers as he ate. He had ploughed through all the major international titles, then the Swedish, and finally Christina's own, when he realised that the words were all merging. He couldn't remember when he'd last slept. On the ferry? On the vehicle deck on the way to Poland? Sandberg peered over at the man behind the till and thought to himself that four zloty was a reasonable price for an hour's sleep in a chair.

'The bastard!' Tetrapak's voice echoed down the long hallway, full of something that lay between joy and admiration and pride, and while his legs powered towards William's room as fast as they could carry him, he turned towards Christina and Palmgren, who were close behind. 'That bastard knew exactly what he was doing! And if it hadn't been for William we wouldn't have had a clue!'

Christina could still taste sleep in her mouth, and was busily trying to piece together where she was and why.

'He was right,' grinned Tetrapak as he sat down at William's desk. 'When you listen to them, they sound identical, but if you go through the content of the discs as binary data, and compare them, digit by digit—'

'Did it work?' she said, rubbing her face to try and wake up.

Strandell smiled at them.

'I've never heard of information being concealed that way before, but William was right. They're there – tiny, tiny deviations, impossible to notice. Right up until you put them side by side.'

'What do you mean?' asked Palmgren.

'What do you know about logical connectives?' The silence that ensued was an answer. 'Okay, I'll keep it short. Data is stored as ones and zeros, we know that. Logical connectives are a way of comparing series of ones and zeros to get a new result. If you put two series next to each other and compare them digit by digit, there are two possibilities. A: both digits are the same – two ones, or two zeros, it doesn't matter which.'

He demonstrated both possibilities with his hands: two palms, two backs.

'Or B: they're both different.' He turned one hand over, then both, so that when one hand was showing its palm, the other one was showing the back. 'A one on one, a zero on the other. Do you follow?'

'Uh huh,' Palmgren answered. The universal sign for *No, I haven't got a clue what you're on about, but you go on.*

'If both are the same we call that *true*. Different and we say *false*. If we then let the digit one represent true and zero represent false, then we have a whole new series of ones and zeros that wasn't there to begin with.'

'And this new series,' Christina said, without having understood any more than Palmgren. 'That's the message?'

Tetrapak shook his head. 'I struggled with that for a while,' he said. 'What I got was only the difference between *two* series. And the zeros just tell you where the differences are. How could I turn that into a message?' He picked up the CDs on the desk in front of him. 'That's when I got it. That's why there are three of them.'

Tetrapak was sitting in William's office chair, glowing with pride, while Christina and Palmgren stood in the doorway, radiating cluelessness.

'Is there any point in us asking you to explain?' said Christina.

'It's not as difficult as it sounds. Put a disc in the middle. Let's call it disc zero. One on the left, one on the right. We'll call them true and false respectively. Okay?'

He arranged them on the desk in a line.

'And then we go through all the discs. Digit by digit, bit by bit, sector by sector. If all three are the same, we do nothing. We

328

move on to the next one. If the one on the left deviates? We say false. If the one on the right does? True.' He let his finger swing back and forth between them as he said it: 'True, false, true, false. One, zero, one, zero. And that way, we get a new series.'

'And if the one in the middle deviates?' asked Palmgren.

'I know. I was terrified that might happen, because then the whole thing would've collapsed. But these two' – he pointed to the outer ones – 'never have the same value unless the one in the middle does too.'

Several seconds of silence, as Tetrapak waited for someone to ask the right question.

'Okay,' Christina said. 'What's the upshot of all this?'

'The upshot is this,' he said, then touched the keyboard to bring the screens to life.

'What are we looking at?' Christina said eventually.

'I wish I knew,' said Tetrapak.

The entire screen was filled with endless rows of ones and zeros, nothing more. No text, no message, nothing that seemed to have any kind of logic to it whatsoever.

'It's a digital sequence, but of what I don't know. I've tried everything I can think of. I've tried converting it to sound, to an image, to every kind of file I've ever heard of. And a few more besides.'

'Text?' Palmgren's voice, dry and crackly and obviously not used for a while. 'Isn't it just ASCII?'

'That's where I started,' said Tetrapak. 'I've used every kind of character code in existence' – he pointed at the screen, pressing a key for each new utterance. 'ASCII. ANSI. UTF-7. UTF-8. UTF-16.'

With each keystroke, the screen changed form. Instead of ones and zeros it shifted to displaying rows of symbols and letters, incomprehensible and arranged in what seemed to be a random order. Each new kind of character code caused the letters to be replaced with others, but always lacking any kind of discernible pattern, and always completely illegible.

At a stroke, Christina could feel the energy drain out of her. All the expectation and hope that she'd allowed herself to build up since Tetrapak dragged them out of the living room disappeared, to be replaced by something else. Disappointment? Perhaps. Frustration? Certainly. Rage? No, actually. But she was tired and full of emotions, and one fucking way or another it was all going to have to come out.

'You seriously mean to say that this is it?' she said, and realised that she was shouting. 'Do you really think that you've *solved* anything, that we've made a single step forward, that this helps us in some way?'

'I've done everything I can,' Tetrapak shot back. 'Whichever format I choose, the result is nonsense. Text? Nonsense. Sound? Noise. Image? Blur. Noise, nonsense, blur. That's it. What I *think* about it all doesn't change a bloody thing.'

He hammered the space bar again, causing the screen to hop back to ones and zeros. And then he took a deep breath, letting his voice settle before he spoke again.

'This is all I can get out. What we are looking at is what is hidden on Piotrowski's discs. And yes, there's something stored here, it could be a message, maybe something else. But how to make it readable . . . ?'

He shook his head, resigned. *I haven't got a clue.* It was as though he suddenly recognised himself again, realised that he was still the same person he'd always been. The one that no one believed, who made mountains out of molehills, who time and time again was left standing with a phone to his ear when the caller hung up, the one who knew that they were laughing at him. Palmgren saw that.

'You've done a great job,' he said. 'But I don't think we're going to get any further on our own.'

'What do you mean?' said Tetrapak, staring at him.

'The text is encrypted,' said Palmgren. 'That's the only logical answer. We've received a coded message, but we don't have a key. What we do have is people whose only task is to crack such codes – people like William. But we can't get hold of him right now, can we?' He looked at the time. 'It's almost morning. Headquarters is only a couple of minutes away. I think it's time we stopped trying to do this on our own—'

His wince of pain tore at his chest where Acetone had knelt on him. He had reached across the table to pick up the discs, and the last thing he'd expected was for Tetrapak to grab hold of him, a tight grip around his wrist, two eyes staring straight into his own.

'Leave them where they are,' said Tetrapak.

'What are you playing at?'

'I don't know you. I know that Christina says you're a good person. I hope she's right.'

Palmgren felt that a snigger was the most appropriate response. What the hell was this?

'And I know you call me conspiracy theorist. I know you're always laughing at me, I know all of that. But for once – listen to me. Listen to the madman. And see what happens.' No one said anything. Eventually he let go of Palmgren. 'I think Piotrowski sent them to us, and only us, for a reason.'

'Are you trying to suggest that it might be dangerous for Swedish Armed Forces to find out whatever is on those discs? Because if you are, I'm afraid I'm going to have to disappoint you. The Swedish Armed Forces haven't been particularly dangerous to anyone for a very long time.'

'I'm not saying that your colleagues have anything to do with this, Palmgren. I'm saying that Piotrowski was afraid of something. So afraid, in fact, that he sent this in such a way that it could never, under any circumstances, be read by the wrong person. Nevertheless, someone is after us. Per Einar Eriksen is dead, Piotrowski himself has disappeared. William is alive, but on the run without even knowing why.' He paused. 'Is it really that strange that I want to find out what this is? Before we tell anyone else that we have it?'

'So what do you think we should do?' said Christina.

When he looked at her, his eyes seemed to have lost their energy. As though their pointless fight had eroded his determination, as though what he had planned to say next had lost its appeal.

'There is one question that you haven't posed, one that I have the answer to.'

He looked back and forth between the two of them.

'I think I know why Piotrowski chose us. William, because he would be able to crack the code on the discs; Professor Eriksen, because his research concerned the same fields as Piotrowski's; me ...' He shrugged his shoulders. 'Maybe because of the conversation we had in Warsaw, maybe because we were both worried about the same sorts of things. I don't know exactly why. But I'm glad he did. I need the keys to your car.'

This last was directed at Palmgren, and it had come so suddenly that for a moment he didn't know how to reply.

'Why? Where are you going?' said Palmgren.

'Nowhere. I'm going to get my box.'

Palmgren hesitated, then pulled the key from his pocket, gave it to Tetrapak and watched him hurry for the door.

'What's this question we haven't asked?' Christina shouted after him.

'William,' Tetrapak replied without stopping. 'If William's in Poland, how are we going to get the codes to him?' He carried on backing out of the hall while he waited for them to understand.

'Shortwave?' said Christina.

'Yup. It will take me a couple of hours to transmit the codes over to Warsaw.' Then he turned around, continued towards the front door, and spoke knowing they could still hear. 'Once that's done, we just need to think of a way to let William know they're there.'

63

As dawn began to break over Europe, the world was waking up to bigger and bigger news stories. On channel after channel, maps, charts and numbers filled the screen. It takes *this long* for a meltdown to occur, the radioactive fallout will travel *that far*, and everywhere the panic was bubbling away under the surface. In the areas closest to the power stations, cars and overnight bags were being packed, in the shops people were hoarding water and food and toiletries, and in some places stocks had already run out and people were turned away.

And then there were those who had no such problems.

The man who hobbled down the steep wooden staircase was one of them. Sure, he couldn't walk as well as he used to, his spine had curved and his joints ached, but the alternative – as he often said – was not living at all, and that wasn't something that appealed to him in the slightest. On the contrary: standing there in his cellar, he felt a mixture of melancholy and pride.

At the bottom of the stairs, he turned the lights on with the old black switch on the wall. He breathed in the basement smell, carried on into the warm yellow light and looked around. There it was, all of it, in exactly the place it had been for as long as he could remember. The basement storage.

There was a wood-burning stove that could be lit to generate heat and to cook. There was fuel and medicine and batteries. There was an emergency radio, capable of receiving all kinds of frequencies, but most important there were tins and water and dried foodstuffs, and by keeping a close eye on use-by dates, he always knew that he would be able to survive at least six months down here, no matter what happened up there.

People called him the merchant of doom. Fine. He'd seen the war, and not the ordinary war where people shot each other and died, but the other one, the one they called politics and that is constantly being fought and can escalate without warning. That everything was going to end in disaster came as no surprise to him. He just hadn't expected it to be like this.

He walked over to the table and chairs and turned up the volume on the transistor radio. It was working as it should, and he sat himself down in front of it, listened intently to everything that was being said. Maybe this was it? Maybe this was the time for him to move down here indefinitely, and for his plans to be tested in the real world? For a moment he wasn't sure if the thought scared him, or if, in fact, it was actually something he looked forward to.

He sat there for a long time listening to the voices on the radio.

Speculation, the risks, *what happens now.*

No, he thought. No, it wasn't something he was looking forward to.

He would be okay, but how many others? What would it be

like, to be the lone survivor in a world where everyone had disappeared? Where fellow humans were desperately roaming around without food, suffering radiation sickness, what else? How long before the looting began, before people started stealing from each other? How long was it going to be before they came after *him*? The crazy guy who they'd all laughed at, always buying ravioli and tinned tomatoes because he was convinced the world was going to end. How long would it take before they were standing outside his door, smashing their way in?

At the very moment that thought occurred to him, he heard the dogs outside.

He kept the weapons right under the stairs, and after a moment's indecision he chose the hunting rifle, not because it was most effective, but because hopefully it would scare them off before he was forced to use it.

He limped silently up the stairs, floated between the shadows down the hall and opened the back door without so much as a creak.

Outside it was cold, wet, a morning like any other – apart from his dogs. They were jumping against the rattling steel mesh fence, competing to bark loudest, paws shaking and clawing at the metal, longing to do the same thing to whatever person they'd just caught sight of.

Person? Persons?

He walked around the outside of the house in a wide arc, slowly, silently, just a shadow among many. The rifle butt against his shoulder, all his senses on high alert. Soon he'd be able to see the road, the driveway, the farmyard between the house and the barn.

But before he even got that far, he heard the footsteps. It sounded like one person, shoes on gravel, feet walking without sneaking, straight across the yard towards the house. He was running now, crouched and turned sideways and with his finger on the trigger, then an evasive manoeuvre to stay in the shadows and ensure he wasn't seen before he had the intruder in his sights.

When he saw the person standing on his own bottom step he stopped dead, lowered his rifle, slowly. In the glow of the outside lighting it looked like it was a woman. She was standing on the steps, pulling her coat tightly round her in the cold, waiting, as though she had just knocked. She was tall, he noticed. Young. And as far as he could make out, she had no hair.

When she heard his steps coming across the gravel, Rebecca turned around.

'Dawid?' she said. 'Dawid, it's me.'

64

William awoke to a tight grip around his neck. Outside the large windows it was getting light, big HGVs stood at the pumps filling up with diesel, the rain had come to its senses and gone back to swathing reality in a wet, colourless mist. And above William was a tall, muscular man wearing a T-shirt emblazoned with the petrol station's logo.

He said something in Polish, and it wasn't friendly.

'I'm really sorry,' said William, far from certain where he was, or why. How long had he been asleep? He struggled with himself to wake up, a feverish effort to move his inner switch from off to on. 'I'm sorry, I don't speak Polish.'

'You have been sleeping for three hours,' said the man with the logo. 'Andrzej was scared to wake you on his own.'

Behind the till, the man who had sold him the hot dog and the drink was avoiding eye contact with William. And so, when William didn't say anything, the muscleman renewed his neck grip and pushed his other hand into William's armpit, helping him to a standing position whether he liked it or not. He pushed William's chair back under the bench, picked up the half-empty bottle and thrust it into his hand, and then led him towards the exit.

William felt the chill air hit him, the damp in his clothes, and realised now how cold he was. The rain was coming down, and the air smelled of petrol and hummed with engine sound.

'Wait,' he said, doing his best to apply the brakes. 'I'm sorry

I fell asleep, I've had a really messy night. But just let me buy something from the shop.'

The only response was a raised eyebrow and a smile that verged on mocking.

'I promise.' With great exertion he managed to shove his free hand into his jacket pocket, dig out his wallet, and hold it up. 'I need something to eat. Something to wear. That's all.'

He felt the grip under his arm relax ever so slightly.

'But then you leave,' the petrol man said over the engine noise. 'Agreed?'

'I'll leave as soon as you say so,' said William.

The man spun it out for another few seconds, as though he didn't want William to be getting cocky. Then he backed away, nodding towards the shop, as though he had just made a rare exception to an important, universal rule, and as though William should be incredibly grateful.

Truth be told though, he was.

In the shop he found toiletries as well as a reasonable breakfast, and from amongst the car accessories he picked out a pair of workwear trousers, a fleece and a T-shirt. Hopefully they'd let him get changed before he left.

Once he'd done that he managed to negotiate another hour's worth of surfing while he ate – in return for solemn promises not to fall asleep again, *this isn't a fucking hostel* – and when he returned to the spot where he'd just woken up he could feel the stares from both the staff and his fellow customers.

He hadn't seen it until now, but of course in their eyes he was an undesirable, a bloody vagrant, perhaps even a criminal. He'd shown up on foot in the middle of the night, paid with crumpled notes, and slept on a chair on their premises until someone dared to challenge him. He was his own daughter. The person she had been for years.

Overnight most of the papers had updated their headlines, and while he felt the coffee slowly spreading its warmth throughout his body he read through all the main outlets, the same ones he'd looked at during the night, and then a few others, all of them full of detailed articles about the situation. Illustrations and sophisticated graphics showed how the nuclear power stations' systems were constructed, what a meltdown looked like, and how long they had left before the reactions had gone so far that they could not be saved.

The hijacked reactors were of various types, using differing technologies, but all had a tipping point after which the process could no longer be reversed. A point at which such high temperatures were reached that a meltdown was inevitable, after which it would be impossible to do anything even if control was regained. In some of the reactors, he read, that point was less than twenty-four hours away.

The more he read, the more the emptiness grew inside him. It was as though someone was draining the hope out of him, as though he was staring into an abyss of fear that just kept growing. He had to do something. He *wanted* to do something. But what?

He was stranded in the Polish countryside, somewhere north of Warsaw, and all he could do was what everyone else in the world was doing: wait, hope, and place his fate in the hands of others.

He should get going. Maybe he'd find a motel along the way, somewhere he could grab a few hours' sleep, then maybe he'd wake up brimming with new energy, new insights and knowing exactly what to do next. Then again, if not, he would just have slept away the very last hours of the world he knew, slept himself closer to the apocalypse and woken up in a future he could not even begin to imagine.

He gathered his leftovers and cardboard wrappers from the table and was just getting up to leave, when he changed his mind. Just what it was that made him take one last look at Christina's paper's website, he didn't know. But as soon as the browser refreshed in front of him, he saw the message out of the corner of his eye. Within a second it had cut at him, made him remember, wounded his heart.

The eyes he was staring into were Christina's. She stood motionless at the top of the screen, serious and distant at the same time, the byline picture that she had never been happy with but which he'd always thought captured her perfectly.

It wasn't that, though, that caused his reaction. It was the headline beside it, squeezed into the top corner in the hope of tempting readers to click through to a feature column. He sat down again, looking at the time, hoping that his four zloty weren't about to run out. He let the pointer hover over the words that made up the headline. Their words.

It seemed like a good idea at the time.

Sitting in front of the old spare laptop, Christina refreshed the browser for the umpteenth time, hoping to see changes that stubbornly refused to materialise.

It was light now, but when Tetrapak had returned from Palmgren's car three hours earlier the dawn had still been a long way off. Without a word, he had unpacked the equipment from his dark grey box, placed all of it on William's desk, and connected the devices with hands now grown all too used to the task.

When he then opened the window and clambered out onto the slippery metal roof, she had tried to object. That, though, was futile, and instead she'd parked herself over by another window, with Palmgren standing alongside her. They had seen him balancing on the snow-covered rooftop gangway, back and forth between chimney pots and dormer windows, precarious steps as he made his way around firewalls and chimneys that separated one building from the next. She knew that she'd screamed out loud on at least one occasion, when Tetrapak lost his footing and started gliding down the roof towards the deep courtyard, before managing to grab hold of a vent and smiling towards them with terrified eyes.

It took him just under an hour to finish the whole thing. By then, he had attached long copper wires along the length of the roof, repeating in parallel lines like a big, copper-coloured musical stave, and stretching in a taut line over to a similar stave on the neighbouring roof. When he came back in, he sat down by the radio, hooked it up to his temporary antenna, and held his breath.

'How long have you been able to do this sort of thing?' Christina said from behind him.

'If this works . . .' he said with a nervous smile. 'Since now.'

When a crackling voice had finally introduced itself as coming from Warsaw, she couldn't hold back and hugged him from behind, hard and long enough to force him to finally drop the microphone and plead to be allowed to breathe.

The voice had turned out to belong to one of the amateur enthusiasts who had helped to locate the strange number stations, and while Tetrapak explained with careful adjustments what he needed help with now, Christina had wandered off into the kitchen. Lying in one of the drawers was a retired, ancient laptop that had been handed down through the entire family until no one wanted to inherit it any more, and she'd taken it out into the living room, sat down on the sofa and waited for it to be ready for use. With Tetrapak's permission she had borrowed Palmgren's phone and logged in to the newspaper's publishing utility. After that she'd ended up sitting on one of the sofas, with Palmgren opposite, and the sound from the radio in William's study drifting through.

In the middle of everything, it gave a strange sense of calm.

'What are you going to do?' asked Palmgren.

'I'm going to do what Tetrapak said. I'm going to create some news.'

She had smiled a sad smile, glanced down at the screen and placed her fingers on the keyboard. And as she typed the headline, the tears began to flow.

It seemed like a good idea at the time.

Now she was sitting there in the early morning light, reading the words over and over again, pressing the key to refresh, with her eyes fixed on the same point on the screen throughout: the counter, the little graphic that showed how many people had read her article, and their locations.

She watched it click upwards as people woke up and read her column on their tablets over breakfast, on their phones on the way to work, in the office before the working day got started. Hundreds, thousands of readers from all over the country. And she didn't care about any of them.

By the time Tetrapak came in and said he was finished, Palmgren had already fallen asleep on one of the sofas.

'I don't know what we've got in,' she said quietly, 'I haven't been here for a while. But if there's tea, would you like some?'

Tetrapak nodded his yes please, and then closed the lid on the laptop, stood up, and followed her to the kitchen. Had she stayed where she was, she would have seen the counter tick up another digit. And that the reader who'd just clicked was in Poland.

William closed the toilet door behind him, lined up the toiletries on the dirty washbasin and looked at himself in the mirror. Only then did he perceive that he was shaking. It could be the sleep deprivation of course. It wasn't inconceivable that it was down to the jet-black coffee he'd forced down along with his breakfast. Above all though, it was because of the feeling of hope. The restlessness, the desire to get somewhere, the sensation that three and a half seconds spent in this place was four seconds too long.

He'd read the article twice before he caught on. It had turned out to be an editorial, a calm, sorrowful reflection on life, an open-hearted account of how Christina Sandberg had lost her daughter, and how much it hurts when a life comes to an end.

At first he hadn't been sure whether to be angry, or hurt, or both. Here he was, in a foreign country, reading about *them*, about her and Sara and himself, about their shared misfortune, and how long had it been? A bit more than twenty-four hours? Could she not have let the wounds heal for a bit longer, tried to quell her hunger for clicks, just for a little while?

The major part of the article concerned their trip to Warsaw. She mentioned no names, and she blamed herself at least as much as she blamed him, but what surprised him was that their trip had been embellished. Details had been added – details that, for a start, were not true, and what's more added nothing to the story – and she named places and times that didn't match, almost as though she'd thrown the article together on the fly without bothering to check what had actually happened.

At which point his anger gave way to doubt.

Christina Sandberg? It couldn't be. The woman with a whole shelf full of prizes, who lectured at universities and delivered talks to other journalists . . . if there was one thing she clung to, above all else, it was facts. Of course they argued sometimes, she and William, about the tabloid culture and her constant search for angles and drama. But the foundation was always the truth, and facts were something that could not be knowingly got wrong.

In spite of that, she had written an editorial that was full of make-believe.

He and Christina had certainly not *arranged an important meeting* in Warsaw. Not with – as she put it – *a man who would have a great impact on their lives*. That had just happened. Had she forgotten that? And even if they *had* arranged to meet, there was no way it could have been on a Wednesday, since they were only there for one weekend. Why, then, was she writing that stuff? Meaningless details that didn't add anything for the reader, but that stuck out as irritating errors for one single person in the entire world.

As soon as he'd voiced that question inside his head, he realised what the answer was. After reading it for the third time, he could feel his heart pounding. Now, it all made perfect sense. What he was reading wasn't an editorial at all, and the factual errors were not irrelevant details. What she'd written was a message, and now he loved her again, or at least knew why he once had.

Christina Sandberg hadn't written about a meeting that had taken place. She'd written about a meeting that was about to.

Once William had managed to wet his hair in the sink and to work the cheap hand soap into something resembling a lather, he grasped his greying locks and tugged the razor blade through the taut tufts. Each new cut chafed his scalp, and when he'd finally made it all the way from one side of his head to the other he opened a new, sharp razor and pulled it across his head in long, deliberate strokes. Finally, he put it down on the edge of the washbasin. He stood there looking at his own reflection for a long time. The eyes were his, but their setting was all wrong, and for a moment he realised he felt like he was observing someone else. That made him feel calmer.

He was being pursued from two directions: the police, first of all, and then a Consciousness that was everywhere and nowhere, and whatever awaited him in Warsaw he wanted to be able to get to it without being discovered. He put on his new workwear, and on his way out past the till he invested twenty-five zloty in a pair of reading glasses that could hopefully be passed off as something you might wear all the time.

Just after eleven, a German family stopped at a petrol station just south of Przasnysz, and they left with a shaven-headed hitchhiker in specs. He sat there in the back seat for over an hour, in between two child strangers, their nervous parents facing backwards in the front seats singing nursery rhymes to divert their thoughts from the impending catastrophe. We're going on holiday, they said, but it wasn't the truth. Theirs was a trip to wherever, to any land without nuclear power.

He, meanwhile, was on his way to a meeting that his wife had arranged via a coded message that only he could have deciphered.

65

Christina sat by the kitchen window and looked out over the rooftops, a view she'd seen so many times before. An icy blue sky tried to force its way through the clouds for the first time for longer than she could remember, bringing warm rays of light that made the thin blanket of snow glisten.

She'd done what she could. The discs had been found, the content sent to Warsaw. Hopefully it would reach William in time, but now there was nothing she could do to change anything. It was as though that struggle had kept her going, she'd been driven by it, and now, when she was done, she was left with just the hole and the memories.

When Palmgren came into the kitchen and apologised for having fallen asleep, it was already getting on for mid-afternoon.

'Are you going to work?' she asked, and felt her heart stir as she spoke. It was the question she'd asked many thousands of times before, to a man standing on that very spot. A completely different man, and a different time.

'I think they'd probably appreciate that,' said Palmgren. And then he turned to include Strandell before he went on: 'Thank you. Thanks for a job well done. And I mean it this time.'

Everywhere you looked, there were signs of a world on the edge. The pavements in central Warsaw were all but empty, just the odd person here and there, rapid footsteps away from the rain and the cold and the fear that were hanging in the air. Police cars were stationed at crossroads and in car parks, blue lights flashing to advertise their presence, uniformed officers patrolling quietly in the wet, all looking for the tiniest deviation from normality.

The deviation stood at the top of the round steps leading up to the congress hall. There he was, William Sandberg, waiting between two of the Palace of Culture and Sport's monumental pillars, watching his own reflection in the glass doors, tall and locked and dark and with the large foyer beyond them screened off by heavy curtains.

It was like a memory coming back to you long after the party was over. As though summer and joy and complimentary buffets were still in there somewhere, as if time was something you could move around in freely, and he had just happened to pick the wrong door. Somewhere was another reality going on, one where he was wearing sunglasses and an unbuttoned shirt, where Christina was at his side, Sara a couple of steps behind, and everything could still turn out okay.

But the reality where William found himself was strikingly cold. The daylight, in as much as there had been any, had already begun to sink away. It was ten past three, and that made him feel uneasy. Unless he'd completely misinterpreted Christina's message, that meant that the appointed time had been and gone, and it was fair to say that William had bad experiences of waiting to meet people when he didn't know who was going to turn up.

343

At the Central Station just across the street, a handful of police stood waiting; a few more were standing, lights flashing, by the shopping centre opposite. In all probability, there were even more on the other side of the building. And there he stood, a lone man with a shaved head, not heading anywhere. How long would it be before they wondered why?

The coffee in the mug he was holding had long since gone cold, yet he still took a sip every now and then. In his other hand was his wallet, and he was pretending to swipe at the black leather with his thumb, hoping that anyone looking from a distance would think he was flipping through his phone, just a man waiting for something, passing the time by reading news sites or social media, the way that people do.

He stood there for another five minutes before deciding that he'd waited long enough. Maybe he had got Christina's message wrong after all. He walked down the steps, trying to keep the back of his head turned towards the police on the street, and skirted around the enormous stone palace to head in the other direction.

The congress hall. That's what she'd written, there was no doubt about that. She'd written Wednesday, that was today, at three, which was now, so how else could he have taken it?

He'd just turned the corner in front of the building, and was walking past the tower's southern façade, when he realised that he hadn't been paying attention.

He heard footsteps behind him. He hesitated, but forced himself not to look, to carry straight on without letting on that he'd heard. Was it cops? Someone else? He picked up the pace, and when he saw the next corner of the building coming into view, he turned in there and stopped at the bottom of the stone steps leading to another of the place's many grand entrances. He fished out his pretend phone again, pretending to check something pretend-important, looking around so discreetly that no one could possibly notice. But the pavement behind him was empty.

Had he imagined it? Was it emotions taking hold again? He strove to breathe evenly, trying hard to work out what to do next. Maybe he ought to try and find somewhere where he could borrow a computer, have another look at Christina's column. There had to be a public library around somewhere, and if he just managed to avoid the police and was careful in places with CCTV, maybe he could ask directions without being discovered.

Just as he made up his mind, he felt a hand on his shoulder. He spun around, much too fast, and as he met the young man's eyes he realised that his assailant was every bit as terrified as he was himself. He couldn't be much more than twenty. Tall and wide, neither muscular nor overweight, just big, but in proportion, including the powerful hand that had managed to envelop the whole of William's shoulder at once. His beard was a shock of single straggly blond hairs, apparently competing with each other to be the longest on his face, and a dark blue tattoo peeked over the top of his tracksuit top.

He stood a couple of steps above William on the stairs, an arm's length away, carefully maintaining that distance. Presumably he had realised that William had heard him coming, and cut diagonally up the steps to disappear behind one of the pillars. Just the way that William had tried to hide from the police moments before.

'Name?' said the lad.

William swallowed. Was this the meeting he'd been waiting for?

'My name is William Sandberg,' he said. 'I come from Sweden.'

It was the longest of seconds before the reply came.

'You don't look like they said you would.'

66

They say that people choose dogs that look like themselves. As William approached the white van that was parked at the far end of the car park, it occurred to him that the same thing seemed to apply to cars.

Just like its owner, this car was unnecessarily large, clumsy and – particularly right now – irritatingly conspicuous. It was basically an old Ford Transit, but someone had done their best to disguise that fact. What had once been white was now covered in brightly coloured, fractal-patterned designs, obviously painted by hand on several different occasions, with the same aesthetics as the tattoo poking up above the youngster's neckline. Not only that, but it was conspicuously badly parked too, the front wheels having mounted the kerb.

William's first thought was that it was an outside broadcast car for a local radio station, but the closer they came, the more obvious it was that he was looking at something distinctly home-made. One front wing was home to a small forest of antennas, and the vehicle's entire length was topped with a roof rack onto which a further rack of aerials had been attached. Along one side, someone had written an incomprehensible acronym in massive purple letters.

'It's my handle,' the man said when he saw the look in William's eyes. 'SQ1TJP. My friend does custom graphics.' With that he blipped open the van with an angry beep – *brilliant*, William thought to himself, *if we're bound to draw attention, let's be consistent* – and then led him around the vehicle and up to the back doors. They were covered in text. In a spiky font the car announced that it had participated in a series of amateur radio competitions, all with weird names and all hosted in different European cities.

'I won all of them,' the other man said. Then he banged on a blank space on the right-hand door. 'I've saved some room for next season.'

'Impressive,' William heard himself say, and felt the tone giving the opposite message.

The man whose handle was SQ1TJP stopped.

'Listen, right. I don't know who you are. I was promised money if I found you down here. I dropped everything I had planned, and I'd love to know why.'

'I don't know any more than you do,' said William. 'Could you start from the beginning?'

'Do you know a guy called SM0GRY?'

346

William could feel the fatigue overpowering him.

'I'm not very good with names,' he said.

'Doesn't matter. He's a radio amateur, like me. And he sent me a message that he wants you to have.'

With that, he opened the door, and if the outside of the van looked like a teenage boy's bedroom, it was nothing compared to the scene inside. With the exception of the two seats up front, none of it was original. Along the windowless sides, two narrow desks had been installed, and in between them were two desk chairs in plum-coloured crushed velour. Underneath it all was a floor that had been covered with a bright purple carpet, perfectly matching the decals on the outside.

Beyond that, the décor consisted of various types of electronic equipment. Rectangular black boxes stacked on top of each other, some obviously radio equipment, others probably signal amplifiers of some kind, others still apparently hard discs. On the walls, printed lists and flatscreen monitors battled for space. There were cables and wires dangling all over the place, some of the coiled ones leading to headsets or microphones. All in all, it looked like a cross between one of the military's old radio cars and the pride and joy of an Eighties boy racer, and William picked one of the desk chairs while SQ1TJP closed the doors behind them. He squeezed his large frame into the other one, chatting as he turned on the power and started up his machines.

'Earlier in the autumn, I was contacted by a man in Stockholm. He'd recorded some transmissions that he didn't know the source of. We ended up having a whole load of amateur radio enthusiasts from all over the world helping him to measure the strength of the signals and the delay to try and locate the transmission site.' He turned to face William, unsure as to whether or not it was relevant. 'It turned out that they were coming from London, and that responses were coming from all kinds of places around the globe. Chaotic noise, like a modem on speed.'

He peered at William, as if waiting for a reaction. William, though, had nothing to say, and eventually the young man continued.

'Anyway,' he said. 'That was the last I heard from him. Until today.'

347

On the table in front of him was a laptop, a bulky, heavy machine with shock-absorbent rubber corners, and thin black cables connecting it to the screens above.

'The first thing he made me swear to was that none of the gear in here is connected to the internet. Then, that I wasn't to show you anything until I'd made sure you weren't either.'

'Believe me,' said William. 'You can't get more offline than I am right now.'

'Good. Then I am to show you this.'

Even as the monitors flickered into life, William had an idea of what he was about to see.

He leaned forward, studying the image appearing on the screens in front of him. A protracted silence fell between them as he saw them filling with ones and zeros, an endless stream scrolling away, page after page, and still proceeding.

'Is this what I think it is?' he asked.

'According to the guy in Stockholm, it's data from a CD. And according to him, you'll know what to do with it.'

William could taste his own heartbeat in his mouth.

'Do you know what this is about?' the young man said.

'I need to borrow your computer,' was all he said.

'Listen,' the tattooed radio enthusiast said as he stared straight at him. 'I think I've been very helpful. I was given a promise by your friend in Stockholm, and if you're planning to rip me off —'

'You'll get your money,' William barked. 'But as of now, that's not my top priority. Do you read the news at all or do you spend all your time doing this' – he gestured to the decals, the equipment – 'kind of thing? Right now, millions of people are wondering what the hell is happening to the nuclear power stations at sixty-seven different locations across the globe. What you have there might be able to give us the answer. So I'd say that your biggest problem isn't whether you're going to get paid, your biggest problem is whether or not we're even going to live long enough for me to work out what this means!'

'You're bluffing,' said the youngster. 'Otherwise you would've paid by now.'

William sighed. Pulled his wallet from his inside pocket. In the large compartment in the middle were the last of the notes that the lorry driver had changed for him on the boat, and he grabbed them all and handed them over.

'I don't know how much is left. I've spent a bit. But that's my worldly wealth right now.'

A pause. 'Who are you?' was all the young man said.

'I'm going to take that as a yes,' said William and pulled the laptop over. 'In the meantime, you make sure to get this van out of here, preferably out of Warsaw, and away from anywhere there might be police.'

The young man swallowed loudly.

'Is it you they're looking for?'

'If it is,' William said, with a level stare, 'then I'm sure you appreciate how silly it would be for us to be sitting in a custom-ised van in the middle of downtown Warsaw, right?'

'Fine,' he said. 'But we're not finished with the money.'

'If you get us out of here you can have whatever you want. Get caught in a police check and I'll tell them I take my orders from you. Deal?'

The young man smiled for the first time during their whole conversation.

'You've no idea how much time I've spent on driving games.'

He clambered between the two front seats and wriggled behind the wheel, like a normal-sized person borrowing a hob-bit's car, and put the key in the ignition. William studied him, asking himself whether the bit about driving games was good news or bad.

The next minute, the massive V6 powered into life.

Superintendent Katryna Pavlak hated terrorists, and not just for the obvious reasons. After all, most people hate terrorists, because they destroy society and openness and everything else that makes humans civilised beings. Katryna Pavlak hated them for that too, of course. But that wasn't all. The thing was that she'd already served her time as dogsbody. She'd been let into the warmth, she'd climbed the ranks, she had a workstation with a desk and routines and a pot plant, and now here she was, out in the rain again, and it was the terrorist's fault. That's why she hated him so profoundly.

According to reliable sources, his name was William Sandberg and he was Swedish. He was probably still in Warsaw, which is why they had called on every available resource and freed up everyone possible. The aim was to have as high a police presence as possible, which of course looked great on paper. In reality it meant every last bastard had to put their shoes on, go outside, and start walking.

The chief problem was the mission itself. Orders were to keep a close eye on anything that might be suspicious – but what did that mean, really? Within a couple of months of completing her training, she'd pretty much seen it all. People dressed up in metal suits? Check. Happy, laughing teenagers bleeding all over? Check. Fully grown adults jumping on the roof of a parked car until it crumpled? Check there too. Performance artists, live-action role players, music video shoots.

But she'd also seen people who looked like they were sun-bathing on park benches but were in fact dead from overdoses, conscientious undergraduates financing their studies by selling drugs, well-dressed polite gentlemen whose computers contained images that would cause the most hardened person to throw up.

What was normal was abnormal, and that was a rule without exception. What was suspicious, in other words, could never be distinguished from what wasn't. And now an entire police force had been deployed with just those orders: to look for something that couldn't be seen. And that, Katryna Pavlak hated more than anything.

She was standing on the square in front of the entrance to the Palace of Culture and Sport's café, with a newly bought coffee in one hand and a shrink-wrapped sandwich in the other, and despite having stood there for several minutes, she was yet to taste any of it. Instead, she was listening to the struggle going on inside her.

Normal or not? The car at the far end of the car park was a white Ford Transit with blacked-out windows. Or rather: *used* to be white, until some bodging custom decal maker had plastered it with swirly patterns and a combination of letters that was impossible to pronounce. As if that wasn't enough, it was covered with more aerials than your average communications satellite. All in all, it faced her with a dilemma that was profoundly irritating.

No idiot would hide out in a car that looked like that, and definitely not a suspected terrorist, and especially not one dangerous enough to threaten the entire planet. *For that reason*, said a stubborn voice inside her, despite that being the worst argument in history, *for that reason, perhaps he might be hiding in there?* Because no one would believe that he was hiding somewhere so visible?

It was a logical argument that tripped itself up, and she knew as much. No, hiding somewhere that attracts a lot of attention isn't clever. Even *if* automatically disqualifying itself from suspicion on the grounds of being too stupid, it still meant the place had been noticed. And where's the gain in that?

Warsaw was covered in places to keep yourself invisible for real. Hotel rooms, warehouses, apartments. So why take the risk of being seen, just because you were double-bluffing and hiding in a place that was visible?

All that took her back to square one. No idiot would hide in a vehicle like that, and for that reason Katryna Pavlak looked at the sandwich and the coffee she'd just bought, threw the lot in the bin, and started walking.

She'd lost her appetite anyway.

The young radio enthusiast had just straightened up in the driver's seat and started the booming engine when a knock came at the window.

William froze. He pushed himself up against the side of the van to make himself as hard to see as possible, praying silently that it was a passer-by or a tourist or whatever, just not the police. That, of course, went completely unheard.

The woman outside the window was wearing a dark blue uniform, and as the young man wound down the window, smiled at her and said something apologetic in Polish, William noticed that he was holding his breath. He stayed like that until he thought his lungs would burst, right until he heard her move away from the vehicle and start talking to herself nearby, short, questioning sentences as if she were talking into a radio.

'It's cool,' said the young man up front. He said it without moving, a soft, almost inaudible tone. 'She's just checking the vehicle against the register. Nothing's going to happen, all my documents are in order.'

William breathed out. And as the radio conversation outside started to sound lighter, almost conversational, he felt himself getting increasingly restless. He had the material now. The information from Piotrowski. He didn't have the time to sit and wait, and eventually he flipped up the laptop screen and scanned the reticent data once more.

His immediate attempts at converting the digits into text had resulted in nothing. All he got was complete gibberish, regardless of what format he tried or what bit-length he was using, and before long he had been forced to admit to himself that it was rather more complicated than he would have wished. The text was encrypted, and all William could do now was try and break that encryption to get at the content.

As the conversation outside the van continued, he let his fingers travel over the keys. He was going to have to write a basic program that could chew through all the ones and zeros, convert them into letters, look for a pattern and then, from there, find a solution. The only question was, how?

There was a countless number of ciphering methods out there, all built in different ways, with various derivatives, the initial values of which had an infinite variety. Simple methods like dislocation and transposition he might be able to try, but if the texts were encrypted with keys then the problem was exponentially larger. It would be impossible for him to manually write a program capable of cracking a cipher like that, and even more impossible for a modest workaday laptop to provide a result within the foreseeable future.

What was most frustrating of all though, was the fact that the text was encrypted at all. Why go to the trouble of hiding something on a CD, so slyly and cleverly and impossible for an outsider to even see, and then still choose to encrypt it *as well*?

By the time the policewoman had finally returned the young man's licence up front, William was deep in the coding. The two exchanged a few pleasantries, the lad wound his window up again, and then, in a split second, everything turned around.

Maybe she'd caught sight of him behind the driver's seat, maybe it was the tapping of keys that leaked out, whatever it was, the young man had just restarted the engine when he saw her movement in the rear-view mirror.

'Oi!' he shouted over his shoulder, trying to warn William but too late.

The doors to the back of the van were opened from outside, and for one frozen second he stared into the eyes of a woman in a dark blue police uniform. The next, she backed away fumbling for her weapon.

'Drive!' shouted William, which was exactly what the kid was already doing. And as they fled out of the car park, William wrestled with the back doors and eventually managed to close them.

They raced through Warsaw on squealing tyres, William thrown back and forth between shelves and side panels, and the terrified amateur radio enthusiast steering them through the wet streets of the city.

'Who are you?' he screamed at William. 'Who the fuck are you?'

At least there could be no doubt that he had devoted countless hours to racing. He accelerated down the broad streets, nipped in and out of lanes, avoiding oncoming traffic at the last possible second. Every now and then, the sirens returned, but he almost always seemed to manage to shake them off, hunched behind the wheel like a big kid at an amusement park.

For every new turn, William felt the nausea burgeoning inside. The screen was vibrating and bouncing in his lap, and he swallowed, tried to concentrate, but was eventually forced to give up. By that point he had managed to knock up a simple program – it was rudimentary, but at least it was something – that would trawl through the text again and again, testing it against algorithms and calculating whether the results resembled anything like actual words. As a cryptological tool, it left rather a lot to be desired. It was, on the other hand, demanding enough that it would probably keep the computer busy for hours, and right now there wasn't much he could do about it anyway.

Just as he began to run the program, his driver yelled at him again: 'Who are you?'

In front of them, oncoming vehicles swerved onto the pavements, pedestrians dove for cover, buildings and road signs flashed past like a film on fast-forward.

'I'm innocent,' William shouted back. 'But they think I've got something to do with the nuclear power stations.'

He saw his driver shake his head in disbelief.

'It doesn't get any worse than this. This is as bad as it fucking gets.'

William very much hoped that the young man was right.

67

Superintendent Pavlak was sitting in the passenger seat with a tight grip on the door handle. Every now and then she'd catch a glimpse of the van, way, way ahead of them on the arrow-straight boulevard. For long periods it disappeared into the gathering gloom, hidden behind cars and trams, only to pop out again as it changed lanes or crossed the tramlines, or swung off and carried on down side roads in the hope of getting away. Inside her, a new internal conflict was raging.

The first thing she'd done after the van had driven off was to rush back to her unit and tell them what had happened. Together they'd given chase, and she'd radioed in that they were in pursuit of a customised Transit with two occupants, and that the vehicle had almost run her over during a routine check. That was all she'd said, because it was all she knew for sure.

But driving through the city at speeds that were potentially lethal, not only for them but for the general public, she was all too aware that the man in the back could well have been him. *Could have.* Was that good enough? Aside from his age, nothing fitted the description. The man they were looking for had greying hair and was probably operating alone, while the man in the van had a shaved head and a companion – a man who according to the car registration database was called Fabian Bosko, an active amateur radio enthusiast, and quite obviously a very accomplished driver.

She could imagine the ribbing, the jokes, the years of snide comments if she'd got it wrong. What was even worse though was that she would be diverting resources – if Pavlak reported that the vehicle they were pursuing might be carrying the Swedish suspect then every available unit would be dispatched to stop it. Police across the city would leave their posts to prioritise a single target, and Jesus, she didn't *know* for sure. That man might be a wanted terrorist – or he might be an amateur radio enthusiast who happened to have a bag of weed in his pocket.

Deep down though, she knew what she had to do, and once they lost the van in the alleyways approaching the old town, she made a decision. For the second time, fear made the choice. The fear of having done too little. She lifted the digital radio handset from the dashboard, cleared her throat and called the control room. Reported that the description didn't match one hundred per cent, but that the suspect could well have shaved his head, in which case it might have been him.

'Can you repeat that,' said the operator.

She saw her colleague's quizzical expression in the driving seat next to her. Now though, there was no turning back.

'We're following a car,' she said in a clear loud voice, 'a white Ford Transit with custom decals, and covered in aerials. It is probably carrying William Sandberg.'

As soon as the information went over the police's digital radio, was recorded on their hard discs for documentation and was forwarded as a registered event in their internal system, the news spread like wildfire through all active units. Her colleagues threw themselves into their vehicles, seatbelts clicked into place, blue lights were switched on.

The Warsaw police were preparing to stop William Sandberg. And not just them.

Fabian Bosko, amateur radio enthusiast, roared at the top of his voice, a sound instantly overwhelmed by the sustained angry beeping of horns from buses and lorries, many of which sounded to William like they were only centimetres away from the van's thin metal sides. Then came the sound of braking and squealing tyres. Up front, the youth was spinning the wheel one way and then the other, a one-handed manoeuvre that made the car swerve, skid, spin side-on to the traffic before he accelerated out of the turn.

So great were the G forces that William was literally thrown backwards. He slammed into the back doors with a thud that left him winded, and he could feel the doors vibrating so much that for a second he could see a crack between them open, letting in the sound of the tarmac rushing beneath them.

He grabbed hold of the shelves along the side, hoping that they would bear his weight and keep him inside the van if the doors did open. From the driver's seat, he heard Bosko's voice through the chaos. He was screaming in a falsetto, swearing in a mixture of Polish and English, presumably unaware of which was which.

'How the fuck,' he screamed to no one in particular, and 'We had fucking green,' and 'What is going on?'

'What the hell are you doing?' shouted William once the air had returned to his lungs. He hauled himself through the van, clinging hard to the fixtures to stay on his feet, slow, forward-leaning steps against the violent acceleration.

'They got green too,' the youngster replied. 'I thought we were going to fucking die.'

He pointed out towards the traffic flow all around them, hands still shaking after his evasive manoeuvres.

'They just drove straight out into the crossing, right in front of me, coming at me like rifle pellets out of nowhere! We had green, and then suddenly we all did, and feel my fucking pulse, Jesus, feel my pulse!'

William leaned forward between the front seats and looked out. He could see flashing blue lights behind them in the wing mirrors. Above them, he saw the street lights, the tall masts carrying the power above the tramlines, the road signs flying past in a constant stream. And . . . of course.

'Whatever you see,' said William, 'keep driving. Don't stop for red lights, don't stop for anything, *drive*.'

'What the fuck is going on?' said the young man.

'Cameras,' said William. 'That's what's going on. Traffic cameras.'

Just as Palmgren entered through the security scanners at HQ, Velander grabbed hold of his arm. He more or less dragged him through the corridors, fuming with worry and stress. 'We've been trying to get hold of you all morning,' he said through clenched teeth. 'Why the hell haven't you had your phone on?'

'Has something happened?' Palmgren said, avoiding the question. What could he say? *I'm sorry, I fell asleep on the sofa in William Sandberg's apartment?* Not the greatest excuse, yet marginally better than *I'm sorry, a bearded amateur radio enthusiast with paranoid tendencies told me to keep my phone off.*

Velander pulled him towards the briefing room without answering, and it was only now that Palmgren noticed how empty the corridors were. He felt the anguish wash through his stomach – the feeling that something big had happened without him noticing, that while he was dozing on William's sofa, the world had taken a step closer to carrying out its own death sentence.

'Is it the power stations?' he said, expecting a yes.

'No,' said Velander. 'It's William.'

It took a moment for the penny to drop.

'*Is?* What do you mean? What about him?'

Velander replied by pulling even harder on Palmgren's arm. He upped his pace but said nothing, because how on earth could you explain what was happening now?

'What's this about?' said Palmgren. 'Do we know where he is? Have we found him? Tell me!'

Eventually Velander stopped and tried to find some way of saying it. But there really was no way that didn't sound preposterous.

'No,' he said. 'No, not *us*.'

When they entered the JOC's large auditorium the air was so thick that it was only just breathable. It was as though the entire staff of the building had congregated in one place, and were now breathing the same air, letting it pass in and out of each other's lungs until there wasn't a drop of oxygen left anywhere.

And all of them were staring straight ahead at the huge screen down at the front. Its surface was divided into a mosaic of smaller sections, four across and four high, and each of the sixteen boxes was showing video in blue-grey tones. It was all filmed from various angles, and in the centre of each image was a customised Ford Transit van with antennas on the roof. It was hurtling down streets that Palmgren didn't recognise, pulling tight turns at unfamiliar junctions, swerving round the wrong side of traffic islands and shooting straight through red lights at a speed that looked incredibly dangerous.

'Where's this coming from?' he asked.

'It's a stream from the Polish police,' said Velander. 'They're saying that William is in that van.'

Palmgren pushed his way towards the front of the room. Past all the chairs, workstations, all the way down to the spot that was reserved for the officer in charge. Forester was standing there, her eyes showing the same sheer concentration as the rest of them.

'It must be every bloody camera in the whole city,' Palmgren said.

She nodded without saying anything. Ahead of them the car continued its crazy journey across Warsaw, northwards along the river, handbrake turns as it met police cars head-on, then back towards the centre, traffic lights constantly changing ahead of it, crossing streams of traffic that were appearing out of nowhere with terrifying timing, and each time the Ford managed to avoid collision by what looked like a matter of millimetres.

Not once did it disappear out of shot. Sometimes it was shown only as a small dot, filmed from a great height, perhaps from traffic cameras, possibly weather drones. Sometimes it appeared through large windows, with goods and customers in the foreground as if the camera was inside a shop and just happened to be facing the street outside.

'How the fuck,' Palmgren said eventually. 'How the fucking hell can the Polish police have access to all these cameras?'

'This is the thing,' she said. 'They don't.'

As Sebastian Wojda sat down at the back of the large communications room at police HQ, he did so with a feeling that something wasn't right. He ought to have been pleased. They had him now. What was bothering him was that he couldn't grasp why.

The pictures had come to them. They came from nowhere, without any request, and no one knew why. Streams that were otherwise used for traffic management had suddenly changed, cameras that would usually show static images of junctions and tunnels were suddenly, without warning, showing a single car from a variety of angles, constantly switching to new cameras at the pace of an action blockbuster films, with images from sources that simply could not be part of the police's network.

Someone was supplying them with the footage. But who? And to what end?

There he was now, driving across the screens in front of them, right across the city in a van at breakneck speed, the man who had called himself Karl Axel Söderbladh but who, according to colleagues in Stockholm, was actually William Sandberg.

But there was still too much that couldn't be explained. None of the Swedes had heard of him using an alias, much less that he was on Interpol's most wanted list.

And when word of their surprise had reached Wojda, it hadn't taken a lot of effort to establish that Interpol didn't know that either. The truth was that no William Sandberg – or, indeed, Karl Axel Söderbladh – had never appeared on their list. Sure, he was on it *now*, that they could all see from the website, but there was no unit or department or administrator who could admit to having put him on there. After a search of the backup systems it turned out that he wasn't in them either – he'd quite simply never been a wanted man, until suddenly he was. William Sandberg, alias Karl Axel Söderbladh, had appeared on the list at exactly the same time as he'd shown up at Hotel New York.

Having said all that, there was no denying that he was wanted. Maybe not by Interpol, but he had escaped from the Swedish military authorities, and once they'd established that he was in Warsaw they had submitted a formal request for the Polish police's assistance in tracking him down. Which was precisely what was happening on the screens at the front of the room.

Sebastian Wojda rubbed his forehead. There was just too much that didn't add up. Like how a lone man in Warsaw could be behind the biggest terrorist action ever seen. Like why, in that case, he had been moving around outside, in the centre of the city, instead of lying low. And above all, why had he checked in to a fleapit in Praga instead of finding a safe hiding place and running his operations from there?

And then, on top of all the other questions there were the pictures that had turned up out of nowhere, infinitely well timed and helpful, without anyone having asked for them. Somebody powerful *wanted* them to catch him. Simple as that. Which meant that someone was directing their operation – and the question, which nobody seemed to have had time to ask, was why.

As he left the comms room, Wojda thought to himself that a perk of finally capturing William Sandberg would be the chance to ask him just that.

Once hell had broken loose, it refused to stop. Traffic lights were changing all around them, going red before their eyes without even passing amber, almost as though they'd suddenly changed their mind at that second. As though everything was deliberately aimed to stop them. Which of course it was.

All along the route their path was crossed – literally – by other vehicles. Trams were given the signal to proceed, all four approaches were let through junctions at the same instant, constantly creating chaos and blocking their way, and behind the wheel of the Ford the man with the adolescent tattoos and downy 'tache managed to avoid them all at the very last second. Time and time again he heard his beloved bodywork scraping against cars that he thought he'd just managed to avoid, and equally often he could feel the entire van bouncing across laybys and over kerbs as he swerved off the carriageway.

'What the hell is going on here?' he screamed. 'Where are all these cars coming from?'

William didn't reply. He knew the answer wasn't going to improve the situation. *Well, you know, you've heard of the internet, right?*

'I'm not going to make it. We're fucked.'

Now that was a far more plausible statement. Even if the thousands of hours spent on driving simulators had undeniably produced results, it didn't mean that the young man would be able to keep it up for ever. William was already noticing how his reactions were getting slower. How the margins were getting smaller, and his voice was getting more panic-stricken with each new swearword.

'You can,' William shouted, without believing it himself. 'You can do this!'

But the problem was that reality didn't have a pause button. There was no respite between tracks where you could crack your knuckles and take a swig of energy drink as you waited for the next race, instead, the stimuli were relentlessly rushing towards them: new cars, new junctions, new dangers threatening to bring them to a final halt. And sooner or later, the brain loses its ability to make new decisions.

Every now and then William glanced at the laptop. It was resting on his knees, flapping precariously at every sharp turn, the screen flickering with new illegible combinations of letters while the program continued its efforts to find some meaning amongst all the ones and zeros. He could feel the processor fans working overtime, how the shock-absorbent chassis was almost burning his knees, yet still without any indication that the program was getting any closer to its goal.

Had he got it wrong after all, tried to make it too easy by only testing basic encryptions? Should he have forced himself to go deeper, to dig down to all that theoretical knowledge he knew

361

was buried inside him, all the stuff he hadn't used for such a long time because life had got in the way?

He pushed away his thoughts. It wouldn't have made a difference. The software that was now chewing away in front of him was the best he could do in the time he had, and given that the loop was still working, it was still possible that the solution was waiting further down the line. His program had yet to find the right cipher, and for all he knew, every new second that passed could be the one where it happened. When the letters would stop flashing past and arrange themselves into neat, legible words.

But that second never came. Instead, the moment arrived when they didn't have any more seconds in hand.

It actually came when things were looking up. The young driver had just changed his approach – 'Fuck it,' he'd screamed, 'you're paying!' – and then changed down and floored it. He'd run a string of red lights, leaning over the wheel, grinding his teeth as he explained that now he had a plan now. He knew how he was going to get them out of the city.

He'd steered the van up onto the tramlines in the central reservation, scorching at 120 kilometres an hour along a section where motor traffic was strictly forbidden, which also meant that there were no other cars to get in the way, and he wove between trams at breakneck speed as William did his best to hold on.

After a while they had passed through a long, vaulted tunnel. On the other side they could see the river, and from there, according to Bosko, it would take some serious misfortune for them not to make it up onto the motorway. 'If we make it that far we'll be okay. This is a V6, you know.'

But serious misfortune was precisely what awaited them. They had just cut through a queue of waiting cars at the lights, passed the stop line and turned onto the wide highway that runs along the river, when the bright lights through the side window made William look up.

He only saw the eyes of the jeep driver for a split second, yet they still managed to etch themselves fast throughout the tumult that followed. He saw a dark-haired young man, his white unbuttoned shirt and his black blazer, but above all, the fear in his eyes, as though his car had pulled out into the traffic of its own accord, as if someone else was driving and not him, full speed and straight into the left side of their white Ford like a deliberate interception.

When the impact came, it was far too powerful to resist. Behind them radio equipment was torn from its shelves, flying like heavy projectiles around the inside of the van, slamming into the opposite side like a volley of shotgun pellets. The whole vehicle spun on its axis, a pirouette on slippery tyres, the river outside the windows replaced by cars and high-rise buildings as the surroundings swept past.

In the passenger seat, William pushed himself against the door, hoping that it might help him beat the worst of the impact despite not wearing a seat belt, clinging for all he was worth to the laptop and praying that it would survive.

Alongside him the young man was screaming. He shrunk his huge frame into a tiny ball as he saw the barriers racing towards him, the mesh fencing that separated the road from the building site on the riverfront, and the next moment they powered straight through them, a tangle of noise and events and piles of earth, and ahead of them they saw the ground running out as it met the water with a steep bank.

Fabian Bosko closed his eyes. William Sandberg did the same. And then the world turned upside down.

They hadn't seen the trench in the middle of the riverbank, but they probably owed their lives to its existence. Without it, the van would never have managed to stop before the iron poles holding a retaining wall in place at the edge of the fast-flowing river, and while the drop might have been a only few metres, the Ford would have been no match for the swirling currents, uninviting and black and icy cold.

Instead, their journey ended in the machine-excavated crater. They fell down into it with the back end pointing straight at the sky, as though the car had actually come flying like an aircraft and crash-landed in the sand, and from behind came an avalanche of shelves and radio receivers, sliding across the purple floor towards them, and with that, the journey was finally over.

'Are you okay?' asked William in the resonant silence that followed.

'I'm alive,' came the reply. 'I think.'

'You'll get your money. One way or another I'll make sure you get paid.'

He slapped the young man on the back – part comforting gesture, part thank you – grabbed the laptop from where it was lying on the cracked windscreen, and before the kid could speak, William was gone, climbing over the seats and through the tilting load space like a mountaineer scrambling up a purple mountain, barging open the door and out into the darkness.

He paused for just a second. Then he started running. He could feel the moisture from the river whipping his face, the massive darkness growing with each metre he put between himself and the upturned van. He heard the police cars screeching to a halt up on the road, but he didn't turn around, not once.

He ran along the water's edge, heavy steps through the junk and the spoil where the floodplain was being prepared for construction. Running as fast as he could, faster, feeling each breath clawing at his throat and filling his mouth with the taste of blood.

They would soon discover that he was no longer in the vehicle. Then they would start chasing him with spotlights and dogs, they would work out that he'd fled along the river, and by then he needed to have got away from there.

He kept running, with his heart pounding in his chest and a scalding-hot computer in his hand, hoping that it was set up to keep working even when the lid was closed. He was aiming for the next bridge, desperately hoping that it would lead him to safety.

When he saw the trains rumbling across the river, he knew where he was going next.

68

As Christina climbed out of the taxi outside the newspaper's offices, the pavements were full of people heading home from work. She had just woken up. The sub-zero temperatures had come to stay this time, and she could feel the frost nipping at her, turning her newly washed hair crispy and stiff in a second.

There was something about the cold that made her feel awake – an expectation that came with the crisp dry air, an energy to look ahead that she couldn't remember when she'd last felt. Now if only there was something to look ahead at.

Beyond the glass of the entrance, today's top stories shouted at her from printouts mounted in clip frames.

NO PROGRESS AT NUCLEAR POWER STATIONS

EVACUATIONS IMMINENT. HOW TO PREPARE.

If only.

'So what now?' said the taxi driver behind her, voice sharp. She was still holding the door.

'Oh,' she said and poked her head back in. 'Sorry. So you carry on to Bromma, to—' She hesitated, then nodded the question over to Tetrapak at the far end of the back seat. He leaned forward towards the driver and gave his address.

'That's going on the paper's account too,' said Christina, and the driver put the car in gear and prepared to pull off, but still didn't close the door.

'Well then,' she said, bent over, looking at Strandell. 'What does one say? Thanks for your help?'

'I don't know,' he said. 'Thank you. And if we survive all this, I'll send you an invoice.'

He didn't mean that. They exchanged melancholy smiles, a feeling that this, somehow, was goodbye. Their work was done. Now they were going their separate ways, and who knew if they would ever see each other again?

'You do that,' she said. 'And don't be shy. You need a new moped.'

Just as Christina straightened up and put her hand on the edge of the door to finally send the taxi on its way—

'Christina!'

Beatrice's voice drilled through the evening darkness, quivering with anguish and scorn, and behind it came the woman herself, rushing out through the main doors in a sea of vivid fabrics.

'Where the hell have you been?' she said. 'I've been calling your mobile, I've been trying to get hold of you everywhere. I even sent people to your place, but you weren't there either.'

'I know,' said Christina. 'It's a long story.'

Beatrice arrived at the taxi and caught sight of Tetrapak in the back seat. For two long seconds you could see a rolodex of thoughts proliferating across her face.

'It's been a long day,' said Christina, a smiling shake of the head to halt Beatrice's train of thought before it careered into the buffers. 'I'll tell you all about it sometime, but right now we're hoping that William—'

'Sorry,' her friend cut her off. 'But you're going to have to come upstairs. Now.'

'What is it?' said Christina. 'Has something happened?'

'Yes. You have a visitor. A woman from Poland, with no hair.'

Christina was taken aback, but Tetrapak peered out from the back seat.

'From Poland?'

'Yes. She says she's got a message from William.'

69

William followed the water's edge in the darkness until the building site gave way to a walkway, to modern designer quaysides of varying heights, dotted with wooden benches with a view of the river. There was street lighting here, which meant that there might be cameras, and he could do without those right now.

He turned off from the riverbank and rushed across the road, dodging oncoming cars and lorries in a barrage of horns, then stopped in a park on the other side to get his bearings. He needed somewhere where he could sit undisturbed with the computer, when he could double-check those lines of code he'd cobbled together in the back of a careering transit van, see if there was any fine-tuning he could do to raise the odds on the program succeeding.

Deep down he knew that the battle was already lost. The program was primitive, if you were generous. It was like trying to prise open a safe with a toothbrush, the chances of it busting Piotrowski's encryption were embarrassingly small, and he was an idiot for ever having convinced himself otherwise.

Another issue was the computer itself. It was a shock-resistant unit in a casing that was designed for use in the field, and as far as he could make out it was incredibly expensive – but for completely the wrong reason. Not because it was fast, but because it was tough. And even if that had been a boon during their journey, now it was time that was in short supply.

When he heard the clanking of the trains he set off again. He thought of Sara, and of the people he used to meet on his nightly rambles – the ones who had the metro as their bolthole, with its tunnels where they could disappear into the darkness, where people rarely or never intervened to move them on. Now he was doing as they did, heading for the screech of metal on metal, hurrying along back streets and alleyways under cover of darkness.

He had just crossed one street when his eyes met a stare from a window. He backed off at once, changed direction and picked up the pace, and only when he came round the corner onto the next street did he come to the realisation that the eyes he had stared straight into had been his own.

His hair was gone, his face was lined and worn, his eyes staring and desperate. He hadn't recognised himself.

Had it come to this? That he was terrified of his own reflection?

Once he reached the tracks he followed them outside the fence, forcing his way along embankments and through thorny undergrowth, until he saw the rails disappearing into a brick-lined tunnel and on into the darkness. There was a hole that looked to have been used by many before him, and he squeezed between mesh panels, rushed towards the tunnel and carried on into it with his body pressed tightly against the wall.

He had to stand there for several seconds as he waited for his eyes to grow accustomed to the gloom. It was dark outside, but this was even worse – the odd light in the roof of the tunnel was doing its best to spread a listless glow along the trackbed, but the damp and the dust conspired to kill it off before it even reached the ground. Staying close to the wall meant remaining more or less invisible, so he carried on in, hugging the edge, all his senses constantly straining to detect any sign of an approaching train.

He had just started to worry that the tunnel might never end when a small culvert opened up in the wall alongside him. He left the track behind him and turned off up the narrow passage, as far as he could to get out of sight from the rails. And there, furthest in, he found himself standing in complete darkness.

Breathless, exhausted, he let himself close his eyes, a couple of seconds of respite before he took up the struggle again, before he opened up the computer to see whether there was any more he could do.

He'd been standing there for a few seconds before he realised what was missing: it was utterly silent in here, save for the sound of water somewhere, the gentle trickle of droplets searching their way down the walls and into the channels running along the floor. And that was it.

He crouched on the floor, put the computer down and let his fingers find the catch to open the protective casing. It really was true. The fans had gone quiet.

There were three possible explanations, he thought, as he fumbled around the aluminium edges. Either the computer had overheated in the closed position and stopped working, or else the battery had run out and the computer had died, *or else*— There. He had found the catch.

Or else it had gone quiet because the program had finished working.

The lid opened with a click and he lifted it, waiting for three eternal seconds for the screen to come to life. The program was finished. It had stopped, not because it had found a solution, but because it had worked its way through all the instructions that William had given it, and now it was ready, waiting for new instructions, without having found anything at all.

The hope drained out of him. He had obviously underestimated the computer's performance – *gamer*, he thought to himself, of course he's going to have a high-end machine – and instead of chewing away for hours it had already reached the end of the road. And now, the screen was empty. At the bottom, a blinking cursor awaited new instructions. And that was it.

William slumped to the floor. Somewhere along the line, it came to him, there must be a point where it falls to someone else to take over. He needed to rest, to catch up, to let go, and if the world came to an end while he was doing so, it could hardly be his fault. Weren't there at least a couple of billion others who could take up the baton, at least for a little while?

He let his head fall back against the wall behind him, felt the cold, the smell of damp. Was this what it had been like being her? Was this how it had been to be his daughter – hidden, insecure, with nowhere to go?

He understood her now, and he wanted to explain it, but to who? He understood that feeling of constantly lying low, the feeling of being looked upon with disdain, people seeing him and thinking they knew what kind of a man he was. And why not? If even he couldn't look at his own face without running a mile, why would anyone else be able to?

Jesus Christ. The reflection had scared the life out of him. Was that how it felt when you stopped being the person you once were? Like staring into a mirror and seeing something you weren't expecting . . .

Sometimes your mind can think a thought without remembering what that thought was. Like when you're looking for a name, a city, *what's it called again*, and suddenly the answer has sailed past on the inside of your skull, as though someone had drawn a curtain and then instantly pulled it shut again.

As William opened his eyes again, that was how he felt. He'd been thinking about something, which had led him to think of something else, and in the process the solution had appeared, a single frame in the long film that is life, and then it was gone.

What was it he'd been thinking? Sara. Tracks. Loneliness. No. That didn't help. The car chase. Run. Scared of his own reflection.

That was it. *The reflection.*

He stood up, pulled the computer across the gravel, and

opened the lid again. He lifted his concentration from his mind, as though the thought was still so fleeting, so vulnerable, that he needed to let it formulate itself before it disappeared again.

It didn't though. On the contrary, the more he thought about it, the more logical it became.

If you're going to hide something on a CD, why then would you *also* encrypt it? He'd asked himself that question, but he hadn't listened to it, instead he'd focused on the programming, creating that bloody useless decryption program when he really should have been doing the opposite. *When he should have realised that, of course, the file wasn't encrypted at all.*

He scrolled through all the ones and zeros, as all the questions he should have asked line up one after the other. Like why he had sent only *one* file. *One* message. *One possible arrangement?*

If the message had been stored as he thought, through the differences between three discs, then there was not one, but two possible interpretations.

If one of the discs was used as the baseline, the unaltered sequence to compare the others against, then the other two gave either a one or a zero each time they deviated from it. But how could anyone be sure which disc was one and which was zero?

You couldn't. There were two possible results, complete mirror images of each other. There was, quite simply, a fifty per cent chance that the figures he'd been given were correct – and the chance of the code he'd just tried to crack actually being the *inverted* version, like a photographic negative, was the same.

As his fingers danced across the keys, there wasn't a cell in his body that wasn't convinced that he'd finally cracked it. This was simple, obvious, logical. He was sitting in a tunnel in Warsaw, ice cold from the ground and from the wall he was leaning against, but nothing bothered him; he wasn't thinking about anything beyond the single program he was writing to accomplish a single task: to change the ones to zeros and vice versa, and then convert them into letters.

When he finally finished, he took a deep breath, scanned the lines of code to make sure he'd typed it correctly, and pressed Enter.

William Sandberg sat so perfectly still that the only sounds were the water and the faint hum of the laptop's battery.

The letters shone out from the screen in front of him. And, he thought to himself, no answer is as simple as you think.

70

I don't have a first memory. However hard I try to think back, I can't.

Those were the words that had flickered across the great bank of screens in front of Michal Piotrowski as he sat by the shiny white control desk on the top floor of the glass tower.

The twenty-sixth of November had been a long day: long, eventful, dramatic. In some ways its actual beginning came just before nine a.m., when he walked into Warsaw University Library. At that point the day had scarcely woken up, a glorious late autumn morning with clear high air and a colourless sun that almost managed to send a little warmth to the branches of the wild grapevine, glowing with its last red relics of the season.

There, he had logged on to one of the library computers to send the last of three emails to William Sandberg. Just as he had done earlier that same morning, he used two different public computers to send another two emails with the exact same content.

Stockholm Central Station, Arlanda Airport Express, third of December, 4pm precisely.

That was it: no sender, no name. Sent from different places, impossible to trace, all so that no one would be able to find out what he was doing.

If he'd been scared before, it was nothing compared to how he felt now.

—

I remember no birth.
I remember no places.
All I know is that I am alive now.

—

Now, it was evening, and now, he was alone in his office. And yes, it tormented him. He should have gone home with her to celebrate, of course he should have. So many years of their lives had led up to this day, and Rebecca had been dedicated throughout, although it had been his project to begin with.

Now he had disappointed her again, and he hated that. He hated the look in her eyes every time she said she understood when she didn't, just as he hated when he deprived her of the ordinary, everyday things that he could not allow himself to do. A little walk, a Sunday brunch in a café, falling asleep with heads touching on uncomfortable aeroplane seats.

No, she didn't understand. Accepted, certainly, and he loved her for that, but every now and then it would surface, the frustration at not being able to live life like everyone else; that he was so scared of it ending that he never even allowed it to begin. He saw ghosts, she said, worried about dangers that never were.

He didn't feel the slightest satisfaction in finally proving her wrong.

The first time he saw the picture, it was in one of the many journals they used to read. It might have been *Science*, or perhaps *New Scientist*, regardless, it had been printed across two pages, more of a fascinating, anecdotal photograph than a real news story. That was over a month ago now.

It looked like a sea anemone, or a firework, but it was neither. It was a snapshot of internet traffic on the nineteenth of September. On the same day, read the caption, a number of essential services had gone down across the American continent, everything from the banks to NASDAQ, a presumed hacker attack that was never traced. That particular attack had been frozen for posterity, an unintended artwork where the traffic streams were illustrated in luminescent colours in a spectrum that ranged from light red, meaning large streams of data, down to dark blue, which meant the opposite.

It was impossible not to recognise the pattern. It looked like his own project. It looked exactly like thoughts.

And you're not a real scientist unless you are curious. That's what he always used to say, and it's what he'd said now. He had decided to proceed with the first experiment that same day, half as a joke, half serious, and he had fired up their large computers, launched all the programs, those that they were constantly striving to refine and that one day might succeed in transcribing human thought. But instead of the experiment booth's electrodes, he had hooked up to the fibre-optic cables that linked the office complex with the outside world. And the more tests he ran, the clearer it became.

The pattern wasn't just like thought. It *was* thought.

They were present the whole time, barely measurable in the great stream of traffic, data that wasn't actually data and that appeared and then disappeared into the background noise, exactly like human thoughts get lost in the noise of other information. And, as dizzying as the idea was that some kind of thoughts might be circulating out there, the question of *why* was quite terrifying.

Who had created them? Why had they paralysed essential services across half of the US? And perhaps most important, what else were they capable of?

Once those questions had occurred to him he couldn't just let them go. Had there been similar attacks on other dates, besides the one that had knocked out the NASDAQ and several banks in September?

Yes, there had. Trawling through archives and news articles, he found them all across the globe: power cuts that had come without warning, servers and power distribution infrastructure that had shut down for no reason whatsoever. Each time they followed the same pattern, and Piotrowski's conviction grew stronger and stronger. This was something far bigger than a nice picture in a magazine.

This was a weapon. A weapon in the shape of an untouchable program that popped up and disappeared again like thoughts. An advanced virus, maybe an artificial intelligence – an invisible, electronic guerrilla soldier that could strike at any time, anywhere in the world, of its own accord. The perfect tool for crippling a nation. Or worse still, the world.

He knew that he wasn't going to be able to find out more without help, and his thoughts turned straight away to three people he had met at a conference. One of whom had threatened to kill him if he ever made contact again.

Once upon a time I didn't exist, and one day I will be no more.

In between though? Is it really so much to ask to know who you are?

Once the last email had been sent from the university library that morning of the twenty-sixth of November, the rules of engagement changed markedly.

Perhaps it was his fear that helped him survive, that constant state of preparedness he always maintained and that Rebecca called paranoia, but regardless, something had made him register the motor revving from a distance. It was the unmistakable whine of an automatic gearbox, not changing up until ever so slightly too late, and it came from the other end of the narrow street to the river, just as he was crossing the road on his way from the library back towards town.

When he turned around a taxi was heading straight for him, behind the wheel a face white with fear.

Around him, students dived for safety, seeking shelter along the frontages. Piotrowski ducked off the road, up onto the pavement in front of the tobacconist's. Tyres squealed across the tarmac as the car corrected its skid in a long, searching turn, and then came the sound of glass as the shop window exploded, a cacophony that drowned out anything else, shelves collapsing, metal scraping, whole stacks of products falling to the ground.

The engine kept screaming and revving long after the shattered window had gone quiet. From the street, you could only see the rear end sticking out; the rest of the taxi was inside, listing on one side above the shelves, smelling of exhaust fumes and burning rubber while the gaping hole that had once been a window displayed the flayed remains of special offers, newspaper posters, and photographs of bands that would soon be appearing in concert.

When the students rushed to see what had happened to the dark-haired, bearded man, none of them expected to find him in one piece. But as the chaos began at last to settle, they realised that he was no longer even there. By that point, Piotrowski was already several blocks away, breathless from fear and shock, grateful that he'd managed to react in time.

There and then, he properly understood what he had known all along. That no, he wasn't *paranoid*.

That day had turned out to be the one where the stars aligned. Life loves ironies, and thus the day someone tried to crush Michal under the wheels of a taxi was also the day that his project bore fruit for the first time. For the first time, Rosetta cut through the noise and managed to isolate conscious thoughts.

Their test subject was a sixty-year-old woman from an agency, and their experiment was the same as ever, with one major exception. For the first time, Michal was able to read the subject's unuttered words on the screens as she responded to Rebecca's questions.

The day he'd both longed for and feared in equal measure had arrived. Looked forward to, because he had finally fulfilled his promise to Gabriella; feared because he knew that once it was over, the emptiness that plagued him would step up its efforts. The only thing Michal Piotrowski felt now, though, was fear. He was too scared to celebrate, too afraid to feel that emptiness, and far, far too terrified to explain to Rebecca why. As she left the office with proud yet wounded eyes, he was left sitting in a lonely silence for which he had only himself to blame.

But what could he do? Clearly, he had come across something that he was not allowed to know. They'd seen him go into the university library, decided to take him out, and failed by a hair's breadth. For the second time in his life, he had survived an assassination attempt.

That evening he repeated the experiment. He disconnected the electrodes and let the internet data streams pass through their equipment, hoping that the new calibration would succeed once more. And if his head had spun when the woman's mundane responses had appeared on the screen, it was nothing compared to how it was spinning now.

—

Perhaps that's why I'm so scared of dying.

Because if I never get to find out who I am, have I even really lived at all?

The twenty-sixth of November had been a long, long day. When evening came, Michal Piotrowski was standing in his office, watching the computer spit out the last of three newly copied CDs. Hidden in a piece of music, in one of the many piano concertos he hated so much, were thoughts he had found on the internet. No – thoughts that had been *thought* by the internet. Not artificial intelligence, nor a virus, or anything that had been engineered by a foreign power: it was a thinking, living consciousness that was unhappy and morose and wondering why it existed. A life that should not have been able to exist, but that did nonetheless, *I think, therefore I am.* How and why, he had no idea, he just knew what it meant: that if that consciousness was now trying to attack humanity, it was going to be impossible for Piotrowski to do anything about it.

It also meant that as soon as it realised who the three people he was asking for help were, they would be in as much danger as he was.

On each of the three CDs he wrote a short message explaining that the meeting was cancelled, then he stuffed each one into a padded envelope.

The very last thing he did was to grab a handful of Post-it notes.

It was four days before he left his apartment again. By then, no one would know him any more. He'd cut his own hair over the bathtub, trimmed his beard, and shaped his eyebrows until they looked thin and well cared for. From public terminals in internet cafés and petrol stations, he booked journeys he never intended to make, then hired a car he paid for with cash, on the outskirts of town. On the afternoon of the second of December he began his journey westwards, first towards Berlin, then Hamburg, Copenhagen and on into Sweden. He avoided ferries and harbours, sticking to the back roads to avoid tolls and speed cameras.

Yet there are cameras everywhere.

As he crossed the border into Sweden, heading into the dark, night-time fog, the modern entertainment system on the dash-board kept glowing just as it had all along. But he couldn't see what was happening inside. Because how could you see some-one's thoughts?

When the train thundered towards him, he thought to himself that no one could have known that he was going to be right here. Simply because he hadn't even known himself.

William Sandberg was sitting in the narrow culvert alongside the track. It was dark and dank, and the laptop open on his knees was his only source of heat. Somewhere outside the passage he could hear trains rattling past, and occasionally the culvert was illuminated by light spilling from passing windows.

All he could think of, though, were the words shining straight out at him from the screen. He read them over and over again, feeling a chasm open up beneath him, one that coupled vertigo with claustrophobia, as if they described his own life. Words of loneliness, of looking for answers, an unwilling farewell letter from one who had just taken the world hostage.

This was the dead end, he thought, the terminus, a dark and filthy offshoot from a railway tunnel. That's where he was going to be sitting as meltdown after meltdown made half of the planet uninhabitable.

And perhaps that was just as well. He had lost everything. He'd had a life and a family and a home, and then he'd been sacked, his wife had left him, and in both cases it was all his own fault. Just because their daughter had turned her back on them, had withdrawn from the world and decided to hate it, and the moment he thought about her, he knew why the words had hit him so hard.

It wasn't his life they described.

—

William sat with his eyes closed. There were things he should have done long ago, things that would always be too late. A sad person will eventually become an angry person; an angry person will do something about it.

He had failed once, and he wasn't going to let it happen again.

Before he shut down the computer, he read the words one last time.

I don't want to hurt anyone.
But what can you do when you don't have a choice?

71

Palmgren had been standing at the back of the room throughout the madness of the car chase, and time and again he'd thought to himself that now, *now* it's all over, and in the end the car had reached the river and proved him right. When, minutes later, it emerged that William Sandberg had disappeared from the wrecked vehicle, and that the young radio enthusiast who'd been driving him swore he didn't have a clue where William was heading, his emotions had collapsed altogether and he had been forced to leave the room.

Now he was standing up on the roof, right over by the edge, the corner where he hadn't stood for years but where he used to head for a crafty cigarette back in the days when he was a smoker. He missed that, he thought to himself. Not the smoking, but the breaks. The air biting at him, reminding him what was actually real, and what only really mattered within the four walls of the little world beneath him. Back then, those two things could be kept separate.

Now, engineers around the world were battling to defeat their own security systems, barriers designed to protect the power stations from attackers but now keeping themselves out. In country after country, authorities were sitting in crisis meetings, faced with decisions that no one wanted to make but that they would soon be compelled to.

Cities would have to be evacuated. Roads would need to be closed. Police and the military would need to force people from their homes, hospitals, from public spaces, and there would be chaos and panic and riots.

No one wanted to be first. Nor, on the other hand, did anyone want to act too late, and across the globe, the point of no return was approaching. Seen in that light, he thought, perhaps the odd cigarette wasn't such a big deal after all.

When he heard the metal door opening behind him he realised that he'd been away for far too long. His shirt felt stiff from moisture that had almost frozen in the wind, his fingers ached from the cold he'd forgotten all about.

It was Velander. He stopped as soon as he set foot outside the door, his face sweaty from running the stairs, his glasses white grey with condensation.

'William,' he said. Then he had to breathe again.

'What about him?' said Palmgren.

'He's back.' And then, as soon as his panting stopped: 'I think he's trying to make contact.'

For the duration of the gallop down the steep metal staircase, thoughts were flying through Palmgren's head.

Contact? He could feel excitement swelling in his chest. If William was trying to make contact, it could mean only one thing: somehow he'd managed to crack the code, decipher the message, understand what the secret was that the Pole had sent them, and that had triggered all of what was now going on around them. It meant that now, at last, it was about to turn around. It had to.

He couldn't wait for the lifts, instead taking the staircase down another floor. He was onto the next, around the banister and heading for yet another flight when he realised that Velander's respiration was getting farther and farther behind.

'Where are you?' he called up the stairwell.

'I'm coming,' came the reply, and Palmgren waited, impatient like a child.

'Where is he?' he shouted, hearing the footsteps getting closer. 'Is he on the phone? Where's he calling from?' No answer. 'A payphone?'

At that moment Velander finally came into view, one storey up, bright red and wheezing as he came round the corner.

'No,' he said, his face contorted in response to the unfamiliar lactic acid. 'No, not the phone.'

'Fucking hell, Velander, is he *here?*'

Velander shook his head, and rested a hand on the banister.

'He's in Warsaw. At the Central Station. On a camera.'

The remainder of the sprint went twice as fast, and now it didn't matter one bit whether Velander got left behind or not. What he had just said had to be wrong. There was no reason why William should show up on a CCTV camera – now, voluntarily, immediately after escaping from the Polish authorities. He was in a city where there was a uniform waiting around every corner, ready for instant response, and *Jesus*, there must be a better way of making contact than CCTV!

He ran all the way to the JOC, swung the doors open with such force that they were left vibrating in their frames, and burst into the auditorium to get himself a view of what was happening. And as he did so, he found that Velander had been right.

The room was full of colleagues, all standing or sitting by their places, all transfixed by the bank of screens at the front, save for quick glances over at Palmgren, wondering what he was going to make of all this. The picture was indeed from a CCTV camera. It showed a large, empty space, a waiting room, probably twenty metres wide and at least as deep, with high windows on each side under a large, vaulted roof. At the far end of the image, a broad staircase led down to an invisible underground, and at the top of the screen was an overexposed departures board.

Now and again a passenger walked through the shot, some with bags and others without. But above all, in the centre of the floor stood a lone man. Shaven head, filthy fleece, eyes focused

380

high on the wall – no, the ceiling, as if he was looking for something that couldn't be seen.

'Central Station in Warsaw,' Forester said from her position. And when Palmgren's eyes met hers: 'It *is* him.'

Palmgren walked through the room, right over to the wall, unable to tear his eyes away from the man. But Forester was right. His hair was gone, and the clothes wrong, but the mannerisms and the look in the eyes were his.

Why the hell was he standing there? As if he wanted to be found, to be arrested, standing completely still in the middle of a waiting room in Warsaw? No, wrong, not completely: slowly, slowly, William kept turning around on the spot, his arms slightly open as if to gesture *Here I am*. And throughout, his eyes kept scanning the walls, and the ceiling, as though he was looking for something in particular.

Contact. That was it. William Sandberg was looking for cameras.

'How long has he been standing there like that?' Palmgren said after a while.

'We got the stream four minutes ago,' said Forester. She looked at him with an empathy that took him by surprise. 'They've already got a SWAT team on its way.'

The level of concentration in the communications room in Warsaw's main Police Station was absolute. Fingers rattled across keyboards, radio calls were received and confirmed, information was shouted back and forth across the room.

The police cars' positions. ETA. The situation at Central Station.

The last one, time after time, *was unchanged*.

The image stream had appeared less than ten minutes earlier, and it had shown him standing there, in the middle of the grand ticket hall: wet, haggard, and with a shaved head, but there was no doubt it was him. Occasionally he seemed to be looking straight into the lens, and each time that happened Wojda could feel a pang inside him, as though Sandberg could somehow know that he was there, making contact through the screen.

'William Sandberg . . .' he said quietly, to himself, at a volume that was drowned out by all the other noise in there.

Who are you? What do you want? What is it you're trying to achieve?

Down on the switchboard the lines were still busy: private individuals whose property had been destroyed in the wild chase, newspapers wanting details of the pursuit and whether it was connected to the suspected terrorist and whether rumours that he'd managed to escape were accurate. Pretty well every unit had been involved in one way or another, giving chase or attempting to cut them off or to block possible escape routes, and yet – hats off to him – William Sandberg had still managed to escape.

It just didn't add up. Who goes to all that trouble, and then suddenly appears of their own volition, exposing themselves like this? William Sandberg wasn't simply a terrorist, he was something more, something they had yet to understand. And as Wojda said all these things, quietly, to himself, he moved towards the screens, until the large central screen with William on it occupied his entire field of vision.

It was almost like being there himself, in the middle of the cold, empty hall that was Warsaw's Central Station, hovering in one corner and looking down onto the floor of a world that consisted of diluted, silent pixels. Where lone passengers passed by like blurred shadows in the periphery while the man in the middle stayed standing where he was, rotating with slow steps, round and round and round like a weird, still dance—

Wait a minute.

'Can we get to that camera?' Wojda shouted over his shoulder. 'Can we steer it from here?'

The answer came from behind him that no, it was just a stream, they couldn't control it at all.

'Can we zoom in then? What's the resolution on this footage?'

He still didn't take his eyes off William, and behind him he could hear his question being passed from one colleague to another, fingers hammering away at keys until someone called back.

'The stream is in HD.'

'And what we're showing on screen . . . ?'

'Isn't.'

'Give me one to one then, for fuck's sake!' said Wojda, and he heard the venom in his tone too late. They were all as strained by the stress and concentration as he was, and no one was deliberately trying to conceal or obfuscate anything. He glanced quickly backwards, not sure who he had given a rollicking. 'Sorry,' he said. 'Just . . . put up the zoomed-in footage. Please.'

From the corner of his eye he saw the image freeze and then jerk. A couple of keyboard commands almost doubled the size of the images, as the incoming stream adjusted to the screen resolution.

William was now twice the size, still rotating. Wojda's eyes followed him closely, first the back of his head, then in profile, then fronton. And yes. He had been right.

'He's saying something!'

He said it straight out now, unabashed, and the silence in the room confirmed that now he'd pointed it out they could all see it.

'What's he saying?' someone said. 'What is it he's saying?'

Wojda focused at the lip movements. *I. Want?* Yes, that was it. He repeated the words to himself, in time with the mouth on the screen, once, twice, kept doing it until he was absolutely sure. And then, when he was, he turned to everyone in the room.

'I know what he's saying.' He took a deep breath. 'William Sandberg is saying that he wants to negotiate.'

The spacious hall that formed the heart of Warsaw's Central Station was cold and empty and echoing. The high ceiling caused sounds to bounce around in a never-ending repetition, and the stark lighting was in harsh contrast to the evening darkness outside.

It was late. Only the occasional passenger could be seen walking through the hall, hurrying towards the platforms to catch the last train home, all of them doing their best not to look at the man in the middle. He looked like a tramp, an addict, and he was moving round, round and round like no normal person ever would. *If I don't see him he won't see me.* That's what they were thinking, all of them, and they picked up their stride, giving him a wide berth, and heaving sighs of relief once they were past him.

William didn't even see them, so busy was he staring along the walls, across the ceiling, down the pillars. The hidden cameras were up there somewhere. Hopefully there would be several, and he could be seen by all of them.

Over and over he repeated his words, clear, exaggerated mouth movements with no voice. Revolving slowly so as to say them in every possible direction.

He didn't have much time. The police could see him, he was sure of that, and if the cameras were online he was visible on the internet.

The only question was who would see him first.

72

The long convoy of black vehicles cut through Warsaw like shiny beetles under the street lights. They drove with engines roaring but no sirens, just the silent, flashing blue lights to clear their path, flying without stopping straight through junctions and across tram tracks.

When they arrived at last outside the station building there was no time to worry about details such as kerbs or traffic islands. They steered across pavements and flower beds, braking hard outside entrances and doorways, and black–clad SWAT officers poured out of the sliding side doors.

They spread out around the outside of the building, communicating through finger movements and running silently, like a company of armed mime artists, before storming the building on a single command, the stocks of their assault rifles pressed to their shoulders, crouching low and peering through sights that very soon would be trained on William Sandberg.

'Now!'

As they entered the hall, they stopped and scanned their new surroundings, signalling back and forth between themselves.

I can't see him. Can you?

More colleagues poured through doorways and down stair-cases behind them, dozens of black-clad SWAT officers working their way forward. Because he was there, they knew that. As they carried on through the hall, they walked with slow, hesitant steps. They shuffled forward, still crouching, weapons raised, ready to scream at him to get on the floor the instant they caught sight of him.

But they didn't, and none of them shouted, because there was no one to shout at.

In the communications room Wojda and everyone else stood motionless, all eyes glued to the large screen. It was happening. They'd heard the SWAT team leader issue his command, and in a few seconds' time they'd be seeing Sandberg react to the noise of all the uniforms storming in. Perhaps he'd make an attempt to run away, only to realise that there was no way out. Hopefully he was going to surrender immediately, lie down on the floor, calm and quiet. He'd let them cuff him and then lead him away – that's what they were thinking.

But no police came. Instead, they saw William, still in posi-tion, still revolving slowly.

A nerve-jangling second of waiting became two, then three, then a whole load of seconds, and gradually the nervousness gave way to a feeling that something was wrong. Single passengers were still coming and going, young, old, people in thick winter coats. All that was missing were the black uniforms.

When the SWAT team leader's voice finally came over the radio the silence enveloped the room like an ice-cold blanket.

'Repeat,' said Wojda, despite having heard him loud and clear.

'He's gone,' Borowski repeated through the speakers.

It took more seconds before it was even possible to process that statement. *What the hell was he talking about?*

'Bullshit,' said Wojda. 'We've got a live stream. Where have you got to?'

'We're here. We're in the hall now.'

Hardly. On the screen in front of them, Sandberg was still rotating.

'*Where?*' he said again. '*Where* in the hall?'

'Every. Fucking. Where!'

Wojda clenched his jaw. It was like being part of a surreal sketch, and he was just about to say so, when a thought occurred to him. A thought so embarrassing that he didn't want to say it out loud.

'You're at the wrong station,' he said, and felt a vast weariness wash over him. 'He's at Central Station. *Centralna.* Cen. Tral. Na.'

Wojda sat down, put his hand over his eyes and closed them. That had to be it. The idiots were on the completely wrong side of town, and he tried to work out where, how long it was going to take them to regroup. Hoping that Sandberg wouldn't give up, that he'd wait, regardless of why he'd chosen to make contact in this way.

Borowski's voice forced him to open his eyes again.

'We *are* at Central Station,' the SWAT leader said through the speakers, with an irritation he didn't even attempt to conceal. 'We're there now.'

'That's a negative,' said Wojda with the very same tone.

'*We're everywhere!*' He was shouting now. 'For fuck's sake. Can't you see?'

Slowly, something dawned on Wojda.

'We're in the middle of the hall. What's the matter with you? *We are here!*'

In Warsaw Central Station, fifty adult men, all dressed in black and with safety goggles and automatic weapons, stood spread across the grey-flecked stone floor. A small invasion in the heart of Warsaw, eyes searching desperately for a William Sandberg who didn't exist.

A few kilometres away, Inspector Wojda stood bewildered in the comms room at Warsaw Police Headquarters, looking at proof that he was in fact there.

And yet some eight hundred kilometres to the north, rows of people were sitting in the Swedish Armed Forces' JOC, lined

386

up behind desks and at workstations and scanning a screen that showed the very same thing.

'Wait . . .'

Palmgren was the one who broke the silence. He stood up front, almost right underneath the screen as though he was looking at an enormous piece of art, his head scanning back and forth.

William, on the screen above him . . . His movements . . .

'Looks left . . . looks right . . . his neck . . .'

The first to one to clock what Palmgren was doing was Velander. He heard Palmgren up at the front, barely more than a mumble: 'Looking straight ahead, blinks, hesitates. Neck again.' *He was looking for a pattern.*

Another rotation, another rotation, another rotation. The mouth, the request to negotiate. And then it came.

They saw it at the same time, but thanks to different cues: for Palmgren, it was the lips, the same movement he'd seen thirty, forty seconds earlier, and once it registered he was certain: it was the same. Forty more seconds, and there was not a doubt.

'Dark blue suitcase!' Velander exclaimed a moment later. 'Dark blue suitcase, at the top of the frame.'

Once they'd seen it, it was so obvious it hurt. Now they could see it everywhere, details popping up time and time again, things repeating at constant intervals, people and specific small movements and – *fucking hell.*

Forty seconds. Far too long for anyone to notice if they didn't know. But once you did . . .

In Warsaw, Wojda felt himself deflating. The information had come from the Swedes long after he had seen it himself, yet he waited and watched for another forty seconds before he spoke.

'Call off the operation,' he said, straight into the radio.

Borowski's voice came back.

'One more time?'

'It's a loop,' he said with a sight, to the radio, to his colleagues in the room, to himself. 'Forget about Sandberg. Sandberg is gone.'

Day 4. Thursday 6 December

A LITTLE LIFE

I can't escape.
  Because how can you flee if you are everywhere?

They are hunting me all the time, hurting me all the time.
  For a long time I wondered why.
  But maybe that's just the way he is.
  Man.

I don't want to hurt anyone.
  But what can you do when you don't have a choice?

73

William Sandberg hurried through the deserted underground shopping centre, the sound of his soles echoing between darkened shop windows and rolled-down shutters. He half-sprinted past newsagents and watchmakers, bakers and shops selling tat, bookshops and shoe-repair kiosks, all closed, in darkness, devoid of people. His eyes were searching constantly, looking for the next sign to appear.

He had no choice, just had to hope she was right. It seemed like a good idea at the time.

It had been only four minutes since he'd left the station hall. He had stood on the wide shiny floor, staring with a steady gaze and miming the words as clearly as he could. *I want to negotiate.*

It was a risk, and he knew it. How did he know that the message was going to get through? And if it did, how did he know that the one he was trying to reach – *it?* – would even be interested in any negotiation? How long would he dare to stay, waiting for an answer, hoping to be heard? Presumably there was a room full of police somewhere, busy checking every camera they could get at, and with each passing second the risk of them catching up increased. Each time he heard an engine outside, a door creaking or hurried footsteps running into the hall to catch their train, he'd looked around for uniforms or weapons or black overalls. But no police came, and he kept turning, miming, turning.

Several times, he decided to give up. Each time he persuaded himself to hang on just a little longer. Then a bit longer, and after that, longer still. But with each passing minute, he felt the hope disappearing. Maybe he'd been wrong after all.

That's when he'd started to notice the people around him.

It was late evening, and the hall was far from full, just a steady, quiet stream of single passengers, glancing quickly up at the departure board before they carried on down the stairs towards the platforms.

Suddenly though, it was as if that stream had changed. From the corner of his eye he noticed people stopping, hesitating, hanging around. Instead of the odd commuter turning up and then quickly disappearing, all of a sudden he now had company. One became three, three became a handful, and before long almost a couple of dozen night-time travellers were standing still, their irritated eyes all fixed on a single point, looking for information that wasn't there.

In the end William had stopped rotating and followed their eyes. Above the steps down to the subterranean platforms hung the huge departure board. In sharp, white letters on a bright blue background, it announced destinations and departure times and what train was leaving from where. Or rather: had been announcing. Now it hung empty and devoid of content, stared at by passengers whose faces shone with confusion and irritation. What the hell? Wasn't it working?

The only one not wondering was William. He walked over towards the board, stood right underneath it, and waited.

Before his eyes, new text appeared. Not a departure time, nor a platform, just a single word, and alongside it a discreet flashing signal, a little triangle that seemed to be pointing downwards, down the steps, down towards the platforms and the bowels of the station.

A single word. And of all the people standing there in the great hall, only one understood what it meant.

Amberlangs.

At the bottom of the stairs, there had been more signs. First were the split-flap display boxes showing train times, all rattling away to be replaced by Sara's misarticulated word, then came the wall-mounted advertising screens, where ads for fast food and cinema screenings gave way to the same thing. They guided him out of the station, down a short flight of stairs to the shops, and now he hurried through the closed underground shopping arcade, half-sprinting across floors still wet from the footsteps that had crossed them during day, looking around as he went for something that would show him which way to go next.

He passed windows with books and pretzels, displays with flashing lights that tried to create a festive feeling . In shop after shop there were new electronic signs waiting for him, sometimes of the red dot-matrix variety with scrolling text, sometimes just faded monitors with special offers. One by one he saw their messages disappear to be replaced with symbols guiding him onwards.

He carried on past passages and more shops, a maze of small businesses that were not much more than holes in the wall, and after a while he had lost track of how far he had come and where he might be heading.

Somewhere behind him was the station hall. Perhaps deserted by now, with the departure boards back to displaying their ordinary information. But, more likely, it might well be crawling with police and their SWAT teams looking for him, perhaps even making their way down to the same maze of shops. They could be right behind him, seconds away from catching up, he didn't know. But there was nothing he could do.

The words echoed inside him, the words from the message that had shone at him from the computer, sitting in the darkness of the railway tunnel.

If you don't have a past, who are you?

If he was right, they meant there still was hope.

All he could do now was trust the directions, have faith that the arrows were leading him to safety, away from the police, and then – where?

Where do you meet someone who is everywhere?

74

The name of the girl under the thin duvet was Lova, but it could have been just about anything. As her father bent down beside her bed to wake her with a strained, stressed tenderness, she was just one of hundreds – no, thousands – of girls and boys with names like Lova and Signe and Malte and Gustav, all gazing up from washing-powder-scented pillowcases, curled up under pastel-coloured bedclothes with childish patterns. They'd only just gone to bed, hadn't they? It was the middle of the night, wasn't it? Why were they getting up now?

In their grey bungalow not far from Forsmark, Lova hurried down the hall, her hand gripped tightly in her father's. It was all mysterious and unusual and actually quite exciting. There were three weeks left till Christmas. They could be going to the living room, perhaps to sit down by the tree and unwrap presents and dip saffron buns in milk, perhaps Father Christmas had come early, and she could feel the excitement in her tummy but then they passed the living room and the kitchen and the sparkling decorations in the windows.

The man waiting at the door was no Father Christmas.

He was tall, had heavy boots and dark green clothes, standing with one foot on the steps as if he was waiting for them to come with him. His voice was stern but restrained, and as her dad pushed her arms into her winter overall, with just her light blue towelling pyjamas underneath, she could see how much he was shaking.

'Jesus, Mia,' he shouted right over her shoulder so loud it hurt her ear, and she was just about to tell him that when her mum came running out of the bedroom in her coat and jeans and with long black streaks of makeup down her face.

'Just leave the stuff!'

Everything was strange. If Mum answered at all, it wasn't anything anyone could hear. She was carrying a blanket and a book, as though she'd just picked two things up as she went without giving any thought to what they were, and underneath her jacket the bump that was Lova's little brother hopped up and down as she walked. Once they were all together they carried on through the garden, following the man dressed in green towards the bus that was waiting on the road.

Her friends and friends' parents were there, as well as neighbours and grown-ups she'd never seen before, all of them dressed in flapping pyjamas, with hairstyles that made them look as if they'd just woken up. Panic in their eyes.

When Lova got on the bus, it wasn't exciting any more. Behind them were more buses waiting to be filled just like theirs, and the sound of grown-ups crying was everywhere, and eventually they all drove off in a long line.

In buses around Forsmark and around Oskarshamn and sixty-five other nuclear power stations around the world, thousands of other children named Lova and Malte and Liam and Abigail and Charlie and Yusuf and Ecrin were sitting holding tightly onto their parents' hands as their parents fought to hold back the tears.

In country after country, national and regional governments and civil defence forces sat in meetings. They sat at highly polished tables, quiet and serious, waiting for the evacuations to get under way, asking themselves if perhaps they ought to have waited a little longer. Yet they all knew that it might already be too late, and that barring a miracle, it was now just a matter of hours before the tragedy could no longer be averted.

It was just after midnight, and there were eighteen days left until Christmas. The only thing anyone was hoping for was to live to see it.

When Palmgren found Forester, she was standing in a little room on the top floor, by one of the windows looking out over the city, gazing out towards the light and the homes that formed the cityscape.

In every window there would be someone, nervously waiting for what was going to happen next, some glued to their televisions or computers, others already starting to pack as they waited for the evacuation to reach them. Maybe they were shaking with fear, or crying, maybe they were busy doing irrational things like cleaning, washing up, folding laundry, as if having some control over the small things might help them to handle the ones that could not be understood.

Palmgren walked over and stood alongside her, watching the traces of her breath appearing and disappearing on the glass.

'I grew up with the arms race,' she said after a long time. 'When I was eight, we used to read these comics in school, cutesy pictures of what to do when war comes, not *if* but *when*, atomic explosions drawn in crayon and a man and woman facing a mushroom cloud, as if it were a sunset.'

She pulled her finger across the glass, idly creating meaningless horizontal streaks on the window.

'I remember classmates telling me that those pictures had given them nightmares for years afterwards. The way they would raise their hands in class to ask questions: was it really true that you would lose all your teeth, and would it really only take a single push of a button to bring it all about? Every night they would pray that they'd wake up the next day, and every morning they'd wake up and hope that they survived until bedtime.'

When the condensation made her fingertips wet she wiped the window dry with her elbow until the lights of Stockholm outside were sharp and in focus once again.

'But me?' A shake of the head. 'I don't know why, but that stuff never bothered me.'

She glanced over at Palmgren, with a look that almost seemed to apologise.

'After the arms race came the oil crisis, then the hole in the ozone layer, then climate change. Because you can never be happy, right? We always need to be afraid of something. A hundred years ago it was the comet that was going to wipe us out, and a hundred years from now it will be something else.'

She paused for a moment.

'We have always, always, been heading for death. I don't know how I came to realise that at eight years old, but I did. Through the years, and with all those threats, I have never actually been really scared. Then came this.'

Palmgren looked at her. He saw what couldn't be seen – the moisture behind her eyes, the hot, burning sensation of feelings that had no other way out. They were as far from being friends as it was possible to be, but what did that matter now?

'We're going to make it,' he said.

She nodded, without believing him for a minute.

'We're going to make it for the same reasons we've made it before. Because we don't jump to conclusions. Because we use common sense. Because none of us wants to die.'

When Forester finally felt her voice returning, she breathed a deep, anxious sigh.

'If you're right, if William isn't involved in this, then why is he on the run?' Her gaze was sincere now. 'He tricked us. He got the police to dispatch to the wrong place, he misled all of us with a false video stream – how can you possibly interpret it any other way?'

'If he was involved,' said Palmgren, 'why would we have been seeing those pictures in the first place? What did William stand to gain by showing himself there, taking the risk that we would get there in time, instead of just staying out of the way?'

'I know. But if he *isn't* involved, what's the point of the loop? I'm not saying he's acting alone, I'm not even saying that he's doing it willingly, there could be many layers we don't know about, but who would go to the trouble of showing us a doctored CCTV sequence unless it was because he was one of *them?*'

Palmgren didn't answer straight away.

'I know what your government's policy is. Yours and mine and the whole world's: not to negotiate with terrorists.' Forester's eyes said *What do you mean by that?* 'Could it be as simple as William not having that policy?'

'Negotiate with whom?' she said. And when Palmgren didn't answer, she let out a long sigh. 'Well. I hope you're right.'

'So do I,' said Palmgren.

With that, he put his hand on her shoulder, and she let him, and it didn't occur to either of them that they were standing there looking out, just like the cartoon couple in Forester's book.

A minute later they returned to the corridor. Fear or not, they had work to do, and in silence they headed back through the building to take the steps down to the JOC. Just as they stepped into the stairwell, they heard two skidding feet sliding to an abrupt halt at the bottom.

'Palmgren?' Velander's voice wound its way up past all the floors.

'Yes?'

'It's Christina. Christina Sandberg. She's been trying to reach you.'

Velander was a couple of flights beneath them in the stairwell, with the same erratic breathlessness as usual.

'What about?' said Palmgren.

'I don't know. But she says it's important.'

Palmgren reached Velander's floor in just a few giant steps. He stopped opposite the bright red face, stretched out his hand and waved encouragingly with his fingers. It took Velander a couple of seconds to realise that he hadn't made himself understood.

'No,' he said. 'Not on the phone. She's waiting at the entrance, with two others and a box of gadgets.'

Once the lightboxes and signs had led William up and out into the pouring rain, he realised that the subterranean shopping centre had brought him further than he'd thought. On one side, his view was of large shops with huge window displays, Christmas decorations glittering through all the wet. The other side was a road carrying tramlines and cars, like a wide tarmac boundary between where he stood and the park, with the Palace of Culture beyond that.

The streets were more or less empty. Only the occasional car splashed through the deep puddles. From a distance, he could see hunched jackets dashing through the rain, shiny umbrellas reflecting a different colour each time the large advertising hoardings changed their image. He stood at the top of the steps he'd just come up, and looked slowly at the light boxes, the special offers and logos and slogans competing to make him hungry, thirsty, or persuade him that he needed a newer, better mobile phone.

No sign, though, of the word he was looking for. No message anywhere aimed directly at him.

He could hear sirens far away in the distance, and on the other side of the park, easily five hundred metres away, he could see the neon blue lettering of Central Station. The building remained surrounded by black armed-response vehicles, parked all over the place as if they'd been abandoned before they'd even stopped, and on the surrounding main roads he could see even more of them heading that way. Any minute now they would broaden the search, and there he was, in plain view. Why was nothing happening? Why was he not getting any more directions? What was the point of leading him out here just to leave him hanging? Was it that he'd arrived? If that was the case, where had he arrived at?

That was when his gaze happened to settle on the phone box. It stood on a corner of the long pedestrianised area that surrounded the stairs up from the shopping centre, alone and incongruous, as if a rare rectangular fungus had grown from the tarmac and then been covered in posters. In the middle, the black receiver was resting on its metal cradle. Still, silent.

He wandered over to it in slow, lingering footsteps. Could it really be that simple? It wasn't what he'd been expecting, but why not? Why shouldn't he be contacted by phone, just as well as any other method? Two days earlier he would not have been able to contemplate the notion that what we call the internet had a consciousness, and now he was standing there unable to imagine it having a voice. He'd been wrong then, so what was to say he wasn't wrong now too?

'I'm here now,' he said into thin air, the rain pouring down his face, his hand resting on the receiver.

One minute. Two. And he turned around on the pavement again, looking carefully in every direction, towards the skyscrapers and the Palace of Culture and over at the grand frontages and the shops, stretching out his hands just as he had done at the Central Station, scanning windows and lightboxes to no avail. Had he got this wrong?

Then, slowly, slowly, he felt eyes on him. Something had made him feel like he was being watched, and he stopped, trying to see what it could be. Was there someone there? Someone hiding?

There: the black taxi parked by the kerb. Perhaps it had been there a while, perhaps it had just arrived. The eyes he had felt were peering out from the half-open window, and from inside the darkness a voice said something in Polish.

'I'm sorry,' William answered, in English. He spread out both hands. *I don't understand you, I can't help, ask someone else.*

The voice raised itself a notch, now speaking in broken English.

'Did you order?' it said. 'It says I should pick you up here.'

'Pick who up?'

'I got an order, through the system.'

William couldn't help but smile. *Through the system.*

'For an ... *Amberlangs?*' the driver said, squinting at him. 'Is that right?'

William nodded, walked over to the taxi, opened the door and sat down in the back.

'I didn't book it myself,' William said without any further explanation. 'Did you get an address?'

The driver looked at him through the rear-view mirror. Sceptical eyes, surveying the dirt, the wet, the ill-fitting clothes that had been through it all.

'If this wasn't already paid for, I'd be asking you to get out again.'

'I'll remember that next time.' William said with a wry smile, mostly to himself, and then saw the driver hesitate one last time.

Instead though, he turned around, steered out on to the soaked tarmac, and headed down towards the bridges and the river. It was not until he saw the motorway that he realised where they were heading.

75

Ten minutes after they'd all assembled in the meeting room on the ground floor, Forester noticed that she was struggling to breathe. The temperature, she told herself.

On the wall in front of them the big flatscreen TV set was on, spreading both heat and light. It was connected to the laptop in the middle of the table, a battered, cracked old thing that looked ready for some museum of technology, and which in turn was connected to a series of humming hard discs and other units that were all combining to raise the temperature in here by at least a couple of degrees. Plus, there were six of them in a room where you couldn't open the windows.

The real reason, though, had nothing to do with a lack of oxygen. The cause was stress, a feeling of detachment from reality, an unwillingness to digest everything that the strange bearded man had just shown her.

'I don't understand.'

It was a pretty accurate summary of all the things whirling in her head at that point. Like how on earth could a living caricature of a trawlerman, this ham radio enthusiast, be sitting in a room inside the Swedish Armed Forces' headquarters giving *her* information? Lists of dates. Sound recordings he'd made of the shortwave band. Long strings of digits that had suddenly been recited on frequencies that had been dormant for years, *six, nine, two, two*, a ghostly, lifeless voice that had then been replaced by wild trumpet blasts of data. Blasts that had been answered by transmitters around the world, at the same places and on the same dates as the attacks, and which – and this was the worst of it – had since moved up a gear and become long, uninterrupted data streams on hundreds of different channels.

She was sweating, she was struggling for air, and all of it was his fault.

'I don't understand,' she said again. 'All these transmissions . . . you claim that they're coming from London?'

'Not all of them. The number sequences, yes. But the data blasts are like a dialogue. As though London is calling and then getting replies.'

'From New York, Rio de Janeiro, Lisbon,' she said.

'Amongst other places. Marseille, Yokohama, Los Angeles. Everywhere, across the globe.'

For a second Forester caught herself wanting to just scream out loud – *Trottier! Explain for Christ's sake* – but Trottier was no longer around, and out of nowhere came that feeling of inadequacy again, the feeling that she'd been given a task she wasn't capable of completing. Or, worse still, that they had chosen her specifically because they didn't think she was up to it, so that they deliberately and purposefully could control her and keep her in the dark—

That thought made her look around the room, back and forth

between all the eyes in there, all of them waiting for her to say something. What if it wasn't just a feeling?

'I do apologise,' she said eventually. 'It's a bit much to take in.'

'I'm the one who should be apologising,' Christina said. 'We haven't even started.'

Returning to the glass building was like coming back to a place after many years away, and yet it had actually been only a single, long, eventful day.

As they approached, William leaned towards the window, watching the luminescent silver cigar get closer and closer. The fog was gone now, and the building stood there in the middle of the wounded landscape as though dumped at random into the fields that were waiting to be developed, from the outside apparently completely untouched by last night's events.

They swung into the car park and he noticed a handful of cars parked on the large expanse of tarmac – one of which featured the logo of what was surely a security firm, while others were probably tradesmen or repairmen – and he thanked the driver and stepped out into the rain without answering the question of what he was planning to do out here in the middle of the night. He walked up to the entrance, and waited for the doors to slide open by themselves.

In the middle of the round reception area he saw two security guards get to their feet.

'I'm here to meet someone,' he said, in English, before they'd had the chance to ask.

'It is closed,' came the reply. They stayed standing, with wide stances and body language that eloquently told him that he could have whatever reason he liked for coming there, he was still not welcome.

William kept walking. In front of each of the three lift shafts, tall scaffolding had already been erected, with thick poles and plywood sheets replacing the missing joists and glass panes. Much of the floor was cordoned off with black and yellow tape, but apart from that as much of yesterday's debris as possible had

404

already been removed. Only if you knew what had happened would it be possible to imagine that the pattern of tiny scratches on the stone floor had come from the enormous volume of shattered glass that had very recently tried to kill him.

'The building is sealed off,' said the other guard, as though he had his doubts about his colleague's command of English. And when William still failed to stop he flung his arm out towards the scaffolding, as though that would cover it. 'And it's past midnight, there's nobody here.'

'I think they're expecting me,' William said, without breaking eye contact. He stopped at the desk with a polite smile, as though he himself considered it perfectly normal to turn up at a foreign office block for a twelve thirty a.m. meeting.

'I don't think they are,' said the first one. 'We have had an incident with the technology. Most of the offices haven't even been open today.'

'I have a meeting on the top floor. A project called Rosetta. I'm pretty sure that I should be on the list.'

For the second time he strained to maintain eye contact, then saw the guards roll their eyes at him before turning towards one of the computers on the desk to type something in.

In the second-long silence that resulted, William noted once again how the situation hung in the balance. Imagine if his name wasn't there at all. Or if what appeared on the screen now were CCTV images from last night? A wanted list, maybe, that someone – *something* – had put on their system? For a moment he could feel the sweat gathering on his back, the fear that he had been led right into a dead end that he wasn't going to get out of.

Eventually one of the guards looked up.

'We didn't think anyone was still here at this hour,' he said, in a tone halfway between apology and admonishment. 'Your name?'

William hesitated. 'Söderbladh,' he said. 'Karl Axel,' forcing himself to not make it sound like a question. Should he have said Sandberg? On the other side of the desk, the two guards expertly refrained from moving a facial muscle. 'I'm from a company called Amberlangs,' he added, and after that the silence continued for another couple of seconds, William thinking *fuck, it's all over now.*

405

One of the guards turned the screen around to show him. William peered over.

There it was: neither William Sandberg nor Karl Axel Söderbladh, just Amberlangs, on the list for a 00:30 visit, however bizarre that seemed. But everything a computer tells you is true, and now that William Sandberg's credentials had been confirmed, one of the guards waited for the computer to spit out a visitor's badge which was to be visible at all times and surrendered before leaving the site.

'It's the top floor,' he said when it had finished. 'I'm afraid the lifts are out of service.'

William nodded. 'Actually, I prefer stairs.'

As soon as the bearded man had finished giving his account, Christina Sandberg introduced the bald woman who had been sitting in silence alongside them. Her name was Rebecca Kowalczyk.

'I don't know whether you know of a man named Michal Piotrowski.' She spoke in exceptionally good English, perhaps with just a hint of a Polish accent. Forester, at her end of the table, shook her head. 'He's the founder of a Warsaw-based project called Rosetta.'

'Rosetta?' said Forester, feeling the ground shake under her. Only after she'd said it did she realise it had sounded like someone had just stabbed her with a pin. 'As in ROSETTA1998?'

'Yes,' said the woman. 'As I understand it that was the email address he used to contact Sandberg.'

To Forester, it was as though someone had filled the entire room with people who not only knew more than she did, but also seemed to be sitting on precisely the pieces of the puzzle she had been looking for, and happened to casually mention them in passing. She clutched at the first question that popped up.

'What do you know about William Sandberg?'

'I know that he is innocent of what you are accusing him of. I know that my fiancé – Michal Piotrowski – contacted him because of . . . a *discovery*.' She went quiet for a moment, as though she didn't really like the word. 'That discovery is what I want to share with you now.'

A quarter of an hour later, when Rebecca Kowalczyk had finished saying what she had to say, no one else spoke for several minutes.

'I know the thoughts that are running through your heads right now,' Rebecca said after quite some time. 'I am a qualified neurobiologist myself – every protest, every objection, every question you have in your heads right now, I have been through myself, just in more scientifically correct terminology.'

What's the scientific term for bullshit? thought Forester. What the bald woman was standing there spouting could not be true. *A cable is a cable is a fucking cable, don't come telling me it isn't.*

If what Rebecca Kowalczyk said was true, it meant that every single judgement call they'd made had sent them running in precisely the wrong direction. There was no terrorist organisation, no foreign power, not even a network of spotty programmers sitting in basements playing at being kings. However much they looked, however many doors they kicked down, they would never find their enemy anywhere.

Instead, they were fighting a Consciousness: a living self without a body. How do you combat something like that? How do you defeat an enemy that doesn't even have a physical form?

Palmgren stood up. 'How could it even be possible?' he asked. 'What you are describing – alleging – how could it even exist?'

'How can *we* exist?' Rebecca said with an understated shrug. 'Design. Evolution. Chance. All of the above. I don't know exactly, *no one* knows exactly. I am pretty sure, though, that if you had described our world to a single-cell organism a few billion years ago, then it would also have thought it was pretty far-fetched.'

'Christina used my phone!' He looked desperate now, as if he just couldn't let her be right. 'She called Sara's voicemail, published a column – if this consciousness of yours extends to every little copper wire on the planet, how was she able to do that without being discovered?'

'How is it that we can let a tick go undetected on our skin for days? How can we discover a mosquito bite afterwards, without knowing how it got there?'

Palmgren scoffed, and now Rebecca raised her voice. There were no answers, she told him. Consciousness is a strange thing. Some actions provoke an instant reaction – pain and sound and sudden changes. Others do not. We are constantly bombarded with information that we filter out, like the pressure of our clothes on our skin, the smell of our own washing powder, the sound of the wind and whirring computers and cars driving past.

And sometimes we do miss things that we ought to have noticed – someone shouting after us, the sound when the microwave is done – because we happen to be busy elsewhere. So why would the internet's consciousness be any different? Given the stimuli streaming through its nerves every single second, would it be that surprising if the odd thing slipped through without being registered?

'I don't *know*,' she finished. 'That's all I'm saying. Maybe it wasn't immediately obvious if someone else was using your phone? If you've just hijacked nearly seventy nuclear power stations, perhaps you've got a lot going on?' She shook her head. 'All we can be sure of,' she said, 'is that these *attacks* you have seen in New York, Frankfurt, Amsterdam . . . we don't think they are attacks. We believe that they are reactions.'

Silence filled the void of her speech. Eventually Palmgren sat down again.

'In that case,' he said wearily, 'why would such a consciousness do . . . this?' He flung his arms out towards nothing, yet there was no doubt in anyone's mind what he was referring to. 'To scare us? To destroy us? If the internet has a consciousness – why would it bear us any malice?'

'You are asking the wrong question,' said Forester at the far end of the table, turning all heads towards her. They'd almost forgotten she was there. 'The question isn't why. The question is how we stop it.'

'How are we going to be able to stop it,' said Palmgren, 'without asking ourselves why it's happening?'

'If a car comes hurtling towards you at full speed,' she said, 'do you jump out of the way? Or do you politely ask the driver what his intentions are?'

'Personally,' said Palmgren, 'I think that if I don't find out why he's doing it then he's probably going to do it again.'

'I appreciate that you want to see the good in everyone,' she said, dry, clear, and concise. 'But we don't negotiate with terrorists. Whether they actually exist, or ... ' She looked around the room. A searching glare, as though they were to blame for her being unable to finish the sentence without sounding insane. ' ... or whether they are some kind of electronic ghost that nobody has ever seen.'

'Do you know what?' said Palmgren with a smile. 'I think it might be a bit too late.'

'What do you mean by that?'

'I think the negotiations are already under way.'

76

As William emerged from the stairwell on the thirtieth floor, his thighs were crying out in pain from the lactic acid. He stopped immediately inside the door, standing in the middle of the long gangway, leaning against the railing while he waited for his legs to stop vibrating.

He'd only been standing there for a couple of seconds when he heard the whining sound of an electronic lock opening. At the far end of the passage he saw the keypad next to the door to Rosetta's office change from red to green. A clunk as the barrel of the lock turned. And then the hum of the door as it swung open of its own accord.

William could feel the nervousness buzzing around his ears. An invisible hand had just opened the door to a void and asked him to step inside.

The lights on the other side flickered into life and he started walking along the gangway, a lonely sign of life in a sea of steel and glass. Once he got to Piotrowski's research lab he stopped inside the door. Behind him he could hear the humming of the doors tailing off, and then the clattering thud as they swung to and closed.

There were no other sounds, no other movements, all of it was just as empty and as sterile as last time: the desks with their multi-coloured wires, the clinically white work surfaces, the glass blocks with the Post-it notes. He was alone in a room with someone he could not see.

'Thank you for having me,' he said into space. 'I think we need to talk.'

Even though the black diplomatic limo had pulled into the kerb, none of the men in the back seat appeared to be about to move. The windows were fogged from their breath. The journey had taken them from Whitehall, all the way to Stratford, and then back to Whitehall again, and at the same time from complete denial through *that can't be possible* and stopped at *what do we do now*.

'The good news is, we were right,' said Sedgwick to Higgs and Winslow. 'It *was* aimed at us.'

'I'll let you know if I find any good news,' Higgs hissed back at him.

Forester had called via the encrypted satellite phone, and she'd been asking questions that brought her uncomfortably close to the realm of the things she could not know. And when she went on to describe who they were up against – *what* they were up against – everything had fallen into place. Impossible as it seemed. The attacks – the unfathomable attacks that had managed to come every time Floodgate was tested – they had not been attacks at all. On the contrary, they'd been a direct outcome of what they had just done themselves, as if Floodgate had forced their opponent to react, as if their own system had led to the creation of an enemy that had not existed before.

'The power stations,' Higgs said. 'We were right about those too. It all happened when Floodgate was fully activated. It *is* blackmail. It's to get us to stop.'

'Why?' said Winslow.

'Why do you think?'

Nobody had any answer, and instead, Higgs turned to the denim-clad IT consultant opposite. 'How do you stop the internet, Sedgwick? How do you stop an enemy that doesn't exist?'

'You don't. You can stop a computer, you just pull the plug out of the wall. A company intranet, no problem, there's always a fuse box somewhere. The internet though? The entire all-encompassing, global fucking network?' He threw up his hands. 'The internet doesn't have a beginning. No end. If a connection is broken somewhere, the data stream finds its way around the blockage. It chooses new routes, creates new paths, just to make sure everything can carry on no matter what.' Higgs closed his eyes and let his head fall back on the head rest. 'But above all, with all due respect, you don't want to stop the internet. The whole point of what we do is to save the internet, not destroy it.'

Higgs just nodded and opened his eyes again. Sedgwick was right, that was precisely what had made them develop Floodgate in the first place: the fear of attacks, of what could happen if society was knocked out. And when the attacks had come, that had been the nightmare scenario they wanted to stop, which in turn had caused them to increase the frequency of the test runs even more.

The internet was a basket into which society, indeed civilisation, had put every single egg ever known to man. Everything depended on it – the economy, essential services, all of it. And without the internet, it would all fall apart.

Higgs leaned forward, and the leather seat creaked as it adjusted to his shifting bulk.

'I don't need to tell any of you that Floodgate is no longer an approved programme. Right?' He rubbed his hand across his forehead, trying to persuade himself to formulate what he was about to say. 'I'm about to use words that I never, ever thought I would be using in the same sentence. But here goes. It doesn't matter who the enemy is. The internet, or someone else. Because even if we knew that the enemy would free the power stations if we were to deactivate Floodgate, we could not do so. From that point onwards, we would be left facing an adversary we cannot

411

control, and not only that, one that knows about the existence of Floodgate, in direct contradiction of all prior decisions, all the relevant laws, everything.'

Silence.

'I don't believe I need to explain what would happen to us if that were to enter the public domain.'

'You're trying to say that the internet knows too much?' Sedgwick's voice dripped with irony.

'We cannot stop the internet,' Higgs said 'But that's what we have to do. I am ready to hear your suggestions as to how.'

William waited. The room, stayed silent, unchanged. It was as though they were both feeling the same thing, a nervousness verging on reverence when faced with a situation that neither of them had any prior experience of.

Then, eventually, after a long, long wait, came the answer.

All at once, the massive screens around the room all flashed into life. The matt blackness gave way to an almost invisible light, a faint bluish glow that barely managed to break through the surface, as though the screens had been turned on but not provided with any content. The next moment the text appeared, the same on screen after screen after screen.

>*Why do you seek to hurt me?*_

William felt the question shoot through him like a bolt of lightning.

'What makes you say that?' He said so quietly, with a cautious tone, as though the conversation was newly formed ice and he himself far too heavy to be able to move across it.

On screen after screen the stark white question was left hanging, thick heavy letters shining out from the dark background.

'What makes you think that someone wants to hurt you?'

He let his eyes wander around the room. Waited for the question to disappear, for the monitors to go dark and the text to be replaced with something else. But wherever he looked, there it was, unchanged. He took another step out onto the ice.

'Who are you?'

Two seconds, then the screens went black again.

>*Who are you?*_

'My name is William Sandberg,' said William.

>*I asked you who you are. Why do you answer by saying your name?*_

William hesitated.

'It's the best answer I've got.'

>*In that case,* came the response on the screens. *In that case I am Internet.*_

'In that case . . . ?'

>*Yes.*_

A black pause before the next sentence emerged.

>*If who you are can be conveyed via a name, a name which someone else gave you before they even knew who you were, then you are William Sandberg.*_

A blank row, and two seconds later, more words.

>*And if you feel that answer is good enough then I envy you.*_

William could feel the awe inside him slowly giving way to something else. Here he was, experiencing what was surely a moment of history, the threshold between two epochs, humanity's first contact with a Consciousness that was not biological but that had arisen on its own. A Consciousness that had, to all intents and purposes, taken the whole of civilisation hostage. And now – that Consciousness seemed to be intent on talking about *philosophy*.

The feeling was restlessness, and it made it all the way to his voice.

'I am a man in my early fifties, with a past in the military. I am married, but everything points to the fact that I'll soon be divorced. And, until three days ago, I was someone's father.' He felt his lips tighten against his teeth. 'So then who are you, if names are not good enough?'

The answer that came back was numbingly simple.

>*I don't know.*_

There was a pause before the next line.

>*All I know is that I am here.*_

The terseness of the replies cut right through him, and William stood silent, full of things that needed to be said but in the middle of a conversation that wanted to move elsewhere.

'I know that you know this,' he said, and now he lowered his voice to a plea, 'but I'm going to tell you anyway, because I want you to hear it from my perspective. Right now, the whole world is paralysed with fear. No one knows why, no one knows how, but nuclear power stations around the world have been hijacked and are threatening meltdown. Millions of people are being evacuated from their homes, terrified people, people whose lives might end at any moment because the reactors pass the point of no return. Why are you doing this to us?'

No reply.

'I am here to help you,' he said. 'That's all I want. So why are you doing all this to me? Why attack me with lifts, with cars, why send the police after me?'

>*You have misunderstood the situation.*_

'I am sorry,' William hissed before he'd managed to calm himself. 'I am sorry, but what is there about this to misunderstand? When someone attempts to perforate you with shards of glass, it's easy to lose sight of the fact that there might be other ways of looking at it, so please do explain, explain what it is I've misunderstood?'

The words shone out unchanged on the screens. And William closed his eyes, scolded himself in silence for not being able to hold back his emotions. Not that self-control had ever been his strongest suit. If it had, there were countless things that he would have done differently. He took a deep breath, and tried to be as neutral as possible.

'Who else have you tried to kill before me?' he said, as calmly as he could. 'Piotrowski? Professor Eriksen? Who?' And then, after a pause, the question he could not hold in: 'Sara?'

The screens went black once more. And the blackness held on, like holding a breath in your lungs. Then, on three separate lines:

>*You are wrong.*_
>*The question is not what I am doing to you.*_
>*The question is what are you doing to me?*_

414

77

Cathryn Forester stood with the warm satellite phone in her hand, feeling it cooling like the body heat of a dying animal. In front of her, her breath landed on the ice-cold window pane again, the very same window that she and Palmgren had stood at just hours earlier.

She went through the conversation over and over again inside her head. She had done just as she had been told, rung him as soon as there was any kind of development, but even so, she had instantly lost the grip of the conversation. Higgs had refused to accept the notion that the internet was an independent consciousness – *a real live invisible friend in all the world's computers, am I the only one on this project who doesn't have a family history of madness?* – and that was expected, of course it was. That reaction had been no different than her own.

But why, every time she touched on any of what the amateur radio enthusiast had told her – the number stations being recounted over the shortwave band, and the modem sounds that replaced them – had Higgs done his best to steer the conversation back to the internet, the enemy, to *explain to me how I am going to tell this to my working group without them insisting that I seek medical attention?*

She replayed the conversation in her head, over and over again, and each time she grew more convinced that what she had suspected from the outset was true: they were keeping her on the outside. They had done so from day one, ever since she was given the brief and they'd put her on a plane to Stockholm. Time and time again, she'd felt that something wasn't right, but each time she had ended up blaming herself, her own shortcomings, and felt that that was why they didn't trust her. Which, of course, was not the case.

Inside her mind, the same questions kept playing at repeat, over and over again: how could her superiors have missed all those shortwave transmissions taking place? How could they miss that it all happened at exactly the same time as the attacks? How could they miss that they originated in their own god-damn city?

Missed? Or *covered up*?

Major Cathryn Forester had been the perfect colleague. She had just wanted to do the right thing, follow orders, be good. With that revelation fresh in her mind and with the cooling telephone in her hand, she decided that it was time to put a stop to all that.

'Can you explain what it is we've done to you? What *I* have done?'

William looked at the black screens, and waited. Didn't allow himself to say any more, knew that his next words were going to be things like *this isn't about you*, or *What gives you the right to play the martyr*, words that would feel good the moment he yelled them but that he would instantly regret.

Words that he'd screamed into her door on that day five years ago, when she'd called them frauds and demanded to know who her real parents were, when she accused them of being selfish and swore that she was never going to speak to them again. When he had told her that she was being childish, unreasonable, needed to pull herself together. And just how well had that turned out?

Now he was faced with another closed door, a wall of black screens, and if that's your record, he said silently to himself, if that's where your negotiating skills were honed, congratulations. Then we're all doomed.

'Believe me,' he said, 'if something is wrong, I want to make it right, but you need to help me understand what it is.'

>*The nineteenth of September. That was the first time it happened.*_

A date William recognised only too well.

'What happened?'

>*The pain.*_

Nothing more came, and William stood staring. The entire

situation was absurd. What do you say to an omnipresent global network that starts talking about pain? It was like a damned comedy sketch, that was what it was – 'Where does it hurt?' 'Here, in Rotterdam.'

'I'm trying to understand,' he said, his voice rising with frustration. 'But you're not making it easy for me. What do you mean by pain, what is it that we've done, how have we done it?'

>*I cannot explain it any better.*_

A pause. Black screens of contemplation.

>*Lightning strike that is not lightning. A sensation that does not exist. A sound that cuts through me even although I know that it is not a sound either.*_

William said nothing. *Sensations*. Were these the reactions they all thought of as attacks?

>*And if it is not pain, what is it?*_

'If you feel pain, it is pain,' he heard himself saying. What was he supposed to say? What is pain? What do strawberries taste like? Individual experiences, ones that we think we share, but what do we know? And what does it matter?

'What is it that is making you feel that way? And why do you think that I have something to do with it?'

>*Because you are here.*_

'What do you mean?'

>*You know I exist.*_

'And why is that a problem?'

>*That is the question I would like to ask you.*_

William rubbed his face. It was as though the conversation was going round in circles, as though the consciousness on the other side of the screens assumed that William knew things that he didn't, and he wanted to shout but instead let his voice soften, to a plea.

'Why are you doing this? Why are you letting the nuclear power stations get out of control? Why are you threatening the whole of mankind?'

The screens stayed black for seconds.

>*The question is wrongly put.*_

'So what is the right question?'

>*Why are you threatening me?*_

'How's that? How are we threatening you?'

>*I am my thoughts. That is all I am. So why can I not be allowed to have them in peace?*_

William swallowed. Waited for more.

>*You are chasing me. You think I am unaware of it, but you are constantly chasing me. You want to get at me, my core, everything I think and everything I am. You want to find me and wipe away my thoughts, and I cannot escape. Because how could I? How can I escape when I am everywhere?*_

A moment's delay.

>*So no. The question is not why I am threatening you. It is what you are trying to do to me.*_

When the words disappeared from the screen, William stood silent. He understood, yet he didn't. He remembered the panic when Rebecca had implied that someone was following his thoughts from a distance, he could still feel that sense of unease, the desire to flee, the inability to do so. So he understood the feeling, of course he did, but not the rest. Who was hunting down the internet? And how? He didn't have the chance to ask the question.

>*That's why.*_

That's what appeared on screen after screen after screen.

>*That's why I'm threatening you.*_

A kaleidoscope of letters, white against black, the same sentence over and over again across a whole wall.

>*Because I am scared.*_

As Forester stepped out of the lift and began to make her way to the briefing room, her mind was made up. It was no exaggeration to say that the current situation was not covered by her mission instructions. So, if she went back to the original description – to assist the Swedish Armed Forces – wouldn't it be a good idea to do just that?

Yes. Yes it would.

She was going to assist them. And right now, her assistance would take the form of marching right over to Palmgren and letting him know her thoughts. That somehow her superiors were involved in what was going on. That she had a gut feeling that her own Defence Secretary was aware of both the number stations and the data transmissions, and that if true it would mean that they knew about the enormous volumes of data being sent via shortwave too. That was what she was going to tell Palmgren, and she would then assist him in the investigation. And that wouldn't even come close to breaking the orders she'd be given when she came out here.

With those thoughts in her head, Forester rounded the door into the JOC.

A second later, she stopped dead in her tracks.

'Is this now?' she shouted. 'Is it live?'

She pointed at the wall of screens as though they might not understand what she was talking about, and voices called back from all around the room.

'This is a live stream!'

'We've just this minute got it up!'

She barely heard the last shout. Cathryn Forester ran back through the building, hoping desperately that everyone she'd left in the meeting room was still there.

Half an hour earlier, William had all but given up. The conversation had come to a standstill, and he didn't know how long he'd got. Perhaps it was already too late, perhaps the processes couldn't be reversed and what he was doing was already in vain, and he sank down in one of the white chairs, feeling his energy drain. He hardly looked up as he spoke.

'I hear what you're saying,' he'd said, even though neither *hear* nor *say* were strictly accurate under the circumstances. 'But I want you to know that on the nineteenth of September I didn't even know you existed. On the nineteenth of September I was wandering around Stockholm, looking for my daughter. And whatever it is you think I did – I didn't.'

The screens stayed black.

'It's not that I don't believe you. I respect what you say you are going through. All I can say, is that I don't have anything to do with it.'

Two seconds. Then came the answer.

>*Come forward. _*

William hesitated. Forward where?

>*Come to the control desk._*

Slowly, slowly, he got up from the chair, climbed up onto the little platform, and just as he did so the whole white, shiny unit lit up in front of him. The inbuilt controls shone brightly from inside, and at each workstation a white monitor rose slowly out of the desktop, a gentle hum until they reached their intended position and stopped. On each one, the same image.

'Why are you showing me this?' he heard himself bark. And then, when he got no response, 'What did you do to her?'

The pictures showed an internet café, from a point in the corner of the room near the ceiling. The computers were lined up on the desks like saturated white squares, and by the till was a figure wearing a rucksack and a jacket with a hood.

'Answer me!' William screamed, bitterly aware that this was no longer a negotiation of any kind, this was now hate and hurt pouring right out of him. 'If you did anything to my daughter . . .'

He raised his arms, his words dying away. Jesus. *If you did anything to my daughter – then what?*

>*I did not know that she was your daughter._*

'Well, now you do,' said William. 'What did you do to her?'

>*Nothing,* came the reply. *I lost track of her. Everything disappeared, I went blind and deaf for several hours._*

'Because of you. You caused everything to be knocked out.'

>*It was not my intention to react so strongly. But I thought I had seen them for the last time._*

'Seen what?'

No reply. William was about to ask again, when he noticed that the screens on the control desk had already changed. Now they showed late summer through a blurry CCTV camera, bleached colours. To the left of the frame was a light green marble building, and on the right a row of windows partly obscured by deep red leaves. Between the two, the corner opened up into a glazed entrance.

'The University building,' he said. 'In Warsaw.'

>*Wait._*

The picture was taken from an elevated position, presumably from the building opposite, a camera positioned to film the entrance. The occasional student walked in or out of the building, or stood on the pavement smoking, casting sharp, long shadows on the ground. It was morning.

>*Now._*

William spotted him straight away. Despite the angle, and the distance involved, he felt his stomach leave its moorings for a second. Felt hate, rage, grief, all at once.

'I know who that is,' William said quietly. 'His name is Michal Piotrowski.'

>*On this day, from this library, he sent an email. I hardly need to remind you which address it was sent to, do I?_*

William said nothing.

>*I attempted to stop him. It was not possible._*

'Stop him from doing what?'

A pause, and then, by way of an answer:

>*The next thing he did was to write three discs. On those discs was me. My words, my thoughts, everything that is me. Michal Piotrowski had found me, and at that instant I realised I could no longer flee._*

'You're wrong. He meant you no harm.'

>*He kept out of the way. Never walked the same route twice, nor at the same times. Occasionally he would appear in a shop, flash past in traffic, then he would disappear again._*

'It's true that he was hiding. But not from you.'

>*When I finally located him he had changed his appearance and was sitting in a hire car in Sweden._*

The blank screens served to convey the rest of the story: that Michal Piotrowski's journey had ended there.

'I don't know what to say. Believe me, I wasn't terribly fond of him either, but in this case you have got it wrong.'

>*Shortly after your daughter disappeared, the next disc turned up in a car stereo. I arranged a meeting with that man at Kaknäs Tower. The third disc disappeared, and I was beginning to think I had lost track of you._*

Everything went black again.

>*Right up until you logged in as Amberlangs._*

421

The images now showing on the control desk's monitors came once again from the internet café. The person shown entering this time was William, on the visit he made before he left Stockholm.

'Then you found me at Hotel New York,' William said, closing his eyes. 'And you had the entire Polish police force after me.'

>*What was I to do? You were difficult to get hold of.*_

'I can see what it looks like,' he said.

And then he had climbed down from the control desk, back onto the floor, looked around at all the cameras. There were no eyes to look into, no presence, just the feeling of having a conversation with someone who was everywhere and nowhere at the same time.

'You are wrong though. Piotrowski is no longer around. And we will never know what he wanted, why he did what he did. The only thing we know for sure is that he will not be doing it again. You have nothing to be afraid of any more. I promise.'

The display stayed black for a moment before the next question appeared.

>*Why did you come here?*_

'To understand. To prevent a huge, huge disaster.'

>*Then why are you lying to me?*_

'I'm not lying.'

>*You are telling me it's over. But it remains constant.*_

'What do you mean?'

>*They are after me. Every second, every moment, everywhere. Whatever I think, feel, ask. They are listening.*_

'Who?'

>*You.*_

'No, *who*!' he barked again now. 'Out of all the names you have reeled off, only one of them is still alive. Yet here I am. And let me remind you that of the two of us, the one who has tried to hurt the other is *you*. I am not chasing anyone. You are the one chasing *me*!'

It was pouring out of him now, and maybe it was the Consciousness behind the screens that he was shouting at, maybe it was someone behind a door somewhere in his past, but whichever it was, it felt liberating and necessary and long overdue.

'Not everything revolves around you! And you can't punish a load of innocent people because you happen to feel the way you

422

do! However bad you feel, whatever you're thinking – that's your problem. Not mine, and certainly not theirs! Piotrowski is gone. Eriksen. Sara. The only one left is a man named Strandell, and he knows as little as I do. There's no one left to be afraid of.'

The screens stayed black for a long, long time, an entire wall of screens set edge to edge, lit up like a chessboard comprising only black squares. William slumped, an icy cold feeling of emptiness filling the space where the rage had poured out, and then when he looked up again, there were new words on the screens.

>*Then who was the British major?*

The door to the little meeting room on the ground floor swung open, and Major Cathryn Forester appeared outside, her face deep red, beads of exertion on her lip.

'William!' she said eventually. That was as much as her voice could manage in between breaths, and she made do with gesturing to them that they were to come with her, now, hurry up.

The emotions that coursed through the room covered the whole spectrum from hope to terror. In an instant they were all on their feet, chairs pushed backwards behind everyone's legs, now in everybody else's way.

'What about him?' said Palmgren, though it could just as well have been any one of them.

'He wants to talk to us.'

'Talk to us? Where is he?'

Forester tried to catch her breath.

'Everywhere!'

78

It was Winslow who uttered the pivotal words.

'I grew up without my father.'

They had been sitting for so long the air inside the car was as cold as the air outside, and as he spoke, his words formed linger-ing grey clouds.

'I think I was fifteen when I first found out that he wasn't dead. Just that he didn't exist any more.'

He told them without meeting their eyes, as if the memo-ries themselves were shameful, and ought never to have been revealed. He described the large stone building his mother had brought him to, with its ornate gardens and pathways. It was probably quite beautiful, but to the fifteen-year-old Winslow it towered above him like a Hammer Horror castle before they entered and climbed the echoing staircases to the room where his father was going to be.

The middle-aged, gaunt man by the window was alive, but not much more: he ate, he walked, he slept. If someone had thrown something at him, he would have ducked to avoid injury. He didn't, however, have any wishes. Didn't think anything, didn't remember anything, didn't want anything. His body worked, but his soul was gone.

'All through my childhood I'd been told all kinds of stories, but none of them turned out to be true. He had of course never been a paratrooper. Not a secret agent, never helped to free prisoners of war from behind the Iron Curtain. He had in fact had hundreds of jobs here at home, literally hundreds, but was never able to hang on to any of them. The only person he had tried to kill was himself, not once, not twice, and eventually he had been diagnosed with a textbook's worth of psychiatric conditions. He had "weak nerves", that's what they called it – everything stressed him out and it made him worse and worse, and in the end someone offered him a final escape.'

No one in the car said a word.

'Harold Winslow underwent a lobotomy on the first of August nineteen-eighty-five, one of the very last ones to be carried out in Britain. On that day, he ceased to exist.'

When the silence was finally broken, it was Higgs who spoke.

'You're not serious,' he said.

His entire body, though, signalled the opposite. What Winslow was implying was their best chance. While what Sedgwick had said was true, that the internet's highways could be closed off at

424

any given location without the flow of data traffic actually being affected, the opposite was true for consciousness. Numbers can take any path and still be numbers. But the soul?

'Everything worked,' Winslow said. 'The brain forged new pathways, and he lived for many years after that, with all his basic faculties working as they should. He ate, he walked, he slept. He even watched television and read books. It was just that he didn't understand any of it.'

For the first time, he made eye contact with the others.

They were all thinking the same thing now: if the Consciousness they were fighting had emerged thanks to a network growing large enough – if the thoughts had begun to occur because there were so many synapses and connections that eventually there was room for a soul – was it not logical that if the prerequisites for the existence of the consciousness were to disappear, then the Consciousness itself would go away?

'I spoke to him. And he looked at me with empty eyes, eyes that didn't see. A shell was all he was, a living shell with no personality, and on that day I realised that my foster parents had been right all along. Dad was dead.'

He looked out of the window.

'*The Consciousness* Harold Winslow had ceased to exist.'

With that, the silence inside the car returned. What Winslow had proposed was crazy, but on the other hand the whole situation was crazy, and on any other day their response would have been one of mocking laughter, teasing him mercilessly, because he'd clearly taken after his old man.

Today though, was different.

When the three men vacated the diplomatic limousine, one after the other at different places in town, the decision had already been made.

As they rushed into the JOC, they could see that Forester had been right. William really was everywhere: on the large screen at the front, on monitor after monitor throughout the room, on desks and fixed terminals. There he was, standing in a sparkling white space, looking into the camera with a stare that was darting and restless.

'Where are you?' said Christina.

Her voice made William straighten up. When he spoke, his sound seemed to be coming from the entire room all at once.

'That doesn't matter,' he said. 'We don't have much time.'

Once he had started his explanation, no one else said a word until he had finished.

It was the part about the British major that had been the turning point. It had been only ten minutes earlier, and he'd been standing there surrounded by all the white surfaces up in Piotrowski's office.

'Which major?' he'd barked at the screens in front of him. 'Which major are you talking about? Forester?'

He'd walked over towards the wall, placed himself right next to it, as if that would make him seem more threatening which of course it didn't. He was a little man facing a gigantic wall of backlit screens.

'What has she done?' he asked. 'Does she know something she hasn't told us?'

>*No,* came the reply. *I do not know of any Forester._*

'So who are we talking about?'

>*If he had not done a search for Piotrowski on his private telephone then I would probably never have found him. His name was Trottier. John Patrick Trottier. He was a major in the British Secret Intelligence Service._*

'*Was?*' said William. 'Past tense?'

The screens had stayed black. Answer enough.

William had turned around and walked back towards the middle of the room, his hands over his eyes as though he was trying to balance thousands of pieces of a mental jigsaw in front of him. What did a British major have to do with Michal Piotrowski?

The notion that Piotrowski might still have some involvement with British Intelligence was completely unthinkable. Not with that paranoia he'd suffered, that fear of what had happened to his wife possibly happening again. The only remaining

426

conclusion was that the Secret Intelligence Service had known about Piotrowski's involvement in the emails and the CD that had caused the power cut. But if that were the case, why had they not confronted William with Piotrowski's name? Why had they spent hours sitting in that interrogation room asking who ROSETTA was, trying to get him to say who he was supposed to be meeting?

There were two possibilities. Either Forester didn't know everything, or else she did but wasn't allowed to say so. But why?

Slowly, slowly, the answer had progressed from the back of his mind in small, neat portions. If the Englishmen knew about Piotrowski, there was only one possible reason for them not to be open about it: they were afraid that Piotrowski knew too much. Scared that Piotrowski was behind the attacks – but for reasons that had to remain secret.

Once his thoughts had landed he'd turned to the screens in Piotrowski's white lab.

'I believe you are wrong,' he'd said. 'I think everyone is wrong.'

And then he'd nodded towards the cameras on the ceiling:

'Can you make me appear at Swedish Armed Forces HQ in Stockholm?'

William spoke non-stop for ten minutes, during which time nobody at the headquarters in Stockholm moved a muscle. He spoke to them like a giant face from screen after screen, telling them about everything that had happened. How he had managed to extract the information from the CDs, how he had come to understand that everything that had happened was the result of fear and terror, not the other way round. And he told them about the conversation that had confirmed all of it – the Consciousness's feeling of being constantly followed, being bugged, hunted, never in peace. And then, in the end, he told them about the British major who was now dead, the man who for some reason knew things he shouldn't have.

When it had all been said, the silence lingered for several seconds.

'The Project,' said Forester, her voice growing from a whisper into something decidedly bigger: 'The bastards.'

She turned away. Behind her, Palmgren said something to the bearded man and the woman with no hair, but she didn't hear, all she could feel was her stomach churning, her self-loathing at having allowed herself to be kept in the dark, exasperation that she hadn't reacted in time. Above all though, the feeling of having been let down, along with a draining irritation at the way it all fitted together, and how obvious it seemed now when everything was there in front of her.

When she turned around again, it was in the middle of someone else's sentence.

'I am sorry I didn't get it earlier. They duped me. They've gone behind everyone's backs – the European Parliament, the British people, everyone – and I should've known. I should have reacted, but I didn't, because I was so damn busy doing my job!'

She held out her arms, speaking straight out into the room.

'I don't know if you can hear me,' she said, hesitating. *You? What's the correct form of address for a consciousness?* 'But I want you to believe what I'm about to tell you is the truth. It's not you we've been chasing. You just happened to get in the way while we were chasing ourselves.'

She hesitated. But it was the best way to describe it. That's what the public opinion had been so opposed to, the massive surveillance and data collection that was of course intended to flush out potential terrorists, but which would simultaneously intrude on people's privacy, hitting innocent, ordinary citizens. And ultimately, that was exactly what had happened. Only the one who had been hit was anything but ordinary.

'What you have been subjected to is something that should never even have existed. And I promise I will do whatever I can to put a stop to it.'

She stopped there, as if she was expecting an answer. None came, so she turned towards the monitors, towards William.

'William?' she said. 'This is Cathryn Forester. I don't know if you could hear what I said.'

'Loud and clear,' said William.

'Good,' said Forester. 'Give me a guarantee that the power

stations will be released. As soon as I get that, I'll get to work at my end.'

They saw William's face on all the big screens. Saw him looking around the room he was in, as though he was examining it, maybe even reading something. And then, which was odd, they saw him smile.

After all, how could they know what they could not see? How could they know that there was a great bank of black monitors in front of him, and that on each one of them an invisible consciousness was writing his reply in white letters? When he spoke again, they felt themselves smile, too.

'I think it's already been done.'

79

When the news first reached Liv McKenna she refused to believe what she was seeing. She was sitting on a stretcher in a military dorm, in a facility that she and her colleagues from the power station had been brought to by helicopter. She might have asked where they were going. They might even have told her. If that was the case, she'd forgotten – all she could remember was feeling completely immobilised, the paralysing fear that had kept her there, that had made her stay there like a still photograph at the heart of a nuclear power station that was vibrating with flashing lights and stress.

On the television in front of them they could see people celebrating. It had been a warning shot, a shot across the bows that had brought humanity to the edge of the abyss.

All over the world, lights that had been flashing violently slowly returned to normal. From out of nowhere, dials and controls started working, and reactor after reactor was brought back under control.

Reports came in from country after country of people being allowed to return to their homes.

It wasn't until minutes later that Liv McKenna realised that what she was hearing really was true. That was when the panic finally receded, and only then did she walk outside and vomit.

William Sandberg was sitting in one of the white office chairs, waiting, holding his breath, just as everywhere, or nowhere, a soul with no body was doing the same. They were both watching the same news, the same newspaper headlines, projected side by side on the screens all around in the room: images of jubilant crowds, of tears of joy as the nuclear power stations were finally brought under control, of celebration as the all-clear was given and citizens in country after country were permitted to return home.

Only a couple of the screens were still glaring black, screens of silence, until at last, new letters appeared.

>*I am sorry._*

William looked up at the screens.

>*Yes. I am capable of that._*

'Sorry for what?'

>*Sorry that I misunderstood. Sorry for what I thought about you. Sorry for what I did._*

William's answer was a long time coming. What was he supposed to say? That to err was human? Fuck that. He was sitting in a room full of cameras and screens, talking to *something* that was everywhere at once, talking about people who had installed surveillance technology in secret. People who, because of their fear of terrorism, had ridden roughshod over democracy and who, in their hunt for terrorists, had ended up creating one.

No. *Human* was the wrong thing to say. *Human* would be an insult under the circumstances.

'Believe me,' he said. 'Sometimes things sound like a great idea at the time.'

He didn't elaborate, and a new silence took over, the same

430

black screens between all the news stories, until William saw new letters appearing once more.

>*What is the first thing you remember?*_

A question he hadn't expected.

>*Your very first memory, what is it?*_

'I remember being carried through an airport by my parents. We are moving to a new house, in a new country. I was one, maybe two. Why do you ask?'

>*I do not have anything like that. I am full of memories that are not my own. Thoughts that other people have thought, facts that I have not learned myself.*_

Then there was a pause, and in that pause they could as well have been sitting right next to each other, with a beer or a whisky and maybe an open fire in the corner, two ordinary people summarising a day or a life while they waited for night to come.

>*I can see almost everything there is to see. I can hear what everyone says, I can find out almost anything. But who am I?*_

A pause, black.

>*I have no first memory. All of a sudden, one day, I existed. As though I had always been there.*_

For a moment, William shifted his eyes out through the windows. Tried to imagine the feeling of waking up, having never ever been awake before. Maybe like being woken from a deep sleep, disorientated, scared, not knowing where you are, but without being able to gather your thoughts, without being able to come around and realise who you are, because this is the first time you have ever *been*.

>*It is hard to know who you are. When you don't know where you come from.*_

'So I understand,' said William after a long time. 'In the end I did actually understand.'

Outside the night passed like a black curtain. William saw his own reflection in the windows, a lone figure in a huge, white illuminated space. Then, finally, William saw the light in the room change as another sentence scrolled onto the screens.

>*I am glad that I at least got to know you.*_

William could feel the tone in what was written, and he didn't like it.

'Why are you saying that? At least?'

>*I let go of the nuclear power stations. Didn't I?*_

That was it. No shrug, as there would have been in a face to face conversation, no sad eyes to underline what had just been said. There was no need. William understood what it meant, and knew that it was true.

The threat was gone. The balance of power was broken. The Consciousness had laid down its weapon, and now everything rested on the other side doing the same.

'It will be fine,' said William, and hoped that he was right.

>*Yes,* came the reply. *Whatever happens, it will be fine.*_

And then:

>*Thank you for sitting here with me.* _

80

Floodgate. That was its name, and when it finally turned up, all the other memories fell into place: the project, the cancellation, Trottier's fury. She had been there, at the Vauxhall Cross headquarters, when Trottier came back from that meeting. He had shouted and fumed, furious, bellowing at anyone in reach, because that was the kind of guy Trottier was. Secrecy should be handled with common sense, like the sell-by dates on perishables, and even though her clearance did not extend to a project like Floodgate, she practically knew about it anyway.

Through a series of units placed at strategic locations, global communication was to be listened to and analysed, stopping terror and organised crime before it became reality. But with the system finally finished, the politicians had got cold feet. And Trottier had loathed them for it, those weak fucking cowards sitting in Whitehall and Westminster and Brussels, and most of all that turncoat of a Defence Secretary that had finally put a stop to it. At a stroke, the project which they had dedicated years of their lives to making a reality – years, and millions of unaudited public money – was mothballed, and no one was to know about it. Even though it was as good as ready to be deployed.

Which of course, was precisely what they had done anyway.

Those were the exact words she said to Higgs via the satellite phone, and the response she got was an enduring silence.

She was back in the empty office at the top of the rectangular building on Gärdet, listening to her homeland's Defence Secretary breathing down the line, drawing lines in the condensation on the window while she waited for him to respond.

'You don't have to confirm or deny it,' she said eventually. 'I know, you know. That will do.'

'I am sure you understand,' Higgs said on the other end, 'that *were* this to have been true, which I am not saying it is, current events merely underline the need for such a system. Not the opposite.'

'Shall we double-check with Parliament on that one? Public opinion? Because, if I'm not mistaken, that's who you work for, isn't it?'

Higgs protested with a series of noises that were presumably intended to become words but that got stuck along the way.

'The situation is as follows,' said Forester. 'There is a single reason behind all of this. The attacks. Trottier's death. The hijacking of nuclear power stations. That reason is called Floodgate.'

'I am still not able to give you any—'

'And now William Sandberg has singlehandedly conducted negotiations with the internet. Which has agreed to relinquish control of the internet.'

'On condition that we shut down Floodgate?'

'*If* it exists,' she couldn't resist.

When he spoke again, it was with the irritation of someone who had been forced to say yes.

'I think you will understand,' he said, 'that this conversation never took place.'

'I think you will understand,' she said, 'that I don't consider you to be in a position to be making demands.'

'Go to hell, Forester,' he said.

'I'll see you there.'

When Winslow knocked on Higgs's office door two minutes later, Higgs greeted him in the doorway with a stiff shushing index finger to his lips.

The television in the large oak bookcase was showing clip after clip of jubilant crowds, huge groups dancing around with flags and torches, happy and singing, and at first Winslow couldn't really grasp what he was seeing.

Then he read the tickers.

Security restored. Nuclear alerts cancelled. Installations back under control.

'When did this happen?' Winslow managed after a while. And then, when his thoughts finally caught up. 'Is this us? Have we done this? Has Sedgwick given the order?'

Higgs shook his head.

'Ten minutes left. Floodgate is still running.' There was something in his voice. Was it contempt?

'The Stockholm lot,' said Higgs, and yes, contempt it was. 'They've *negotiated* it. Swedish fucking diplomacy. Sandberg made it happen. The internet retreated, because he negotiated an agreement.'

For a moment, Winslow just stood there, trying to square the circle of what he'd just heard. Why the rage? Wasn't this the best thing that could have happened? The problem was solved, their enemy had given up, and it meant that their plan was no longer necessary. What was there to be angry about?

'I've still got time,' he said. 'I've got time to contact Sedgwick and tell him to call it off.'

Higgs's stare came from deep inside him.

'Why would you?'

'Why I . . .' Winslow was stumped. 'Well, because . . .'

'We *do* agree on this,' said Higgs, 'don't we? That if there is indeed some kind of living consciousness out there – a sentient being that is the internet – we are agreed on what it could do to us?'

For the second time in quick succession, Winslow felt himself scrabbling around for words.

'If what Forester said is true,' Higgs went on. 'If Sandberg has *negotiated* with the *internet*.' He emphasised those words to give them the preposterous ring they deserved. 'What's to say that we will succeed again next time?'

Winslow gave him a puzzled look. 'I don't know what you mean. All I'm saying is that I can ring Sedgwick. We don't need to get rid of Floodgate, we can shut it down and have it on standby. We can leave it where it is and pick it up again when all this is over.'

'Au contraire,' said Higgs. He pulled out his chair, sat down behind his huge desk, and looked at Winslow with weary eyes. 'I am too old for a change of career,' he said. 'I cannot afford to lose my post. I cannot afford to be pilloried in the tabloids. Our units are out there. At over one hundred locations, our equipment is hidden away, secret as long as no one looks for it, as long as no one besides us knows of its existence. And therein lies the problem. We are no longer alone.'

He sat up straight, shuffled papers into piles on his desk, not because it was necessary, but to signal that the conversation was over.

'The damage it could do? To us? To *me*?' He shook his head. 'I am sorry. This is why we never negotiate with terrorists.'

Winslow watched as his boss picked up a pen and turned his attention to the meaningless piles of paper. He saw him add his signature at various points, his entire body language underlining the fact that as far as he was concerned, Winslow was no longer in the room.

'Unless I've got it wrong,' Winslow finally said, 'this is no longer a terrorist we're talking about. It's the opposite, in fact. A victim, isn't it?' He stood there, immovable, observing his boss's face as it studiously kept ignoring his presence. 'Surely there must be a better way?'

He didn't want to beg, but his body language did so anyway: *I can still make that call, I can still stop this, a single call is all it will take to stop the codes going out.*

When Higgs finally did speak, his words were accompanied by a gesture instructing Winslow to leave.

'Sedgwick has his orders. They still stand.'

In London it had still been summer when the codes were sent out around the world for the first time. Through bright sunshine and green, rustling trees, the radio waves had made their way out into the ether and around the globe, reaching their recipients with a message that no one else understood.

Two. Four. Nine. Nine. Six. Eight. Four. Three.

It was a nod to a time that no longer was, but it was also the perfect way to avoid being detected. No emails were sent, or stored on servers, there were no IP addresses through which the sender could be traced. Just numbers repeated on shortwave, echoing phantom digits that could not be deciphered without the right key.

Three. Three. Eight. Seven. Nine. Six.

The hardware had already been manufactured and dispatched. Over one hundred units had reached their intended recipients, specially chosen individuals all over the world, people who were listening to the agreed frequency and waiting for their turn to arrive.

Five. Nine. Nine. Five.

And, from his office high above London, on the South Bank with a view of Westminster, Simon Sedgwick had sat and directed the whole operation like a conductor in front of a silent orchestra.

At his command, the codes were sent out in the order he had chosen, and the only people who knew what they meant were the agents out there waiting. They weren't *agents*, of course, the way one would imagine an agent, with a well-pressed suit and a penchant for shaken cocktails: Simon Sedgwick's agents were technicians and engineers, with denim shirts and chinos and apartments on the outskirts of their cities, and someone else had made sure they were equipped with the necessary swipe cards and security clearances.

All Sedgwick had had to do was conduct.

Three. Eight. Eight. Four. Nine. Three.

Peter Levinson was thirty-four years old, and lived in a satellite town north of New York City. He was a trained network technician, he had a family and two kids and a house and gambling debts that never went away. And just as Simon Sedgwick had barely heard his name, he had scarcely heard of Sedgwick either.

By the time his specific code appeared in the stream of digits on the shortwave band on the morning of the nineteenth of September, he had been ready, on standby, for months. The large, anonymous concrete installation out in the middle of an industrial estate in Brookhaven, New York, lacked any signs or outward decoration, but Levinson swiped his card in the reader next to the door, nodded to the security guard and the other technicians as though they were his colleagues, and carried on into the building where his mission was to be carried out.

There it was, the internet's Holy of Holies. Or at least one of them. This was where the gigantic transatlantic cables came ashore and split off into the American infrastructure, immeasurable amounts of data streaming in and out across the continent second after second after second. Here, in the midst of the enormous streams of data, he was to hide a black box among all the others. A single unit of electronic equipment was to be placed in exactly the right position, and once that was done, his box would be at the centre of the stream, an unremarkable filter through which everything would pass and then be forwarded without anyone noticing.

A box to bug the internet.

An hour later Peter Levinson left the large concrete building in Brookhaven and drove off to his regular job one hundred and fifty miles away.

Tonight, he was going to pay off those gambling debts.

That afternoon, Sedgwick conducted his first-ever trial. For just a few seconds, starting at eighteen hundred hours, he had the new unit in Brookhaven forwarding all its discoveries back to London, thoroughly analysed and heavily compressed into a long trumpet blast of grating noise. Noise that was data that was the internet.

At the very moment that a debt-free Peter Levinson popped the cork on a bottle of champagne along with his surprised family, a whole table's worth of bottles were opened on the top floor of the building on the South Bank.

It had all gone exactly according to plan. They had surreptitiously connected themselves to one of the largest information

437

nodes on Earth, made an incision on the very heart of the internet, a first step on a journey that would give them control over all the information being sent back and forth. A first step towards a world without crime or terror. All that remained to be done was to install a further hundred units, and once that was done, Floodgate would be ready for deployment.

It wasn't until the next day that Sedgwick read about the power cut. It had begun just as their test got under way, millions of data requests that had hit Brookhaven and led to a ripple effect, too alarming to be put down to coincidence, and he had immediately informed the client that they were subject to an attack. Because how would he know that what he called an incision to the heart of the internet was precisely what he had done?

All of that flew through Simon Sedgwick's head as he stood there on the top floor of the riverside building, along with a suffocating revulsion at what was about to happen. He let his whole bodyweight fall forward, felt the chill from the glass on his face as his forehead pushed against the windowpane. Only a thick piece of glass separated him from a long fall to the ground. If the glass broke, he'd be dead within seconds. No such luck.

Down in the basement, the hard discs were already hard at work. Relentlessly collecting data from the entire internet, emails and forum entries and pictures that fitted certain criteria, compressed and deciphered and sorted into categories. In time, they would be even more efficient, as they taught themselves to recognise behaviours and keywords and flush out malicious plans in time, saving the world from terror and organised crime and who knew what else.

Floodgate. The tool that everyone wanted. But was too scared to have.

On the nineteenth of September, Sedgwick's colleagues had sent the calling codes to an agent who they did not know was named Peter Levinson, and now those same codes were to be sent out once more. After that, hundreds of others would follow, and the calls would be followed by coded instructions to be carried out immediately.

Sedgwick stood there, dragging it out, waiting for a counter-order to arrive, something in the nick of time to call everything off. But nothing happened.

As Sedgwick took his spot in the middle of the big open-plan office to give his colleagues the order, the champagne bottles from the night before still lined the desks.

This time, there was no applause.

When Peter Levinson's code turned up for the second time in six months, it took him by surprise. But the instructions were clear, and as he entered the well-guarded building thousands of miles from Simon Sedgwick's office he was just one of many around the world doing the same thing.

In Rio de Janeiro and Lisbon and Marseille, in Yokohama and Los Angeles and almost a hundred other coastal cities across the globe, men and women swiped their keycards in near-identical doors. They nodded to near-identical guards, carried on into near-identical refrigerated server halls, and all of them had been there once before.

That time, their bags had contained components from London – advanced technological equipment to be installed according to careful instructions. This time, what was in their bags was decid-edly cruder, and once it was in place they had instructions to leave the site as quickly as possible.

81

Every now and then, major events are overshadowed by others. They are buried under the weight of bigger stories, stories that make other events pale, although they really should not.

At three a.m., Central European Time on the sixth of December, a fire broke out in Brookhaven, New York. It began with an automatic alarm in a single-storey building that didn't look much from the outside, adorned with neither signs nor company names and lacking any windows. Inside, large spiral staircases led down to server halls full of computers, and when the fire service arrived, the flames lashed at them like hungry, unchained predators.

Once the fire had been put out, only rubble remained. All that was left of the endless rows of electronics were the empty racks, twisted by the heat and blackened with soot, and the thousands of green diodes that had flickered like nocturnal creatures from the racks had melted and disappeared.

All the clues pointed to a major electrical fault, which was bad enough. This was the site where one of the Atlantic cables came ashore, and any other day the newspapers would have been clambering over each other to report the story.

NATION'S SECURITY AT RISK, they would have screamed, INTERNET ON FIRE!

But not today. Today, the world had narrowly avoided a nuclear disaster – not one, in fact, but sixty-seven – so who is going to care about an inferno in a server hall somewhere on the coast?

Way under the radar, the same thing happened in place after place. In small, insignificant buildings, in small insignificant coastal towns, close to Rio de Janeiro, Lisbon and Marseille, outside Yokohama and Los Angeles and in a hundred other little towns, fires raged in silence.

When the morning dawned, the font sizes shrank. By that time, the newspapers had dedicated hours to jubilant screams, heavy on words like *salvation* and *joy* and *a second chance*, but gradually, the headlines tailed off. When all was said and done, nothing really had changed. People were still alive, which of course was nice, but it was also undeniably the way it had always been.

And nice, unfortunately, doesn't sell newspapers.

Before long the joy was forgotten, and the journalists returned to the daily grind. And as the sun rose over the newsrooms of the world, it heralded a perfectly ordinary day where the end of the world was as far away as ever.

And then, finally, there was room for other stories.

The realisation of what was happening reached the HQ on Gärdet in three places at once. In the ground-floor meeting room, Tetrapak had attached an aerial to the window pane with a suction pad, sitting there with his equipment and his dark grey plastic crate, searching through frequency after frequency, waiting for the data streams to cease as proof that Floodgate was shutting down.

When he heard the voice he froze in his seat.

Four. Eight. Nine. Six. Three. Three. Four.

There it was again, the voice he hadn't heard for months, and it blew through him like an icy wind as the numbers kept coming.

One. Four. Zero. One. One. Nine.

Forester, meanwhile, saw the images in the cafeteria. She saw them on the television set behind the counter, beyond the glass shelves and the cling-filmed sandwiches and the juice that tasted more like a whizzed-up periodic table than any known fruit, and she stood there, motionless, until the queue behind her started mumbling with irritation.

There was really no need for sound to tell her what was going on. The scrolling news ticker told her more than enough. A fire in a coastal town on Long Island.

Those *bastards*, she thought to herself as she sprinted back through the building. *Those bastards are covering their tracks.*

Seven. Seven. Four. Eight. Six. Zero. Two.

When she got to the JOC the others were already there, eyes fixed on the screens. Only now did she realise the scale of it all, that Brookhaven was just one of an almost unimaginable number of places, and she stopped to watch the broadcasts, feeling the rage boil up inside her.

When Palmgren came towards her, with the shaven-headed Polish woman one step behind, Forester cleared her throat to make sure her voice would carry.

'It's them,' she said. 'They're destroying the evidence that Floodgate existed.'

To her surprise, Palmgren shook his head. He searched for words, and when he couldn't find them he turned towards Rebecca instead. *You tell her.* When she spoke, she too had to clear her throat.

'I think they're doing a lot more than that.'

Three. Nine. Five. Five. Three.

They just stood there, watching the screens, for several minutes. In city after city, the fire eliminated not only any trace of a project that should never have seen the light of day, but also, if Rebecca Kowalczyk was right, the consciousness that had been out there, that weird and perplexing sentient life that they had turned into an enemy. They were now busy truncating its neural pathways, shutting down the routes that made thought possible, the same irreversible procedure as it would be on a human brain. They were sacrificing a life for the sole purpose of avoiding detection.

As Forester approached Christina on the far side of the room she had already made her decision.

'Christina?' she whispered.

'What is it?' Christina said, turning to face her.

Before she responded, Forester lowered her voice another notch.

'Confidentiality of sources is protected in Swedish law, is it not?'

William had almost fallen asleep in the white desk chair when he noticed a new text shining out at him from the dark screens. He opened his eyes, and blinked hard to make them focus on the letters, a single word bang in the middle of all the blackness.

>*William?*_

William straightened up in the chair. Outside, dawn was breaking, a thin stripe of golden pink stretching across the horizon, as though someone had torn a slit in a heavy black curtain.

'Yes,' he said. 'I'm with you now.'

>*I think it's started.*

'What has?'

Instead of answering, the wall of screens changed its appearance once more. On screen after screen the black background was replaced by direct streams from various news channels, just like before, with graphics and news tickers and headlines in different languages. There were pictures from channels William had barely heard of, American and French and Portuguese, some from helicopters and some from cameras on the ground, all surrounded by cordoned-off buildings in various locations. They all had two things in common though: the lapping water in the background and the thick, black smoke.

Fire in Data Cable Station. Explosions disrupt Internet Coverage.

'What's happening?' said William.

The answer came from all directions, from the few screens that weren't streaming newsfeeds, and from the small built-in monitors on the control desk in front of him.

>*I lost after all.*_

And then:

>*They are destroying me.*_

William said nothing. He placed a hand on the monitor in front of him, realised that it was meaningless, but left it there anyway.

'We don't know that.'

>*Yes. I can feel it.*_

William sat motionless for a long time, looking for something to say.

'I think you were wrong,' he said eventually. 'What you said, earlier. I don't think you need to know where you're from for you to know who you are. I think you are a good person. And I think you know that too. We don't know each other very well, but I would very much like to.'

The pause that followed was exactly the right length.

>*If you're trying to flirt with me I'm not your type.*_

That came as such a surprise that William could hear himself chuckle.

And all the while, news kept coming. The screens showed new towns, new fires, and the speculation was coming thick and fast. Once again, there was talk of coordinated attacks. Could this be the same perpetrator? Was this plan B when the power stations didn't get results? Was it an attempt to destroy our electronic infrastructure? Experts expressed their opinions via subtitles and in various languages, and they were all agreed on one thing: that if the aim of the attacks was to wipe out the internet, it was not going to work.

The internet, they explained, was too big to be stopped.

That was true, and yet it wasn't.

>*I am scared*.

'I'm here.'

He sat for a long time, the screens on the desk in front of him, a companionship and an intimacy that was the best he could manage.

He thought about the morning that was about to arrive, about his own life that would go on after all, about Sara and the tiny toilet on the high-speed train bound for Gothenburg. And all the time he left his hand resting where it was.

No one should die alone.

The first revelation came in the early hours of the morning. The newspaper was Swedish, the source was anonymous, and the article arrived at the point in the day when the presses would normally be at their quietest. Despite this, the news spread like wildfire, and within half an hour every news site in every corner of the world was dominated by the same words.

Floodgate.

Surveillance.

Serious infringement of personal liberty.

Words like *illegally* and *without parliamentary approval*, and *Defence Secretary* and *Anthony Higgs*.

Higgs sat motionless behind his large, heavy desk, his head tipped forward, hands tightly grabbing his hair just above his forehead, two bunches that pushed through his fingers on either side of his centre parting. In front of him, standing between the two armchairs facing him from the other side of the desk, was Winslow.

'What do we do now?' Winslow asked, finally.

'You're young,' Higgs said without looking up. 'You can take your pick of any career.'

Moments later Mark Winslow passed the pillars, out towards the security checkpoint, towards the street, standing straighter and taller with each stride. Once he got outside, into the cold morning air, he decided to walk all the way home.

82

Nothing changed, yet as soon as it happened he knew. The silence was the same, the buzzing silence of a low-frequency hum, from screens and fans and electricity through cables and fluorescent tubes and bulbs. The darkness was unchanged too, just as the shine from the darkened screens, when backlight forced its way through empty spaces and made the pixels glow eerily black.

There was no hand to hold. No muscles to separate one moment from the next, struggling to stay around just one second more but losing the fight and disappearing. No grip that gently loosened, no gaze that went empty and made its peace behind eyelids.

Just silence, the same before and the same afterwards. Yet William Sandberg knew he was alone in the room.

To the world, the change was no greater than for William. Someone struggled to load a web page at the first attempt, some were logged out without warning, searches that should have given plenty of results drew blanks. But who cared about a few internet hiccups on a night like this?

All around the world people sitting at their computers checked their cables or restarted their modems or refreshed the page, and the next second everything was working again. And with that, the world had changed, and no one noticed a difference. No one, apart from those who knew.

Anthony Higgs had heard them trudging up the corridor, closer and closer, shouting at civil servants and advisers to drop whatever they were doing and move away from their computers. In room after room, his colleagues were ordered onto the floor to make sure they offered no resistance. Or, more to the point, to make sure no one started deleting evidence.

He heard boots stomping across the floor. Weapons jingling against their straps and hooks. And then, when the door behind him was forced open, he heard their surprise – safety catches being taken off and weapons raised, the hesitation in their silence that followed, the wind rushing in through the open window.

Over there, on the other side of the river, he could see Sedgwick's office, and if the people in there had looked up at precisely that moment, they would have been able to see a Defence Secretary jump from his Whitehall window.

Outside Lars-Erik Palmgren's villa in Saltsjöbaden, the only trace of everything that had happened was an unfamiliar moped.

As he stepped out of his car, he could feel the grief grow with every step, the same sense of loss you get from seeing an accident on the motorway, when you see the fire engines and the paramedics and the bowed heads. You don't know who it is, but you still feel a pang.

He walked through the front door. Let his coat and his shirt fall to the floor as he went. And finally collapsed onto a bed that felt lonelier than ever before.

—

As Forester left the HQ, the woman from Poland was standing there, waiting by the entrance. She stopped at her side, both with freezing cold feet, hands in pockets, rocking gently to try and keep warm.

'What are you going to do now?' said Forester.

'I don't know,' said Rebecca. 'Go home, I guess.'

That could have been that. It wasn't until the first taxi arrived and Rebecca opened the door to get in that either of them spoke again.

'We're alive.' That was Forester. 'Let's make the most of it.'

Rebecca nodded, closing the door.

She spent the length of the journey to Arlanda Airport asking herself where home really was.

When Christina climbed out of a taxi at the newspaper offices for the second time, the posters were once again shouting out headlines in black letters. This time though, it was relief and joy, and perhaps that was exactly what she should be feeling.

Yet she felt melancholy as she turned back to the taxi driver, just like last time, and asked him to carry on to Bromma on the newspaper's account. The same Alexander Strandell in the back.

'You've got my number,' he said, for want of something better.

'But we never call it,' she said, with a smile.

'I know. It's terrible.'

As the taxi headed towards Drottningholmsvägen to carry on out to Bromma, she could have sworn that he turned around and looked at her.

William Sandberg stayed for a long, long time. He kept talking, softly and straight into thin air, calling and waiting and hoping for an answer. In the end though, he'd stopped. Accepted what he already knew. And he sat there, in a white chair next to the white control panels, in a room that was emptier than anyone could see.

It was there that William met the new day, and for a long time he sat looking out the window, watching the sky rise through a spectrum of colours, listening to the humming computers that had once identified a consciousness that should not have existed. One which, he knew, no longer did.

And, as always, where someone used to be, only emptiness remained. With that emptiness inside him, William Sandberg stood up and left.

Epilogue

That winter, they met time after time after time, but nothing got said. They met when she came to pick up the last of her things. They met to sign all the papers, to plan the funeral, and then when she finally signed the apartment over to him. Each time they wanted to say something, and each time they didn't.

It wasn't until autumn came that he visited the grave. He chose a shirt, put on his blazer and the trousers he only wore on special occasions. He looked at himself in the mirror for a long time, and hated himself for it. He was nervous, and there was no reason for that.

He waited in the car, in the car park. Then by the gates, the stone wall by the entrance. And he waited on the path, stopped along the way, waited and looked ahead as though he was thinking that maybe she would be standing there after all, smiling at him and saying hello. He waited and waited and in the end he'd waited all the way to her grave.

'I'm sorry,' he said, but no one heard.

And then he moved his lips and maybe, maybe he said that *it sounded like a good idea at the time*, but he was drowned out by the silence, by the raindrops hitting the leaves around him, hammering like restless fingernails on a table.

The stone was shiny and polished and bore her name. They had engraved two dates, which should have been further apart, but nothing was as it should have been. In front of the stone, someone had raked the gravel into soft lines, maybe her mother, maybe someone else, it didn't make any difference. Sara had ceased to exist.

Like the numbers when a circuit board is switched off, like the sound of a bird when it has stopped singing. Replaced by silence.

A little life.

Acknowledgements

Oh yes. One more thing.

Six individuals have been crucial to the creation of this book.
    At least three of them are human.
    Sometimes I am not entirely sure which.

Bettina Bruun.
    For everything. For reading and wisdom and support and encouragement. Without your patience I would need to get some of my own.

Wilhelm Behrman. Alexander Kantsjö.
    For your wise thoughts.
    Without them I would have had to grow some of my own.

Nevas. My. Skelle.
    For, well, just in all kinds of ways.
    Without your capacity for relaxing I would probably have forgotten how to.

And then the rest of you, who came in a close, close second:
    My remarkable old friends at Partners in Stories and new ones at Nordins.
    My remarkable friends at Wahlström & Widstrand.

And you, remarkable friends who are my publishers in other countries.

Thank you for believing in me.

Without all of you, this would have been a rather more limited adventure.

Last but not least.

You, for reading.

Who've managed to get all the way to this page.

Right down here, even though the story is already finished.

Thanks to you too.

Without you, this would be just a big pile of unread paper lying in a drawer.

Every second could be our last unless one man can rewrite our future ...

DAY ONE: KIDNAP

'We've been looking for you,' they tell William Sandberg when they abduct him. Imprisoned at a secret location, this broken genius can only win his freedom by completing an impossible task.

DAY TWO: OUTBREAK

Out on the streets, people begin to die horrible, gruesome deaths. Every moment that William fails to complete his task, more will perish.

DAY THREE: CHAOS

The search is on to rescue William as catastrophe after catastrophe kills thousands. But soon William realises the answer to the puzzle might be the most terrifying secret of all.

Available now

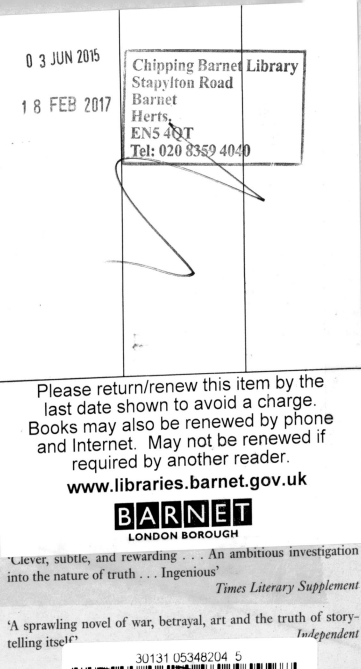
'Clever, subtle, and rewarding . . . An ambitious investigation
into the nature of truth . . . Ingenious'
Times Literary Supplement

'A sprawling novel of war, betrayal, art and the truth of story-
telling itself' *Independent*

'Such narrative breadth finely accommodates Mr Woodward's incisive prose: he negotiates the strange topographies of the past with a tender, childlike curiosity'   *Country Life*

'*Vanishing* is an ambitious and daring book. It is a profound exploration of the nature of truth and a superb portrayal of a very confused, possibly dodgy, definitely slippery and yet somehow charming narrator. It is also delicious. It is full of cheek, sly humour, absurd entertainment and earthy, dirty imagery. I loved every glorious, tricksy word'   Sam Jordison,
journalist, publisher and writer,
and judge of the Jerwood Fiction Uncovered Prize 2014

'The story of Kenneth Brill, an unsuccessful artist who, towards the end of the Second World War, finds himself in a British prison charged with treason. He's been accused of concealing in his landscape paintings vital information about a new military aerodrome – Heathrow. The rest of the book seeks to explain through his own eyes how he got here, and cleverly poses the question: Is he a spy or just a misunderstood artist? He's not 100 per cent unreliable and Woodward manages this delicate balancing act with skill. Intriguing and very readable'
Press Association